Patchwork *to* Healing

BOOKS BY KAREN COULTERS

YORK HARBOR SERIES NOVELS

Hope from Daffodils

When Cookies Crumble

Patchwork to Healing

PRAISE FOR KAREN COULTERS NOVELS

HOPE FROM DAFFODILS

IAN Book of the Year Finalist

Karen Coulters is my new favorite author! At once charming, vivid and delightful, *Hope from Daffodils* has a natural movement with a suspenseful build-up that kept me turning pages well into the night. Set on the seacoast of Maine, I could picture myself by the water, in the bakery, smelling the flowers and watching the events in the beautiful barn. I fell in love with the characters and miss them already.

Jenny Bruck, Author, *52 Vitality Tools*

Hope from Daffodils brought me through a wave of emotions that kept me from putting the book down until I was done! Each character is so well developed and rich, you become invested in each of their outcomes. Thank you for the journey, Karen!

Caleigh Flynn, Amazon

Hard to put down…I enjoyed reading every part of *Hope from Daffodils*. You really come to like the characters and before the book ends, they feel like old friends. Reading this book feels like a mini-vacation.

One Girls Opinion, Goodreads

I felt I knew the main characters as well as if they had been long time friends of mine. The conversations throughout were natural and never contrived, giving me the sensation, I was present as a silent partner. I was delighted that I never knew exactly where Coulters' was taking me, but I willingly turned the pages to find out!

Connie Evan – Author, *The Pine Tree Riot*

A grieving widow. A disillusioned attorney. Set along the idyllic Maine coast, *Hope from Daffodils* is about how we lose our way in the world and find our way back. Coulters delivers a romance both twisty and heartwarming. A charming debut!

Lorrie Thomson, award-winning author of
A Measure of Happiness, What's Left Behind, and *Equilibrium*

WHEN COOKIES CRUMBLE

Romance with a mystery built in. When I started this book, it was 1:30 AM before I put it down! The characters are very likeable and right away you are rooting for good things to happen to them. There are some lovely descriptive phrases in here and it is obvious the author has a true love for this local New England setting. If you are looking for a relaxing read that takes you away from today's hustle and bustle, this book is a good choice. You will not be disappointed.

Sharon Czarnecki, Director of Weare Area Writers Guild

I could not put this book down!!! I loved that *When Cookies Crumble* has characters that are so relatable to real life experiences and responses that I have felt. This is a heart-warming well written story. You won't be disappointed!

Cindy Mills

Wonderful book! As with her first book, it is hard to put down. The storyline, the development of the characters, the descriptions of the scenery and the events held at Proposals all are extremely well done. Can't wait for her next book!!!

Susan L.

A wholesome and satisfying mystery, thread through with love. When baker Emily Vassure's mother, Helen, dies, she leaves Emily with the mystery of her paternity, and a mistrust of men—due to Helen's poor choices. Until Duncan Philips comes into Emily's life—a stranger with whom she feels an instant connection. Much like a favorite recipe, the mystery unfolds step by step until it arrives at its satisfying and delicious conclusion.

Lorrie Thomson, award-winning author of
A Measure of Happiness, What's Left Behind, and *Equilibrium*

Another great beach read! Number two in the York Harbor Series; what's not to love?! Situated in the lovely York Harbor area, our friends from the first book *Hope from Daffodils* are seen in a mysterious back story that just keeps unfolding and unfolding. You will have a hard time putting this down. I loved it!

KGG

Once again, Karen's expressive and descriptive writing puts the reader into the story and lives of the characters. We want to know them or already think we already do.

Susan Hudson

Patchwork
to Healing

A York Harbor Series Novel

K A R E N   C O U L T E R S

Howland
Press

Howland Press

18 Loudon Rd. # 494
Concord, NH 03302

WWW.KARENCOULTERSAUTHOR.COM

Library of Congress Cataloging-in-Publication Data

Names: Karen Coulters, Author

Title: Patchwork to Healing

Book 3 in the York Harbor Series

Description: First edition. | New Hampshire: Howland Press, 2022.

Identifiers: LCCN 2022909103 |

ISBN 978-1-7336460-6-2 (softcover) | ISBN 978-1-7336460-7-9 (eBook)

Our books may be purchased in bulk for promotion, educational, or business use.

Please contact your local bookseller or Howland Press via email @ HowlandPress@KarenCoultersAuthor.com

Cover & Book designed by: My Custom Book Cover

Editor: Roxana Coumans

Image Credits: Canva: cat, quilt patch, chapter heading

Printed in the United States of America.

First Edition: 2022

10 9 8 7 6 5 4 3 2 1

Dedicated to all the beautiful people that deeply care for kids that are entrusted to them, and to the kids that endure and excel under circumstances that most could never imagine.

You are wonderfully made.

You are not a mistake; you were born on purpose.

You were born to be great.

Acknowledgements

You've heard the expression: never have I ever; those words could not be truer for me. Never had I ever imagined that when I first started writing in 2016, that I would by 2019 have my first novel published, let alone three.

Patchwork to Healing, I confess, brought me to a place of immense appreciation for those that care for children who were not born to them. This story incorporates the magnitude of pain that the characters, Rebecca Mills and Benjamin Daly, went through at having been placed within the foster care system. However, it captures the love given to them by one of their foster care providers as well.

There is a calling, placed on one's heart, that pushes those to care for these precious children in need of a loving and nurturing home. Bravo to you, if you have! I pray you will be blessed with immeasurable joy at doing so.

I learned long ago that success grows not from the strength of one, but with the strength of many. Those that lift us up, cheer us on, and advocate on our behalf are essential in having a fulfilling life. Success in life also takes sacrifice of self and willingness to accept help when we need it. My characters navigate through these insights, but so have I. I owe tremendous gratitude to Ellen Reed for teaching me about the ins and outs of quilting so that *Patchwork to Healing* will ring true… Thank you from the bottom of my heart. Thank you as well to author Sylvie Kurtz for taking my manuscript of *Patchwork to Healing* and helping me make it shine. Most importantly, thank you, readers, for embracing my works, for it is you that brings my writing purpose.

For those of you who foster, or have lived within the system; for those that have suffered a tremendous loss of loved ones, for those that find purpose in the giving of your talents to help others, to those that simply need to find peace and strength to get through another day, to those that move beyond their pain so they might help others who are going through the same; It is my hope that *Patchwork to Healing* will open your eyes and your heart to heal and grow in the truth that you were born with a purpose. You are gloriously and wonderfully made. You have been given a gift of having gone through something, and you now have the ability to flourish despite it. You are treasured.

Patchwork to Healing is set in York Harbor, Maine, as is *Hope from Daffodils* and *When Cookies Crumble*. I'm often asked if the locations in the books are real; some are and some are simply made up. In this book, the following locations are actual places in York Harbor:

York Harbor Inn, Ship's Cellar Pub, Rick's Restaurant, Foster's Clambake, York Harbor Beach, York's Cliff Walk, Nubble Lighthouse at Cape Neddick, and LaBelle Winery (Portsmouth). Should you decide to visit these places, I hope they provide you with the same sense of pleasure as they do me.

One of the highlights in my writing is getting to read comments from my readers. I have the most wonderful readers on the planet, and your remarks inspire me and keep me going. Thank you from the fullness of my heart.

Blessings,
-Karen

Chapter 1

Rebecca tucked a loose strand of hair over her ear and rolled the steel wheel across the fabric, cutting images of kittens playing with balls of yarn into squares. A wisp of a smile washed across her face as she thought of the six-year-old foster child named Jessica, who would receive her gift. Rebecca had been told that she adored kittens, but more importantly, she was as sweet and loveable as the cats she adored. After a few more cuts, she decided the special message she'd embroider onto the special quilt: *I, Jessica Finch, am purrrfect just the way I am.*

Sunshine dancing across the swatches gave the illusion of warmth, but the chill in her apartment's workroom made its way to her bones. Fall has always brought on a cloak of melancholy that she couldn't shake, but keeping her hands busy, making quilts on her days off, and creating wedding bouquets at Proposals, squelched the ache.

Over the past few days Rebecca had been reliving the anniversary of a day that changed her life forever. The death of her parents, brought on a weight and foreboding that rocked her to her core. She'd tried over the years to go on trips to escape the pain, work from dawn to dusk busying herself, or simply take a couple of sleeping pills to sleep the day away, but nothing would ease the gut-wrenching pain that filled every atom of her being.

Rebecca cut the last square, and she sat back to observe the stacks of fabric with a sense of accomplishment. She had lost count of the number of quilts she'd created. If she had to guess, it would be nearly one hundred. Rebecca used to count, but it was too sad to think about, even though they were gifts with a purpose.

She glanced down. Her alarm would sound any moment now, so she readied herself for work. It would be the first day back since her mini-Thanksgiving time off. She had completed the floral arrangements for the holiday and events that had been planned, but as soon as those responsibilities had been done, she'd bailed. Her direct boss, Sophie; and her partner, Emily, were understanding of her absence each Thanksgiving. They assumed that she'd be spending her Thanksgiving with family. She saw no harm in their belief, so she didn't correct them.

She unplugged the sewing machine and took a cursory look at her quilting room. The stacks of colorful fabric, patterns, and partially completed quilts tugged at her senses. She wanted to stay and play awhile longer, but begrudgingly turned off the light and shut the door behind her.

Rebecca dashed down the hall to jump into the shower so she wouldn't be late for work.

She shed her gray sweat pants and oversized t-shirt, dropping them to the floor around her feet. Steam curled over the curtain and in her haste, she stepped into the shower.

"Damn it!" she shouted as the scorching water sprayed across her scarred body, instantly transporting her back to a hell of pain. She jumped back, tangling her toe in her t-shirt, and went down with a thud, leaving her shivering on the bathroom floor in a pool of tears.

"When will it end?" she sobbed. "I just want it to stop."

Rebecca looked up toward the heavens with a quivering lip. "Please make it stop."

The memory of seeing her parents' nearly unrecognizable charred bodies, billowing black smoke, and angry flames was unbearable. No human being should ever have to feel that kind of anguish. Rebecca wished she could turn back time, change the past and erase the guilt of what she had done.

She rose from her fetal position on the floor and caught sight of her naked body in the mirror. The right side of her neck, chest, torso, and arm bore scars that appeared raised in some places and smooth in others. Purply, red colors splayed across each surface in varying degrees. She ran her hand across her patchwork skin and felt the thick, fibrous texture that coiled under her touch. No amount of wishing would ease her pain. Rebecca draped her flowing chestnut-brown hair over her scars, then wiped her tears away. She did what she always did; she stuffed the pain down.

***

Rebecca didn't live far from Proposals. She'd found a small rental right there in York Harbor. In as much as she hated the fall, she was relieved to have the village quiet once again, as most of the tourists were now long gone.

Rebecca approached the driveway to Proposals. Sophie

uncovered the massive pots of mums that adorned the signage and main entrance. Despite the fall season and its chilling frost, the arrangement was rather pretty. She gave a wave, and Sophie waved in return.

Flowers of any kind were beautiful in her eyes, which was a good thing, because flowers had become her profession. Rebecca was most grateful for the opportunity Sophie had provided her when she'd needed it the most. She still couldn't believe that it had been nearly two and a half years since she'd started working there. It was the longest place she'd lived or worked since she was fourteen, and that was sixteen years ago. She was saddened by this realization as she'd often wondered what her life would have been like had her parents lived, and yet part of her was happy as well. She enjoyed her work and sensed she was on the right path; a path that brought joy to others.

Rebecca stepped out of the car, and a gust of wind gripped her. She tightened her jacket's belt. She scurried toward the shop and around the fall décor near the entrance. Daisy, Sophie's cat, leaped off one of the small bales of hay, seeking her attention. Rebecca gently nudged Daisy aside with her foot. Daisy was declaring her indignation with a string of meows, then strutted off toward the main house's porch.

Proposals, with the smell of cinnamon and baked apples wafting through the air, Sophie's wave, Emily's smile, and even Daisy's annoying hello, made her feel like she was home—like she belonged. She couldn't help but grin as she thought back to when she'd first arrived. Emily wasn't what you'd call a warm and fuzzy person. In fact, at first, she didn't think that Emily cared for her at all, but Rebecca had earned her trust, and she was grateful.

Emily retrieved pumpkin muffins from the counter. "Well, well, look who the cat dragged in," Emily said with a smile. "It's good to have you back."

"It's good to be back." *Really good.* She hadn't been far away, but walking into Proposals gave her consistency, and a place where she felt needed. *Yes,* she thought, *I'm home.*

***

The next morning, Rebecca sat in her tufted chair with the sound of jostling leaves blowing outside her living room window. She embroidered the last stitch of the last letter on her latest patchwork quilt, then checked her handiwork.

I,

Kimberly Fields,

was born for a purpose.

Kimberly, an eleven-year-old, was in foster care, and Rebecca considered it her mission to make a quilt for those kids in that system. A quilt that belonged to only them, one that was small enough to move from home to home without too much difficulty, and one that brought them comfort, warmth, and the sense that they were wrapped in love, and that they mattered.

She carefully and lovingly folded the finished quilt and carried it over to her kitchen table. She wrapped it in tissue paper, then tied it with a ribbon. A sense of satisfaction and pride washed over her. *Another one done.* She'd deliver it to Mrs. Getchel, who would hand it over to her contact at the Office of Child and Family Services after she left Proposals for the day.

At these times, she felt renewed, energized, and a little less guilty. She pressed the wrapped quilt in her arms, holding it to her chest. Yes, she thought, Kimberly will love it. She'd made sure to piece the patchwork quilt in her favorite colors. It included something that made her happy—ballerinas in different poses, using purple, pink, and red fabric.

Rebecca looked at the time and had the fleeting thought of stopping by Mrs. Getchel's house before heading to work instead, but decided against it, as she was cutting it too close. Today, Sophie had forewarned her, she'd fly solo, designing a wedding bouquet for a client, along with six bridesmaids. Sophie would only have to handle the boutonnieres and corsages, because she had already booked some other commitments. Rebecca was happy for the task, as it would take her mind off her heavy heart. Nope, she'd decided she'd see Mrs. Getchel on her way home when they would have more time to visit.

Mrs. Getchel had played a pivotal part in her upbringing. She was Rebecca's 'Grandma' figure, and Rebecca cherished their relationship. Rebecca and Norma Getchel had come to know each other when Rebecca had been a teenager. She'd opened her home to her but Rebecca hadn't appreciated it as much as she should have. In fact, it wasn't until her adulthood that they'd really become close. They stood more on an equal footing now. *It's funny*, she thought, *how the older we get, the less far apart in age we become.*

Rebecca placed the package in the back seat, tossed her handbag on the passenger seat, and made the short distance to Proposals for her morning shift. As she pulled into her parking spot, she took in the well-appointed Victorian that had become Proposal's bakery and florist shop. To her left, was the refurbished barn, turned event center. The barn sat majestically overlooking the Atlantic, and the sun shone upon the stained glassed windows, giving it the appearance, it was waiting for a celebration to begin. She eyed Agnes Templeton, out of the corner of her eye, carrying her little bag of pastries and cutting through the path between Proposals and her home.

Rebecca opened her car door and felt the warmth of the autumn sun upon her face and breathed in the aroma of fresh baked apples that filled the air.

Yep, today's going to be a good day.

***

Rebecca was invigorated as her productive work day came to an end and she looked forward to seeing Mrs. Getchel. She stepped out of Proposals and the night sky took her breath away.

Like icing on a good day, the brightest orange hues that she'd ever remembered seeing painted the sky. She stood in the driveway and looked around her in amazement. Sophie and Brady emerged to see the spectacle, and Brady lifted his camera to capture the breathtaking moment.

"It's stunning," Sophie said in awe.

Behind Rebecca Brady's camera shutter clicked away as Emily jutted out of the shop to catch a glimpse.

"Beautiful, isn't it, Emily?" Rebecca asked, almost in a whisper, afraid that if she spoke too loudly, the magic would break and the sky would turn dark.

"Sure is. It just goes on and on as far as the eye can see."

Rebecca continued to gaze at the sight, thinking that it was as if God was putting an exclamation point on the end of the day, but she just couldn't shake the unsettled feeling that it was too good to be true.

"Hey, Beck," Emily said, "it's five o'clock. Didn't you say you needed to be somewhere?"

Rebecca pushed up her sleeve to see her watch.

"Oh, wow. Thanks Emily. I told a friend of mine that I'd drop off a gift, and she'd invited me to dinner. Could this day get any better?"

"Well, get going—you're late!"

"I'm going!" Rebecca gave quick hugs goodbye. She climbed into her car and made her way to Mrs. Getchel's home, singing *Good Day Sunshine*, along with the radio, at the top of her lungs.

Before long, the orange sky combined with red and blue streaks. She slowed to a stop, craning her neck out the driver's window to see what was going on up ahead. The bright glaring flashes of red and blue lights blinded her. She shielded her eyes to get a better look. An ambulance.

No, this can't be happening.

She gripped the wheel. *This can't be happening.* A whirl of fear coursed through her body and she shook. She closed her eyes, willing the scene before her to go away. *Please be okay, please be okay. I can't lose you too, Mrs. Getchel, you're the only family I have. I can't...* Tightness in her chest gripped her as though her heart was trying to purge itself from her body. As she burst out of the car toward Mrs. Getchel's home, her pulse quickened.

"What happened?" she shouted, grabbing at the arm of one of the first responders. "Please! Tell me what happened!"

"I'm sorry Ma'am, are you a relative?"

"Yes," she lied, "she's my—my grandmother."

"It appears that your grandmother had a heart attack, and I'm sorry, but we couldn't revive her."

Rebecca fell back to a time and place that spun her life into chaos. A paramedic pulled a sheet over Mrs. Norma Getchel's motionless body.

She's dead.

***

Rebecca stood on the side of the road, in front of Mrs. Getchel's home, in a daze. She looked on as they rolled Mrs. Getchel's lifeless body into the ambulance. She was unsure of what to do, where to go, or even how to breathe. Norma Getchel was the only 'family' that she had, and now she was gone. The crippling realization of this numbed her as sorrow wrapped itself around her with inescapable pain of loss. She was alone once again.

Her gut roiled, and all she could do was to lash out and scream at everything and everyone around her. "No! I can't do this anymore! Haven't I paid enough?"

As she clutched her breast, an animalistic, anguished wail escaped her. She fell to her knees on the pavement.

"Ma'am, are you okay—ma'am, can I help you?" Rebecca heard the paramedic's voice, but she didn't register what he was asking. She just wanted to be left alone.

"Ma'am, can I call someone for you?" This time, his words were loud and clear.

"There is no one!" she shouted. "No one at all—they're all dead! All of them!" She continued to sob uncontrollably and, as the paramedic tried to comfort her, she pulled away. "Just leave me alone."

Again, he tried to console.

"Don't touch me—please, don't touch me," she said as she attempted to push his hand aside. She was limp with exhaustion and she had no more fight in her. She resigned herself to allowing him to ease her off the ground and walk her toward the ambulance, providing her a more comfortable place to sit.

"What's your name, ma'am?" he asked with tenderness as he handed her a tissue.

"I'm Rebecca Mills." She took the tissue that he handed her. "And her name is—was—Norma Getchel." She sat there quietly, and wiped her nose, trying to recall what he'd previously told her about Norma's death, but it was a blur and the details were lost on her.

"Please tell me again what happened?"

"We received a 911 call from dispatch. She was having a heart attack, and unfortunately, we couldn't make it on time. Please know, Miss Mills, that we tried everything we could to revive her."

As she caught her breath, Rebecca's heart rate slowed. She shivered from the cold. She wiped her nose and the gnawing tug in her gut gripped her with guilt once again.

"I was late—I got held up because of a stupid sunset. I should have been here."

"Ma'am, I don't think—"

"Don't you see? If I'd been here, I could have helped her until you arrived. It could have saved her." Tears ran again and the icy wind chilled them to her cheeks. *I should have been here.*

"Are you sure there isn't someone that you'd like to call?"

She thought of calling Sophie or Emily, but she would have too much to explain. They knew Mrs. Getchel as her dear friend and not as her foster mother. "I'm sure," she said as she stuffed the wadded-up tissues into her pocket and stood. "Do you think it would be okay if I go inside?"

"Of course. It's probably best. We turned off the oven and the stove, but if you feel up to it, the food should be taken care of—wouldn't want it to go bad."

"Sure." Rebecca wiped her hand across her jacket and extended her hand. "Thank you," she said. "Thank you for trying—to save her."

With that, she approached the lit porch, took in a deep breath, and made her way up the stairs; the same stairs that she'd climbed a thousand times before.

She recalled the first time she'd climbed these stairs in utter despair. She'd been unsure of what lay ahead as she'd stood there, holding a half-filled pillow case of her meager belongings. It was her third placement in the system. She'd been demeaned, ridiculed, abused, and unseen. She'd become a shell; a corpse that housed nothing but what she'd deserved—loneliness, shame, and a pain that settled so deeply within her she'd doubted she'd ever be able to truly live again.

She remembered standing with her sack, afraid to look up as the front door creaked open. A matronly pair of laced-up, black shoes with short blocked heels came into view. The ankles were thick and the knee-high stockings sagged low. It was only then that she dared to look up.

Mrs. Getchel stood on the top step, wearing an apron and a kind smile. Her stocky, outstretched arms spread open, welcoming, and ready to embrace her. Rebecca tentatively approached this woman's awaiting arms. As they wrapped around her with a gentle strength, she could finally breathe. Rebecca's head had rested on the woman's full-bosomed chest, and the scent of sugar cookies met her.

She'd felt safe—for the first time, since her mother's arms had held her—she'd felt safe.

CHAPTER 2

Ben Daly watched the sunlight breaking through the warm water of the Pacific. He steadily rose to the water's surface. In his solitude, he reflected on the depth of what he'd just witnessed. *How does one grasp the imminent, powerful grip of death?* He crested the line between water and air with a heavy heart. Yes, he was happy they'd found the helicopter, submerged, and lying at the bottom of the sea, because it meant closure. But he always had a hard time seeing the bodies of those that hadn't survived. Next would come the careful task of retrieving the lost souls and the helicopter's wreckage. It was his life now—drifting from place to place as a salvage diver, without a place to call home. He gave the crew a thumb's up and swam toward the boat.

The captain shouted from the bow of the boat, "What are we looking at, Daly?"

"In one piece, but upside down. It's just teetering there on the edge of a ledge." Ben hopped up and sat on the landing, then took off his fins. "It should be an easy one to grab, though."

"Bodies?"

"All three accounted for, Captain."

Within minutes, the rest of the team joined him on the boat deck, anchored just off the island of Kauai. Before long, they were coming up with a plan to bring the bodies and the helicopter to the surface before the impending hurricane's arrival.

"If we don't beat the storm," Howie said, with concern, "it could fall off the edge to a much deeper bed."

Ben brushed off the concern as always. "If it does, it does—we'll get it."

"You've got a death wish, don't you, Daly?" Smithers said, "it's gotta be five to six hundred feet down!"

"Ah, water's warmer here," Ben said as he pealed his wetsuit off, down to his waist. "Besides, I could use a little euphoria nowadays."

"Speak for yourself. If you want to feel drunk, have a six-pack."

Ben laughed off Howie's tease, then looked at their plan. "Let's just pull the wreckage up. There's a shattered woman waiting for her family's return."

***

Ben ducked to stand under the steaming water in his cramped one-bedroom bungalow. He rinsed the salt off his body, wishing that he could also wash away the vision of a wife, mother, and grandmother being reunited with her beloved family. Her anguish echoed through his mind.

The only thing that brought him a sense of peace was

that he wouldn't have to experience the loss of a loved one, nor would anyone cry for him. Benjamin Daly was alone in the world. He'd become an orphan at the age of four and cast about as a ship on the sea, drifting from port to port without an anchor. It was the only life he'd had until his late teenaged years when he'd lived in Mrs. Getchel's foster home. Outside of that, he knew nothing different. He didn't have anything to lose.

Ben had always acted recklessly. From the time he could remember, he pushed the limits. Sometimes it would help him excel, but most times it caused him trouble. He was born to a drug addict, and had been found in the backseat of a car, with his parents' overdosed bodies slumped over in the front seat. The courts had placed him in the system, and there he remained until he aged out. Carrying the label of damaged goods with him—which meant he was worthless. For a brief time, he'd thought he might as well live up to the label he wore, but it never sat well with him. Not until he joined the Navy at eighteen did he feel as if he fit in and could turn his life around. Now, here he was, retired from service, and still spending his life salvaging lost things in the depths of the seas, pulling up pieces of lives lost.

A bang at the door jolted Ben from his memories.

"Hold on a sec!" he shouted as he finished drying off and threw on a pair of shorts. The bangs persisted, but with less intensity as he drew closer to the door.

Ben gave Juno, his neighbor from a few doors down, the once over, taking notice of her shapely body in her floral wrap dress. Her long black hair blew in the breeze across her face. She moved it aside with her slender fingers and smiled, her lips ripe like strawberries.

"Hey, what's up?" he said as he welcomed her in.

"Heard the news—so sad about that family. Wasn't sure if you'd be up for it, but I thought you might like to grab a bite?"

With Ben's hesitation in responding, Juno twirled her fingers around the tips of her hair. He'd learned her nervous tick and wondered what she'd be nervous about.

Juno lived in a condo unit, around the corner, and they'd become friends during the short time he'd lived on the island. He sensed she wanted more out of their relationship, but having any kind of lasting relationship was out of the question because he was constantly on the go. Dinner, however, sounded great. After the dives, his stomach growled with hunger, and having her for company wasn't a bad idea.

"Sure, why not?" Ben ran his hand over his closely shaved head that was still damp to the touch. "Just give me a minute." He sauntered back toward the bathroom, then turned in her direction. "Grab yourself a drink."

"Can I get you anything to drink, too?" Juno sauntered toward the kitchen.

"Nah, I'm all set." He grabbed a dressier shirt out of the closet, slipped on a pair of leather flip-flops, then brushed his teeth before joining Juno on the patio. She held a glass of white wine as a warm breeze whisked through her long black hair. The curves of her petite body created perfect proportions. She was beautiful. Maybe, he thought, they should just skip dinner altogether. Juno turned to face him. Her full, red lips parted ever so slightly before they turned into a sultry smile.

"You ready?"

"Absolutely," he said as he approached her.

She moved toward him and licked her lips. He stepped closer, welcoming her into his arms. He took in the aroma of melon as his hand ran through her hair. Then he cradled her head in the palm of his hand and brought her lips to his mouth.

"Let's skip dinner and just jump to dessert," Juno said with a whisper before she led them to his bed.

***

The next morning on his way to the dock, Ben's phone rang.

"Damn it." He hit ignore for the fourth time, and shoved his phone back in his pocket.

Ben took in a deep breath and slowly let it out. He felt like a jerk not answering Juno's call, but she wanted more than he would give; they always did.

She was beautiful inside and out, but she deserved better than him. He wasn't willing to commit to her—or anyone for that matter—and her persistence was pushing him away. He could feel her need for more creeping in and his need to flee was growing stronger. Their relationship, if he could call it that, had run its course. Once again, Ben didn't have the gonads to be decent and break it off, face to face, like a good man should. No, he was a coward.

He tapped ignore once more, and jogged to the truck that sat idling outside his bungalow.

Holokai, one of his dive team buddies, sat behind the wheel, and he didn't want him waiting for him any longer. He threw his dive gear in the back end of the truck and swung into the seat. Then they made their way toward the docks at the southwestern side of the island.

"Good day for a dive," Holokai said with a couple of nods of his head.

"Yep."

Holokai glanced over at him. His head cocked and his bushy brows furled before turning back to the winding road.

Holokai's gruff exterior was a far cry from who he was as a human being. His manner was pretty much matched that of a Saint Bernard, whose bark was worse than his bite; he had a gentle spirit. Ben had learned that Holokai's name meant a seafaring person, which Ben thought was pretty cool, given he'd chosen the sea as his life's mission. He'd learned that the meaning of names was taken seriously in Hawaii, and Holokai had certainly lived up to his name. Ben often wondered if Holokai chose his life, or if his life chose him. Either way, he was happy to serve with him.

The ride wasn't long, but it gave Ben a chance to think. He tapped his fingers on his legs as if tapping out a tune. He looked on at the row of sightseers lined up to board the catamarans. The surf was quiet, and the seas were still, so the tourist should be fine, and enjoy the Napali Coast.

Ben's phone rang again, and he retrieved it from his pocket, ready to hit ignore once more when he'd noticed it wasn't Juno calling; it was his friend Jason, from back on the mainland. He rarely heard from Jason, and he answered with an uneasy feeling in the pit of his stomach.

"Hey, Jason. Good to hear from you, man."

"Hey, Ben, you still diving in the Pacific and workin' your charms?"

"You bet I am. What's goin' on?"

"Yeah—so I wish I was calling with some better news." Ben's mind raced as Jason continued. "It's Mrs. Getchel."

Ben's heart sunk, knowing what was coming next. "She's gone, isn't she?"

"I'm afraid so. She had a heart attack at the house."

Jason went on to tell of the upcoming services as Ben's mind whirled about with fleeting memories of Mrs. Norma Getchel. He hadn't seen her, but she'd never been far from his thoughts. She'd been like a mother to him. *She's gone.* His regret at not keeping in touch sat in his stomach like curdled milk.

Jason sat quietly on the other end of the line when Ben realized he was waiting for a response, but to what? He hadn't been listening.

"Ben, are you still there?"

"Yeah, I'm here." Ben weighed his options: to go to Maine or not to go? He owed her that much, but he was hesitant. "Can you text me the info?"

"Sure thing—and Ben, I hope you come. It would be good to see you."

Ben ended the call and looked out the passenger window. The sunny day had become overcast, and the narrow winding road matched his mood; a feeling that at any moment, he'd fall off the edge of the cliff.

Mrs. Getchel was gone.

Ben's tapping fingers moved to the door handle.

"You're going to wear the leather right off if you keep that up," Holokai said. "What's up?"

"It's nothin'."

"Na, it's somethin'."

Yes, Ben thought, *it is something; another loss in my life.* A loss that hit him hard. He cursed himself for not writing more, for not calling more, for not telling her how much she meant to him. She was now another life that he'd taken for granted.

Ben bit his lower lip. "Someone pretty special to me just died—back on the mainland."

"Well, that sure as hell categorizes as somethin' in my book."

"Yeh, I guess."

"You goin' back?"

"Not sure."

"Not sure! You just said this person was pretty special to you." Holokai shook his head. "Man, you are dumber than a rock if…"

"I know." Ben held up his hands in surrender. "I should go, but I gotta work—you know?"

"There's always work, Daly." Holokai shot him a stern look.

"Just watch the damn road, will ya," Ben said as he leaned back in the seat.

"Juno's still chasing you down, right?"

"Yep."

"Seems to me that having to head to the mainland makes for a great excuse to say aloha, seeing how you're afraid to tell her you aren't interested in her anymore."

Ben cringed. It pissed him off that he was that predictable, and his defenses shot up. "I'm not afraid, you good for nothin' piece of sh—"

"Ah, seems I've hit a nerve, my friend." He laughed.

Ben threw his arms up in surrender. "Would you stop focusing on my love life and get us onto the friggin' boat?"

Holokai once again chuckled at Ben's obvious lady troubles. With a roll of his eyes, he said, "I'd hardly call it a love life—it's more of a lust life if you asked me."

"I didn't ask you! Good Lord, man—will you just drive already?"

Within a few moments, they were lugging their duffels out of the back, removing their shoes, and clanking across the gangplank. *A short day—in and out.*

All he wanted to do was focus on the dive and retrieval of the vehicle that lay in the bay. At least this time, it was just a vehicle. No bodies.

His mind kept shifting to what Holokai had said, that if this person was that special to him, he should go. The question that kept floating in and around his thoughts was, which person? Mrs. G. had died, and he wanted to pay his respects; she deserved it. After all, if it hadn't been for her, he probably would have ended up a juvenile delinquent.

But it was the other, someone special, that tugged at him more.

She could be there.

Ben didn't know how to face her if she was. He'd turned his back and walked away just as he'd always done. But it was better that way. The question was, he realized, was who was it better for?

He shook off what he knew in his heart to be true and booked a flight.

***

Ben walked out of Boston's Logan Airport and crossed the walkway toward his rental. The icy temperature and bitter wind cut deep, making him realize he was under dressed for the New England climate. He pulled his jacket collar up and wheeled his bag toward his car rental, taking a mental note to purchase a heavier coat and gloves. He threw his luggage into the trunk and started his hour and a half ride up I-95 to York Harbor, Maine.

As each mile brought him closer to his destination, he thought of the possibility of seeing Becky Mills again. He never could forget the look of her standing in the driveway at Mrs. G.'s house with tears running down her cheeks. He could still hear her yelling for him to not leave her. It broke his heart as well as hers, but he'd left and there wasn't anything he could do about it now.

He'd last seen Rebecca Mills eighteen years ago. She'd still been a kid. Come to think of it, he'd been one too, even though he was a couple of years her senior. She'd been mature for a sixteen-year-old, but still way too young. Besides, he'd been a menace to society back then. It was as if he had a grudge against the world and he wore it like a badge of honor. Only Becky and Mrs. G. saw through his front, even if he couldn't.

Mrs. G. had had to deal with his troubling antics more than he cared to remember. He was ready to age out of the system, and she'd encouraged him to join the military. She'd said he needed the discipline and structure to succeed in life. As much as he hated to admit it, it had proved true. He'd really had no better choice but to leave York Harbor and make his own way, whether he liked it or not. He'd had no money. No skill. Nothing to give Becky the life she deserved.

He remembered that day like it was yesterday. Mrs. G. had given him a deep and lasting hug, as if it were to last him a lifetime, but he didn't know how to move forward without Mrs. G's love and care, and so he'd remained stiff-armed, and detached, not hugging her in return. Saying goodbye was too hard. He'd fought back tears, determined to not show how scared he really was. But Becky couldn't hold her tears back. She'd begged him not to leave. She hadn't understood that he had to.

Instead of explaining, he'd turned his back on her and walked away. He could still hear the last words she'd shouted at him that day, *"You're a lousy, good for nothing piece of crap, Benjamin Daly!"*

Her words had hurt. He'd heard that he was worthless too many times before from too many people. What he was doing was for the best, even if she wouldn't understand. He wasn't good enough for her then, and he probably wasn't much better for her now. What had she expected him to do back then? They'd been kids. Her angry taunts haunted him still. She'd said she hoped she'd never have to see him again for as long as she lived, then slammed the door behind him and on the life that he'd leave behind.

He couldn't help but think that his ride to Maine was the calm before the storm. He had no idea of what awaited him once he returned to York Harbor. For all he knew, Becky Mills could live on the other side of the planet, and therefore, all would be well.

He'd just touch base with Jason Fisher, who'd told him about Mrs. G's passing. Jason was one of his foster brothers, who, as it happened, had turned into a Navy buddy. To his delight, Jason was now stationed in Portsmouth, New Hampshire. He'd stay a few days in York, connect with Jason, then hike back to the island.

A quick in and out.

CHAPTER 3

Rebecca pulled into the portico of the funeral home and received parking instructions, then proceeded to her directed parking spot. She sat there and stared at the funeral home. *Well, this is it. It's the last time I get to see you.* Rebecca dabbed the corner of her eye and hoped that the undertaker had done a good job. Mrs. Getchel liked her hair loosely rolled, and she'd want her lipstick. At least it was sunny; she would have liked that.

Rebecca was pleased to see the number of vehicles and wondered if the cars belonged to anyone she knew. If she knew them, she may not even recognize them after so many years. Mrs. Getchel had touched a lot of lives and had made friends along the way. As far as Rebecca knew, Mrs. Getchel didn't have any family. Her only "family" came and went with the wind just as Rebecca had, and she was sure there were too many to count.

Rebecca was grateful that she could take the day off to say goodbye to Mrs. Getchel. She hadn't told Sophie and Emily how she knew Mrs. Getchel because, in doing so, she'd have to reveal too much, and she wasn't ready to open that wound. They did, however, know that she was her dear friend and gave her all the time and support she needed.

Rebecca grabbed her handbag, silenced her phone, checked for tissues, and sighed with the realization that she only had a few left, then slowly made her way to the front door. A man with sad eyes, dressed with a black cap and overcoat greeted her with a nod.

She tried to stuff down the memory of missing her parents' funerals all those years ago when she'd been in an induced coma at the hospital. Her pain felt just as raw today as the day she'd found out she'd missed it—a pain that was all consuming and lingered every day of her life since. She quietly counted to three to ground herself, then trudged into the foyer.

Elevator music filtered throughout the halls. The forlorn expressions on familiar faces, and the clustering of whispers engulfed her. She gave a stiff smile at Mrs. Getchel's kind neighbor that had come over for tea from time to time, and nodded at several former foster kids that she'd recognized over the years, but she couldn't bring herself to chat with anyone. She was determined to keep herself together. So many people filled the space that she wanted nothing more than to quietly back out of the room and flee, but the sight of Norma Getchel lying there beckoned her forward.

A multitude of red, yellow, and white roses, chrysanthemums, gladiolus, and orchids surrounded Mrs. Getchel's casket. She was pleased to see that lilies were few as Mrs.

Getchel never liked lilies precisely because they reminded her of death. Rebecca grinned, imagining what Mrs. Getchel would do if she were there. She pictured her plucking out the lilies and throwing them into the shrubbery out back.

Rebecca recognized a handful of the arrangements that she'd fashioned and hoped she'd made Mrs. Getchel proud. She'd considered it an honor to create them, but was relieved that she hadn't had to plan the service. Mrs. Getchel had pre-planned every detail to not be a burden when her time came. Her church made sure that they followed every detail to perfection.

Rebecca wasn't sure what to do when she looked down at the casket. Should she kneel, stand, talk to her? She wasn't much for praying, praying never amounted to anything as far as she was concerned. God had made it abundantly clear, long ago, that her requests fell on deaf ears. No, she concluded she'd just stand there and take in the lips that had kissed her goodnight, the hands that held hers, and the shoulder that she'd cried on more times than she cared to admit.

Rebecca's chest became heavy and the urge to cry welled up in her throat. She reached down and touched the loose curl of her bangs. *They did a nice job.* She whispered a thank you and said her last goodbye, then took a seat near the back. In the back, she could be invisible. Rebecca hated the feeling of people looking at her—watching her—seeing her vulnerable and raw. She sat at the end of the aisle, hoping above anything that no one would sit next to her. She needed her safe space to mourn and take in the fullness of the service without distraction.

The pastor eloquently spoke about the impact that Norma Getchel had made in the community as a foster mother or friend, and Rebecca recognized that she had the privilege of having Mrs. Getchel as both.

She'd exhausted her tissues, resorting to using her sleeve when someone's arm reached forward from the bench behind hers to accommodate her need. She wished she could say a few words, too, but she couldn't bring herself to step forward. Besides, she thought, she'd simply cry.

Mrs. Getchel's friends and former foster kids stood and spoke of how Mrs. Getchel had changed their lives for the better, how she'd accepted them with all their faults and scars. How she'd dedicated her life to bring hope and love to others, and how she would never be forgotten. When Rebecca realized that she felt as they did; that she hadn't been alone. For a moment, a terrible thought crossed her mind. She'd been no one special or unique to Mrs. Getchel. She was just another recipient of Mrs. Getchel's good nature, like all the others. She wiped her face of the sadness that poured down her cheeks.

Again, the man's arm reached over the back of her seat and handed her another tissue. Then six men, including the man that had been sitting behind her, stepped out into the isle to make their way toward the front to accompany and carry the body of her dearest friend toward her final resting place. Rebecca recognized Geoffrey and Aiden who were a couple of her foster kids from the past; Thomas, Mrs. Getchel's Pinochle playing companion; Sal, who'd taken care of odd jobs over the years, another gentleman whom Rebecca hadn't known, and then the kind man who'd handed her tissues.

Rebecca couldn't breathe. It was as if she'd momentarily forgotten how.

No, it can't be.

She was lightheaded and the need to flee intensified,

but she would be darned if she'd let the likes of Benjamin Daly keep her from saying goodbye to the one person who'd saved her.

Ben Daly wore a stoic expression. He dressed much like the funeral director with his long black overcoat, that accentuated his broad shoulders. He wore a black-and-gray tweed driving cap atop his closely shaved head. His tanned face didn't have its once youthful, skinny, blemished markings; it now bore a carefully manicured brown goatee on a strong, chiseled chin. His lips were relaxed and his eyes seemed to drift away. He seemed confident and strong; unlike the scrappy kid she remembered. As a teen, he'd tried to act like he was a tough guy, but she had known him too well. Now, he had grown to be a gorgeous man—a man entrusted to carry their beloved surrogate grandmother and caretaker to her final resting place.

Never in a million years had she expected to see him again; he'd been a ghost. Now, here he was in the flesh. In some regard, she was happy to see him. After all, she could honestly say she'd loved him back then. Sure, it had been young love, which was fleeting. But he was her first love, even though he'd been oblivious to that fact. He'd left an indelible mark at a time in her life when she'd needed to feel alive and accepted.

Over the years, she'd often wondered what had happened to him. Had he gone down a path of destruction, or had he made something of his life? More so, she'd wondered if he'd ever thought of her, that long-ago girl who'd seemed lost and brokenhearted, the one that still lived in her. Seeing him here and now, however, ripped at her heart because she now realized that she'd meant nothing to him. If she had, he would have kept in touch. It was obvious to her that someone knew how to find him. And that someone wasn't her, and that realization tore at her soul. He had purposefully ghosted her. She was a nobody to him—he'd discarded her as if she never mattered or existed.

She looked on as the procession made its slow progress toward the back of the room to the awaiting double doors and hearse. They stopped to remove the casket from the wheeled cart, and Ben stepped aside. His deep brown eyes caught her gaze. As a glimmer of recognition crossed his face, her pulse quickened, and after a moment, he shifted once again to his task of carrying their beloved Mrs. Getchel out the door.

Rebecca escaped, at long last, out into the fresh, crisp air, then retreated to her awaiting car that now bore a magnetic flag on its hood.

The cemetery had turned bleak. Even the flowers seemed to fade into the shadows, leaving the scene as if it, too, were mourning. The pastor read the ritualistic reading: 'Though I walk through the valley of the shadow of death, I will fear no evil: for thou art with me: thy rod and thy staff they comfort me...' But the words didn't ring true. God couldn't be farther away than He was right now. So, she quietly turned and strolled away.

Rebecca made her way back to the long line of parked vehicles that filled the narrow cemetery roadway. She opened her car door and sat. It hadn't occurred to her she'd be stuck. Rebecca laid her arms across her steering wheel, rested her head on them, and wept. The song, *Amazing Grace*, drifted through the air, causing an anguish that she hadn't felt in a long time. It was always on the cusp of breaking through, but she'd buried it down deep, hoping to keep it at bay.

A knock at her side window broke through her labored

and jagged cries. She raised her head and Ben's warm brown eyes stared back at her.

Rebecca wished she could jump out and punch him in the gut and slap him across the face for leaving her, for staying away without so much as a word. For coming back. She wanted to kick and punch until she didn't have any punch left, but all she could bring herself to do was shake her head and turn away. His large shadow cast over her, and his weighted presence pressed against the window. So, she gave in and looked back at him. Her adrenalin spiked at the sight of him.

Ben stood firm, his gloved, open hand on the glass. His deep voice, which was foreign to her, only said, "Please."

Rebecca slammed her fist on the steering wheel, then cracked the window just enough for him to hear her.

"Please what, Benjamin Daly?" She didn't wait for a response, nor was she looking for one. "Please forgive me? Please, what?!"

"Please, let me in," Ben said in a calm tone. "Please, let me in."

"And why should I do that, Ben?"

"Because we need each other, Becky."

"How dare you speak about what I need!" She clenched her fists, reaching her boiling point.

"Becky—"

"No! You lost the right to need anything from me a long time ago." Her lips quivered and her throat tightened. *No, don't you do it, Rebecca Mills. Hold it together. Don't you dare let him see you cry because of him again.* She pulled in her anger just as the line of cars moved ahead of her, then rolled the window back up, put the car in gear, and drove away. In her rearview mirror, he stood with his hands in his pockets, becoming smaller and smaller, then he disappeared, leaving another scar that wouldn't heal.

Becky drove silently, with no direction or place in mind. She just drove. The next thing she knew, she sat in a parking spot overlooking the Nubble Lighthouse on Cape Neddick. Gray, angry waves crashed on the rocks, sending breaking water skyward.

She slid out of her seat and stood with the wind in her face, causing her tears to freeze and sting her cheeks. She ventured toward the flat surface of the rocks.

The sea beckoned her. The wind's groans and moans billowed around her as if to say, "Come."

She took a few more steps, teetering on the weathered rocks, moving toward the ones that awaited her where the ocean waves swirled and grew angrier. Still, she moved closer and closer toward the sea. She could feel an internal tug pulling her ever so gently forward, and all she could think about was that she would be in no more pain. That knowing allowed her to take another step forward. Then a voice rose out of the wind, a gentle and kind voice, a voice of tenderness and love. "Go back," it whispered ever so quietly in her ear, "Go back."

Rebecca's phone buzzed in her pocket. She glanced down at a number that she didn't recognize and hesitated to answer until it dawned on her that Benjamin might have gotten her number.

"Hello?" she asked in a hush.

"May I please speak with Miss Rebecca Mills?"

"Yes, this is she."

"This is Attorney Larry Howard from Howard Law Office." Hearing that it was an attorney's office on the other end of the line piqued her curiosity. "I'm calling in regards to a Mrs. Norma Getchel."

When the gentleman on the other end of the line mentioned Mrs. Getchel, she realized the call had to be about Mrs. Gtechel's estate, but she couldn't fathom why he'd be calling her.

He spoke with a warm, yet matter-of-fact tone that was precise. "I'm sorry for your loss, Miss Mills. Would it be possible for you to stop by our office tomorrow morning at nine?"

Sophie had told her to take the day off to grieve her friend. "Sure, I can do that." She nodded and climbed back up the rocks. "Tomorrow morning at nine—I'll see you then."

Rebecca hung up and pressed the phone to her heart. A whirlwind of thoughts swirled around in her mind. *What have you done, Norma Getchel?*

CHAPTER 4

Ben drove out of the cemetery gates but circled back. The chill in the air, especially having lived in a warmer climate, penetrated his new overcoat. Even his toes were cold, but nothing beat the chilly reception he'd received from Becky Mills.

When he'd seen her sit in front of him at the church, he wanted nothing more than to talk with her, but the timing wasn't right. All he could do was offer tissues from the box that sat next to him. He had a hard time taking his eyes off her, and he'd made a point to seek her out afterward. He'd hoped that she'd join him for a cup of coffee and have a cordial conversation to reminisce. But as soon as he'd taken one look at her, the sight of her glassy, almond-shaped, green eyes had nearly put him over the edge. She was hurting and angry, and her anger toward him made him want to pull her out of the car and hold her tight and never let her go.

He'd always cared for Becky, but having been away for so long, he'd still envisioned her to be a kid. The kid that followed him around, believed in him, that made him feel like he set the sun and the moon. Seeing her sitting there had sent a shock through him. She'd literally taken his breath away. He couldn't blame her for hating him. He'd let her down, but he couldn't turn back time and change it, nor would he even want to. Ben had done what he needed to do at eighteen.

Ben stood back as he watched dirt fill the hole in where Mrs. G. lay. He owed his life to her. Without her, he had no doubt that he'd have turned into a delinquent, or worse. She'd given him wings to fly the nest. He'd left with rebellion and anger. He hadn't wanted to leave, but his time had come. He'd aged out of the system and the Navy offered him his best chance at a bright future. He'd have discipline and greater opportunities, Mrs. G. had said, and it would be good for him.

Kids in high school were excited for their eighteenth birthday, but Ben dreaded and feared that day. These kids could go back home, but he would no longer have a place to call home. He'd truly be alone in the world and he'd have to make his own way.

Ben never admitted his fears to anyone. No, he'd played it cool. He wouldn't even admit it to Becky. In fact, with Becky, he'd never even broached the subject. To him, it was like finding out there wasn't a Santa Claus before your younger sibling, and choosing to keep it a secret to protect their innocence and excitement. Of course, she had to know she'd age out at eighteen, but when he was her age, it seemed far away and it was easier to pretend it wasn't going to happen. At least she got to stay until she graduated high school, especially because she'd only arrived there less than a year before. She deserved more time with Mrs. Getchel.

Being a foster care kid was never a label he wanted

to wear, however, it was one he'd worn for most of his life. It wasn't so much the label as it was never having control over where he'd stay or for how long. Oh, how he'd longed for a permanent home that felt safe, and where his belly would be full. Looking back, he supposed he'd made it harder on himself than need be. Maybe, he'd thought, if he'd just behaved better, they would have been kinder, and he might have been adopted.

Ben's thoughts drifted to Jason, who'd been like a brother. He'd lived in Mrs. G's home, along with him and Becky. Outside of Becky, Jason was the only one Ben cared to talk or see while he was in York. He was disappointed when he realized Jason hadn't been at Mrs. G's memorial service, but ventured to guess he simply couldn't get leave.

Jason had been a follower, and Ben had felt responsible for protecting him. Ben thought of all the times Jason had wanted to tag along when he was up to no good, but he'd encouraged Jason to be better than he was. The one thing Ben couldn't discourage was when Jason had also joined the Navy. He turned out okay, Ben thought, and he missed him.

Ben shook off the memories that flooded his mind. He was here to send Mrs. G. off. The one woman in his life that made him feel special and cared for.

The workers smoothed the crunchy earth above her grave, and now the work was complete, except for a headstone. He imagined her headstone would read: *Here lies, Mrs. Norma Getchel, a mother to none, yet a mother to all.* He stood staring down to where Norma now rested. That was it. She was gone. Would he ever come back to see her name engraved on her stone, a monument that said she'd existed—that she'd lived? No, he thought, he'd just prefer to get chucked into the sea.

No need for fanfare or farewells. After all, who would come? He was alone in the world and, once he was gone, he was sure he'd never be missed.

Ben drove to the York Harbor Inn and checked in. He threw his coat, gloves, and hat on the bed, and made his way to the main floor. He was pleased to find a warm fire burning so he could get rid of the chill that still clung to him. The smell of the burning wood and the hint of smoke filled him with a longing for home. He hadn't realized until now, that he'd never considered anywhere in particular to be his home until now.

Home wasn't a house or a place, he thought; it was more of a feeling. He sat down on the overstuffed cushioned chair and rubbed his hands across the wooden arms. They were warm and smooth to the touch. Above him, exposed beams reflected the flickering flames, and at his feet dark-stained floorboards showed wear. He leaned back and crossed his ankles to take in the comfort. This, he thought, must be the feeling of being home.

Ben's phone went off and he hurried to quiet the noise. "Hello, this is Ben."

"Hello, Mr. Daly, this is Attorney Larry Howard."

Ben listened and agreed to meet the attorney at his office in the morning, then ended the call.

A meeting at 9:00 in the morning. He shook his head in disbelief. He couldn't begin to imagine why he'd be needed at Mrs. Getchel's attorney's office, but figured he'd do his part and show up.

He reluctantly escaped the comfort of the chair. His stomach churned and the aroma from the pub was getting impossible to resist, so he descended the stairs. The special on the board was a turkey sandwich of stuffing and cranberry sauce. A smile emerged. He'd forgotten Thanksgiving had only been a week ago, and his mouth watered at the thought of sinking his teeth into one of those sandwiches. First, a bowl of clam chowder called his name.

A tall, slender woman approached to take his order. Her hair was dark brown, but in this light, it could have been blacker than he supposed. She had a turned-up nose and full lips, much like Becky's. Ben wished he'd seen that woman's bright smile on Becky. A smile that, despite the circumstances, had flooded his memories for years. Remarkably, he'd never pictured her as a grown woman. In his mind's eye, she was still a stubborn teenager. Now, she had a natural beauty about her—still stubborn—but beautiful. He could still feel her green eyes looking into his, and that nearly took his breath away all over again.

Ben emptied the small bag of oyster crackers into his steaming bowl of chowder. He blew on his spoon and tested the heat on his lips, then licked them with satisfaction, savoring every spoonful until his spoon clinked at the bottom with nothing left to taste.

The server placed a stacked turkey sandwich in front of him. The sandwich filled him with memories of his last Thanksgiving at Mrs. G's place. He and Becky had made a wish as they each pulled on the wishbone Mrs. G. had saved especially for them. When the wishbone snapped in their grasp, he'd gotten the larger portion, which meant he'd get his wish. Becky paid him back by splashing him with a sink full of soapy water. He'd retaliated until Mrs. G. gave them "the look" as her way of reprimand, but he didn't miss her slight grin as she'd turned her head away.

Ben took a hefty bite of the impressive sandwich as his thoughts continued to wander. That was one thing he treasured most about Mrs. G.; she never yelled. She always got her point across without the use of harsh words or gestures. Because of that, he'd tried not to disappoint her. Unfortunately, he hadn't always proved successful in that regard.

He hadn't realized until now how much Becky had meant to him. Thinking back, she was the person he was closest to. Out of all the other fosters that had come and gone, he'd favored Becky. She was who he had missed the most. He'd thought so many times of writing to her, but he couldn't bring himself to follow through. He'd figured she was better off forgetting all about him and assumed she'd done just that.

With his stomach full, and the warm atmosphere, his eyes grew heavy. He ordered a nightcap of Crown Royal to, hopefully, help him forget Mrs. G's still face and Becky's sad eyes.

CHAPTER 5

Morning broke with a freezing rainfall that had apparently continued throughout the night. The trees hung heavy over what was left of fallen leaves. Rebecca would have to get ready earlier than she'd expected to scrape off her windshield and head to her appointment with the attorney. She was grateful that Sophie was once again gracious in providing her with the time off that she'd needed, but concerned for the million and one things that were adding up on her to-do list at work.

Rebecca took another sip of her steaming coffee, warming her hands. She was sick of feeling cold. Her apartment was a nice size, and she loved its location, but it was drafty, and she had a hard time shaking off her chill. Her overly loved slippers were matted down and ugly as sin, but at least they kept her feet warm. She had a hard time letting anything go. She shrugged off her propensity of holding on to material things and moved as a snail to the shower. She dreaded the task because it would entail the removal of her night clothes, thus making her shiver that much more until the heat of the shower could warm her up.

Rebecca stood under the heat as the water ran over her face, and cupped her hands under her breasts, catching the warmth within her hands as the water overflowed to her feet. She'd just finished lathering on the shampoo when the lights flickered. Panic washed over her as she raced with nature to rinse the shampoo, but she was too late. Off the power went as she stood there, covered in suds from head to toe, cursing that fact that her apartment ran on an electric water pump and wasn't a part of the town's water supply. The only thing she could think to do was to rinse with the gallon of water that she kept in the fridge.

She stepped out of the shower, grabbed her robe, then slid her way across the linoleum floor to the kitchen. *I hate my life,* she thought as she laughed at her situation. Then she poured ice-cold water over her head and screeched with every pour. *Okay, it's as good as it's going to get.* Then realized she wouldn't be able to dry her hair either. *"Dang it! Of all friggin times."*

Rebecca shivered with her wet towel wrapped atop her head, stomped into her bedroom, and pulled the chain to turn on the closet light. "You're an idiot," she said as she stood staring into her dark closet in search of something to wear.

What does one wear to an attorney's office? All she knew for sure was that she wanted to be warm. Rebecca tried on a pair of black leggings and a herringbone patterned, black-and-white skirt, then whipped them off in a huff and threw them on the bed. She dug around until she pulled out a pair of black slacks. At least she hoped they were black. They could have been navy. She paired the slacks with a burgundy turtleneck sweater, then hoped for the best.

Before long, she stood in the freezing rain, with a still wet head, and her teeth chattering, but thankful the warmth from the car would rescue her from her predicament. Unfortunately, it wouldn't be for long; the attorney's office wasn't that far away.

Rebecca pulled in and cautiously stepped over the ice-covered parking lot until she reached a sanded section and entered the foyer, grateful to see that the lights were on. A matronly woman, who sat at the front desk, greeted her with a kind smile and offered to take her coat.

"No thanks, I'll hang on to it." Rebecca wasn't about to remove her coat or her woolen hat. No, she thought, her hat was covering her mangled hair, and she'd be darned if she'd make a spectacle of herself while Mrs. Getchel's will was being read.

The kind lady escorted her through a heavy door. Before her sat a gentleman with soft eyes, wearing a zipped-up sweater, much like Mr. Rogers had worn. He stood and offered his hand.

"Hello, Miss Mills. Thank you for making the trip here on such a day. Please have a seat." He gestured toward one of the two cushioned chairs opposite his desk. Before her bottom could rest in the seat, the door opened again.

She gasped as Benjamin entered, looking as well put together as the day she'd seen him at Mrs. Getchel's funeral service. *Why is he here?* She staggered to her seat, missing the cushion, and caught the arm enough so that she plopped into the chair off kilter, having to brace herself with her hand as it slammed onto the desk. Rebecca stiffly sat, pretending that the entire episode never happened. She rolled her eyes back in complete humiliation, but Ben and the attorney carried on as if nothing had happened.

Rebecca could barely bring herself to look in Ben's direction. None of this was making any sense. Why was she there? Why was Benjamin there as well? Ben hadn't just left her all those years ago, he'd left Mrs. Getchel, too. She couldn't reconcile why Ben, of all people, would be at the reading of her will.

"Ah, Mr. Daly. Welcome—please have a seat." Again, he extended his hand for a shake before Ben moved to the chair within inches of hers.

He smelled deliciously masculine, she thought. She couldn't help herself, she sneaked a peek and got caught. His gaze met hers as he took his seat. How was it possible that she could despise someone and still feel something for him at the same time? She pondered this thought as her pulse quickened, and her internal heat rose. By now, she was so warm that all she wanted to do was shed her hat and coat but shook off the idea. She'd look foolish sitting there with no coat and still wearing her hat. So, she just sat there staring into Ben's big brown eyes, unable to speak. When the attorney addressed them again, she pulled her gaze away from Ben's responsive stare.

Rebecca's hand clenched the arms of the chair as the attorney read the typical boiler plate introduction to Norma Getchel's will. Mr. Howard stopped, made sure he had their full attention, then continued.

"Item one: I, Norma Getchel, bequeath my home, its contents, and vehicle to Rebecca Mills."

Rebecca felt as if the floor fell from beneath her. Her

mind spun with confusion and could barely comprehend the magnitude of the words on the page. "I don't understand. Why would she do this? Surely, she must have some family or someone more deserving?"

"I can assure you that she has no family, at least not in the traditional sense, and I understand that this is a lot to take in, but if you'll allow me to continue, Miss Mills—"

"Oh, sorry, of course," she said, then motioned for him to continue.

"Item two: I, Norma Getchel, bequeath the sum of my retirement account, savings, and checking accounts, to Rebecca Mills. Said accounts will be held in a separate trust and released when, and if, certain conditions have been met."

Rebecca's breath caught, and she gasped for air. "Conditions? What conditions?"

Attorney Howard raised his hand. "I'll explain momentarily, but I must continue."

"Of course." Rebecca nodded, but she was having a hard time understanding. He sounded as though she were in a *Peanuts* episode and his words were unrecognizable mumblings.

"Item three: I bequeath the sum of my stocks, to Benjamin Daly with conditions. Said stocks will be held in a separate trust and released when, and if, certain conditions have been met."

Ben's eyes grew wide and he sat up straighter. "I'm with Becky. What conditions and why us? Does she say why?"

"Please allow me to proceed, and hopefully, it will answer some of your questions, but before I continue, you must know that I am Mrs. Getchel's trustee. Understood?"

Ben nodded and swallowed hard, and Rebecca stared blankly.

"I manage Mrs. Getchel's funds," he said awaiting their response. Ben and Rebecca nodding.

"Item four: I, Norma Getchel, bequeath and devise, the full sum of my trust fund to, Rebecca Mills and Benjamin Daly equally and jointly with the stipulation that it is used for the sole benefit of those within the foster care system."

Rebecca squirmed in her chair. *This is too much. I can't breathe.* She had the sudden urge to run.

Mr. Howard scanned the will for a minute, then peeked over the top of his glasses. "In a nutshell, the stipulations say that the two of you," He pointing to her and Ben, "must develop and operate this entrusted endeavor for foster care kids, jointly, and you have one hundred and eighty days from the date of her passing to abide by the terms, or I, as her trustee, have been instructed to dissolve the trust account, its assets, along with her savings, checking, retirement, and stocks will then be bequeathed to the Office of Child and Family Services."

Ben shot Rebecca a look of panic before he turned toward the attorney. "But I can't. I have a life. In Hawaii! What happens if we can't?"

Rebecca couldn't take it anymore. She leapt from her chair and paced back and forth like a caged animal. *This can't be happening.* Her stomach turned somersaults, and she thought she might throw up. She leaned against the wall and placed her hands on her knees to brace herself for more to come.

Rebecca was lightheaded. She might faint right then and there. She numbly wandered back to her chair. Her mouth was dry, and she couldn't bring herself to respond when the attorney asked if she had any questions. Her hands gripped the cushioned arms of the chair and she stared blankly at his questioning eyes.

"So, the bottom line is that Becky and I have to get this foster care program of some kind up and running—together, to your liking, within one hundred and eighty days, or we don't get the money?"

"That is correct."

Rebecca could sense Ben turning toward her, but she couldn't move. This was all too much to take in. She was overwhelmed and tried to regulate her breathing. *Why?* She could feel herself getting even more lightheaded, and she rested her head in her hands. *Why would Mrs. Getchel do this?*

"Becky, are you alright?" Ben placed his hand on her back. "Beck?"

Some of the tension from her shoulders relaxed, and she finally could bring herself to speak. "I'm okay." She nodded, as if convincing herself that she was okay. "I still don't understand why she would choose us?"

"Perhaps this will help explain." The attorney took out a handwritten note from his file and was sure to capture their complete attention before he read.

Dearest Rebecca and Benjamin,

Have you ever felt something so strongly in your heart that you had to act on it? Well, I have. You may not see your future as I see it, but I know you are the ones to fulfill my greatest desire. I chose you because I believe in you. I ask that you continue my legacy of caring for and nurturing the next generation of foster kids. You can bridge the gap of instability to ability, and I hope that you will also bridge the gap between yourselves.

I know I should never have had favorites, but I knew from the first time I laid eyes on the two of you that you would be just that.

I love you, Rebecca, and Benjamin, as if you were my own daughter and son, and I hope that through this endeavor, you will feel my love and grow to be truly happy.

Norma

Rebecca couldn't stop the silent tears that slipped down her cheeks. Norma's words stunned her. *She loved me, and I wasn't there for her when she needed me the most.* It didn't matter that she'd just inherited Mrs. Norma Getchel's home, its contents, vehicle, and a possible fortune. All she wanted was for Mrs. Getchel to hold her in her arms once again. She'd learned long ago that material things didn't matter. She missed her dear friend and just wanted her back.

Ben grabbed hold of her white-fingered grip on the chair's arm. He leaned in and wiped her tears with his thumb. "Are you alright? Do you need anything—water or something?"

"No—yes, I'm okay. I'm just—"

"I know—me too." Ben squeezed her hand. Rebecca slid her hand out from under his and rested it on her lap. Her feet bounced with nervous energy. She looked in the attorney's direction as he now continued with instructions. She and Ben collected paperwork and shook hands with the attorney, who then escorted them toward the door.

"What just happened, Benjamin?"

"As God is my witness, I don't have a clue. I mean, what she did for you, I completely understand. You were there for her. I wasn't."

No, I wasn't. Not when it mattered the most.

Rebecca and Ben stood on the walkway, sleet pelting down on them. Ben's shoulders hunched over and stuck his hands in his pockets. "Have you eaten?"

Rebecca shivered and wrapped her arms around her waist. "No—just coffee. I lost power. It was all I could do to get here on time."

"What do you say we head over to Rick's for a bite? We should talk about all of this." He tilted his head in the direction of the law office.

"I can't—I don't—I don't even know what she was thinking. How could we possibly..." Rebecca was angry at herself, and angry with the overwhelming responsibility that Mrs. Getchel had just laid on them. She didn't understand why she'd think for one minute that she and Ben could do this. They hadn't spoken to each other in years. They lived a world apart. She was now freezing. Her mind raced. Ben's larger-than-life presence stood between she and her car. "I can't do this."

CHAPTER 6

Rebecca considered her options as she and Ben stood outside the attorney's office. Ben placed his gloved hands on Rebecca's shoulders and turned her toward him. "Becky, you're shivering. You probably still don't have power, and we need to talk about what just happened in there."

His firm, yet gentle voice brought her to her senses. They needed to talk about how they would navigate this monstrous undertaking together. Going back to her cold apartment made little sense, either. She was hungry. Eating had become a calming force for her. Not in a negative sense, but in how her mom would make her soup and grilled cheese on a cold autumn day. Yes, she thought. A bit of comfort food would probably do her some good.

"Fine. I'll meet you at Rick's." With that, she removed Ben's firm hands from her shoulders and precariously made her way to her car. It took several tries before her old Toyota started. The engine sputtered, just like her thoughts, as if it too was too cold to function. She waited for the car to warm up before heading to Rick's. As she pulled into the back parking lot, turned off the ignition she just sat there, trying to force herself to vacate the car. The urge to flee pressed in on her. She wasn't ready to dissect this monumental situation, especially not with Ben. Not yet. She needed space to understand what had just transpired.

Rebecca reached to turn the car back on just as Ben tapped on her window. She looked up at him through the steamed up side window. He stood with his hands in his pockets and expectant eyes, and she couldn't say no. She slumped in defeat and placed her key back in her handbag, then retreated from her seat.

"It's pretty slick." Ben offered her an arm. "I thought I'd walk with you."

She looked at his outstretched hand, then glanced down at his feet. "You're wearing loafers. I hardly think you'll be able to walk yourself, let alone help me."

He gazed down at his feet on a thin layer of ice, freezing rain tapping on top of the leather.

He lifted an eyebrow. "You could be right. But the way I see it, we're in this together. I figure we could hold each other up."

That'd be a first. Ben's act of chivalry wasn't lost on her. He'd abandoned her when she'd needed him the most. "Sink or swim, Benjamin. After all, you're used to doing things on your own. You don't need me."

She was being petty, but seeing him acting all gentlemanly didn't sit well with her. Rebecca trudged to the main entrance of Rick's, leaving Ben slipping and sliding behind her. Rebecca didn't wait for him to be seated and took the table near the old paned windows. She was previewing the menu when Ben stepped in, brushing sleet from his overcoat. She didn't bother to wave him over; the place wasn't large enough to require it. He removed his coat and slid between the planked table and large, paned window.

Rebecca removed her hat and set it on the chair next to her, then shrugged off her coat and rested it behind her before once again reaching for the menu. Ben burst into laughter.

"What's so funny?" Rebecca asked, irked he could find anything funny on a day like today.

***

Ben bit the inside of his cheek to keep from laughing aloud. He didn't mean to laugh at her. In fact, she couldn't have looked more adorable. Her dark hair was an absolute disaster. It lays flattened, actually, more pasted at the top of her head where her hat had covered it, and a clumpy mass of a mop below. But he couldn't take his eyes off her. Even in her disheveled mess, she melted his heart. By now, her deep green eyes narrowed at him.

"You might want to um…" He gestured toward the bathroom door that stood about fifteen feet behind her, then pointed to his head. She brushed her hand through her hair and urgency flashed across her face.

"Oh! I lost power when I was in the shower—I, um." Before finishing the sentence, she slid her chair back, nearly toppling it over, and scampered off to the restroom, latching the door behind her.

Ben asked for a couple of coffees. He wished they'd ordered before he'd said anything about her hair, but if she'd realized it any later in their brunch, she'd have been even more embarrassed. That would just have added to the many reasons she shouldn't give him the time of day. And they needed to talk about Mrs. Getchel's will.

Ben leaned forward, playing with the paper from his straw. He reran the events of the morning in the attorney's office. Mrs. G. had left him a decent sum of money, with the caveat that he and Becky create a program. *A foster program. What does that even mean?* This so-called venture could mean so many things and he wished Mrs. G. had given them more guidance. This would not happen. He had a life outside York Harbor, Maine. He didn't have time to delve into some kind of crazy venture, nor did he have the desire. The only connection he wanted, when it came to the foster system was to never look back.

The bathroom door squeaked open, and Rebecca shyly peered out from behind the door. She ran her hand through her hair and sat down.

"You're an ass," she said before looking him in the eyes.

"I'm sorry I laughed. It's just that you looked—"

"Horrific. Go ahead and say it. I looked like a clown, Benjamin Daly, and you laughed at me!" She leaned forward and now spoke in a more quiet voice. "Out loud, in public!"

"Yes, I did, but you looked so damned cute. I couldn't help myself." He also couldn't help but grin as she cracked a smile.

"I'd hardly say I was cute, but thanks for bringing the abomination of my hair to my attention." She picked up the menu and stood it up between them. "I'm starving."

They ordered and gulped down coffee before a word of what the attorney had told them came up. They agreed they had no idea what Mrs. Getchel had been thinking to give

them what she'd given them, and hadn't a clue regarding the
foster care situation, but thought they needed to give it some
time to adjust to their situation. When they'd finished eating,
silence fell over them. Ben shifted in his seat and picked up his
empty coffee mug to take a drink. He placed it back down and
tapped on the side of it with his worn, copper ring, oblivious
to the clinking.

Rebecca reached over and steadied his hand. "So, we
have a lot to talk about and get through, and yes, we need a
breather—over the next week or so—to put some thought
into everything that's been thrown at us. But we shouldn't
drag our feet too long. One hundred and eighty days will go
by fast." Rebecca cleared her throat. "When are you going
back to Hawaii, anyway?"

"Soon," he said, without thinking about his reply. Soon,
was the first response that came to mind. Rebecca's demeanor
changed in that instant. She bit her lip and retrieved her
purse. She fumbled around in it, then slapped a debit card on
the table. "No, I've got this, Beck."

"Nope. We're going Dutch," she said coldly.

"Sure. That's fine—we'll go Dutch."

"Of course, it's fine. I don't need your approval, Benjamin." She gave him a questioning look. "How soon is soon?
Are you thinking about the next day or two? One hundred
and eighty?"

"I haven't really thought about it. I've got to get back for
a job that's been in the works, and I've got some things I need
to attend to, and—"

"So, safe to say, this week, then," she said in a voice colder
than the sleet outside.

Ben didn't want to lie, but he wasn't sure what to make

of everything that had just happened to them. He needed to get back to work. After all, he'd only come to pay his respects to Mrs. Getchel, and hopefully run into Becky. He hadn't counted on her gripping him quite the way she had. In this brief time, she'd somehow invaded his mind, and he wasn't quite sure what to make of her or his feelings. And now, with this inheritance thing to work through, he didn't know what he thought. All he knew was that he had a life away from here, so he shook off his rambling thoughts. "Yes, that would be safe to say."

"Ben, we need to talk about the will. You can't just run away! Don't you see? There's too much at stake. You heard the attorney. We have less than six months to meet Mrs. Getchel's timeline."

Her eyes were pleading with him. He'd seen that look before; the desperate need for him to stay. But he couldn't. "Becky, I have to figure things out with my own life before I—"

"Well, I won't keep you," she said through gritted teeth and slapped her napkin on her plate. "I suppose we'll just touch base somehow, if something comes to mind about the foster care thing."

With that, she stood and grabbed her coat from the back of her chair, stuffed her hat back onto her head before realizing that she hadn't given her debit card to the server. She hastily grabbed her slip and headed toward their server, who met her in mid-stride with a smile. The waitress took her slip, then continued toward Ben. Rebecca stood near the doorway to await her receipt.

Ben couldn't help but watch Becky as she teetered back and forth, avoiding looking his direction. He kicked himself for what he'd said to bring on her change in demeanor. He thought things had been going well until she asked when he was leaving.

It never occurred to him she'd be taken aback when he'd said he'd be leaving soon. What did she expect him to do? Drop everything and bend to Mrs. G's literal will immediately? He was living out of a suitcase, and he had a life away from there. He'd thought she might even be relieved that he'd leave for a while. He had obviously annoyed her, that much he was sure of.

The bright-eyed server brought back his slip, he scribbled on a tip, signed, and pulled on his coat, while Rebecca signed. Ben gave her time to head out, then realized that she'd beat him to their cars sooner anyway, knowing that his shoes were more like skates. He didn't relish the thought of walking across the iced parking lot again.

Ben was right. She was at her car before he'd even climbed the small exterior stairs. They'd salted and sanded the parking lot while he and Becky ate breakfast. He pulled up his collar and waved his goodbye as Rebecca drove by him. She hadn't even glanced in his direction. *Unbelievable.* Ben took in a deep breath, exhaled, then surefootedly got to his car, and turned on the engine before realizing that he didn't have anywhere to go but to his room at the York Harbor Inn, and that didn't interest him in the least.

Ben sat while the car warmed up and ran his work schedule through his mind. The timeline of what he would need to do if he were to take on this project that he had no desire to do. *I'm a diver, not a friggin' caretaker!* He slammed his fist on the steering wheel out of frustration because he had no choice but to settle things about Mrs. G's will. He couldn't stay, but he also couldn't leave Becky to handle the entire project on her own.

We have to do it together, but how?

Chapter 7

Rebecca was grateful that she had the day off work. Her goal was to finish straightening up Mrs. Getchel's house by emptying the fridge, doing some laundry, taking out the trash, and doing whatever else she felt should be done. It was the least she could do after everything that her dear friend had done for her over the years.

As she took the corner, Mrs. Getchel's Victorian home stood to her right. The large porch and the handsomely curved archway above the staircase were a welcoming sight, even though Mrs. Getchel wasn't there to greet her.

Inheritance!

In that instant, it hit her like a ton of bricks, and she hit the brakes. Rebecca pulled over and stepped out of the car. She stood with the impressive home before her. *This is mine now.* She thought gaining a place to call home would make her happy, but all she could think about was how huge of a house this was. She couldn't manage, maintain, and live in. The taxes alone would empty her bank account. Somehow, she and Ben had to make the foster care venture work, or she'd lose the only home she had left. Her brain couldn't register all that had happened in just a few days. Having this home seemed like a dream a few hours ago, but now, she had absolutely no idea what to make of it all.

Rebecca lay a handful of tote bags on the porch swing and opened the door with the hidden key that had its place under one of the stones in a flower bed. Norma's house had rarely ever been quiet, and the eeriness of the silence didn't escape her. She meandered through the living room, remembering the voices of the children that had once occupied the room. Four other kids had lived there when she'd moved in. Benjamin, who was the oldest; Jason, who's birthday closely followed Ben's, then her, and two much younger kids: Frida and Amy. Rebecca smiled at the memory of Ben playing the piano while the two little ones played Candyland on the coffee table.

A loud car drove by, snapping her out of her thoughts, and so she traipsed to the kitchen. Rebecca started with the fridge. Handling food didn't seem as intimate of a task. She dumped leftovers and opened containers into the trash. She gave pause when she'd seen the chicken and rice soup they'd shared. Mrs. Getchel had wanted her to take the leftovers home that evening, but she'd insisted that she leave it there, that they'd finish it together. Rebecca swallowed the lump in her throat. There would be no more sharing of meals.

She placed the now-empty containers into the dishwasher before removing any items she could still use. *Okay—good— making progress.* Becky reached to retrieve one of the totes before realizing that she'd forgotten them on the front porch.

She worked her way around the full trash bags, skidded to

the porch, then opened the storm door with a burst, pushing it directly into Ben Daly's forehead.

"Oh, my gosh! What are you doing—I didn't even see you there?" Becky said with a start. Ben, who now rubbed the crease that was forming down his forehead, stood dazed for a second.

"I was just about to knock when you—"

"Sorry about that, but I guess the better question would be. Why are you here?" She said propping the door open with her foot and crossed her arms.

"I wanted to—well, I guess you could say—I wanted to…"

"Spit it out for crying out loud." Rebecca's patience was waning, and she had better things to do than stand there listening to Ben stammer.

"I was just being nostalgic. Wanted to see the place, you know. I intended to just drive by, maybe even park for a minute." He shrugged. "But I saw your car there, and figured I—"

"Oh, you just figured you could just waltz in here and—"

"I was about to knock, remember? It wasn't like I was just going to let myself in, you know, Rebecca. I don't know what has happened over the years, but you sure as hell have a pretty big chip on your shoulder. And for your information, my being here has nothing to do with you." His steely gaze glared at her with the intensity that she'd seen years ago. He was no longer playing Mr. Nice Guy, and that calmed her down. Being furious with an ass was easier than being angry with someone she thought she'd once loved.

"Well, since you're here already, I suppose you may as well come in." She stepped aside, and with a wave of her arm, he stepped through the door. Ben stood in the entry, his mouth taught and his hands stuffed in his pockets.

He glanced around the living room. "Hasn't changed at all, has it?"

"Not really." Becky hadn't really thought about changes because she'd visited so often over the years. She, too, looked around the room, taking it in. She pointed to the spot in front of the fireplace. "I remember you burning the rug over there."

"Becky, I told you then, and I'm telling you now, it wasn't my fault. The log fell out onto the floor."

"Yep, but it wouldn't have happened if you'd listen to Mrs. Getchel and not built the fire in the first place."

"I guess you've got a point there." With a sideways smirk, he took a few steps, stopping in front of the piano. He touched a few of the portraits of Mrs. G's "kids" that hung on the wall. "There's a lot more of those though," he said with a bit of tenderness when he found the one of himself.

"Not too shabby for such a geek," Becky teased, but secretly she thought he'd been the most handsome boy she'd ever known.

"Takes one to know one." Ben pulled the one of her off the wall, hiding it close to his chest.

"Yes, it does, okay? What can I say? It was during my awkward phase."

"Sure was!" Ben laughed.

Becky gave him a punch in the shoulder before taking the frame from him and hanging it back on the wall.

"Do you still play?" he asked, lifting the lid over the keys, then tinkering out a tune.

"I haven't played in years," Rebecca said as she ran her hand along the curve of the piano, "even though she said I could come and practice anytime I wanted. It just didn't feel right. Besides, I'd really just gotten started with my lessons, anyway."

Ben patted the bench next to him, inviting her to sit. She hesitated, then scooched to the edge of the bench while his fingers tapped the keys, testing each one with expertise.

"Not too bad. I figured it'd be out of tune," he said with a nod, then he began to play. The melody took her back to another place and time. She'd always loved the tune as it was thought provoking and stirred in her what she'd considered a spiritual awakening.

"I remember that song," she said in a hush. "It's from the movie *The Piano*."

Ben turned to her while he played. "Sure is," he said, with a glimmer in his eyes. "I've always liked the name."

"What is it, I forget?"

"*Big, My Secret*, by Michael Nyman." He continued to play, and for a while, she thought he'd forgotten where he was. He seemed lost in the music. She happily moved there with him, until he stopped abruptly, then shut the lid, and stood. "Not sure Mrs. Getchel would approve, though."

Becky sat astounded by his turn-of-a-switch attitude, but tried to brush it off as best she could. "I don't think she would've minded. She loved to hear you play. She taught you well."

"Sure, but not that one. Remember, she always said it was an adult song, because of the movie."

"You're right, I forgot about that!" Becky stood up and pushed the bench back into place. "Of course, we had to watch the movie to see why we shouldn't."

The lightheartedness settled in momentarily until a

silence fell between them. Rebecca shifted her feet and pushed her hair behind her ear. She walked toward the kitchen, then turned back toward the front door, nearly bumping into Ben. "Forgot my bags on the porch." Rebecca, do-si-doed around Ben's sturdy frame. "Do you think you could carry some trash out for me?"

"Absolutely."

Before long, they wrapped up the kitchen, and Rebecca felt satisfied with their teamwork, other than they'd barely spoken as they'd gone to task. She imagined what it would be like being in business together. Would they be this in tune with each other's movements, and succinctly and instinctively tackle what was needed doing? At this point, being in business together was a big stretch. He was leaving.

She couldn't get over how tall he'd grown. He'd reached the top shelves with ease. She thought for sure that he'd caught her checking out his biceps. Rebecca had a million questions for him--like where have you been, what are you doing, and are you happy? But the questions would have to wait, if she ever got to ask them at all.

Ben took the last load out to her car. She pulled back the drapes from a living room window to watch him. He'd taken care to organize the packing efficiently, then shut the trunk. Rebecca quickly backed away from the window.

"We've been at it all afternoon," Ben said. "Would you like to grab some dinner?"

Rebecca hesitated before responding. She desperately wanted to say yes, but to what end? He'd just leave her again, and the more she thought about that, the more the pain of his leaving all those years ago plunged her right back into her bitter mood.

"Nope, I'm good. I think you should just go."

Ben's questioning gaze penetrated hers. *Why did you have to grow to be so darn good looking?* His stare continued as she shifted her feet and cast her eyes toward the floor; stuffing down her mixed emotions.

"Um, I'm not hungry," she said, lying through her teeth. In fact, she was absolutely famished. "I still have things I want to get done around here. But, hey, thanks for your help."

"Okay, well, since you're going to be awhile, why don't I go get us something and bring it back here? That way, by the time I'm back, you might be ready to eat, and I could help some more." Before Rebecca could think of a response quickly enough, Ben added, "Yeah, I'll do that. Be back soon."

He grabbed his coat and was gone, leaving Rebecca standing there feeling like her head was spinning.

What just happened? She shook her head. *Why can't I ever say no to that man?*

She plunked on the sofa, the same worn sofa, and afghan that adorned the back since heaven knows how long. She pulled the afghan over her lap and a warmth grew through her. *He's coming back.*

Rebecca's mind drifted off to the first time she'd sat there. She'd placed her small laundry sack, containing all her worldly possessions: a few items of clothing that others had donated to her, some toiletries, a pair of slippers, a robe, and a small, treasured quilt that her mother had handmade for her. Rebecca absentmindedly rubbed her shoulder and arm as if the pain still existed, then shut her eyes, recalling more.

She'd been so afraid. Oh, the house was pretty from the outside. It offered a large porch with a swing, table and chairs, and a doormat with the words, "Welcome Home" at its center, but none of those details brought her comfort. As she'd learned, the outside can be lovely. What was on the inside held the truth. This place had been the fourth such place in just a little over a year. If her first three were any indication, she'd run from this one as well.

Mrs. Getchel had greeted her warmly, then led her to the sofa. Her large, plump frame sat down next to her, and she kindly offered her a cookie from the decorative plate that sat in the center of a frilly doily on the coffee table. The voices of other kids drifted from upstairs and more distant ones came from the backyard. She wished she could see them to know if they seemed happy. They were probably just as good at masquerading reality as her former foster parents had been.

Mrs. Getchel had called a boy named Benjamin into the room. She'd asked if he'd fetch a glass of milk to go along with the cookies. He'd been tall and scrawny, his black hair stuck out in every direction, but he was otherwise well dressed and groomed. What calmed her more was Mrs. Getchel's soft touch on his arm, and the thank you she'd given him when he'd handed over the milk. His bright smile was contagious, and Rebecca, for the first time in a long time, smiled in return. She'd remembered feeling hopeful, but still cautious.

Rebecca's thoughts went back to the decorative plate. She got up stiffly from the sofa, feeling her achy muscles from squatting and lifting Mrs. Getchel's belongings, then walked to the hutch in search of the plate. It had resided there since she could remember, and hoped it was still there. *Yes!* She carefully opened the glass-framed hutch door and removed the plate. Its inscription was almost worn off by now, but she could still read the words. She ran her fingertips across the lettering.

In this home...

We do real.

We do mistakes.

We do I'm sorry.

We do second chances.

We do hugs.

We do together the best we can.

"Thank you, Mrs. Getchel," Rebecca whispered and quietly wept. A tear trickled down her cheek and fell on the plate. She wiped the moisture from its surface with her sleeve and reluctantly put the plate back in its proper place, but made a mental note that if she couldn't live up to Mrs. Getchel's expectations about the project, and lost the house, she would keep the plate as a treasured memento.

Out front, a car door closed, then Ben's familiar footsteps took the stairs two at a time. She smiled at this memory, but it faded quickly for all the times that she'd wished she'd hear them after he'd left her.

"I got you an Italian sandwich from the pizza shop," he blurted out before the door finished shutting behind him. "Hope that's okay."

"Actually, that sounds perfect. Thanks." Rebecca gestured toward the kitchen, then an uncomfortable feeling crept up her spine, recognizing that she was already acting as if Mrs. Getchel's home was her own, and stopped before moving. "Ben—where do you think we should sit? Feels kinda funny—doesn't it—just making ourselves at home here without her?"

"I doubt Norma would see it that way. Besides, I think of this place as home, don't you?"

"Yeah, I guess," she said hesitantly. *It was exactly that when we were all sitting around the table together.* She pushed the thought aside. "It's just that eating a meal at her table seems a bit—I don't know—like we're overstepping."

"Tell you what, would you feel better standing at the counter? As I recall, you spent more time sitting on the counter eating than at the table, anyway? Would that make you feel better?"

I loved sitting there. Mrs. Getchel would cook and we'd talk while I nibbled. She'd swat at my hand and tell me to get down, but it was all part of the charm. Oh, how I miss you, Norma.

"I don't know," she said with a sigh. "Sorry, but all this just seems so strange."

"I hear you," Ben said with a shrug. "The table then?"

"Yeah, I kinda think she'd rather me be sitting at her table than on the counter. I used to get reprimanded for that."

"True story. So the table wins?"

"Table it is."

Ben set the bags ceremoniously down on the table. They unwrapped their sandwiches and sat in silence. Rebecca, occasionally, watched him as he tucked the salami into the bread, picked fallen black olives off the paper, took large bites, devouring it at a ravenous pace. She realized she had only eaten about a third of hers. *I've missed you, Benjamin.*

Rebecca marveled at the changes in his now adult appearance. She'd thought him so mature when he'd left as an eighteen-year-old. Rebecca had perceived him as so worldly.

She grinned at her own naivety. His jaw was strong, and she couldn't get over the facial hair that framed his bright smile. Even when he was brooding, she'd found him attractive. His hands gathered up the paper and crunched it into a ball before he looked in her direction.

"I guess I was hungry." He laughed lightheartedly, before stuffing the balled-up paper into his plastic bag.

"I guess so." Rebecca wrapped up what she had left of her sandwich and placed it back into the bag. "Ben . . . who told you about Mrs. Getchel's passing?"

"Jason Fischer."

His response cut like a knife. Jason had been one of the older kids that had lived in this house. The kind of kid that kept to himself and more or less just blended into the woodwork. She had no idea that they'd kept in touch. Sure, Jason tagged along with Ben back in the day, but that was about it. She didn't think they were that close. What bothered her the most was that the handful of times that she and Jason had run in to each other, he'd never thought to mention anything about Ben, and Ben had, obviously, never asked about her.

"Oh." She could feel the heat rise on her chest and up her neck. The realization that Jason would know how to contact him was crushing, but the last thing she wanted was for Ben to see her get all teary-eyed over it.

She got up abruptly from the table and pushed in her chair. "I'm calling it a night. I think it's best if we head out," she said in a calm yet cold tone.

She could tell by his tightened mouth that he was perplexed, but she didn't care and didn't feel she owed him an explanation, so she just picked up his coat and handed it to him. His eyes pleaded with her as he backed away from his coat.

Not this time. This time, I say no.

She responded by pushing it into his chest. He continued to stand there as she retrieved her handbag and dug out a ten. "Thanks for your help and the sandwich."

"I don't want your money, Beck," he said, pushing the ten back toward her. "Why don't we just—"

"I really need you to leave, Benjamin."

With that, he squared his shoulders. "I'm staying at the York Harbor Inn for a few days—in case you need me for anything." He gave her a nod, then strutted out of the room and out the front door into the night.

"Jason Fisher? He heard from Jason Fisher!" The realization that he'd known how to get in touch with Ben hurt. They'd remained friends, but he'd kicked her to the curb again, and that tore her to shreds. She was furious with herself for inviting him in, but he had been standing there, with his big brown eyes, and his broad shoulders, and she'd caved.

Not again, Ben—not again.

Chapter 8

Ben pulled up his collar and cursed the bitter cold. He sat in his idling car with the heat blasting, unsure of what to do. Certainly, he hadn't seen he and Becky's night coming to a screeching halt the way it had. He thought they'd had a good day, considering how they'd last left things. All he wanted to do was start fresh, and their pleasant dinner had encouraged him, until she turned on a dime.

Ben looked on as Becky turn off the lights of Mrs. G's place and continued watching her get into her car. She hadn't so much as looked in his direction. She had to know he was sitting there, but she totally ignored him, again. *Rebecca Mills, you are insufferable.*

He sat there as she pulled away, but couldn't bring himself to leave just yet. He stared at the darkened, lifeless house. Even when he'd been unacceptable and unkind, Mrs. G. had made this place a home: a place of acceptance and kindness. Now, it was just a house without warmth, or a soul. He longed for what had been and feared it would never be again.

The moon was full, casting light over the frosted lawn of Mrs. G's empty home, and his mind drifted to Norma lying beneath the frozen ground. He put the car in drive and before long, he ambled through the cemetery to pay Mrs. Norma Getchel a visit. A couple of bouquets lay haphazardly on their sides upon the sod. He stood the flowers up and leaned them into one another, hoping they'd keep each other standing. He plucked a yellow rose and held it in his gloved hand.

"I'm sorry, Mrs. G.," he said in a hushed voice. Ben closed his eyes and played over in his mind, the many times that she'd asked him to come home for a visit. His answer had always been, I can't right now, maybe, or some other poor excuse to avoid going back.

When he'd joined the Navy, Mrs. G. had written him letter upon letter while he was away in boot camp at the Great Lakes Naval Training Center, on the shores of Lake Michigan. It had been the farthest he'd ever been from Maine, and the connection to "home" was abundantly welcomed. It didn't matter that Jason Fischer received them as well. He smiled at the thought of her making sure that they'd each received them at even intervals. They'd never talk about what she'd written. He supposed they needed their contents to remain private. She'd had a way of making him open up, unlike anyone else he'd ever had in his life, and assumed she'd done the same for Jason.

Over the years, he'd let Mrs. G. know where he was. Including the time when he served on an aircraft carrier, the USS Carl Vinson, to provide relief efforts after an earthquake devastated Port-au-Prince, Haiti, killing nearly 230,000 people. She'd remained faithful in writing, but she wasn't one to use a computer. So, sadly, his responses became fewer and fewer, until he'd stopped writing to her altogether.

He often wondered if Mrs. G's unconditional love for him had fueled his drive to save people, and salvage the remains of lost things, making him want to give back, in some small way, a taste of what she'd given him. His angry streak, his rebellious nature, and feelings of self-loathing didn't seem to ruffle Mrs. G's feathers. She was steady at the helm and, without fail, ready to guide and not judge, to seek the truth, to quietly sit and listen, even when he wasn't able to speak. He'd wanted to tell her so much more, but if he'd spoken of his pain and what had happened to him over his tender years, he thought he'd fall apart and crumble like a clay pot that could never be put back together again.

By now, his toes were freezing as the icy air cut through him. "Thank you, Mrs. Norma Getchel, for being my mother, grandmother, teacher, disciplinarian, and trusted guiding light. I just wish I'd followed your advice."

He kissed the rose that he still gripped in his fingers and laid it on her resting place before heading to his car.

The York Harbor Inn was a welcoming beacon. He parked, but he wasn't quite ready to go inside. The heat from the car had finally warmed his feet, so he dared to take another walk instead of sitting in an empty room or small talking with people he didn't know. He crossed the street and meandered down the walkway that led to the harbor.

The full moon shone across the water, giving him that now familiar sense of home. The waves were typically quiet in the harbor, but with the wind, they seemed more alive. He hadn't stood on this beach for years, he'd realized.

Thoughts of Becky flooded his mind. She'd been a lost kid when they'd spent their days cooling off in the water. There, he'd questioned her about wearing long sleeves on such a hot day. If memory served him, it was the first time she'd stepped out of her shell and showed that she had a voice. Until then, she'd been closed off.

She had intrigued him from the first time he'd laid eyes on her. He could tell she had an inner strength. She hadn't shied away from Mrs. Getchel, and she hadn't shied away from him. She'd just sat on the couch with her chin up, as if she were accepting her new reality. He remembered seeing a recognition of sorts, a kindness in her eyes when he'd handed her a glass of milk. He knew right then she was a good person, but just below the surface, she had to have harbored some kind of pain. Most of the kids who ended up inside the system did. It was just the way it was, but he'd held the upper hand because that way of life was all he'd ever known, or remembered. Unlike Becky, who had gotten thrust into it at fourteen. And for that reason, he'd needed to protect her.

The sea breeze stung at his cheeks. The howling wind whistled and moaned as he stood on the path that jutted out to the sand. He could still hear their youthful laughter before he'd asked about her long sleeves. She'd told him it was none of his dang business, as if he'd flipped a switch from happy to anger—much like tonight. He didn't understand it then, and he didn't understand it now.

The clouds moved, covering the moon, and his path back to the Inn grew dark and dreary. Once again, his feet ached, and so he hoofed it back. But before calling it a night, he'd get a nightcap at the Ships Cellar Pub, hoping it would help him sleep.

Ben sat at the bar inlaid with intricate, exotic woods and veneers that created nautical patterns. The mahogany decking and shiplap boards created a rich, warm glow. It was a cozy place with the charm of a sailing vessel. A fire blazed in the fireplace and warmed his bones. He rubbed his chilly hands together while the same slender brunette greeted him with a smile.

"A shot of Crown?" It took him aback that she'd remembered him.

"You know what—I think I'll make it a bourbon and ginger tonight."

"One bourbon and ginger coming up—Mr.?"

"Ben. My name's Ben."

She added ginger ale to bourbon. "Hello, Ben. Where might you be from?"

"A little bit of everywhere, I suppose—miss?" She set the glass of golden liquid and ice in front of him and dropped in a mixing straw.

"Julie." Her smile once again flashed at him and her hair matched the warmth of the mahogany wood. Her eyes danced with the reflection of the flickering flames of the fire, but in that moment, all that came to mind was Becky. It was Becky's smile, and mahogany-colored, long-braided hair that he wanted to touch. He downed his drink, and much like Becky had just done to him, he dismissed Julie as he dropped a ten on the bar.

"Goodnight, Julie." The bourbon would not be strong enough to clear his mind of Rebecca Mills.

CHAPTER 9

Rebecca, exhausted from lack of sleep, then having overslept after finally dozing off, pulled into Proposals. She was furious with herself for allowing Ben to get under her skin and keeping her up half the night. After all, she'd gotten over him long ago, and he had no business taking up space in her head. "Thanks, Mrs. Getchel," she said with a roll of her eyes and a huff.

She grabbed her belongings and retreated from her car. Her plate was full and running late was not on her agenda. She slammed the door shut and scurried into the shop. Once again, Daisy, Sophie's calico cat, greeted her, and circled around her feet, tripping her up.

"Enough already, you stupid feline," she snapped, then pushed Daisy aside.

"Whoa there. Who peed in your Cheerios this morning?" Emily chortled while picking up the cat. "Miss Becky's cranky this morning, isn't she, Daisy?"

"Are you kidding me? It's usually you that has her apron in a wad," Rebecca said with irritation as she trudged inside.

"Ah, I see what you did there," Emily said, standing in the door, her apron adorned with flour. "Seriously, are you alright?"

Emily set Daisy down and closed the door behind them, then picked up a crate of apples that had just been delivered. "You've seemed . . . not your usual self lately."

"Everything is fine." Rebecca knew her response wasn't convincing and tried to brush off the inquisition. She motioned toward the floral section of the shop. "I've got work to do."

"Not so fast. You're scurrying off like Daisy does when Sophie opens a bag of kibble." She set the apples down and pointed to one of the wrought-iron chairs. "Plunk it there, Beck."

"Seriously, I'm okay. Just tired is all. And I've got the Baxter's wedding arrangements to do, like yesterday, an order to place, and—never mind, it's just some personal stuff I'm dealing with."

"Even more of a reason to take a seat," Emily said, her insistent brown eyes staring her down.

Emily would not let her off so easily, so Rebecca resigned herself to taking a seat. Before her bottom hit the chair, Sophie strolled in.

"Ah," Sophie said, "I thought I heard your voice out here, Rebecca."

Rebecca sighed and dropped her shoulders, slumping further into the chair.

"Oh my, you look terrible. Are you okay?" Sophie pulled the other chair out and joined her.

"That's what I was just asking," Emily said from the pastry counter. "Right? She looks terrible?"

"For crying out loud, I'm sitting right here. As I've already said, I'm fine—just fine."

Sophie reached a hand across the table and placed it on Rebecca's forearm. "Fine, isn't how you usually are. Please, tell us what's troubling you. Maybe we can help."

"Something is definitely wrong. You should have seen how she treated poor little Daisy," Emily teased, as she placed a cup of tea in front of Rebecca, then handed her a cinnamon twist and a napkin. Sophie's questioning eyes probed Emily's with alarm. "I was kidding Soph. Daisy's fine."

"Well then," Sophie said with a raised brow, "seeing how everyone is, fine…"

"As you know, my good friend passed away this week, and it's hitting me kind of hard." Rebecca didn't want to expound upon it any further, but Emily caught her avoidance.

"Try again, Beck."

"Emily! She's just lost a friend. I hardly think—"

"Soph, she's angry, not sad." Emily turned her gaze to Rebecca, pulled up another chair, and awaited a response.

"Oh. I see," Sophie said. "Rebecca, we don't mean to pry, but we care about you. So, if there's anything you'd wish to share, we'd really like to help. Please know that we're very sorry to hear of the loss of your friend."

Sophie stood up, circled around to Rebecca, and leaned in to give her a hug.

"Yes, sorry for your loss, Beck. I didn't mean to make light of that." Emily rested her hand on Rebecca's forearm.

"No, it's alright. Honestly, it's kind of refreshing to have some normalcy for a change."

"Okay, so what is it then?" Sophie's soft eyes and tender touch welcomed an answer.

"Another friend came to the service. I hadn't seen him in years, and well," she shrugged, "he kind of fell off the radar. Now, he wants to act like it wasn't any big deal that he'd left—as if nothing he'd done was wrong. He thinks he can just waltz back into my life again, and I'm supposed to forgive him, just like that." She snapped her fingers.

Emily nodded. "I hate to say it, because it sounds so cliché, but men can be really stupid."

Sophie stood up and sauntered over to the counter and filled a mug with hot water. "Emily's right." She dropped a tea bag into the mug. "Sometimes it just takes them a little time, and some directness to help them understand."

Directness, Rebecca thought as Sophie sat down across from her once again. *Sure, I'll just tell him, straight out that he's a selfish ass and only thinks of himself.*

"Perhaps," Sophie said with a nod, "he acts like it wasn't any big deal because he really didn't think it was." Sophie raised her cup to her lips and sipped the steaming liquid. "They can be pretty insensitive without realizing it, you know."

"Maybe." Rebecca considered the idea, but it didn't sit well because if he really didn't think it was a big deal to leave her, then it would mean that she really didn't matter to him. If she didn't matter to him as much as he mattered to her, then his behavior all made perfect sense.

As a guest approached the door, Sophie stood. "My guess is that if he was important in your life, he'll come around." She gave Rebecca's hand a squeeze, then moved to greet the couple. "Welcome to Proposals. How can we help make your day special?"

"Thanks for the tea, the twist, and your thoughtfulness." Rebecca got up and forced a smile toward Emily. Daisy squeezed through the opened door and darted between them, nearly causing Rebecca to trip.

"Don't mention it." Emily gave a wink while clearing the plate from the table. "Word might get out that I've become a softy or something."

"We certainly wouldn't want that to happen now, would we?"

Rebecca appreciated the pep talk, but it didn't alleviate her discouragement or predicament. She sighed and tried her best to push thoughts of Ben aside so she could focus on work.

She reviewed her schedule, then retreated into the walk-in refrigeration to select various orange and yellow rose stems, ranunculus, cymbidium orchids, broom corn, wheat, seeded eucalyptus, and some Italian ruscus to create a texturally rich, yet refined, bouquet for a bride. She lay each stem, cradling them in the crook of her arm, and noted the burnt-orange ribbon she'd use to pull it all together. This, she thought, was just what she needed to take her mind off Benjamin Daly and her dreadful past.

Rebecca stood back to take in the finished arrangement and nodded with satisfaction and relief that she'd turned a corner on her day when Daisy jumped onto her work station. Her purring, furry body brushed the arrangement before she sat to take Rebecca in with her piercing cat eyes. Rebecca's heart pounded, and her mind raced in a whirlwind of scattered memories of her own cat staring back at her; memories that had shattered her world. She wished, with everything in her, that she could bury them away forever.

She closed her eyes and took a few deep breaths before opening them up again. Daisy was no longer there. She'd vanished, just as her childhood had vanished, just as her family had, just as Ben had, and just as Mrs. Getchel had.

***

After the weekend's wedding at Proposals, Rebecca once again sat before her large sewing table, cutting fabric for a young boy by the name of Scotty. She was told Scotty enjoyed playing in the dirt with Tonka trucks, so she'd compiled a couple of yards of fabric that had a variety of trucks she thought he'd enjoy. Rebecca intended to cut out each one and apply them as appliqués throughout the quilt's face. Her special message would be:

I,

Scotty Guthrie

can move mountains.

This message held a special place in her heart, not in the way he'd understand it to be, but in time, he'd learn of its true meaning: anything is possible.

As a teen she'd been determined to make the junior high cheerleading squad. She'd come home without the reward of her hard work. When she hadn't entered the kitchen, ready to share her good news, her father had taken notice. She'd told him that there was a tie between her and her best friend, and they had to do their cheer one more time in order for the judges to determine who'd make the team. She'd told him she messed up on purpose so her friend would be chosen. When he'd asked why she'd do such a thing, she'd said she already had plenty of things that made her happy, and her friend didn't.

She could still remember her father cupping her cheeks in the palm of his hands, but sadly, try as she might, she couldn't remember the sound of his voice, nor could she imagine the feel of his hands. As she held back tears, a lump now formed in her throat.

I miss you daddy.

She closed her eyes, willing herself to see his loving gaze once again. He'd tilted her head up toward him, and with eyes that burned with pride, told her that through that kind of love and sacrifice for other's wellbeing she would move mountains someday; the impossible would be possible.

Rebecca's chest grew heavy at the thought of disappointing her dad. She certainly hadn't lived up to his expectations. She'd only thought of herself and her needs both then and now. And she'd lost everything that truly meant anything.

Rebecca thought her only redeeming qualities were in making quilts and bouquets for others, but now realized not much had changed after all because deep down she knew she made the quilts more to relieve her own guilt than anything else. Yes, she was still selfish, and that thought tore at her heart.

Her hands ached and scissor handles indented her fingers. Rebecca rubbed the indentations as she surveyed the trucks spacing on her design wall.

She smiled. One of Mrs. Getchel's plastic-lined kitchen table cloths now hung on her wall. She'd discovered that the backing was perfect for displaying her fabric cutouts; they clung perfectly to the flannel. The plastic side of the tablecloth was covered in a variety of fruit and prominently displayed a melted ring from a casserole dish.

Rebecca had taken the casserole out of the oven for

Mrs. Getchel, but what she hadn't considered was the lack of a place to put it. As the heat intensified, she'd set it on the table. What brought the smile was the fact that Mrs. Getchel hadn't gotten upset about it. After the smell of melting plastic alerted them to the error, Mrs. Getchel pulled the dish off the table and said, "Well, would you look at that? You made a work of art." Then she'd laughed.

Rebecca had been so taken aback by her response that when Mrs. Getchel asked her to remove the tablecloth and put it in the rubbish bin, Rebecca had collected it and stuffed it under her bed. Looking back now, she realized it had been an odd thing to do, but that tablecloth represented love to her. She wasn't willing to just throw it away.

She stood to switch out a few of the truck's positions and was content with her progress. The yellow trucks on the speckled, earth-toned batik she'd picked out would look great together. She hoped little Scottie Guthrie would like it and heed the message she'd inscribed. Would he really believe one day that he could move mountains? It would take some faith and inner strength on his part, but she hoped he'd find it within himself to do anything he set his mind to. The question that weighed on her now, was could she do the same?

CHAPTER 10

Ben decided to take a drive into Portsmouth when it occurred to him that his buddy, Jason Fischer, might be at the Portsmouth Naval Shipyard and if not, they could meet, grab a beer, and catch up on old times.

Ben no sooner texted Jason when he got a reply. Jason said he was at the shipyard and told him to come on by the back gate. He'd meet him there to escort him in.

As he drove down route 103 along the coast of Kittery, he'd forgotten how beautiful the area was with its inlets of salted rivers, coves, and the Atlantic. Boats speckled the water. A few lobster buoys bobbed on the surface. Seagulls flew effortlessly in the gusty winds. Maybe, he thought, being in this area had lured him into joining the Navy.

He never thought he'd miss it here, and he certainly never dreamed that anything would tug at him enough to consider coming back. The beauty notwithstanding, this quaint, New

England coast represented his past; a past that he couldn't wait to escape.

Hawaii, on the other hand, was a paradise, without a past. It didn't hold his baggage or any pain. It didn't hold judgement. It didn't hold his sense of worthlessness at being a child of stoners that orphaned him and placed him in the system. Anywhere but here, he thought.

His job took him to numerous places, but Hawaii had helped him escape the realness of life. However, something could be said for the change in seasons. The brilliant color of a strong oak, to the now leafless trees; a gray sky, and brown turf, to a blanket of snow still takes his breath away. Maybe, Mrs. G. was guiding him, once again, to take a different path. He was awakening to a new season in his own life—a season of needed change that a week ago he'd never realized he needed.

Jason was true to his word and was waiting for him. Ben checked in at the gate, went through the proper protocols, and then Jason escorted him to the utilitarian rectangle box of a training center that sat in the back of the shipyard at water's edge.

Jason was animated in telling Ben about all the advancements in underwater salvage training since Ben had left the Navy. Of course, Jason couldn't show and tell him everything because Ben didn't have the clearance now that he was a civilian.

Ben watched one of the underwater training drills, and he and Jason had a good laugh, recalling their own inadequacies when they'd been in boot camp. Ben had no hesitation about teasing Jason when he went into an out-and-out panic attack after going underwater in scuba gear for the first time. He' never confess that he, too, had felt that same panic, and Jason was none the wiser.

Jason followed the banter with a slap to the back of Ben's head.

"Do you miss it?" Jason asked.

"Can't say as I do. I mean, I'm still diving and challenged. In fact, not much has changed, except for the fact that I can pretty much come and go as I please. Being a civilian definitely has its advantages."

"So, you're telling me you're really done? No Navy reserves, no reenlisting, nothing?"

"Thought about it a time or two, but I got a pretty great deal going for me on the islands." Ben looked on as a one-man submarine surfaced. "I guess you could say I'm a lot like that." Ben gave a nod toward the sub. "I like doing things on my terms, go where I want to go, navigate my own path, so to speak."

"But you said you work with a team."

"Sure, I do, but I'm an independent contractor. If I don't want the job, I don't do it."

"Sounds like you have it made. No commitments, nothing holding you down. You're livin' the dream, man."

Ben wasn't so sure he was living the dream. More like avoiding nightmares. Even though his childhood nightmares followed him everywhere he went and no depth of the sea could help him escape them. *Except for the last couple of days.* He'd been more relaxed, and at peace, since he'd returned to New England. Even in light of Mrs. G's death, his demons had taken a bit of a reprieve.

"Hey," Jason interrupted his thoughts, "sorry I wasn't at Mrs. Getchel's service; I couldn't get leave. She was a special lady, and I know how close she was to you."

"It's all good." Ben gave him a slap on the back.

"Yeah, I know, but it still sucked that I couldn't be there."

"I hear you," Ben said as they walked along the inlet. "It was nice—for a funeral."

"Have you seen Rebecca Mills? I figured she must have been at the service. Seems like they remained pretty tight."

You don't know the half of it. Ben nodded and wondered if he dared broach the impossible inheritance debacle.

"She sure grew up to be quite the looker." Jason picked a piece of lint off his jacket. "Hear she's made a good life for herself, making flowers. Place is called, Purposes—no, I think it's called Proposals—or something like that."

Ben didn't want to acknowledge what he thought of Rebecca's looks, but was intrigued by her work. He liked to think of her as successful.

"Where is this Proposals place?" Ben asked as nonchalantly as possible. The last thing he wanted was for Jason to get some crazy idea that he was interested because he'd be relentless.

"Somewhere in York—the harbor area, I think. Not far from the village, if my memory has it. Can't say I've been in any need of a wedding, flowers, cakes, or anything even remotely close to that kind of thing. If that day ever comes, be sure to smack me on the back of the head and knock some sense into me."

"Trust me—I hardly need an excuse to slap you upside the head." Ben laughed. "When do you get off? Want to grab a beer?"

"Oh man, wish I could, but I've got a late shift. Raincheck?"

"Probably not. I'm heading out soon." *Soon.* His gut grumbled at the thought. Was it guilt he was feeling in the pit of his stomach? He tried to shake it off.

"Well, hopefully we can grab one in the next decade, then."

"I'll be sure to give you a heads up when and if I'm back this way. So, I guess we can say a raincheck it is." They stood overlooking the dive pool. Jason cleared his throat during the lull in conversation. "Hey, I better let you get back to it."

With that, Ben patted him on the shoulder. Jason signaled to one of the shift workers that he'd be right back, and they headed to the back gate for their farewells.

Ben's stomach was still uneasy as he wrestled with the idea of going back to Hawaii, but he didn't want to stay just because he was feeling manipulated, either. Mrs. G. had certainly contrived an impossible task. He was his own man, and he wanted to lead his own life. Ben had to admit that the venture for foster kids came from a good place. The money he'd inherited would be a big plus, but he wanted his freedom more. And yet there was Becky to consider.

Ben pulled into Frisbee's Pier and put the car in park. He strolled to the end of the pier and grappled with his situation. Being close to the water usually gave him clarity. The clause in the will that he and Becky had to work together didn't affect just his life; it affected Becky's inheritance as well. But, if she loved what she did at Proposals as much as he loved the sea, then she might feel the same way about their forced project. His leaving would give her an out. All he knew for sure was that he'd have to leave better than he had before; Rebecca deserved a goodbye.

CHAPTER 11

Rebecca pulled into her apartment's driveway and gathered the container of coffee she'd just picked up from the convenient store. She was relieved that she hadn't run into anyone she knew, as she hadn't showered and was still wearing her sweatpants and fleece coverup.

Warmth met her at the door. *Aah, now this is what I'm talking about.* Rebecca shed her coat, hat, and tossed her gloves on the entry table. The folder the attorney had given her slid just enough to grab her attention. She picked it up and brought it to the kitchen while she made herself a much-needed coffee.

Rebecca opened the folder. The words *Last Will & Testament of Norma R. Getchel* stared back at her. She ran her hand through her tangled hair and tried to comprehend the enormity of its content. She and Ben had to do this thing together. It was hard enough to consider doing it by herself, but adding Benjamin to the mix made the task seem impossible.

He'd been thrown for a loop when the attorney told them what they needed to do. Ben made it very clear that he had a life, and a job, and it wasn't in Maine.

What were you thinking, Norma? Sure, the cause was a great one; one that was near and dear to their hearts, but this was a huge ask, even for her.

Rebecca's mind shifted to Mrs. Getchel's house. Even if she'd rented out a room or two, she wouldn't be able to keep up with the property taxes and upkeep, but the last thing she wanted was to lose it. That house was the closest thing to home she had left, and she couldn't for the life of her figure out a good solution. *He has to help.*

Rebecca picked up her *Life is Just Better When I'm Quilting* coffee mug and scooted down the hall to her workroom. She opened the door and instantly felt a bit lighter. She needed to get her mind off things for a little while and quilting was just the answer.

Rebecca spread her current work-in-progress out on her worktable. She laid a combination of swatches to use as the border until she was satisfied with her choice. This one was for a little girl of about seven. Apparently, she loved ribbons and bows, so Rebecca selected a ditsy pink- rose print and would embellish it with a light pink satin ribbon that would weave along the border and on each corner, she'd use that same ribbon to tie a small bow.

Time went by quickly as she worked through the multiple steps of the quilt, but she was satisfied with the progress she'd made. She stood back to take in the whole quilt.

Little Amy will be happy with this.

Rebecca smiled as she folded up her work. Before setting it aside, she held it to her breast and thought of what message she should embroider for this sweet little girl.

"Okay, enough of that for the day." She spun on her heels and traipsed to her bedroom.

Rebecca scanned her closet for something more appropriate for work as she was determined to put some hours in, even if only for a bit. She had a wedding order to pull together and didn't want to be too rushed tomorrow.

Now that the pain of Thanksgiving was over, she could finally look forward to the Christmas season. It was her favorite time for weddings. She could consume her time and thoughts with work. Most florists, she imagined, would prefer the spring and summer because there were so many more blooms to pick from, but Rebecca loved the simplicity of traditional greens, and poinsettias, and roses of red. They were almost magical to her. They held tradition and symbolism that gave her a feeling of hope, especially with a new year fast approaching. She supposed Valentine's Day was similar, but for her, that day brought on a heartache of another kind; she'd spend it alone once again.

Rebecca grabbed a lightweight crimson tunic off the shelf and a pair of black leggings, then scuttled to the bathroom for a hot shower.

Rebecca intended to run the floral arrangements over in her mind while she was in the shower, as most of her great ideas started there, but her thoughts quickly shifted to Ben. *He's leaving soon.* She scrubbed her scalp more aggressively as her anger built.

She was furious at herself for caring even one iota if Benjamin Daly stayed or went. It wasn't as if she had any kind of relationship with him. If anything, their relationship was strained from the get-go. He'd always been selfish and self-centered, and she shouldn't have expected anything different from him. For that matter, she shouldn't have had any expectations at all, especially because she hadn't thought she'd ever see him again after all these years. So, the fact that he was leaving shouldn't have any bearing on her life whatsoever. But it did.

Why would you do this to us, Norma?! Making us work together! Really?

She lathered on conditioner and let it set while warm water massaged her shoulders. She and Ben were both loners. He had his life, and she had hers. Besides, they lived half a world away apart. She couldn't fathom how in the world Mrs. Getchel thought they could work together.

I know nothing about taking care of children, Norma, and would wager that Ben doesn't, either.

She rinsed the conditioner off and filled her fluffy loofa with body wash. A fresh cucumber melon fragrance filled the space as she caressed her scarred body.

For crying out loud, Norma, we're both screwed up ourselves.

She thought about all the quilts she'd made over the years. Quilts were just gifts—she didn't have to get involved. Sewing was safe. And Ben hadn't changed. He'd run away then, and he was running away now. As much as she loved Norma Getchel, there was no way that they could honor her wishes. This reality tore at her heart because she wanted nothing more than to make Norma proud. Maybe, Rebecca thought, they'd find a way for her to do the project by herself.

Rebecca flipped off the faucet and stepped out into the chilly room, grateful, once again, that the steam blotted out her image in the mirror and hid her scars. She dried off and slipped on her clothes while attempting to expel Benjamin Daly from her thoughts.

The quick drive to Proposals gave her little time to wrap her head around the floral arrangements she needed to design. She'd made notes, but she usually saw the displays clearly in her mind before starting the assembly. She wasn't even sure if all her selections had arrived and hadn't even thought to question her choice of blooms so distracted was she by Mrs. Getchel's death and Ben's arrival, and now, learning about her inheritance.

Rebecca pulled into Proposals, and it was as if fate was on her side. Duncan Philip's car sat in the parking lot. *Of course!* Duncan was a wiz at numbers, and he had skill in all things to do with investments and whatnot. He could help her make sense of what she had to do to get the project going.

With that bit of relief at having the start of a plan, she gathered her things from the car and eagerly entered Proposals.

Emily leaned against the counter, wiping her hands with a towel. Duncan sat at one of the wrought-iron tables for two, and another customer, with his back to her, sat at the far table clutching his phone. She'd recognize that hand anywhere. *Are you kidding me right now? What is Ben doing here?* Before she could take another step in that direction, Emily greeted her with a mischievous grin on her face.

"Hey Becky," Emily said in a hushed voice. "I wasn't sure if we'd see you today. Sophie's in the back—seems a big order came in, and—" Emily motioned to the man on the phone, and raised her eyebrows in a teasing fashion, "—you have company."

"Em," Duncan interrupted with a shake of his head, a stern expression, and mouthed, "Stop it."

"It's okay, Duncan." Rebecca rested her free hand on his shoulder, then shot a death stare at Emily before turning her attention to Duncan once again. "I'm hoping maybe you could help me out with some financial stuff. Should I make an appointment at your office or…"

"Nah, just give me a couple of time slots that work best for you, and we could just meet at your place, or even here somewhere, if that's better." Duncan's attention drifted away back to his soup, and Rebecca could sense that Ben was now standing directly behind her.

Rebecca couldn't believe the audacity he had in hovering into a private conversation, so she made him wait.

"Thanks, Duncan. I'll text you some dates and times. I really appreciate it—but I don't want to take advantage, so please treat me like any other one of your clients."

"The first consult is always free anyway, but know you aren't just any other client. You are like family, and family doesn't pay full price."

"You're the best." Rebecca leaned over and gave Duncan a quick hug. She was beyond irritated by Ben's behavior. He was nearly breathing down her neck. Duncan's gaze drifted once again toward the interloper. Rebecca shifted to the side and Ben stood there as if he didn't have a care in the world, as if it were perfectly normal to be hovering over her at her place of business.

For the love of all things holy. "Duncan, this is Benjamin Daly. He's a friend from way back in my teen days and a mutual friend of Mrs. Getchel's. The friend who just passed away. Ben, this is Duncan Philips, my soon-to-be accountant, an insane musician here at Proposals, and friend."

Duncan rose to his feet to meet Ben's awaiting extended hand. Rebecca couldn't get over the difference in their size. Ben stood a good foot taller, broader in the shoulder, and his hands were massive in comparison. Duncan adjusted his coke-bottled glasses to take in Ben's dominating presence.

"Nice to meet you, Benjamin," Duncan said, then awkwardly slid his hand from Ben's firm grip. "Sorry to hear of the loss of your friend."

"Yes, and thanks. She was the closest thing to a mother that we ever had." Ben directed his attention toward Rebecca with a tender smile.

How dare he say that Mrs. Getchel was like a mother to me? Grandmother, yes, but mother, absolutely not. Heat rose across her chest and up her neck. She'd had a mother, and she'd been the most amazing and giving woman that Rebecca had ever known. No one would ever hold a candle to her.

You presumptuous, impossible man. She clutched her fists at her side and took in a few deep breaths, hoping that she could hide her anger.

"Duncan, thanks again for agreeing to meet with me. I just need to take care of the Foreman's wedding event, and then I'm all yours if that works for you?"

Duncan slid his glasses up his nose and leaned back to hold on to the back of the chair, as if his knees were about to give out on him. Ben's imposing presence stood steadfast over her shoulder, and Rebecca had a hard time shielding her annoyance.

"Sure, um—that should work, Rebecca," Duncan said, then cleared his throat. "Are you sure there isn't anything else I can do for you? Anything more urgent, perhaps?" His eyebrows rose and he shifted his weight while continuing to lean on the chair.

"I'm sure Duncan, but thanks. I'm all set for now." Rebecca could tell that Duncan was relieved. His shoulders relaxed, but still seemed unsure of what to do.

"Well, I guess I'll finish my soup then," Duncan said, and once again took his seat before nodding at Ben. "I'll see you in an hour."

Rebecca grabbed hold of Ben's hand and pulled him outside, out of earshot of the customers, then put her fisted hands on her hips. "What are you doing here, Benjamin?"

"I don't understand. Why are you so pissed at me?"

"You were looming over me and listening in on my private conversations! How would you feel if I just showed up at your work? And I find it difficult to believe that you just happened upon Proposals. Stalking me isn't a good look, Ben."

"Stalking you?" he said with wide eyes. "Excuse me if I wanted to see what grown-up Becky's life was about. I heard good things—and—and I wanted something sweet to eat."

"Oh, I see. You heard good things. It's good to know that my life was the topic of your conversations."

Rebecca shivered, and she could sense her co-workers staring at them from inside.

"You know what, Ben, I don't need this right now. I came here to work—this is my place of business. Besides, you have important things that you have to get back for, and I hardly think—"

"I don't get you, Becky! One minute you act like you want me around—you know, to help and stuff—and the next minute, you're pushing me away. Do you want my help or not because, for the life of me, I can't figure you out?"

She couldn't even look at him. What he was asking was a perfectly sound question, but she couldn't answer. She didn't want to do what was required of them by herself, but he wasn't dependable. The last time she'd counted on him, trusted him, he'd left her. And he was just going to do it again. At least this time, he'd shown her the courtesy of giving her some kind of head's up that he was leaving.

Ben stood before her, waiting for an answer. Daisy leaped onto the hood of her car and pushed her nose toward his tapping fingers. Without removing his questioning stare from hers, he nonchalantly moved his hand to Daisy's back and gave it several long, slow caresses, then moved to under her ear. Daisy responded, pushing herself closer with a purr.

Rebecca, in that moment, wished that his hand would caress her like that and found herself getting jealous of a stupid cat. "Daisy, down," she said, and nudged the calico off the car. "You're going to scratch it."

The warmth welling within her ebbed, and the momentary distraction cleared her mind. "You know what, Ben. It doesn't really matter what I want, does it? You're just going to do what you darn well please anyway."

"Beck, I—"

"I've got to get to work." With that, Rebecca stepped around Ben, taking only a few steps before Daisy got underfoot.

"What is with you?" She picked up the ginger cat, trudged toward the main house's porch, opened the door, then plopped her inside with a thud. She just hoped that Ben had left because she couldn't face him another minute. Her emotions wreaked havoc in her with a quickening pulse and the familiar knot at her throat. She swallowed hard and forced herself to not tear up.

"I always figured you for a cat person," Ben said as he leaned against the car with his arms and ankles crossed. Once again, Rebecca faced the man she'd tried to erase for the past decade.

"Well, you figured wrong." She brushed her hands together as if wiping the feel of the cat from her. "I thought you were leaving."

"I will, but not before you agree to talk to me—later—after work."

"Why did you come here, anyway?" Rebecca asked.

His long eyelashes accentuated his deep brown orbs, and she swore they could see right through her. He'd always been able to do that, and his perception of her liking cats ripped at her heart.

She used to love cats, until her life changed in the blink of an eye. But she hadn't told a soul, not even Ben or Mrs. Getchel. And she wasn't about to turn into a blubbering fool right there in front of him. Again, she stuffed the urge to cry deep inside, as she'd always done.

"I didn't want to leave on a bad note," Ben said.

"Oh, was that all?" She shoved her hands in her pants pockets and chewed on her lower lip. "Let me get this straight. You came here to tell me goodbye, again, because you feel bad."

"Yes." He took a step closer to her. His musky cologne was intoxicating as he lowered his strong face close to hers. "I don't want to leave with you upset again. I didn't want it before, and I don't want it now."

Rebecca wanted him to wrap his arms around her so she could cradle her head against his chest. Just once, she wanted him to think of her just as she'd thought of him over the years. He was leaving her again. She'd just have to accept that fact. Any amount of wishing on her part was futile.

"We don't need to talk later. Let's just get it out there right now."

"Okay," Ben said with some trepidation in his voice.

"You don't owe me anything. We are just two people thrown together by happenstance. Please don't worry about me. I'll be fine. I'll take care of the project. I always end up landing on my feet."

With that, Ben leaned into her and wrapped his arms around her and gave her a hug that as much as she wanted to push him away, made her weak in the knees. She breathed in the scent of his leather jacket and musky cologne, then gave his bicep a squeeze to indicate the embrace should end.

"It really was good seeing you again, Becky." He pecked her on the forehead. "I'll let you get to work."

"Yep. I really need to get to it."

She could barely bring herself to look at him. She just wanted him gone. Ripping off the band-aid was better than dragging things out.

CHAPTER 12

Benjamin's insides turned upside down as he drove away from the Proposals. Once again, he left her standing alone while he was leaving. This time, she was a grown woman with a life of her own. Becky Mills had grown into a remarkable woman. It wasn't his place, but he was proud of her. She still carried a chip on her shoulder, but he couldn't blame her. All the kids in the foster system had, and if he was any indication, they still did today.

Rebecca had lashed out, then would retreat into her own world where he could never enter. Truth be told, he thought, he wasn't much better.

Benjamin has only vague memories of his parents. They were a shadowy dream in slow motion. He could see their thin bodies in a haze-filled room, moving around the coffee table like rag dolls. Later, when he was four, his father sat hunched over a steering wheel and his mother splayed out on the other side of the front seat. The day had been sweltering and his parents were barely clothed. He had no idea what he had been wearing. He watched the scene as if in a movie, or an out-of-body experience. His mother's eyes looked into some faraway place, her mouth agape. He heard his own voice saying, "Mommy, Daddy, wake up," over and over again. But they never did.

Ben tried over the years to remember a good time with his parents: a smile, a hug, an atta-boy, but nothing came to mind. He only knew the feeling of being afraid, alone, and hungry. For years, the fearful pang of being abandoned had shaken him to his core. As he grew, that fear was replaced with the need to run away from those who claimed to care for him. The system had transferred him from place to place, never knowing where he'd end up or who he'd end up with.

Until he was thirteen and Mrs. G. entered his life that he had the feeling of being wanted, and if he dared say, loved.

His thoughts again went to Becky. He'd been in the system for far too long and he understood the full weight that experience carried. Even though she wasn't in it for nearly as long, her battle scars made up for the time.

If he remembered correctly, she'd arrived at Mrs. G's when she was fifteen. Prior to that, he'd learned she'd had health issues. He and the other kids weren't supposed to ask about or talk about; Mrs. G. made that clear. Apparently, she'd been placed in the foster program around fourteen. He was happy that she'd been placed at Mrs. G's because it offered her a greater chance of success. She was one of the lucky ones.

Joining the military had proved an awakening. He'd had structure, authority figures that he dared not get on the wrong side of. He'd had too many painful experiences of bad actors in his life, so he did all he could do to not bring him any more harm than necessary. In the Navy, he had a real sense of purpose and belonging that was both honorable and necessary to his well-being. To this day, he wondered why he'd left. He supposed it was his freedom and his independent streak that called him to leave. If he were being honest with himself, he'd have to confess that it was those same needs that were calling him to stop salvaging or leave Maine yet again.

***

Ben arrived at his room at the inn. He shed his coat and kicked off his shoes. He cracked open a beer from the mini fridge, lit the gas fireplace, and flipped open the large pepperoni pizza that he'd picked up. The packet of papers he'd received from the attorney stared back at him as if it were taunting him. *You win.* He opened the folder.

The more he read, the more he now had an inkling of why Becky might have been so upset with him. *Of all the presumptuous, preposterous, and downright inconsiderate things to have put on our shoulders.* The magnitude of what Mrs. G. was asking of him and Becky was just too much.

Ben paced the floor. The file folder firmly in his hand, he slapped it against his thigh. He looked up toward the heavens. "I have a life, Mrs. Getchel!" He wheeled the folder over his head. "I don't have time for this in my life. Do you hear me?"

Ben tossed the folder on the coffee table, then plopped into the overstuffed chair and rested his head in his hands, tapping his heels on the hardwood floor. Mrs. G. always had an ulterior motive up her sleeve, but he couldn't imagine what had been on her mind.

He now had a splitting headache and felt terrible that he'd blown off Mrs. G's wishes when he'd first heard them. He'd basically checked out after he learned he'd inherited some money. He and Becky talked about it briefly afterwards, but he had to confess, he'd only half listened to Becky's ramblings about the whole thing. He supposed he was too focused on her adorably messy hair to fully pay attention.

Surely, Mrs. G. hadn't expected him to leave his whole life behind and stay here, and Rebecca had to know that as well. Frankly, he figured she'd just handle the project on her own, and they'd get their money. Now, however, he realized the will clearly stated that to receive any money, they must work together to form the foundation for foster children. Problem was he had no idea how he was going to manage that, seeing he lived in the middle of the Pacific.

Ben needed to call his team in Kauai to see if he could feasibly delay his return. Hawaii was five hours behind east coast time, so he shouldn't have any trouble reaching anyone. Smithers would have a pretty good idea of the schedule for the foreseeable future. Maybe, Ben thought, he could figure out a way to do both.

He paced the floor as the phone rang on the other end. "Hey, Smithers, miss me?"

"You bet your sweet ass I do," Smithers said with a boisterous laugh. "What's up?"

"Got myself in a jam, and I've got to stick around here longer than I thought. Anything going on your end?"

"Nah, just some small jobs—no more superhero crap that we'd need you for. We're actually expecting a hurricane over the next week anyway, so we couldn't go out, even if we wanted to. You say you're in a jam there on the mainland?"

"Seems my old friend who passed away left me in a bit of a bind. I've got to work some stuff out with Becky—another friend of mine."

"That the girl Holokai's been yapping my ear off about? Says you used to be sweet on her, back when you were a pup."

"Yep." He didn't dare encourage Smithers anymore. He had a way of turning everything into some kind of sexual innuendo, and Ben wasn't in the mood.

"Is that what they call it now? Workin' some stuff out?"

Ben rolled his eyes at Smithers' predictable, crass sense of humor.

"I guess a man's gotta do what a man's gotta do," Smithers said.

"Guess so," Ben said. "Hey, can you ask Holokai to swing by my place on the way to the docks sometime over the next few days? I'd like him to take what he wants out of the fridge, and throw anything else out that might spoil?"

"What, I'm not good enough for you to do that?"

"You live in the opposite direction and—"

"I'm just bustin' your balls. I'll let him know." With that, Ben said thanks and disconnected.

Good, Ben thought, that will give him time with Becky, and he had to admit that spending more time with her was definitely a plus. God willing, they'd work out a feasible plan; one that would meet Mrs. G's wishes and still allow him to go back to his life.

A brilliant sunset caught his attention through the window. He slipped on his loafers and grabbed his coat. The temperature surprised him when he opened the door. Maybe it was the calmness, without the Northeastern sea breeze. He ventured across the street to take in the fullness of the spectacular display. Just looking at the water and smelling the salty air relieved his angst, and before he knew it, he was feeling a bit better. Knowing that he wasn't causing any added stress back home sealed the deal that he'd stick around.

Besides, he thought, he owed it to Mrs. G. and Becky.

CHAPTER 13

Rebecca stopped by her new house on her way home. She still couldn't come to terms with the fact that it was hers. As she placed the key in the door, the sensation that she was intruding still lingered. She knew in time that the feeling would abate, but it was strange, nonetheless. Rebecca didn't plan to stay long, but figured if she walked around the rooms, she'd get a feel for what might lie ahead.

She hoped for some kind of epiphany, or that the house would speak to her, but she found herself reliving the past.

Rebecca wandered into the room where she'd slept when she'd first moved in. The room was large with windows that looked toward the street. Two twin beds sat against opposite walls with matching quilts. She bet if she looked closely, she'd see the initials she'd penned on one of the corner squares.

Rebecca sat on the edge of the bed and untucked the quilt from under the pillow. She turned down the edge, and sure enough, a faint R.M. still showed on the square near the binding. She caressed the letters and wondered if anyone ever knew of this secret. The secret that she'd claimed it as her own, in a world where nothing was no longer hers.

The act of scribing those letters may have planted a seed that would spur on her need to make personalized quilts today. She held the corner of the quilt close to her chest, thinking of all the other children who were feeling lost, alone, and afraid, knowing that they'd lost everything that they ever knew.

Rebecca recalled the first time she'd lain on the bed. She repeated the action by lying on the bed with her arms to her side and looked toward the ceiling.

She remembered the unbearable sense of despair, an overwhelming remorse for what she'd done to end up in that bed back then. Rebecca recalled how she'd worn the remains of a few small bandages on her shoulder, right arm, and chest. They weren't nearly as extensive as they had been when she was in the burn unit, but had been tender and a constant reminder of what she'd done.

Coming to terms with the loss of her parents had taken years of counseling, and lessened the burden of guilt. Try as she may, guilt reared its head and consumed her body, mind, and spirit, as if it had just happened.

She once again stared up at the watermarks and faded, stuck-on stars. The ceiling needed a fresh coat of paint, Rebecca decided.

She sat up with a new determination. *Fresh paint. I could do that.*

She needed to do a makeover on the house to make it more to her liking, but first she had to come up with a vision, and that was a challenge, considering she had no idea what that vision was.

If she followed in Mrs. Getchel's path, she'd simply update each room with its current intent, but things had changed. Rebecca should have technology, a learning center, and perhaps even a game room.

Rebecca mulled over the possibilities and became more excited by the minute. Maybe, she thought, she could make the house into a place for teens that would soon transition out of the system; a kind of community center that taught kids how to live successfully on their own. A bridge from foster care to independence. She certainly had the space in the big old house. *Would the town of York approve a transition home?*

Soon her excitement faded. The daunting task became too enormous for her to do on her own. This irked her immeasurably. By all rights, she shouldn't have to do any of this alone, but Ben was leaving. And that was that.

Emily, she recalled, had gone through something similar recently, so she at least had her friend as a resource. As Sophie would always say, "One step at a time." Rebecca would follow that advice.

For now, she thought it best to first figure out where she'd live. She could either move in to the house, or find a more suitable place for just herself, then determined that she really needed an overall plan. Her frustration was settling too deep to think about it anymore for the day.

She flicked off the lights and allowed the ghosts of her childhood to recede into the woodwork.

***

Rebecca, exhausted from the day, couldn't wait to crawl into bed. She entered her apartment and sloughed off her coat, then traipsed to her room to put on some comfy clothes.

She pulled out a pair of worn sweats and threw a hoodie over her head. She slid on her slippers, then headed to the kitchen to make a hot toddy. She added a shot of bourbon to her now microwaved mulled spiced tea, added a squirt of lemon, and a heaping teaspoon of honey. The steam rose to her nose and instantly transported her to a place of comfort. A time when her mom had made her hot tea, and they'd sit for hours in front of the fireplace, piecing together puzzles; a time when crackling fires didn't scare her. As the smooth warmth of the drink ran down her throat, she savored the moment.

Benjamin Daly intruded yet again into her mind. Why couldn't she shake him? It was as though she were back in tenth grade, when her crush over him bored into her inner-most thoughts. Now, she was a grown woman, and her desire for him had grown in ways she never thought it would.

She'd been with men, in the romantic sense. But those relationships had been fleeting and she'd simply gone through the motions, until the boredom of the situation made her call it quits. No one, except for Benjamin, has filled her with desire and want, but he'd been a fantasy. The fact that she never thought she'd see him again made it safe to indulge in those fantasies, but now that he was here, she needed to stuff them down. He wasn't interested in her. Why would he be? He lived on the romantic island of Kauai, filled with beautiful, bikini-clad women. For all she knew, he already had a girlfriend.

Rebecca curled up in her favorite oversized chair and wrapped her favorite fluffy blanket over her lap to enjoy the rest of her hot toddy. Perhaps it was all for the best that he was leaving. No sense having him stay if he was just going to resent it and be unhappy. She cared too much for him to see him unhappy. Rebecca shrugged at the idea that he was remotely attracted to her, anyway; she was damaged goods.

Rebecca tipped her head back to rest it on the chair back. The nightcap was doing its work; her eyes grew heavy, and she drifted off to sleep.

A dream formed. She was once again a kid. She was playing with her cat outside. Bubbles floated in the wind and a cat jumped to pop each one. Eventually, the bubbles turned to cold water droplets that showered all around her. They didn't touch her or the cat, but the feline ran away into the now gray-filled air. The sound of crackling surrounded her and intensified. Flames licked at her, lashing at her arms and legs. She woke in a pool of sweat, gasping for air. Hyperventilating, she fought back the need to breathe with the urge to scream, alone in the dark, once again.

It took her a few minutes to realize that she'd been dreaming. The same dream had haunted her for years, but every time, it left doom and despair in its wake. Terror abated, and anger set in. "For once, will you leave me at peace?" she screamed at the phantom interloper. "Just once, I'd like to sleep! Is that too much to ask?"

She flayed and kicked at the blanket to escape the nightmares. She shook as she made her way to her bathroom sink. Rebecca splashed water on her face to snap out of the fear and to wash away the cold sweat that beaded across her forehead, down her neck, and into her cleavage. She ran a brush through her hair and pulled her hair up in an elastic, then stripped down and crawled into bed, praying above all things that the nightmare wouldn't come again.

Everything was uncomfortable. Her pillow was too stuffed. The bed was too firm. The blankets were too light.

She kicked the blankets off her and threw her pillow across the room--as if any of that tantrum was going to help her sleep.

By now, she was wide awake, cursing at the night. *Well, Rebecca, it only serves you right. You prayed you wouldn't have nightmares, and now you can't sleep. Prayer answered.*

Rebecca threw on her robe and slippers, then trudged across the creaking floors. Her eyes adjusted to the night with the help of the glow from the full moon, which guided her path toward the kitchen so she could get a glass of water. The next thing she knew, she was in her sewing room and perusing her stacks of fabric. She was grateful that she'd thought to put shelving units up before her fabric obsession became too great. Now, she could see all her pink, blues, greens—a rainbow of colors. Creating a new quilt was just a matter of matching designs at this point. She thought of getting a head start for her next project, and pulled a selection of fabrics for the next child on the list she'd received from the Office of Child and Family Services via Mrs. Getchel. Rebecca jotted down a quick note: *see about getting a direct contact with OCFS.*

She'd been told Katrina was a twelve-year-old girl who had a large birthmark that covered a third of her face. She'd been tormented and teased mercilessly because of it, and Rebecca knew her pain too well. Rebecca's own abnormalities were mostly covered, and to this day, she had a hard time wearing anything other than high necks and long sleeves. She hated the questioning looks and assumed Katrina had it worse because she couldn't hide hers.

One positive thing Rebecca had learned about Katrina was that she loved to read. Rebecca had been quite a reader too, but she didn't wise up to that until she was older. Had she realized the pleasure earlier, it would have helped her through some of the worst times of her life. She wouldn't have lain in her hospital bed and foster homes feeling sorry for herself; she would have had an escape from the loss of her parents. Maybe reading would also have given her another way to avoid her deep, debilitating pain and guilt.

Katrina S. would have a quilt that would incorporate two things that would, hopefully, help her on her journey: comfort, and happy ever-afters. Rebecca's creative mind would design what looked like a bookshelf, filled with book bindings--some laid down, some upright, others falling over. The books would appear in many colors, prints, widths, and heights. She would leave the titles blank to show Katrina's imagination. She would embroider only a few exceptions: one book would be titled *Katrina S.*, another would be titled *I'm on Purpose*, and the last, *I Am Beautiful.* All in all, the quilt would contain a hundred books, with twenty-five on each shelf. Rebecca was excited for the challenge of making the shelf unit look three dimensional. She only wished she could see Katrina's expression upon receiving it.

By now, she grew weary, and her bed called her. She was grateful for a slow schedule for the day and only needed to place a few orders and put away some deliveries. Tomorrow, she'd keep it simple. No stress, no overthinking, and no regrets.

Dreams weaved in and out until the break of dawn, but this time, they were as if she were being guided in the way of her future. A vision solidified in her mind that she would build a bridge for kids who were about to age out and had aged out. She wouldn't be a mother figure or grandmother figure. She'd be a mentor, teacher, and caring resource.

When her eyes opened, Rebecca was surprised that she wasn't exhausted. If anything, she was invigorated. She opened the notes app on her phone and tapped in her inspired thoughts about building a bridge for kids so she wouldn't forget. *Yes, this could work.* She could envision each room's purpose—her purpose—and for the first time in a long time, she felt like the shoe was a perfect fit.

Chapter 14

For a change of scenery, Ben popped into the local coffee shop. Grounds was bustling. A gathering of ladies sat at one of the larger tables, chattering away. The smiling server named Jillian delivered another round of hot cocoas. As she set each one down, stating that she'd made them with her special ingredient: love. They giggled their thanks and ate it up.

Ben chose a quiet corner with a comfortable-looking leather chair where he could see out the window. He pulled his computer out of his bag, set out a note pad, and his pen, then meandered through the other customers to find his place in line. Before long, Jillian greeted him with an exuberant hello.

"You're new around here, aren't you?" she asked with a swish of her ponytail.

"Sort of?" Ben replied.

"We haven't had the pleasure of meeting." She stuck out her hand for a shake.

"I'm Jillian, the owner here at Grounds."

"Name's Ben, Ben Daly," he said as he met her hand.

"You seem familiar," she said with an upturned corner of her mouth and a tilt of the head. "Family in town?"

Ben smiled at the use of the word family, but he didn't want to share his life story. "I guess you could say that."

"Well, either you do or you don't, Benjamin." Her use of his formal name and inquisition took him off guard. Outside of his commanding officer in the Navy, he wasn't used to people talking so directly.

"A woman, that could have been my grandmother passed away, and I'm here to pay my respects." He couldn't believe he was answering her questions. It certainly wasn't any of her business, and he owed her absolutely no explanation, but, he guessed, she had a way of pulling information out of him.

"Oh! You must mean dear Mrs. Getchel, right?" Jillian didn't wait for a response and kept on. "She was such a lovely lady in the community. We will all miss her kindness and what she did for all those kids over the years. Are you one of her kids—from the foster program?"

Now Ben was beyond taken aback by her directness.

Before he could get a word in, she jumped in again. "What can I get you? It's on the house. To lose such a person in your life must be sorely felt. Coffee, tea, cacao? I'll even throw in a cinnamon twist from Proposals." She stood with her hands on her hips, waiting for his response, and for the life of him, he couldn't speak. "I'll surprise you.," she said, then spun on her heels.

Ben shook his head in astonishment, then went back to his seat. He wanted to understand as much as he could about Becky's history. He'd found little information online, but Jillian seemed familiar with Mrs. Getchel and her kids.

Maybe she knew something about Becky's past.

A few minutes later, Jillian was at his side with an as promised cinnamon twist, and a mocha latte. "If I can get you anything else, just let me know."

"Yes, actually, there is something."

Jillian's eyes brightened.

"You mentioned Proposals. Do you know them well—the people who work there?" What's good for the goose is good for the gander, he thought as he peppered her with questions.

"Doesn't everybody?" she replied. "They're like family to me."

"Do you know much about Rebecca Mills?"

"Well, I hear she just inherited Mrs. Getchel's home and fortune, and I say, good for her. She deserves it after all that poor thing's been through in her life."

"Oh?" Ben bit back his irritation that word had gotten out; *small towns*. He couldn't help himself but to ask. "What happened?"

Jillian leaned in to whisper in his ear. As if gossiping was more acceptable that way. "I read once—or maybe someone told me…" She cocked her head, trying to recall where she'd heard the information, then waved the thought off with a flit of her hands. "Doesn't matter. Anyway, I think the poor dear was nearly burned alive, along with her parents." She stood to wave at another customer coming through the door, then turned back to meet Ben's gaze. "Can you imagine?"

"No, I can't." A knot formed in the pit of his stomach.

She went on to say how grateful she was that Becky had found her way to work at Proposals. Said they were good people and she should know because she, herself, was practically like family. Seemed she dates Duncan Philips, whom Ben remembered as Becky's accountant friend. As she continued to chatter, her words became background noise; all he could think about was Becky.

He pictured her as a kid dealing with a scary situation like that, and he could only imagine what her scarred body would be like as a vision played over in his mind. If true, he thought, he now understood her need to wear long sleeves. He'd been burned with the butt of a cigarette many times over as a child, and simply couldn't image the pain she must have felt, never mind learning her parents had perished in that fire.

He'd witnessed survivor's remorse, both in the service and search and rescue operations. It was never an easy thing to get over, and he felt for her.

"Well, Benjamin Daly," Jillian said. "I'll check back in with you in a bit to see if you need anything else."

He wondered, as she flitted off, if she repeated names to remember them, or if it was just her quirky nature. He took a bite of his cinnamon twist. Flakey pastry stuck to his fingers, and he licked them absentmindedly.

He'd intended to check his emails and get some work done. He figured it was the least he could do since he wasn't there to help, but Miss Jillian was a fountain of information, and her story piqued his curiosity. For all he knew, it was all rumor, but it made sense, and Jillian had some connection. Even so, he clicked around on his laptop for confirmation. He guessed at the timeline and searched for house fires in Maine with deaths. A headline read, *Devastating Loss of Unbearable Proportions Hits Kennebunk Family*, jumped off the page, inviting him to read more. He scrolled through the article, but no names were mentioned. It simply said, a professor and his wife had died at the scene, and a minor was taken to the hospital with life-threatening burns and smoke inhalation.

Ben leaned back in the leather chair and stretched his arms over his head before settling his clasped hands together behind his head. He looked on as Grounds buzzed with conversation. Jillian strutted her way to his seat.

She peered into his empty cup and picked up his plate. "Can I get you a refill, Benjamin?"

"I'm all set, but thanks."

"Are you sure? I hate to see empty plates and cups."

"Tell you what, I'll take a cinnamon twist to go."

"I should have known. Most people can't eat just one of Emily's twists. I'll get that packaged right up." She scampered off in the direction of the group of ladies, removing plates along the way.

Ben once again leaned forward and clicked on some additional news articles, but no further information regarding the professor, his wife, or the minor appeared, and so he called it a day. Jillian returned with a white paper bag containing his twist. He dug a couple bills out of his wallet and was about to hand them to Jillian, when one of the boisterous ladies approached, swaying her weight around.

"Jillian, I've got this," she said in a commanding voice.

Ben stood to meet her, realizing that she'd been one of the ladies in the group near him. "No, I couldn't—I…"

"Now Benjamin," Jillian said. "Don't take away Mrs. Bennington's joy."

At that, Ben had no response. Jillian's comment completely derailed him and he felt no other choice but to accept the gift from a stranger.

"How nice of you, Mrs. Bennington." Jillian said.

"I confess. I overheard you say you were here to pay your respects to Norma Getchel—God rest her soul." Mrs.

Bennington made the sign of the cross over her heaving chest. "Please accept my condolences. It's the least I can do for one of her *kids*." Her words were spoken so loudly that he was sure the entire population of Grounds heard.

"Thank you for your kindness, Misses...." he hesitated, picking up on a cutting edge to her condolences, while he tried to recall what Jillian had said her name was.

"Mrs. Margo Bennington." She extended her hand, and for a moment, Ben thought she was expecting him to bow and kiss it, but he gave it a shake.

"Mrs. Bennington." He nodded as if to say thank you and good day, but she didn't move.

"It was so good of you to be here for Norma's service." She tsked. "To have one of her poor kids carry Norma to her final resting place would have meant the world to her. Why, I bet most of the people at her memorial were a part of your— *family*." Her pursed lips and her condescending tone didn't sit well with Ben, but he did his best to swallow it down and act unaffected. "Lord only knows what will happen now. I wager to guess her home will become an estate for some nice family instead of—well—you know."

"I wouldn't count on that, Mrs. Bennington. We plan to do whatever we can to bring her home back to life, helping kids from all walks of life," he said with a coolness that made Mrs. Bennington shudder.

"Won't that be marvelous!" Jillian chimed in, oblivious to Mrs. Bennington's condescension. "I'm guessing by you saying 'we,' that you're referring to you and Rebecca Mills?"

"Indeed." Ben reached into his pocket and handed Jillian the couple of dollars that she'd returned to him. "Please use this for my payment. Since Mrs. Bennington here has such a generous heart, maybe she could use her kind gesture toward your tip, or for those less fortunate." He nodded, then turned toward Mrs. Bennington. "Maybe you could even spread your generosity for the needs of kids in the foster program, since it obviously means so much to you."

Her jaw dropped, and for the first time since she'd introduced herself, she was speechless.

"Good day." He picked up his belongings and left Mrs. Bennington to sputter in his wake.

Chapter 15

Rebecca lay in bed as the sun climbed. She continued tossing ideas around about Mrs. Getchel's bequeathed wishes and the inspiration from the wee hour's dream-filled sleep. She concluded it didn't really matter if she did the project alone; if she didn't try, she'd beat herself up, and she'd already done far too much of that in her life.

Rebecca threw off the covers and scampered to the shower, shivering along the way. She clasped her hands close to her chest and teetered back and forth, trying to stay warm while she waited for the water to get hot and regretted not grabbing her robe from the foot of her bed. She was getting colder by the second.

Rebecca darted back to her room to retrieve the robe, but before she could put it on, she slammed her pinky toe into the bathroom's doorjamb, sending excruciating pain through her foot. The pain was so intense that she thought she'd vomit. She dropped the robe in the hallway and crouched against the bathroom wall as her eyes filling up, fighting the urge to hurl.

Rebecca hobbled to her feet and managed to knock her full water glass off the bathroom counter, smashing it to pieces across the tiled floor. She stood leaning against the sink, her pain and frustration bubbled up. She threw her toothbrush, toothpaste, and any other random items sitting on her counter, then burst into tears. "Today was supposed to be a good day!"

She took a frustrated step toward the shower and with that step, pain took her breath and her feet out from under her.

"I hate my life!" she yelled, and continued to wail like a child that didn't want to get a shot.

"Oh my God, Ben!" Shear panic flew through her body. She instantaneously coiled at the idea of him seeing her naked, let alone in the situation she was in. "What are you doing here?"

"I knocked," he stuttered, "I heard—"

"Get out!"

While she lurched for a towel, she slipped again, landed palm down, and slid on the shards of glass. She was absolutely mortified. There she lay, splayed naked on the bathroom floor, with a broken toe that stuck out at an unimaginable angle, a bloodied hand, a runny nose, and was now ugly crying.

Rebecca closed her eyes, as if it would make her humiliation go away. *I give up. I'm done.* She had no more fight. Rebecca slumped in defeat and shivered while gasping for air between jagged cries. She no longer cared at this point that he'd seen her scarred body or what he'd think of them. Her dignity was in tatters. She brought herself to a sitting position on the floor, and shot him a defiant look. *Go ahead and judge me.*

Ben didn't say a word. He simply took hold of the towel and placed it over her body. Then he grabbed the hand towel hanging on a ring, dampened it, then searched for glass chards in her palm before wrapping the towel around her hand.

Rebecca's breathing calmed, and her initial self-pity and frustration lessened. She was in too much pain and too tired to fight. She ran her fingers through her hair to get it out of her face, then pulled a wad of toilet paper off the roll and gave her nose a blow. Rebecca didn't hesitate when Ben reached his hand out to retrieve it. She handed it over and he dropped it in the wastebasket.

"Thank you," was all Rebecca could whisper.

"What else can I get you, Becky?" Ben asked, squatting so near to her, she could feel the warmth of his breath against her cheek.

"I don't know—I…"

"How about we get you cleaned up?" He reached down and placed his arms underneath her armpits and hoisted her up as though she weighed nothing at all.

Rebecca was breathless in his arms as his eyes surveyed hers. It was as if time and space momentarily disappeared as his muscular arms held her in his grasp. In a nanosecond, she was brought back to the here and now when he stood her on the floor, safely away from the broken glass. Pain shot through her foot at putting weight on her toe. She jerked her foot up and grimaced. Ben tightened his grip on her and guided her to the side of the tub to have a seat. "Did you step on the glass?"

"No, I—think I broke my toe." Rebecca stuck out her foot and the grotesque pinky toe jutted out toward the side of her foot.

"Yep, I'd say you did," he said, light heartedly. "I'm going to run the tub and help you in. You can pull the shower curtain closed so you can have some privacy, and I'll take care of the clean-up. Would that be okay with you?"

"Yes—no! I don't know."

"Becky, please let me help you."

His low voice was calming and without judgment. There were no words that she could convey what she was feeling at that moment. He was being anything but selfish and witnessing him in this light was eye opening. The compassion he showed moved her. There wasn't any teasing or condemnation.

"Okay," Rebecca said shyly and trembled as he removed the towel from her hand to examine her wounds.

"Nothing too deep—that's good. I was afraid you might need some stitches. If you can stand it, put it in the water. I'll do a proper cleaning after you get out, and see if I can set your toe."

She complied by turning her body to face the tub. The steam rolled as the water filled the tub, and he eased her in, then he pulled the curtain closed.

"Where do you keep your cleaning supplies, Becky?"

"No—I mean—thank you, but absolutely not. You've done way too much already and—I—I can—"

"I've got it, just relax." Between the care he gave her, the warmth of the tub, the lack of sleep the night before, her toe and hand hurting, and the fact Benjamin Daly was about to clean up her bathroom, she resigned herself to comply to his request.

"Fine. You win," she said as she rolled her eyes. *This can't be happening.*

She told Ben where everything was, including her first-aid kit, and he went to work while she soaked. Perhaps it was sitting in the tub and the talk of bandages that got her mind wandering. With her eyes closed, her memory rushed in again, bringing her to her first foster care home after leaving the burn unit at the hospital. Her upper body was wrapped in heavy bandages that covered her skin grafts. She could smell the medicinal ointment, bandages, and healing flesh as if it were yesterday, but it was the voice that haunted her most.

Mother Roseline was the name she had to call her. The shrill of her voice was worse than nails on a chalkboard, and her hands were boney and harsh. She was a pincher; the kind of pincher that would take hold of the tender parts of her flesh, squeeze, and twist.

While Rebecca took a bath, Mother Roseline hurt her. Rebecca had tried very hard to keep her bandages dry, but the water was deep, and she was used to receiving sponge baths in the hospital. In the blink of an eye, her arm had slipped off the edge of the tub and landed into the tub with a splash. She jerked it out, but not fast enough.

Mother Roseline screeched at her, telling her she was nothing but trouble, and that she'd pay for adding work. Mother Roseline would have to remove the bandage, reapply the ointment, and rebandage her arm, just because Rebecca stupidly couldn't keep her arm out of the damn water. All the while, she'd pinch and twist the remaining healthy skin on her other arm, her back, and the inside of her thigh. Terror coursed through her as she tried to escape the pain being inflicted on her. More and more bandages got wet. The shrilling hatred continued spewing.

Ben's deep, calming voice broke the reliving of her mind. "How ya doing in there? Everything okay?"

She took a couple of breaths before responding, and wiped the tears spilling down her cheeks. "Yep, I'm alright, but I'm ready to get out. Now."

In fact, at this point, Rebecca couldn't get out of the tub fast enough. Thinking now, the last time she'd actually soaked in a tub was in the presence of Mother Roseline. The urgency to get out swelled. Her heart raced, and her breathing shallowed and quickened. She needed air and needed it now. Rebecca tore open the shower curtain to allow the heat to escape into the rest of the room, then tried scrambling out.

"Whoah there, Beck." Ben knelt, then he cupped her cheeks, bringing them face to face. "It's okay, Becky—I'm right here—you're okay."

Seeing the expression on Ben's face as her panic seared through her, she thought she must appear crazy. His gaze peered into her depths. His jaw was tight, and yet his touch was tender, as was his voice. Before she knew it, she was breathing again, and he was carrying her towel-wrapped body across the hallway to her bedroom.

Ben set her down on the side of the bed, then retrieved her bathrobe from the hallway floor. As she removed the towel, he placed the robe over her shoulders, then he wrapped it around her and tied the belt.

"I'll be right back," he said, heading out of the room toward the bathroom.

Rebecca gathered her robe in her fist, as if it would keep her from losing control. It did help her feel grounded. *I'm okay, I'm okay.*

Ben returned with the first-aid kit and removed some tape, gauze, a tiny pair of scissors. "I'm going to set your toe, and it's going to hurt, but I'll be quick."

Panic once again speared Rebecca's chest, and she clawed at her robe. The smell of the medical tape, and seeing gauze and scissors, instantly brought her back to the burn unit. She coiled at the memory of them cutting off her dead skin, piece by piece, then re-wrapping her wounds. She breathed a slow breath in and let it out as she clung to her robe. *I'm okay, I'm okay.*

Ben rested his hands on hers until she no longer needed to cling to a false security.

"Trust me?" Ben asked, making eye contact.

"Yes," she said, but she wasn't so sure she believed her answer.

"Once it's set, I promise you'll feel a lot better. On the count of three, okay?"

Rebecca braced herself and counted along with Ben.

"One, two," Crack went the toe, as fast as a lightning strike. A rush of nausea reached her throat, then subsided.

"What happened to three? You tricked me!"

"It was easier for you that way," he said as he cut a piece of the gauze.

"How do you know how to do all this stuff?" Rebecca stuck out her foot to look at her toe. It was already black and blue and still stuck out a little, but felt better.

"In the Navy." He threaded the gauze between her pinky toe and its neighbor, then tethered the two toes together. "Sometimes with search and rescue, we'd find people who were hurt." He ripped off a piece of tape and secured the gauze.

"So, I'm guessing setting a pinky toe is like nothing for you, then." She could feel her face and neck warm with embarrassment at the silliness of the situation, especially after she imagined he'd seen worse cases than hers in his profession.

"You hurt your hand too, don't forget." He retrieved a tube of bacitracin ointment out of the kit.

She examined her hand as if it belonged to someone else, then took notice of her now bloodied bathrobe. Through her panic attack, she'd forgotten all about her cuts.

"Let's fix that up." His bright smile pleaded with her as he held the opened ointment in one hand and its cap in the other.

"Sounds like a plan."

He went to task, and the urge to explain herself was ever-present, but she couldn't explain her overreaction to herself, let alone to Benjamin Daly, so she let it go. She figured he'd have questions, anyway. By the time he asked, she'd hoped to have a logical answer.

"Have you had breakfast yet?" Ben asked as he applied the last piece of tape.

"No. I'm not really hungry."

"You should eat. How about I scramble a few eggs—that is if you have any? If not, I can—"

"Yes," she said with resignation. "I have eggs, some leftover fried potatoes from yesterday, beans, and bread for toast." She didn't want to argue about eating, and the fact her head was pounding, made her think he was probably right. "I have so much food from Mrs. Getchel's fridge and cabinets that I should be able to eat for the rest of the month before having to think of shopping. I have orange juice too."

"Perfect." His smile was broad and delicious against his tanned skin. Rebecca thought he was all she'd need to fulfill her appetite. "Let's see if you can put some weight on that foot." He helped her up as she steadied her stance.

"It feels pretty good, actually." She was impressed. He was good looking, smart, and had a wonderful bedside manner to boot. She took a few tentative steps and felt comfortable to move about. Her toe was definitely tender, but the pain was tolerable. "Tell you what. Why don't you get started in the kitchen, and I'll get dressed?"

"Sounds like a great plan to me. See you in the kitchen." He turned and left the room, whistling a cheerful tune.

Rebecca removed her robe, and for the first time in a long time, stood naked before the full-length mirror. Her hand trembled as she ran it over her bumpy, scarred flesh. She could barely feel her touch as her hand caressed her once-scorched skin, but the memory of its pain still lingered on. *This is what he saw.* She was neither sad nor embarrassed, as she peered more intently into the mirror. She just felt ugly, and it surprised her that Ben hadn't appeared repulsed by her as others had been in the past. Perhaps he was, she thought, but covered it well. As he'd said, he'd seen a lot. She closed her eyes and turned away from the mirror.

Rebecca put on a pale blue tunic blouse, then, being careful of her toe, worked a pair of leggings up her legs, as best she could, with her bandaged hand. She retrieved a paisley-printed scarf out of her drawer and carefully wound it around her neck just so, then went back to the mirror to inspect her handiwork. Much better, she thought, then gingerly made her way to the kitchen.

The smell of bacon beckoned her. She held back short of the kitchen to take in his strong stature. He moved with ease about the kitchen, whistling as he worked. He took hold of the frying pan's handle and lifted the pan waist high, quickly shifted it back and forth, then flipped four fried eggs into the air. She held her breath until they landed safely back in the pan.

"I'm impressed!" She limped to the table to take a seat. "Let me guess—the Navy?"

"Nope. Just a way to keep myself entertained." He grinned.

He separated the eggs in half, and slid them onto her plate, added the bacon, a couple spoonfuls of reheated potatoes, and placed the plate of toast and butter before her. "I'll have you do the honors of buttering. Do you want jam?"

"No—I'm good, but thanks." She held the now-buttered toast with her non-bandaged hand. Again, he went back to whistling his tune while he poured juice.

"Ben, you never told me why you're here, and how do you even know where I live?"

"Ah, that, I almost forgot about that." He ground pepper onto his eggs. "How did I know? Small towns, but why I'm here, isn't important right now. You look like you're feeling better."

"Seriously? Yes, I'm feeling better." She didn't know if he was referring to her physical or mental health, but either way, he was avoiding the question. "Why are you here, Benjamin?"

"Okay. There's good news and bad news. I didn't want to tell you bad news because—well, you've already had enough bad for one day."

"Ben, honestly, my restraint from wanting to punch you is wearing thin."

"I ran into a lady at Grounds. Her name was Bennington—Margo, I think. She's a real peach," he said with a sarcastic tone and a roll of his eyes.

"Oh?"

"She might be an issue for us and the project."

"I see." A prickly feeling ran down her spine. "That woman is insufferable."

"Yep." He leaned in and glanced down at her plate. "How are your eggs? I took a guess at over medium. Am I right?"

His cavalier question and avoidance were purely for his own entertainment. She wanted to throw her plate at him, but he'd said, us, which wasn't a term he'd ever used before, so she indulged his antics.

"Fine. You don't want to answer. Honestly, I don't really care what that woman thinks or does. I've had worse people in my life than the likes of her." She said it emphatically, but she hated to think what Mrs. Bennington would do.

"Cool." He nodded, then took a bite of his toast. He wore a glimmer in his eyes and a mischievous grin. "You didn't tell me if you like your eggs."

"None of your dang business," she said, then put a fork full in her mouth and gave him a smirk. She'd be darned if she'd ask him what the good news is.

"I was just wondering, because I figured, if I'm going to be sticking around a while, it would be good to know how you like your eggs."

She swallowed her mouthful and her mind reeled with his surprising news. *He's staying—a while.* She took a gulp of juice to hide her wary excitement. *A while is a good start. I can work with that.*

"Over medium works for me, but I prefer my bacon crispy," she said nonchalantly, as her insides burst with joy.

"Duly noted," he said just before she balled up her napkin and beaned him in the head.

Chapter 16

Rebecca's animated chatter about her plans for the house captivated Ben as they continued to eat. He nodded from time to time. Not that he wasn't interested in hearing her brainstorm ideas that had percolated from the night before, but her expressive eyes, bright smiles, and bandaged hand gestures held his attention more than the words she spoke.

Ben cleaned up the kitchen while she continued with her avalanche of thoughts before asking if she'd like a ride to work. He was still staying at the inn, which was practically in Proposals' back yard anyway, and he doubted she'd be able to place her driving foot in an actual shoe. She was adamant that she'd be fine, but of course, he knew better.

Ben excused himself and headed to her room to retrieve her slippers. He peered into the bathroom, recalling how the morning started. His heart sank when he'd heard her cries as he'd approached the front door of her apartment. When she hadn't responded to his knocks and hollering, he knew he'd needed to enter. He was so glad he had.

When he'd turned the corner to the bathroom, Becky's tear-covered face and panic as she'd tried to hide herself from his view had torn something in him. She'd instinctively covered her scars before her most vulnerable private places. Seeing her distorted body had shocked him. He wanted nothing more than to wrap her in his arms and reassure her that everything was alright. Then later, when she'd frantically tried to climb out of the tub with such fear in her eyes, it nearly brought him to his knees.

Ben sighed, with slippers in hand. He took her to be a strong woman, and he presumed she was skilled and respected at work, but he'd never realized the magnitude of her strength until he'd seen her scars. *You're an amazing woman, Becky Mills.*

He'd seen a lot over the years in the service and salvage business, but burns were something that seared into your mind and were hard to forget.

Through her frustration and pain, sat a beautiful woman of fortitude and strength.

He recalled all the times that other kids would pick on her for wearing long sleeves and high necklines in the summer. He wasn't one to tease her, but he did little to stop it, so he was just as guilty as if he'd done so himself. When he thought back of her time at Mrs. G's, she'd never so much as complained about her scars. She had to have suffered in silence, and that realization set heavily on him. In fact, she'd never asked for anything either, except for his friendship and her need for him to stay all those years ago.

He was making his way back toward the kitchen with her matted slippers when he saw her adjusting her scarf in the mirror near the front entry. She stood tall and determined, in her coat, hat, one glove, one bandage, and snowflake socks. Rebecca beamed at him, and it nearly melted his heart. He bent down to slip on her slippers when her muffled glove and bandage clapped together.

"Well, would you look at that? They fit!"

"But of course, milady!"

"You must be my prince charming." She laughed as she picked up her handbag. "Does my chariot await?"

"I'd hardly call me a prince charming. I'd say I'm more of a toad." He batted the front of her hat, which brought it over her eyes, leaving her befuddled and disheveled before he corrected it.

"Yep, you are indeed a toad, Benjamin Daly."

Rebecca reached out to take his awaiting arm. He grinned at the feel of her in his hold. *Yep, I'm a toad just hoping to be kissed*, he thought as he walked her to his car.

They sat silently as they headed toward Proposals. She examined her bandaged hand, then leaned into the seat, appearing content for the duration of the ride.

"Would you look at that?" Ben said as he pulled in. "I got you here safe and sound."

"Indeed, you did."

"But my job is not complete until I carry you over the threshold."

Becky's eyes widened, and she leaned away from him. "You will do no such thing!"

"Okay then, be that way. I guess this prince charming shall just have to settle for walking you in."

"Could be worse, I suppose," she chided. "Better than hopping in, being you're a toad and all."

Ben helped her out of the car and carefully escorted her inside. He wasn't sure if it was because he'd told her he was staying, but it pleased him when Becky reintroduced him to the heads at Proposals: Sophie, Emily, Brady, and Duncan, even little Samantha popped her head in, carrying the calico cat, Daisy. He could tell by their outpouring of support upon learning of her broken toe and bandaged hand that she was in excellent hands, and so he reluctantly saw his way out.

CHAPTER 17

Rebecca's workday finally ended, and she sent Ben a text to let him know she would be set to leave in about twenty minutes. She was happy to see his quick reply. *"I'll be there."*

Rebecca looked forward to seeing him. She was anxious to talk about the project, and she wanted to get more details about Mrs. Bennington possibly posing a problem for them. Rebecca could only imagine what would have transpired between them. Mrs. Bennington had most likely been at the diner with her entourage, whom Emily referred to as cackling hens. *Poor Ben*, she thought as she carried an arm full of stems to the walk-in refrigerator. *He probably doesn't even know what hit him.* Everyone around York knew Mrs. Margo Bennington was notorious for gossip, but no one ever stepped on her toes out of fear of being blackballed—or shunned—by the elite society, which she ruled.

Rebecca sat near the bakery windows with her foot up on an opposing chair, while she waited for Ben's arrival. Her toe and now foot had throbbed for the past hour, and the relief of having it inclined helped. She'd make a point of icing it when she got home.

Rebecca grinned at watching Emily scurrying around while talking to herself. She was putting another tray of cupcakes in the oven, and apparently, the paper liners weren't listening to her. Sophie was meeting with a client, Brady was in his office, going through the photos of their most recent wedding, and Duncan, bless his heart, was hard at work putting together some preliminary business tax, and bank account forms that she, and now Ben, would need to complete.

She hugged herself for making the choice to work at Proposals. It was a happy place, with good people, which, in her experience, was rare. Oh, how she missed Mrs. Getchel, but at least she had Emily and Sophie, and she was reminded of the delights and care she's received from the most adorable lady who lived next door to Proposals, Agnes Templeton.

Overall, it had been a quiet day, with a few exceptions. Agnes had dropped in for a sweet. She typically came in the morning for muffins, but her Frank wasn't feeling so great, and she wanted to surprise him with a dessert cookie or two. Rebecca laughed silently, knowing that Agnes made it a habit of eating a cookie on her walk home, and kept two in the bag for them to each have one later. It was Proposals' and Agnes' little secret.

Agnes had made it a point to seek Rebecca out when she popped in. She shared her condolences and told a few stories of when she and Mrs. Getchel had been in the garden club together. Agnes giggled like a schoolgirl recalling their antics. By the end of the conversation, she was clutching Rebecca's good hand, and stood nearly eye to eye to give her sweet kisses on both of her cheeks before saying she must stop dawdling and get back to Frank.

Oh, to be Agnes and Frank. Rebecca could only wish for a love as great as theirs. They'd just recently celebrated their fifty-second anniversary together, and she couldn't help think that if her parents were still living, that they too might have had a cherished, long-lasting love as the Templetons. Rebecca stuffed down the impulse to self-deprecate. Ben would be here any minute, and she didn't want a sour expression on her face when he arrived. Besides, once she opened that Pandora's box, she'd spiral, and that wasn't pretty.

Yes, Rebecca thought, *I have some pretty great people in my life.* In her daydreaming state, she hadn't seen Ben pull up, but the slam of his car door snapped her to attention. She gathered her belongings and limped to the door and waved goodbye to Emily. Before she could step out, Ben had taken her elbow to assist her.

"I'm perfectly capable of getting to the car, you know."

"I don't doubt it, but I rarely get to be a gentleman. Please don't deprive me of the privilege," he said before giving a curtain-call bow. "Please allow me, milady."

"I suppose I should stick my nose up in the air, like some kind of royalty or aristocrat?"

Ben tapped his finger on his chin a few times. "No, more like a certain Mrs. Bennington."

"Oh, my gosh, that's perfect!" Rebecca laughed, then mimicked Mrs. Bennington by widening her stance and gait, with her bust jutted out, and nose sticking up. She deepened her voice, bellowing as loudly as she could, "I do declare, young man, that you must escort me to the car expeditiously. I have important places to go and important people to see, you know."

She could no longer keep up the charade without breaking out in laughter. Ben joined her, and she couldn't remember the last time she'd actually belly-laughed.

Rebecca latched the seatbelt and settled in before inquiring about the uppity Mrs. Bennington. He'd explained how she'd been eavesdropping and deduced he'd been one of Mrs. Getchel's foster kids. "That woman was so condescending, Beck."

"She is pretty good at doing that." Rebecca said and turned in her seat to better face him.

"She actually told me she hoped the house would become an estate for a 'nice' family instead of for people like us. I told her she shouldn't count on it because we'll be bringing the place back to life to help kids who need it."

"You didn't?"

"You bet I did," he said as he yielded for an oncoming car. "I'll be damned if she'll keep us from fulfilling Mrs. G's legacy." Then he punched the gas.

Rebecca could hardly contain her emotions. She turned to look out the window, and pushed her tongue into her cheek, to keep from crying. Silence filled the space.

"Did I say something wrong?" Ben asked as he slowed the car to enter her apartment's driveway. She swept the corner of her eyes and turned to face him. His deep brown eyes and long lashes stared back at her with concern. She cleared her throat and glanced down toward her bandaged hand that rested across her lap.

"No, not at all."

"Are you sure? Because you seem upset."

"I mean, sure, I'm nervous about what Mrs. Bennington said because she could really cause us some problems. But it's not that."

He reached his hand over and rested it on her thigh. "Then what is it?"

"I'm just happy that you *want* to carry on her legacy with me, is all."

Ben gave her a warm smile and touched the corner of her eye. "So, these are happy tears then?"

"Yes, but if you really don't want to do this, I need to know. You're a loner, I get that. The last thing I want to do is guilt you into doing something that you don't want to do." She turned to face him and his expression hadn't changed from the last time. She'd stared into his chestnut eyes. "It's a big commitment that will take you away from Hawaii, of all places." She threw her arms open in surrender. "If your heart really isn't in it, Benjamin, it won't work, and I will not put myself out there just to have you walk away."

By now, Rebecca was becoming more animated and more passionate as Ben continued to take it all in. "I'm a difficult person, I realize that, and can be stubborn, but I think you already know that. It will take planning, a ton of time, and—"

"Commitment, got it."

"Don't you dare mock me, Benjamin. Because if you can't take this seriously, we might as well stop right now."

"Becky, stop." He gently took hold of her bandaged hand. "I have every intention of seeing this project through until it's on solid ground. Sure, I don't know the first thing about how we'll get there, but I'm willing, so long as you'll trust me. If you can't trust me, then there's no point in moving forward."

"But don't you see, Benjamin? We have to move forward. If we don't I end up..." She cleared her throat and stared him down. "I'll lose the house, because I won't have the money to take care of it, and you'll—you'll end up with nothing."

"You're right." He turned the car off. "I know that I've disappointed you in the past, but I was just a kid, who had an opportunity to escape the only life I'd ever known, and I can't have you making me feel guilty for that anymore. Can you please just trust me, Becky?"

"I'll try, I really will, but I think you'll have to earn that trust, Ben."

"Got it."

"Alright then." Rebecca sat up straighter with a renewed determination. "I'm hungry. I think we should grab a bite to eat, because I don't feel like cooking, and I'm not about to make you cook for me twice on the same day. And we need to talk about all that we need to get done so the trustee can see we're making some progress. I can't even begin to think about what Mrs. Bennington might dream up to stop us."

"Okay. I could eat." Ben had the car in reverse and turned back in the direction from which they'd just come from.

"Where're we going?"

"York Harbor Inn. I've only eaten in the pub, but I think this new adventure of ours calls for a celebration and dinner in the dining room. Sound good?"

"Sounds delightful, Ben. Thank you, but I'm not so sure how they'll feel about me wearing slippers." She stared down at her feet.

"Just wear them with confidence—maybe you'll start a new trend," he said with his eyebrows raised and a grin. "But I caution you to not get the steak, unless you want me to cut it for you in public. If that happens, you know a certain uppity lady will get wind of it, and then the whole town will be in a tither."

***

Ben swished the ice around in the golden liquid, then sipped his after-dinner drink. Becky seemed relaxed and more talkative after having had a couple of glasses of wine. She retrieved a small piece of chocolate that the server had given them off the plate and popped it into her mouth, seeming to savor the flavor of the creamy, raspberry, dark chocolate morsel. Her eyes were closed as she glided her tongue between her slightly parted lips.

"Mmm, this is amazing," she said with a sparkle in her eyes as she looked at him, "you should try one."

"Nah, I think you should have it, since you're enjoying it so much."

"Don't mind if I do." With that, she snatched up the other one, unwrapped the decadent treat, and bit the tip off with a snap. "I think we've really got a chance of doing something pretty great together, Ben."

"I do too." He took the last swig of his drink. "We've made good headway writing our to-do list. What do you say about me getting you home? You've had a pretty rough day and I don't want to—"

"Don't be silly. I'm fine," she said dismissively. "You know what I would like to do, though? I'd like to see your room."

"I'm not sure that's a good idea, Beck." He didn't like the idea of having her in his room. He'd become more intrigued by her throughout the evening. Seeing her relaxed was great, and he was finding it harder to recognize the insecure teen from his past. She'd grown into a confident, feisty, beautiful woman, and he couldn't take his eyes off of her. The last thing he needed was to have her in his room, especially because she'd had too much to drink. But he had a hard time saying no to her.

"In all the time that I've lived in this area, I've never been beyond the main areas. I've always wanted to see what the rooms look like." Her pleading eyes mesmerized him. "Please?"

His muscles tightened with apprehension, then he slid his chair back and stood. *How can I resist?* "Alright then."

"Terrific! I'd like to get some ideas on how we could transform the rooms in the house. Oh, we should come up with a name for the house!" she said as he took her coat and threw it over his arm along with his.

His worries diminished, and he felt like a fool. He'd obviously read into her intentions completely wrong. She continued to chatter about the house as they made their way out the door and across the side street to his unit.

He unlocked the door and escorted her inside. "Wait right here a sec," he said, then went about turning on more lights. "The last thing I want is for you to break another toe."

"Aww, you're the sweetest," she said with a wrinkled-up nose, then wandered around the room. "This is really pretty, Ben. I'd enjoy staying in a place like this."

She ran her hand over the back of the upholstered, high-back, winged chair as she looked toward the high-poster bed.

Ben turned on the fireplace, and in an instant, a cozy glow filled the room. "I have to say, I sure miss having a fireplace. Hawaii has plenty of warmth, but not like this." He rubbed his hands together in front of the fire. Becky came to stand at his side.

"Are you sure you're doing the right thing by staying here? I mean, I know it's not a permanent thing for you. Even so, it's going to take you away from your career." Her concern for him, without judgement or making him feel guilty about eventually having to go back, pleased him greatly.

"I work when and where I like," he said as he guided a strand of hair out of her eyes and tucked it behind her ear. "I'm sure."

She shyly looked away and reached up to retouch her formerly loosened hair.

Ben noticed her bandage as her fingers drifted away from her face. "I think I should take another look at that hand."

He led her to the bathroom and carefully removed the tape and unwound the bandage. He examined her delicate hand in his and was pleased at how well it was doing. The wounds seemed to be closing up nicely. "I'm going to leave this off for now, but when we get you home, we'll get some more bacitracin on the cuts and re-wrap it. By morning, you should be in pretty good shape."

"Thanks. My toe feels a lot better, too. Although it could be the wine." Rebecca let out a slight giggle.

"I think you're probably right." His phone rang. The screen displayed Holokai's name. *What did he want?* "Excuse me for a minute? I'm sorry, but I have to take this."

"Of course," she said with a nod.

"Hey, Holokai. What's up?"

Holokai asked where he could find a piece of equipment. Ben got concerned by the question, because that piece of equipment was only used for dives with a heavy current.

Ben took the call outside, so Becky wouldn't have to feel like she was intruding. He didn't want to take the chance that she'd overhear, then Holokai cut to the chase. Seems Smithers regretted telling him they'd be all set because they needed him, and Holokai wanted to give him a heads up, in case Smithers called.

A good fifteen minutes went by before he stepped back inside. Ben stood in the entry and took in the sight of Becky sound asleep on the bed. She was lying on her side, with her feet dangling over the edge. He considered waking her, but decided to remove her slippers and carefully placed her fully on the bed, then covered her with the extra blanket stowed in the closet.

If she woke up in the night and wanted to go home, he'd take her then. He just hoped she didn't need to be at work too early in the morning until he remembered that she'd said they could meet up for breakfast to see if they could make some headway on their plans.

Ben turned down the lights just low enough to help her sleep, but bright enough that he could dig through his suitcase for some workout shorts. He lifted his sweater over his head, and stepped out of his jeans, letting them fall to the floor, then pulled on his shorts. He carefully folded his jeans and sweater and placed them on top of his suitcase. He reached for his laptop that sat on the nearby table.

Ben sat there in the chair and wrestled with what to do about Holokai's call. He was annoyed that Smithers, who'd given him the green light to stay longer, was regretting his decision. Hurricane season was supposed to be winding down by now, but it wanted to go out with a bang, and the need for divers was great. Boats lost at sea weren't unusual, and he cursed the damn helicopter pilots that insisted on venturing out with tours, despite the warnings. They had to make a living, same as fishermen did, but putting paying customers at risk was an entirely different story.

What's done is done. They've managed without me in the past, and they'll just have to do it again. Ben pushed the thought away and, instead, tried to focus on the more pressing issue; researching foster programs and living facilities in Southern Maine. He wanted to see where their project might fill a gap.

Ben couldn't help watching Becky as she slept. He thought of all the times they'd stayed awake into the night, talking about their dreams of the future. They were usually in his room, because he hadn't had a roommate, and they'd have "privacy." Of course, Mrs. G. made sure they left the door open at all times. He wondered what dear Mrs. G. would think if she saw Becky here with him now. He laughed, realizing this wasn't how he'd expected his day to end.

CHAPTER 18

Rebecca had felt Ben take off her slippers and cover her with a blanket, but she'd been too sleepy to respond with a thank you. Instead, she'd lain quietly, watching Ben as he undressed. He pulled off his sweater, releasing each of his broad back muscles and well-defined waistline. His jeans rode low and snugged his tight bottom. It was all she could do to not give away her secret when he dropped his jeans to the floor. Her heart nearly jumped out of her chest. She lay as still as she could as he bent over to retrieve his clothes off the floor. His muscles bulged as he folded each item with precision, and heat grew between her thighs. As he reached for his shorts, she quickly shut her eyes so he wouldn't catch her peeking. She played the beauty of this man over in her mind, and before she knew it, she'd drifted off to sleep again.

The bright sunlight cast a glow of golden light through the window blinds awakening Rebecca. She stretched and yawned before realizing that Ben wasn't anywhere in sight. She rolled toward the other side of the bed. An imprint of where his head had lain near hers left her feeling surprisingly content. She ran her hand along the sheet that was cool to her touch. She couldn't help but wish he were still lying next to her so she could snuggle into his arms. That would have been out of the question—for him anyway—because he wasn't interested in her in the romantic sense.

This arrangement was strictly for business, which, in the grand scheme of things, was probably the wiser way to go. Especially because he planned on going back to Hawaii once they'd launched the project.

Rebecca sat up and as she did, the pounding in her head began. *Wow, I definitely overdid it last night.* She caressed her temples a few times, then needed to use the bathroom. At first step, the pressure from her stocking foot onto the floorboards shot pain through her foot, reminding her of her broken toe. She retrieved her grubby old slippers and gently slid her feet into them, then hobbled to the awaiting bathroom while lifting a prayer that it held a complementary toothbrush and Tylenol.

Rebecca sat on the toilet just when Ben returned from wherever he'd gone off to. She could make out Ben's voice as he spoke to another man, but she couldn't tell what they were saying, nor did she recognize who it was. Within seconds, she caught the aroma of bacon and freshly brewed coffee. By the time she'd freshened up, she returned to a table set for two and Ben's beaming face.

"Good morning, sleepy head."

She was awestruck by the table before her. A crisp white tablecloth with a vase of winterberry and flower mix sat in its center. Two plates of crab cakes eggs benedict, fried potatoes, and slices of bacon masterfully graced the table. Fruit cups sat on the side. Glasses of orange juice, coffee mugs, and a silver coffee carafe sat in the middle.

"I'm speechless." Rebecca couldn't stop her heart from melting right there on the floor. She'd never in her entire life had anyone do something so special for her. "I honestly don't know what to say." She lifted her gaze to his. "Thank you, Benjamin."

"You're welcome. I figured if you're anything like me, you'd be famished, too. So, I took the initiative. I hope you'll like the selection."

"It's perfect." She took a seat and admired the spread on the table again, then laughed. "You didn't!"

She picked up the tiny plate that sat next to her juice glass as her laughter continued. It contained two aspirins, and two raspberry, dark chocolate candies. "You are too much Benjamin Daly."

He beamed from ear to ear. "I just figured you needed a better start to your day than yesterday."

"Well, I'd say you succeeded." She picked up her juice glass, gesturing cheers, before taking a sip. "Another surprise—it's mimosa!"

"Figured you'd need a little hair of the dog." He raised his glass and his eyes sparkled.

"Oh boy, if Mrs. Getchel could see us now." She giggled.

"I was thinking the same thing! I honestly don't know if she'd be happy to see us sharing a bed and breakfast together, or if she'd be chasing us with a stick."

"She would never chase us with a stick—a hand towel, maybe, but not a stick."

"You've got a point there." Ben stuck a piece of bacon in his mouth.

"I think she'd be happy. In fact, it wouldn't surprise me if she'd planned for this to happen all along."

"She was sneaky like that, wasn't she?" Ben placed his napkin next to his plate and leaned back in his chair. "She certainly had a way of getting what she wanted."

"I was thinking. . ."

Ben leaned in. "Let's hear it."

"I'd really like the house to be a stepping stone toward living a successful life of independence. Kids need a place where they can plan for their future. A place where they can learn unique skills, be exposed to different job training, learn how to handle their money. You know, things like that."

"I know what you mean. We were lucky to have Mrs. G's guidance. She encouraged me to go into the military as soon as I aged out, but others might want other alternatives."

"Yes," Rebecca said. "I was so scared as I got older, knowing that my time at Mrs. Getchel's would soon end. I had no direction or plan. If Mrs. Getchel hadn't recognized my tendencies toward art and design, and encouraged me to go to school, who knows how my life could have ended up? I'm able to do something that I enjoy and can take care of myself. I couldn't have asked for more than that."

Ben sat quietly as he listened to her, nodding now and then. "I think you're on to something here, Beck. Last night, while you were sleeping, I did a little research, and there's just not enough programs for empowering teens for success within the foster system. Not anything as extensive as what you're dreaming up."

Rebecca took a gulp of coffee. "She'd like what we're thinking—bridging the gap-- right? I mean, we're doing right by her wishes, wouldn't you agree?"

Ben leaned in. His eyes burned into hers with a steely expression. "Becky, I have no doubt that we will make her proud."

"Yeah—right—me either." Rebecca took in a deep breath and let it out slowly. *We've got this.* "I'd like the house to have a name. Something that means moving forward, taking the next step, but I can't put my finger on it."

Ben took her by the hand. "You've already named it, Beck."

"I have?"

"Yes, in fact you said it earlier. And the more you speak about what you want, the more I think it's perfect."

Becky played the conversation over and over before it hit her. "Stepping Stones?"

"Yes. Stepping Stones: a bridge to success."

"Oh, Benjamin, it's perfect!" Becky couldn't help herself. She jumped up from the table, leaned over it, then gave him a kiss, smack dab on his juicy, full lips.

Ben appeared unphased, but Becky instantaneously went weak in the knees. His lips were tender. He hadn't pulled back, nor had he leaned in. He seemed to have welcomed the advance, and now she was at a loss. She wasn't sure if she should acknowledge what had just taken place, play nonchalant, or act as though it hadn't happened. She chose the latter. "I'll see about getting a logo made, but first we should get the name registered with the state, and—"

"Beck…"

"Shoot, listen to me. We'll need approval from the town first. There's just so much to think about, and—"

"Becky," he said again, and she could no longer ignore him.

Her hopes of pretending the kiss never happened vanished before her eyes. "I know. I shouldn't have done that. It was spontaneous—I was excited. I mean not excited in that way, but that we'd come up with a name and I—"

"I'm excited too, but—"

"Seriously, it won't happen again. This is strictly a business transaction. I know that. You won't need to worry about—"

"You have Hollandaise sauce all over the front of your shirt." He ran his hand over his own chest, indicating where the sauce was. His smirk grew into a wide grin. "When you leaned over the table, you…"

Rebecca glanced down at her shirt. "I know how it got there, Benjamin!" She was mortified. They'd just kissed, and his lips rocked her off her socks, but the only thing that occupied his mind was the hollandaise sauce that covered her right breast.

He grabbed his white linen napkin and motioned to her water glass. "Maybe if you dab it in the water, you can rub the stain to—"

"Oh, my gosh. I know how to get a stain out." Becky grabbed the napkin out of his hand and dipped it in her water glass, then thought better of it and excused herself as she limped into the bathroom.

"Do you need another shirt?" he asked. "You can wear one of mine."

"I'm fine!" She turned on the water, stood in front of the mirror, then wiped furiously at her bosom. Her once-pale blue tunic now had a gold-smeared stain that was now see-through, making her wish she hadn't left her scarf at Proposals. Rebecca turned off the water, and rested her palms against the counter in defeat. "I guess I will need to borrow one of your shirts after all."

Rebecca pulled her top off and tossed it into the sink to

give it a thorough soak when Ben rapped at the door.

"Here's a sweater for you," he said through the crack in the door. "It's just a pullover, but I think if you—"

Rebecca opened the door abruptly and grabbed the sweater out of his hand, then shut the door in his face.

"As I was saying, if you shove up the sleeves, it will just look like one of those sweater dress things that you ladies are wearing nowadays."

"Oh, my gosh, Ben! I'm not a complete idiot!" She flung the door open again, and he just stood there, dumbstruck. She moved to the left as he moved to her left, and as she adjusted to the right, he too moved to her right.

Ben took her by the shoulders and stilled her. "I'll tell you what, I'll stand over here, and you go that way." Again, he wore his Cheshire cat grin.

Rebecca was exasperated. She'd gone from having an absolutely wonderful morning to feeling like a fool in a matter of minutes. She didn't move in the direction he'd indicated. Instead, she stood her ground. "You must think I'm a clumsy oaf. I recognize that this is the second time in the matter of two days that you've had to come to my aid, but I can assure you, I'm not. I—"

And that's when it happened. He cupped her chin, tilted it toward him, and kissed her right then and there.

She swam in a sea of warm water, then floated in and out of the waves, gasping for air. "I—um—didn't expect that."

"Neither did I, Rebecca Mills, neither did I."

She could taste him on her lips. *Please kiss me again.*

CHAPTER 19

Ben was still kissing Rebecca. *Wow,* he thought as he gazed into her green eyes, trying to get a read on Rebecca's thoughts. She didn't look panicked or angry, but nor did she appear wanting, and in that moment, he knew he'd made a mistake.

Rebecca backed away, diverting her eyes. "We should probably get going. I need to, um—get ready for work."

"Yes, I suppose we should." He gave Rebecca room to pass by. *What was I thinking?*

Not that he hadn't wanted to kiss her. On the contrary, he'd wanted to wrap his arms around her and kiss her since the previous morning. His heart broke for hers when he'd seen her in distress. All he'd wanted to do was help her feel better, and now he had to confess that he cared for her too deeply. He didn't like attachment. Attachment only led to disappointment. And that was the last thing he wanted to do to Becky. He needed to put a stop to his cravings for her. She was his business partner and, anything other than that, would mean disaster.

Their drive toward Becky's apartment was quiet. He guessed they both had had second thoughts about the turn of events.

She said that she'd manage getting herself to Proposals by herself, but he suggested he drive her one more day. Or at least until she could wear actual shoes to work. He followed as she walked up the step to her front door. She still hobbled, and the last thing he wanted to witness was having her lose her footing. As they entered, she gestured toward the living room and told him to make himself at home.

Her living area was welcoming. She had an eye for decorating, which didn't surprise him much. Her profession of arranging flowers was an art form. Everything was inviting, from the comfortable floral pattern of mint green, blush, and cream-colored chair, to the pillows of her linen-colored couch. He guessed the style was what they called shabby chic. A bouquet of similar flowers sat atop of a reclaimed coffee table. Twin built-in bookshelves of ivory stood on opposite ends on one side of the room. He browsed through the books, and noticed that she took great interest in design in its every form.

A stack of quilting magazines was neatly splayed on the shelf, recalling that a floral quilt draped over the back side of the couch. Other quilts of varying sizes hung on the adjacent wall. Each one was so intricately created and told a story. The detail of her work mesmerized him. He pictured her stitching each stich with her slender fingers. The thought of her taking the time to painstakingly applying the detail was beyond his comprehension. He was more about hurry up and get it done, move on to the next thing, then keep moving. Sure, he planned his sea searches with care, but to spend hours and hours creating one small piece of art led him to believe that she had the patience of a saint.

Ben was lost in thought, admiring a small, framed wall quilt, featuring a house.

"What do you think?" she asked, coming up beside him.

"Did you make all these?" He ran his finger over the fabric of the tiny framed quilt.

"Yea, it's a hobby of mine. I've been making them for years."

Ben moved in closer to examine the first quilt in the grouping. It featured a house with wildflowers along its border.

"That one is of the house I grew up in," she said.

"It's so detailed and delicate. You even have a cat in it." He pondered that for a moment before turning toward Becky. "But you hate cats."

"I don't—hate them," she said, but her reply wasn't convincing.

"Then why put one on your quilt?"

"Because we had one, is all. It makes the scene more authentic."

Ben acknowledged the quilt that hung next to the one of the house. It showcased an embroidered inscription and incorporated the same wildflowers. It read, "Like scattered seed, memories bloom forever."

"It's really great that you have a home to remember." A place to call home had always been his wish, one that was never fulfilled. "I bet you had a lot of great times there."

"We did," she said, with a touch of melancholy to her tone.

There was more to the story, but he didn't want to pry. He too didn't really want to talk about something he'd given anything to have had, and so he changed the subject. "I suppose we should take care of your hand and get you off to work."

"One step ahead of you." She retrieved the first-aid kit off the coffee table and handed it to him, then took a seat on the couch.

"You're always thinking." He took a seat next to her, took her hand, then gently unwrapped it. As he held her injured hand, he still couldn't get over how small it was in his. He could see now how she could do such skilled work; her fingers were tiny and delicate. "You should sell your artwork. It's really good, you know."

"Thanks," she said rather shyly. "But I couldn't dream of asking for money for something that I just enjoy doing. I think it would take the fun out of it."

Ben thought about her response and understood. He'd felt like that lately with his diving. He'd been doing it professionally for so long now that he'd lost the beauty in it.

"I enjoy giving them away, though," she said, and he was pleased to hear a brighter tone in her voice.

"That's great. I hope whoever you give them to warrants your hard work." Ben applied the last piece of tape to the bandage and gave her hand a small squeeze. "Speaking of hard work, we better get going, or you'll be late."

"Thank you, Benjamin," she said, then reached toward him and gave him a hug.

As he held her in his arms, and her cheek rested against his chest, he couldn't help but to respond. She was warm and open to him, and it took him back in time. They used to hug like this when they were kids. The kind of hug that simply meant I care, and everything would be okay.

As they headed for the car, he couldn't remember the

last time he'd felt this carefree.

The ride to Proposals was quiet. They each seemed lost in thought. His mind drifted to his and Becky's new venture together. He was enthusiastic about it, but his job, and his team continued to weigh on him.

"Ben, you just drove past Proposals." Becky chuckled at his mistake.

"Seriously! I'm sorry. I was on another planet." He turned the corner to the nearest driveway to turn around and headed back to Proposals.

"Been there, done that," she said, as he approached the drive, then took a cooler tone. "Everything okay?"

"Sure—yeah. It's all good. Just work stuff."

He did not know how to remedy the situation he'd gotten himself into. His job was a huge part of his life, and he was damned good at it. They needed him, but the last thing he wanted to do was leave Becky, especially now when he'd committed to helping with Stepping Stones.

"Here you go," he said as he pulled in and put the car in park.

She gave his hand a squeeze and climbed out of the car. She threw him a beaming smile. "See you around five?"

"You bet." Ben looked on until she'd reached the inside of Proposals and was out of view.

As he turned the car around in the driveway, he could see the horizon over the Atlantic and had the urge to be in the water again just for the fun of it. Just like Becky's quilts. He picked up his phone and punched in the numbers for Jason. Within a couple of rings, he'd answered.

"Hey, Jason, Ben here. Thought I'd be leaving you a

voicemail."

"Perfect timing. Just punched out. What's up? You still on the mainland?"

"Yeah, I'm still here for a little while, anyway. I was wondering if you wouldn't happen to have another dive gear set-up on hand?"

"Always have, always will. You feeling the pull to get in there?"

"Yep. I've got quite a few hours to kill and thought I'd go to the Nubble."

"Want company?"

"Absolutely!"

Ben was excited to dive again with Jason. It had been years, and he figured it was best to dive Nubble with a buddy, it was safer that way. They set up a time to meet, and he was confident that Jason would bring everything he'd require for a cold dive. A good dive was just what he needed.

Being in the water settled him. Out there, it was peaceful. He found a quiet tranquility that wasn't preset above water. This was exactly what he needed. Sharing this outing with Jason made it that much better.

CHAPTER 20

Rebecca still couldn't believe he'd kissed her, and she was having trouble getting that thought out of her mind. She shook her head as if the act of doing so would force the thoughts out. *Focus, and get your head in the game.* She had to make a special-occasion centerpiece and had no time to dawdle.

Rebecca collected two dozen white roses out of the cooler and spread them across her worktable, along with the juniper and cedar greenery, that remained from a prior event. She breathed in the luscious scent as she placed each rose in the wicker basket along with the greenery, and stood back to examine her work. *Nope, it needs something more.* She scanned the shelving for faux red frosted winterberries and handpicked each stem. *Yes, these will do nicely.* Then she grabbed some white bouvardia for added texture.

Rebecca's favorite part of being a florist was creating something from nothing. It gave her a sense of accomplishment, much like her quilting did. She stood at the counter and placed each stem, adjusting them just so. Thoughts of Ben floated in.

She could still taste him on her lips and feel his touch on her face. He'd completely taken her off guard, and she imagined she'd done the same to him. She laughed at the thought of her resting her breast on top of his eggs Benedict. Even the thought of it brought a warmth of embarrassment to her cheeks as she continued shifting roses in the chicken wire framework of the basket.

Her thoughts shifted to her framed quilt, hanging on her living room wall. Ben's curiosity touched her, and he'd even recalled her aversion to cats. Rebecca hadn't always felt that way toward cats. In fact, she used to love them a great deal. She had gotten Greta as a kitten and they'd been inseparable. That was before her life changed in the blink of an eye. That damnable cat had destroyed her life and, the more she thought about that tabby and the events that had transpired since, the angrier she got. Her heart rate shot up. It was all she could do to not scream at the top of her lungs. Lost in the memory, she decapitated nearly all the remaining roses, and then turned her anger toward the pine boughs, leaving them in fragmented pieces on the table.

"Rebecca! What are you doing?"

Rebecca froze as Sophie's voice rang out from behind her. That's when she saw what she'd done, and the shock of seeing where her anger had taken her scared her. She stood staring at what lay before her and couldn't explain herself even if she'd tried.

"I—I'm sorry. I don't know—I...," she said as she fought back tears, but lost the battle.

Sophie carefully took the snipping sheers out of her hand

and set them on the table, then turned Rebecca toward her.

"I'm worried about you Rebecca," she said calmly, yet more sternly than Rebecca had ever heard Sophie's speak. "Why don't you go take a break? Get a cup of tea or something."

"No, I should clean this up and—"

"No. What you should do is precisely what I just said you should do. And if you're not feeling better after that, then you should go home."

Sophie's concern for her seemed to outweigh her anger. Perhaps, Rebecca thought, it might even be disappointment, which made her feel terrible. She hadn't been reliable lately, but what she'd just done made her second-guess her mindset as well. A break would do her good.

Rebecca moped as she stepped toward the bakery, hoping Emily would be in the back instead of at the counter, but no such luck. After just having disappointed one partner, the last thing she wanted was to have Emily wonder why she needed a break now, especially after they'd already given her a lighter schedule. Fortunately, no other customers were in the shop at the moment, so the likelihood of having Emily retreat to the kitchen was more likely.

Rebecca approached the counter and she could tell by Emily's expression that she, too, seemed concerned.

"Don't you look like something the cat dragged in." Emily was busy wiping the counter down and barely made eye contact.

Emily didn't surprise Rebecca much, because her nature was more aloof, but the sting of her statement hit her. Rebecca couldn't let go of the irony of it. Within the blink of an eye, Rebecca let a tear sneak out.

Emily, in all her wisdom, held back from reaching out, for which Rebecca was most grateful.

"Emily, would you mind getting me a cup of tea?" Rebecca gulped down the knot that was caught in her throat. "I'd do it myself—but..."

She couldn't hold it in any more. Before she knew it, the floodgates opened, and she stood like a pitiful child needing to be held and told that everything would be okay.

"Oh my, Rebecca, of course. What do you say I bring it to you in the back room instead? I think you'd be more comfortable there. Besides, you can prop your foot up, and the chair's a lot more comfortable."

All Rebecca could bring herself to do was to nod while Emily went about making her a cup of hot tea.

Rebecca stared out the window, an overarching sadness swept over her. Even the leafless trees seemed to weep, and the gray sky melted into the sea's horizon. She missed her cat, her parents, and her home. She missed her once-wonderful childhood, and on top of everything else, her foot hurt, and she was thrown into a task that was thrust on her out of left field. Part of her wanted everything to go back to the way things were before Mrs. Getchel passed away. Life was simpler then, but she owed it to Mrs. Getchel to keep moving forward.

Emily approached with a small tray of tea and a couple of cookies. "Cookies always make me feel better. Thought maybe you could use a little feeling better."

"They do have a way of doing that, don't they?" Rebecca said, then closed her eyes, willing the memory of her mom pulling a tray of freshly baked cookies out of the oven. She'd always make a 'tester' just for her. It was usually double the size of the regular ones that would follow. It was just her mom's way of making her feel special and loved.

"Would you like to talk about it? If not, I completely understand. It's just sometimes—I think—I think that if you get it out, it helps."

Rebecca wanted to tell her, but talking about the worst day of one's life wasn't an easy thing to do. Sure, she'd spoken to counselors many times in the past, but it didn't seem to help her then, and doubted it would help now. She most certainly didn't want pity; she'd had enough of that to last her a lifetime.

"Thanks, Emily. I've just got a lot on my mind. With Mrs. Getchel's passing and having Ben here. It's just brought up a lot from my past, and I suppose it's gotten to me."

"That makes sense," Emily said as she took a seat on the sofa. "If you don't mind me asking, how do you all know each other, anyway? I mean, I know she was your friend, but I don't recall you ever mentioning this Ben guy before?"

"No, I don't mind," she said, but it tied her insides in knots. She wasn't ashamed to have been a foster kid; it was the why she'd been one that she couldn't bring herself to tell. Rebecca took a moment to collect her thoughts as she stirred the stiff cinnamon stick in her cup. "Benjamin and I met when I was fifteen. He was living at Mrs. Getchel's, and so was I.

Emily's hands rolled her apron's ribbon around her fingers, and Rebecca could tell she was considering what she'd just shared.

"I'm not sure I understand. You lived there too?" she asked, then unwound the apron ribbon she'd been playing with and stood. "You know what? You don't have to answer that. I'm totally prying." She smoothed the apron out. "And it's none of my business."

Rebecca reached out and rested her hand on her arm. "It's okay, really. Sit."

She took a bite of her cookie before proceeding. Emily sat back down, resting her hands on her lap.

"To answer your question. Yes, I lived there too. In fact, I lived with her at the same time Benjamin did, at least until he—well, that doesn't matter." Rebecca could feel her neck and face grow warm at the realization that she was just about to open up about that part of her life. A part of her life that she'd kept hidden.

Emily cocked her head with questioning eyes. "I don't understand. You moved in at fifteen to live with your boyfriend?"

It was all Rebecca could do to not spit her tea across the room. "Oh, my goodness, no, that's not it at all. I would never—"

"I'm not judging—"

"No, I know that," Rebecca said with a reassuring touch of her hand on Emily's knee. "I'm sorry. I didn't make myself clear. First of all, Ben was never, nor will he ever, be my boyfriend. We were, what you might call, foster brother and sister."

"I see."

"Mrs. Getchel was our foster mom, but she was more like a grandma to us. She's taken care of many kids over the years, and I became one of them after my parents died." Rebecca sat, waiting for the pity to start. That look of 'you poor thing,' and an, 'I'm so sorry,' but it didn't come.

"How great for you that you had Mrs. Getchel. She'd obviously made a wonderful impact on your life. Families come in many forms." Emily shifted to face Rebecca straight on. "Yes, you lost your parents, but you'd gained a grandma that could see you through that time."

The chimes rang, indicating the front door had opened to a customer. Emily patted Rebecca on the hand and suggested she finish her tea, and left her taking in what she'd just heard.

Rebecca glanced at the empty plate and grinned. *Hmm, I guess cookies do make everything a little better.* She took the last bite of her cookie, and the last sip of her tea, then made her way back to clean up the mess she'd created on her worktable. To her surprise, Sophie had already cleaned it up. Rebecca was pleased to see that Sophie hadn't built the centerpiece for her as well. She was happy to create a touch of beauty, hoping to cast off the self-pity that was tangled around her, holding on tight, refusing to relent.

CHAPTER 21

Jason met Ben at the parking lot on Cape Neddick, just as he said he'd do. The Nubble lighthouse stood majestically before him, and he took in the sight. *It never gets old.* They gave their usual grab-the-hand and half hug-slap on the back before catching up on the latest goings on. Ben shared his predicament with his work back home, and his newest challenge of staying on the mainland to get a new business off the ground.

"Sounds to me like you've already made up your mind, Bud," Jason stated in a matter-of-fact, hoe-hum manner.

"How do you figure?"

"You've committed," he said as he tugged on his wool socks.

"All I've done was tell Becky that I'd help her with getting the business going. You know, start-up and all that kinda stuff." He huffed as he put on the jacket over his base layer.

"Yep, you're committed, Bud. I can't believe that you'd

consider leaving Rebecca in the lurch like that. This is a big deal. Honestly, I gotta tell ya, if you plan on pulling out after you start this thing, you're better to just walk away now. At least that way, she won't have to do it alone, and everyone would go back to how things were—you know—before Mrs. Getchel died."

By now, they were pulling on their dry suits, and Ben's mind raced at Jason's insistence. Jason was right. If he was going to do this, he had to go all in.

I have committed and I've told her as much. But he hadn't been thinking with his brain. He'd responded that way out of emotion and because of her adorable excitement. She was contagious, and he'd become infected. Now he didn't know how he'd turn back when he'd assured her he wouldn't. This time, he'd stick it out. At least until the project was up and running.

Ben pulled the hooded headpiece up and over his forehead and was relieved that the neoprene suit fit so nicely. He couldn't wait to get into the water. It would clear his mind; it always did.

As the icy wind picked up, it stung his face. He was grateful to have had such a big breakfast, which was essential to keeping warm. He was used to tropical waters, and getting back to cold diving was stretching him a bit. He would take no chances on this dive. By now, spectators watched as he and Jason went about their rituals of suiting up. Ben drank his fill of water, knowing it was necessary to stay warm, then lifted his tank onto his back and secured his weighted belt.

Today wouldn't be easy, Ben thought. The winds were strong and the current moved quickly, but he was skilled, and he lived for adventure; the water was his home. His adrenaline pumped as they made their way over the rocky shoreline. At the entry point in the cove, rock walls below the surface protected the waters. As the rush of water consumed him, it transported him to another realm, a time and place not known to man, but of flounder, rock cod, and sea bass.

Ben surveyed his surroundings in search of Jason, who had followed behind. Jason gave him a thumbs up as they moved through the water. Ben pointed out the wolf eels, then they approached its depths along the bottom. Crabs scurried along the sand. Ben reached to retrieve one. He normally didn't touch the living down below, but the crab grounded him to the turbulence that stirred in him on the surface.

His stressors receded, and he felt light and free. *Yes, this is exactly what I needed.*

After some time, they moved toward the outer walls of the cove into the open waters. Light was fading through the water, and the visibility waned. Ben meandered around the rocks in search of nothing, except oneness with the sea.

Jason signaled he was heading up, and Ben reluctantly followed. He could have spent another hour exploring the bay. Their fins moved gracefully through the water, and bubbles from their breath danced around them. Ben was at peace, and he wanted the tranquility to last longer, but it was time to return to the real world.

As he neared the surface of the rushing current, the waters turned and whirled, pulling them closer and closer to the ledge. A foreign weight hit him on the head and jarred his mouthpiece free. He didn't panic, but this unwelcome intrusion snapped him out of his solitude and contentment.

As his eyes adjusted to the surrounding whirl, he became entangled with another set of arms and legs that thrashed about. They grabbed hold of him and pushed him down. He fought back to reach the surface. A man in street clothes must have fallen in from the rocky overlook. Knowing that sent shock waves through him. He needed to take control quickly, or this man would not survive.

The face of a man flashed before him, filled with fear and panic. Powerful hands clung to him, and the man's feet tried to climb him. Ben pushed against the man with all of his strength and retreated from the flailing man by going deeper and deeper until he was completely free of him. He popped his mouthpiece back in, then kicked to the surface again, coming up behind the drowning man. He latched his arms under the panicked man's armpits, then pulled him toward the surface as fast as he could.

Ben kicked and tugged the now limp body through the crashing waves, dragging him closer and closer to the rocky shoreline. A woman screamed. A crowd shouted over the crushing water. A neoprene-sleeved hand reached out and yanked him and the drowned man on the rocks.

Ben scurried to remove his fins as Jason administered CPR to the victim. All Ben could do was to wrap his arms around the hysterical woman and hold her tight while, saying, "He's got this, he's got this." Finally, the woman retched in jagged sobs and sank to her knees. Ben held on to her tight.

Too much time has gone by, Ben thought. Just as he'd taken a turn with administering CPR, the man coughed up water and gasped for air. The crowd cheered, and the woman rejoiced as she rushed to his side, caressing his matted hair away from his face saying, "You're okay, you're okay."

By now, the local EMTs had arrived. They lifted him onto a gurney. The woman ran alongside as they made their way to the ambulance. Observers said the couple had been standing too close to the edge when a wave swallowed them up. He'd learned that Jason had quickly recovered the woman, but had to fight with her on shore so she wouldn't jump back in and try to help.

The excitement over, the crowd dissipated. Ben and Jason trudged their way to Jason's pickup and opened the tailgate, then removed their multiple layers of clothing. Ben heaved the gear in a duffle, threw on one of Jason's down coats and pulled on some dry socks before everything that had just happened finally sank in. A laugh billowed in his belly and bubbled to the surface. By the time it escaped, he was in full-blown laughter, so much so that his side hurt. Jason looked at him as if he'd lost his mind. Ben's contagious laughter overtook him too, and they stood, gasping for breath.

"When I said I had some time to kill, I didn't mean that literally," Ben said as he held his side to catch his breath.

Jason snorted. "Yeah, remind me again why we dive? Isn't it supposed to be relaxing?"

"I guess I never thought that people would fall from the sky and land on our heads—my bad." Ben's breathing relaxed, and he finally expelled the stress of the moment.

"It was good saving lives with you again, man." Jason gave Ben a sideways hug.

"Yep," Ben agreed, "it was good saving lives."

CHAPTER 22

Rebecca had placed a few more sprigs of greenery in the basket, for the second time, and stepped back to see her progress, thinking that once she was done, her clients would be happy. Just knowing that she'd help bring some joy to someone else helped pull her out of her doldrums.

Focusing on work, instead of being so self-absorbed, helped. In the past, she'd still be beating herself up, but because of Emily and Sophie's kindness, she was able to gulp it down, just as she'd done with the tea. So, she chose to think about the future and all the wonderful things that were happening in her life and not dwell on the bad that had already happened.

Rebecca lost track of time. Before she knew it, she'd placed the last winterberry, and her job was complete. She stood back to inspect her work. *I've still got it*, she thought while she put it, and the other arrangements she'd created, in transport boxes and placed them in the fridge until pickup time.

Rebecca reached for her phone to check the time, figuring Ben would show up before too long, but it wasn't where she normally kept it. She retraced her steps from the refrigerator and all around her work area. When it occurred to her, she may have left it in the back room where she'd had her tea with Emily.

Her phone was right where she'd left it, on the small break table. She breathed a sigh of relief before noticing that she'd missed a call from Ben. She still wasn't used to the fact that he was back in her life, but she was grateful that he was. Rebecca hit play and listened to her voicemail. She was pleased that Ben and his friend were going to go for a dive together at the Nubble Lighthouse. Rebecca smiled at the thought that he'd get to spend the day doing something that he loved so much, and it warmed her heart to know he'd reached out in case she needed him.

Voices from the bakery grew louder by the minute. She couldn't imagine what was happening. Rebecca could make out Mrs. Bennington's distinct voice over the others, and curiosity got the better of her. She hoped that Mrs. Bennington wasn't raising a stink about Stepping Stones, and the thought of disturbing Proposals' business over her personal situation didn't sit well with her. She had to put a stop to it. Rebecca dropped her phone in her smock pocket and stepped toward the bakery.

Mrs. Bennington's eyes were wide with excitement, and she was going on and on about how an ambulance had flown by from a tragedy that had just taken place.

Rebecca hated to admit it, but she was relieved the fuss wasn't anything to do with her.

Mrs. Bennington was animated when she told her group

of friends, and anyone else within earshot of the bakery, that four people nearly died by drowning. Another lady proclaimed that she'd heard that two people died. Mrs. Bennington gasped and took a seat in exasperation. At that point, another customer said that they'd had it all wrong, that one person died and two survived. By now, Emily was scurrying around, trying to help them all calm down.

Rebecca tried to make sense of all the contradictory statements, but they were still talking over each other and the decibels rose higher.

Rebecca grabbed Emily by the arm and pulled her close. "Where did they say this happen?"

"Cape Neddick," she said.

"Cape Neddick!" Rebecca squeezed Emily's arm harder. "Are you sure?"

Emily raised her eyebrows. "Who really knows? These gossiping geese could stir up a bee's nest in the North Pole."

Rebecca froze. *He's okay, he's okay, please be okay.* She stared at her phone in the palm of her trembling hand and proceeded toward the back room.

She sat on her chair and rested her elbows on her knees while clinging to her phone, then finally had the courage to call. *Please pick up, please pick up,* she begged, and it went to voicemail and nausea built. She dared to try again. Still no answer. She left a message. *It couldn't be Ben and Jason, could it?*

She paced, willing her phone to ring when it occurred to her that the York page might have something about the incident on social media. She clicked on the page and read the post, "Two Nearly Drowned at Cape Neddick."

"Nearly drowned—not drowned," she said with a moment's relief, but then again, she thought, if he had almost drowned, he could be unconscious, or in a coma or something. Her panic rose again.

Stop it, Rebecca, she thought before recalling one of Mrs. Getchel's rules: *Get the facts.*

She sat as her legs could no longer support her, then read on. Two heroes came to the rescue after two individuals were swept off the rocks. Someone else had posted a video, but it wasn't clear. As she read on, the poster explained how two divers dove into action after colliding with the couple in the water. Their quick action and skill made the difference between life and death. One person wrote, "I'd hate to think of what could have happened if those divers hadn't been at the right place at the right time."

Rebecca now shook in her seat at the thought of losing someone again. Her throat grew tight with the urge to cry, and yet, she was relieved. These mixed emotions continued to bubble to the surface, and when they finally broke loose, she wailed with tears of relief, pride, and anger for what could have happened. And self-loathing for getting herself worked up before she knew the facts. Trusting social media was an iffy proposition, filled with speculation on who both the heroes and victims were, but in her heart of hearts she knew: one diver was Ben, and she'd have to trust that Ben would call her back when he had a chance.

She pulled herself together and went back to the bakery, where the ladies still prattled all a flutter about the spectacular event. Their speculations had reached near lunacy, and Rebecca had to put an end to it. She rounded the counter, where Emily was frantically doling out sweets. in their distress, they'd requested the confections to soothe their worry.

Emily opened a pastry bag and handed it to Rebecca.

"I found out what happened at Nubble," Rebecca said. "Do you think I could make an announcement?"

"Oh Lordy, please do," Emily said as she stuffed an eclair in the bag. "They've nearly broken me."

Rebecca placed her index fingers in the corners of her mouth and blew. The whistle broke through the noise of the cackling hens and silence filled the room. Rebecca went on to read them the posts and after she'd read them, conjecture and speculation stopped, so they quieted down to a mere chatter.

Rebecca marveled at what a draw tragedy was, and recognized that her behavior wasn't much better than those that speculate and gossip when horror strikes. She could only imagine how people had reacted when her own life's tragedy had hit the news. For the first time in her life, she was grateful that she'd been in a coma when her news was fresh.

By now, the ladies had finished making their purchases and left Emily to retreat to the kitchen. Rebecca too went back to work because she expected the hero himself would pick her up soon. She shook her head at the knowledge of how demanding the last few days had been for him. He'd attended the funeral of a loved one, mended a wounded-hand and broken toe for a friend, and saved two people's lives. Knowing him, he'd just say it was all in a day's work, and it probably was.

Rebecca rolled up to her desk and opened the design app on her desktop. She clicked on a handful of photos, examples for an upcoming follow-up appointment she had with a bride and her mom. She was pleased with their overall vision, as it made it a lot easier when she, too, liked their concept.

Before long, she was on auto pilot, and her mind shifted to all the plans she had for Stepping Stones. She wanted to offer job-skills training, but thought life-skills would be just as important. Hearing about today's events sealed the deal in her mind. She jotted down some notes and, as her brainstorming continued, she flooded the paper with such a wide range of ideas that she ran out of space.

***

A rap on the door drew her out of her focused energy, and she felt guilty for having shifted to her own project. She slid the paper under her client's folder before responding to the knock.

"Come on in."

The knob turned, and the door slowly opened. Ben's deep brown eyes peered around the door before a broad smile emerged. "Hi there, pretty lady."

He's here. She breathed in a sigh of relief. *He's safe.* "I do declare, our local knight in shining armor has come to rescue me from my toils." Laughter rolled off her tongue.

"You heard." Ben's eyes shined, and his grin grew wider across his face. "If by shining armor, you mean wetsuit, then I'm your man."

"I was so worried. I kept calling. You should have called me back, Benjamin."

"Yes, I know, I should have, but I was just too excited to get here and whisk you away."

Before she knew it, he scooped her up and threw her over his shoulder, which instantly brought Becky to a state of panic. The flash of smoke and flames whirled through her mind and she let out a scream.

"Put me down!" She kicked her feet, trying to get loose, "Stop it, Ben!"

"No can do. I'm starving. My white horse is waiting,

and we are going to celebrate saving a life, so—"

"Put me down right now!" Her breath wouldn't come. "I can't—I…" The memory of being flung over the shoulder of a firefighter tore through her. *I'm okay. It's just Ben—I'm okay.*

Ben didn't put her down. Instead, he twirled her around, and his foot tangled in a lamp cord, which caused him to stumble. Ben held on to her tightly, using his body to protect hers. They went down with a bang. His head bounced off the corner of Rebecca's desk, then once again as he hit the hardwood floor. Ben lay in a slump. Rebecca lay sprawled on the floor beside him.

Rebecca scrambled to her feet. Ben wasn't moving. "No—no, no, no, Ben, wake up!" She nudged his arm. "Wake up!"

Panic washed over her, and she crawled away and sat on the wood floor, leaning against the wall. She grew numb as she stared at his still body sprawled across the rug.

The door flew open and Emily stepped in. "I heard you screaming, Rebecca," she said as she scanned the room. "Oh my God! What happened?"

Rebecca couldn't bring herself to say a word. She sat frozen. All Rebecca could do was watch Emily lean over Ben's body and place her ear on his chest, then she checked his pulse.

"He's breathing," she said as she turned to face her. "Rebecca, have you called 911?" Again, Rebecca's words were locked inside, and she could not open her mouth.

Emily made a few steps toward her, then kneeled at her side. "Beck, Honey, I think you might be in shock. I'm going to call 911, and then I'm just gonna step out so I can get a blanket."

Rebecca nodded.

"I'll be right back."

Within a moment, Emily was wrapping a blanket around Rebecca's shoulders. Sophie was waiting out front for the ambulance to arrive.

"Thank you," Rebecca whispered. "He's going to be okay, right?"

"He'll be in excellent hands."

Emily fumbled to the work desk and grabbed the half empty bottle of Dasani water. "Here, Rebecca, take a drink."

Rebecca brought the water to her lips and gulped down the rest of it, then crept over to where Ben lay and stroked his brow. "I'm so sorry, Benjamin. I'm so very sorry. I didn't mean to hurt you. Please be okay."

CHAPTER 23

Ben could feel motion—a sense of rocking from side to side, as if he were in a fog. Nausea hit the back of his throat. *What's happening?* He willed himself to move without success. His body was heavy and stiff, as if a weight lay upon him. His head pounded.

Where am I? The rocking sensation continued. He could hear an unfamiliar voice off in the distance. Beeps, buzzing, and a siren sounded. He willed himself to open his eyes. A muffled, husky voice, talked above him. A man sat at his side.

"Mr. Daly, can you hear me?" he asked. Ben could make out his words, but he was having trouble finding his own. "Mr. Daly, you've had a head injury, and we're taking you to the York hospital."

Hospital. My head. Ben tried to bring his hand to his head, but he couldn't move it. Panic shot through him. "I—I can't move. I can't—"

"We've strapped you down so you can't move, Mr. Daly. We don't want you to further injure yourself."

Ben searched around. His head was securely locked within a brace and strapping. He tried to wiggle his fingers and toes, and a flood of relief washed over him as the vehicle sped its way to the emergency doors. Each motion of the gurney jostled him as the EMTs wheeled it out of the ambulance. The clank of the legs being lowered hammered. The ridged wheels rolling along the floor bumped into his back.

A doctor stepped forward and the EMT filled her in on his state. The words cerebral edema, MRI, and intracranial pressure flew above him. He tried to recall what had happened to him. He remembered being happy, then the next thing he knew, he was in the ambulance.

He just had to concentrate, but the bright lights made his head hurt. Ben closed his eyes. *Focus.*

He remembered seeing Becky with a smile on her face. *She was happy; we were celebrating.*

Intermittent flashes of memory came back. *I was happy.* He'd had her over his shoulder, and she'd shouted. Was it fear he'd heard? *Becky! Where's Becky?*

Another wave of nausea bubbled up from his stomach. He opened his eyes to keep the room from spinning.

I'm going to be sick, he thought, and before he could get the words out, he retched. The room, along with its sounds, faded to black.

Chapter 24

Emily reached around Rebecca and flipped the sign to Closed and grabbed her coat and keys. Before Rebecca knew it, Emily was pulling her out the door and to her car. Emily sped out of the parking lot.

"Don't rush too much, Em," Rebecca said, hands gripping the sides of the seat. "We don't need both of us in the hospital as well."

"You can say that again. You sure gave me a scare back there. I thought they'd be taking you away, too."

"Sorry about that. I'm feeling better now. Just knowing he's being taken care of helps."

"You have nothing to be sorry about. I'm just glad you're okay."

Emily stopped at the hospital's emergency room doors. "Should I wait for you? Never mind, that's silly, I'm sure you'll want to stay awhile. I'll—um—just head back and finish things up at Proposals. Why don't you just call me when you're all set to leave, and I'll come back and pick you up?"

Rebecca knew she could be here late into the night, and it would be out of the way for Emily to go home and then come all the way back.

"Thanks, but I'll figure something out. Like you said, I could be here most of the night." Rebecca patted Emily on the leg.

"Call if you need anything. Anything at all."

"I should—um…"

"Yes! Go! Get in there," Emily said with a wave of her hand. "Rebecca, I will say a prayer for him."

"That would be great, Emily. Thanks."

Rebecca entered the Emergency room. The sterile environment sent her reeling, and an instant ache pierced her flesh. She took a seat to catch her composure before approaching the check-in desk. She explained that Ben had no family, and that she was the closest to a sister he had. After she was done; they were kind enough to allow her entry.

The large U-shaped nurse's station was straight ahead. A robust nurse with a tight bun, wearing light blue scrubs, stood at a rolling computer. *Claire? Is that Claire?* Rebecca's chest grew tight, and she couldn't find her breath. Claire had been one of the nurses in the burn unit. She'd been rough and relentless. *It hurt so much.* She could almost smell her flesh as it was scrubbed to remove her dead skin. She could see the tiny scissors in Claire's thick fingers as she snipped at the remaining pieces of flesh that hadn't come off.

Rebecca was lightheaded, and the room started to spin. The piercing sounds of beeps, pumps, and the cadence of the atmosphere were at a near crescendo. *I need to get out of here. I can't be here.*

Rebecca placed her hand on the hallway wall to steady herself, and took a few jagged breaths, then she ran toward the exit. Everything was whirling, as if she were drunk, and she couldn't find her footing, until she came to an abrupt stop and smooshed into the chest of a robust nurse. Her startled eyes stared back at hers. "You're not Claire."

"No, Lovey. I'm Grace. Are you alright?"

"I'm sorry—I, well, I'm here to see my friend, and I…"

Grace's eyes were kind, and for a moment, she thought she was looking into Mrs. Getchel's thoughtful gaze.

"What's your friend's name, Lovey?"

"Benjamin Daly."

"Come with me," she said as she gave her a sideways squeeze.

Rebecca and Grace walked through the corridor of the emergency floor. Moans and cries drifted as they walked past closed curtains. *Number twelve, thirteen. There, number seventeen.*

"Here we go." Grace said. She gave Rebecca's shoulder a tender touch. "You just let me know if you need anything."

"Thank you, Grace."

The curtain was open, but the bed that Ben was supposed to occupy wasn't there; the room was empty.

Rebecca frantically turned to locate Grace, but the nurse was no longer in view. She walked toward the nurse's station. Staff moved behind the partitions, and sounds grew louder in her head. *Stop it. I'm okay.* She remembered seeing the nurses and doctors scurrying about as she lay in her own hospital bed. *I'm okay.* She took a few deep breaths, then approached the counter.

Her voice shook as she asked one nurse where Ben was.

A young guy, wearing green scrubs, tapped his keyboard for what seemed like an eternity.

"Oh, here we go," he said with enthusiasm. "He's having some tests done and should be back before too long." His lips went tight and shook his head. "That's unless they needed to take him in to surgery. But you can go ahead and wait in his room until they get back, if you'd like."

Surgery! At those words, she no longer thought of her own pain of the past. *He hit his head.* Rebecca remembered him lying unconscious, but she didn't remember any blood. *Oh my God! Did I break his neck?* She was fully in the here and now, and Ben was the one in pain.

Rebecca floated back to the sterile empty room and sat in the metal-legged plastic chair in the corner. She bowed her head and prayed, hoping this time God would answer her prayers.

CHAPTER 25

Ben lay still as they slid him into the MRI machine. It wasn't bad enough that they had strapped him down so he couldn't move, but now he was encased. He recalled the same panicky feeling when he'd scuba dived for the first time.

His team was pumped up on a picture-perfect day for training. They'd done their prior training for scuba, but now they would venture in the depths of the ocean. Ben recalled thinking that going down fifteen feet was nothing. He'd been fine when he'd sat on the boat and going about the routine of strapping on his tank, mouthpiece, and goggles, but when he placed a weighted belt around his waist, his nerves had gotten the better of him. He'd be damned if he'd let it show.

When jumping into the water, adding weight to one's waist goes against nature. Sure, he had his inflatable vest on, but he'd soon deflated that, and then he'd be at the mercy of his mouthpiece alone. Ben could inflate his vest again, if he got too shaken, but again, he'd never hear the end of it. So down he'd gone, lower and lower, hearing nothing but the sound of his own breathing, in and out, in and out. His apparatus and the water trapped him, and panic had washed over him.

Ben's trainer had faced him as he sank deeper. His trainer's eyes shone large behind his goggles. He'd given Ben an okay sign and then waited for an okay in response, indicating Ben was doing alright. Ben had hesitated. He wanted to say he wasn't doing fine, but his shame outweighed his urge. Instead, he signaled the okay sign, and the instructor swam off. To his own amazement, the panic slowly subsided. Maybe it was the tranquility of the sea that overtook him, or maybe the sheer pleasure of moving through the water. Fish were plentiful, and the depths called to him. That dive made him realize he was born to dive.

Ben lay in the machine. He could hear loud clanking noises and feel vibrations. This wasn't below the surface. He could breathe, shallowly, but he could breathe. He lay there, knowing he had a head injury. A head injury might mean he'd never be able to dive again. He'd seen it happen before while he served. As the clinking and clanking noises continued, his heart nearly beat out of his chest.

Who am I if I'm not a diver? It's all I know—it's all I've got. He had to believe that he'd be okay. Becky needed him.

CHAPTER 26

Rebecca sat idly in the chair beside Ben's hospital bed, waiting for him. She'd already called Emily to let her know she hadn't seen Ben. She wished she'd brought headphones or something that could drown out the hospital noises.

An emergency room was where she'd accepted the fact that her parents were dead. She remembered shaking from her trauma, but she still had the ability to scream for them through the pain of her blistering raw flesh. She didn't want to believe it—she couldn't believe their deaths were real. The more she screamed, the more she thrashed. The more she thrashed, the more she'd added to the damage of her body, and the more pain she'd endure, until she passed out.

The next thing she knew, she'd woken up to learn that her parents were already in their final resting place, and she hadn't had the chance to say goodbye. She recalled wondering where that place even was because her parents never talked about such things. Thinking they were alone, buried under the cold ground, had scared her. She'd tried to imagine what had been said about them, who would have been there, and if anyone thought to give her mom flowers.

Rebecca closed her eyes, rocked back and forth in her hard plastic chair, and stuffed down her sorrow.

Voices down the hall got louder. *It's Benjamin, I hear Ben.* Wheels squeaked as they got closer. Ben was coming, and she'd learn his fate. She swallowed hard and, on shaky legs, stood to meet them.

The nurse and an orderly were all business as Rebecca shifted out of the way so they could connect him to all the monitors. There were so many cords. He was no longer wearing the neck brace the EMTs had placed on him, and wasn't strapped down. She breathed a sigh of relief. Ben was right there in front of her; they hadn't needed to take him into surgery. With this revelation, she could stop holding her breath. *No surgery.*

Rebecca approached him, but his eyes were mere slits, and he'd drifted off to sleep. She gasped as she observed the grotesque swelling around his forehead and temple. Tears burned in her eyes.

Rebecca sat back down to collect herself and to not pass out.

"Ma'am, are you okay?" asked the attending nurse.

"Yes, I—ah, I guess I just never expected him to look so awful," Rebecca whispered, hoping Ben wouldn't overhear her.

"Not to worry, hon. He'll be back to being handsome as ever in no time. You wait and see," she said with a warm smile and a tender touch, reminding her of Grace.

The nurse informed her Ben was receiving medication to help prevent additional swelling, but warned, if the swelling continued, they may have to do a Ventriculostomy, which Rebecca learned, was a surgically cut small hole in his skull and a plastic drain tube to help relieve the pressure.

She pulled her chair closer to Ben and held his hand. To think she'd been jubilant when he'd said he'd gone diving, something he'd always enjoyed. He'd been a hero, and now this.

"Benjamin, I'm so sorry," she whispered as tears fell down her cheeks. "This is all my fault."

She breathed in and closed her eyes, reliving what had happened. *If I hadn't hurt my stupid toe, he wouldn't have had to pick me up from work. I should have let him have his fun. It was innocent play. I can see that now.*

Rebecca caressed his arm. "You were so happy, and I carried on like a lunatic. I caused you to stumble. I'm so, so sorry, Benjamin."

She couldn't escape the torment that was building inside her. She was better off alone. It was safer that way. Rebecca wiped her tears away and vowed to not allow anyone to get close again because all she did was create harm. And seeing loved ones hurt was just too painful.

Rebecca gave his hand a squeeze, kissed him on the forehead, and pushed away. Waiting for Emily to pick her up would take too much time. She wanted to leave now. She'd find Ben's keys, then all she'd need to do was walk to Proposals. She could take his car home for now. Rebecca searched through his bag of belongings and found the keys in his jacket. She placed them in her coat pocket and slipped out the door. Next, she left Emily a voicemail to let her know she was all set and that she'd see her in the morning.

Rebecca needed the fresh air; she needed to breathe. She walked, not caring how long it would take for her to reach

Ben's car. She didn't care that the temperatures were near freezing, that she awkwardly limped in her tattered slippers, that her foot ached, or that her toe throbbed. All she knew was that she deserved the discomfort—this pain. After all, she thought, Ben was suffering more than she was, all thanks to her.

***

Several weeks passed since Ben was rushed to the hospital, and the ache of knowing he was still there paralyzed Rebecca from performing her day-to-day activities. Christmas had come and gone without fanfare. She'd been grateful for the distractions of making holiday centerpieces and various other bouquets of red ribbons, bobbles, pine, and candles. The busier she was, the easier it was to keep Ben out of her mind.

Now, she restlessly tried to focus on work, but try as she may, all she could think about was Ben lying in the hospital.

She'd been proud of herself when she thought she was getting over her growing phobia of hospitals. She'd checked in on him every evening. He'd been unconscious, and wasn't aware of her at his bedside. Even so, she was there.

She could only imagine the anger he'd feel, knowing that he most likely wouldn't be able to dive again, and the thought of seeing him in such agony, over that realization, was too much, especially knowing he lay there because of her.

Rebecca's thoughts continued to weave in and out as she wrapped the thin green wire around the floral stems she'd collected. She recalled all the medical wires that were attached to his body, and the buzzing and beeping that played over and over like a record skipping. The sounds wouldn't stop and made her pulse quicken. He'd seemed peaceful, lying there, but her insides had roiled. Her body screamed at the thought she could have lost him, too.

Rebecca was at his side when they'd whisked him off for emergency surgery. She could no longer keep up the charade of bravery. Rebecca feared the worst, and it brought her to her knees.

It took all she had to pull herself together while waiting to see if he would live or die.

Once she learned he'd gotten through the surgery, she'd walked away.

Rebecca thought it was the right thing to do for both of them. She couldn't bear to be there when he learned of his fate. He'd blame her, and rightly so. He'd resent her, and that was just too much for her to take. After all, his career would be over because of her, and so she thought it best to stay away. The last thing she wanted was to cause him more pain.

She placed her now finished floral arrangement in the refrigerator while Sophie and Emily prepared the barn for an upcoming wedding. She was relieved when they said they were nearly done and let her know she didn't need to stay.

Her car was all warmed up, and she was eager to get back to her apartment. It had been too long since she'd been able to sit down and work on her quilting. She'd made a commitment to herself to finish a couple more quilts before the end of the year, and time was running out. Just a bit more stitching and she'd meet her commitment to herself.

As she drove toward the village, she expected Mrs. Getchel's home would be dark, just as it had every day since Ben's head injury. It beckoned her and begged for light and life to fill its rooms once again. Rebecca shook off the ache that lay heavy on her chest. She and Ben should have been making progress on their plans together. They'd had such hope and promise in making the place a sanctuary, but now, with what happened to Ben, all she could bring herself to do was to adhere to the trustee's timeline. She provided some filled-out forms for the town planning department and historical society. Otherwise, she'd put everything else on a shelf, as her heart wasn't in it without him.

As Rebecca rounded the corner, she had to look twice. Mrs. Getchel's house lights blazed. She tapped on the brakes and slowed to a near stop. Ben's car was parked in front of the garage. Her heart skipped a beat, and her scarf grew itchy around her neck. *What are you doing there?* She couldn't wrap her head around how Ben could be there. Rebecca calculated the time from when he went into the hospital to now, and from what she'd learned online, he could be in recovery at home by now.

After her earlier thinking, she was kicking herself for not having been at his side. *What was I thinking?* She felt horrible that she'd left him alone when he needed her, especially after he'd taken such good care of her.

She lay her head on the steering-wheel, gripping it tight. *I'm a terrible person. A terribly selfish person.*

A horn blared behind her, startling her. She flicked on her blinker and turned into the drive, not knowing what to do next. Minutes ticked by as she sat idle, then she put the car into drive to go home.

Thoughts of Ben, doing who knew what, in that big old house by himself, left her feeling guilty, and before she knew it, she pulled over to the side of the road.

"Suck it up, Beck!" she shouted. "Just get over your damned self and face him. You owe him that much."

But how do I face him now, after what I've done?

Now that she had to face him, she realized that her behavior was unforgivable. She took a few deep breaths to gain the courage to see him and his anger. If she didn't do it now, she never would because as time got further away, so would he.

I should have at least called him. Again, she slammed her fist on the steering wheel. *Rebecca Mills, you are a full-fledged idiot.*

The stunt she'd pulled would have alienated him, but she'd done it for the right reason: to spare him. He was safer without her in his life, but how she handled it was wrong. She could almost hear Mrs. Getchel giving her holy grief at not having nursed him back to health. Rebecca tried to push her reprimand from her mind. After all, she doubted Mrs. Getchel had ever been in her shoes. She'd probably never had to face losing her family because of her own selfishness. Mrs. Getchel would understand Rebecca's position if she were alive for Rebecca to tell her about it. Still, she was curious about what Ben could possibly be up to in the house.

Rebecca's heart raced as she backed out into the road and made a U-turn. As she approached the house, the lights were out, but she hoped Ben's car might still be there. Her heart sank, knowing that she'd missed him. She missed him, that much she knew for sure, but that was her selfishness acting up again.

Rebecca pulled into the driveway and slid out of her seat. The wind had picked up, and a bitter edge to the night slapped at her face as she made her way to the front porch. She unlocked the door and stepped inside. The house felt warm. Heating it was costing her a fortune, and she'd made it a point to keep the thermostat low. Rebecca sighed before she flicked on the light, then checked the thermostat. She smiled, knowing he'd turned it back down before he left.

Rebecca pivoted her head from side to side to see what he might have done and noticed nothing unusual until she turned back toward the door. The piano stood along the living room wall, just ahead to her right. The keyboard lid stood open and, resting on the keys, lay an envelope.

Rebecca approached the piano with a sinking feeling. *A dear John letter?* She wouldn't blame him, especially after the way she'd treated him.

She sighed, picked up the envelope and slumped on the piano stool. With hesitancy, Rebecca slid a finger between the seal and pulled out the note. She bit her lower lip and flipped it open.

Becky,

I'm not angry with you for not coming to see me in the hospital, but I am disappointed. I suppose you think I deserve it after leaving you all those years ago, when you needed me the most, but I confess, you've left me confused. I thought we'd gotten past all that. I thought we were moving forward. We had plans. Did I do something more to upset you? I'm at a loss as to how to move forward.

I've moved out of the inn and staying with Jason for now. Since they haven't cleared me to fly home yet, staying at the inn long term didn't make good sense. If you decide you'd like to work this out, please call. If I don't hear from you, I'll take it that our partnership is a bust, and you'd rather lose everything than keep me in your life.

With my deepest regrets, Becky.

Love,

Ben

Rebecca reread the letter a few more times. Their future was in her hands. Still, her heart sank. The few words that hit her the most were that he hadn't been cleared to fly home yet. She couldn't make him stay. He'd obviously preferred to go home, and who could blame him? His friends and life were in Hawaii. She had no hold over him—never did—never would. At least, she thought, he'd written to her this time, and for that she was grateful.

Rebecca folded the letter, stuffed it back in the envelope, and slid it into her pocket. She took in a deep breath, put her chin up, and walked out the door.

If she set her mind to it, she didn't need Ben to make Mrs. Getchel's dream come true. She just had to figure out a way she could carry out the plan by herself. Surely, she could make the trustee understand.

Chapter 27

Ben's head throbbed as he drove toward Jason's place. He had no business driving out to Mrs. G's house, but he had no other way to reach out to Becky, outside of bothering her at work. He hesitated doing that again, especially after the fiasco he'd caused that last time.

It crushed Ben that Becky hadn't checked in on him at the hospital, and he wondered if she even knew he was out. *Could she really be that upset that I'd picked her up?* He wondered if he had pushed a button that he was unaware of. She'd told him to put her down, and he'd ignored her, thinking she didn't really mean it. He thought it was all in fun. *Maybe something from her past?* He didn't know what to make of her reaction, and the silent treatment now ticked him off.

Jason was still at work, and his place off Seabury Road, in York Harbor, was quiet. The wind had died down and a full moon shone. *I need some air.* He threw his coat back on and stepped out the back door and down the set of weathered stairs. Ben stuffed his hands in his pockets as he maneuvered over the gravel road toward the York River.

Ben had forgotten how much he enjoyed seeing his breath. It reminded him of being a kid. He tipped his head back, pretending to blow a smoke ring, then laughed. As much as his childhood sucked, he'd had enjoyable moments, too. He grinned at the thought and breathed in the fresh night air and filled his lungs.

Before long, he stood on an outcropping of dry rocks that led to the water's edge. The tide was high, and the waves lapped the rocks with a lull that was music to his ears. He sat down, brought his knees up, and wrapped his arms around them, then gazed out at the moonlit water. It called to him still as it shimmered and sparkled as if celebrating his return, but a part of him also felt as though it mocked him.

Ben looked toward the night's sky, wishing his connection to the sea could remain as it was. He was at home with the sea. As unpredictable as it was, he respected its greatness—its power—and its lure.

The crisp night turned frigid now and settled in, sending a shiver down his spine. Once again, thoughts of Becky permeated his mind.

Before his accident, he'd had such high hopes for their future together. The Stepping Stones venture was a good one. He'd actually been excited about it and was looking forward to bringing it to fruition. Becky had great ideas, and he enjoyed seeing her happy.

He remembered how rarely he'd seen her happy when they were kids. He'd oftentimes tried to make her laugh, because Becky had been the living definition of sadness. She'd worn it as an invisible cloak, and everyone knew it was there, but sometime, she'd let it slip.

He grinned, recalling her as a gangly teenager. She'd laugh as he played and sang his silly songs on the piano, or mimicked Mrs. G. behind her back. He remembered the time that she seemed happiest back then: when they'd gone to the beach. They'd floated on the water, riding the waves, and looked toward the blue sky, dreaming of their futures.

Becky had dreams of making an impact and doing something important for others. Looking back now, he realized that she'd already done just that. She made quilts for foster kids and created flowers to brighten people's days. Did she really need to do more? Yes, creating a program for foster kids was a condition to Mrs. G's will, but more importantly, she'd thrive if she did so.

The rhythm of the sea sloshed methodically against the rocks. Ben looked toward the heavens once again. *What do you want from us?*

Becky was more than capable of running Stepping Stones without him, and because she'd been avoiding him, it appeared to be her preference. Maybe he could convince the trustee that they had extenuating circumstances. After all, Mrs. G. certainly couldn't have anticipated that he'd have a head injury. At least they had the name, Stepping Stones, and wagered to guess that Becky had ticked off more of the trustee's to-do list while he'd been incapacitated. The biggest hurdle was to have the town accept the plan, and once they got that approval, the actual project could get off the ground. Surely, he thought, that would be enough to fulfill Mrs. G's wishes.

"I've done all I can do," he said to the stars. "Becky

doesn't need me or want anything to do with me." He hesitated, as if awaiting a response. The lull of the water and the sky stilled, and all was quiet. "Do you hear me? I'm done!"

Then, as if it were deliberate, a wave crashed against the rocks, sending an icy spray over him, drenching him where he sat. Ben spit and sputtered the salt water out of his mouth and wiped his eyes with his numb fingers.

"Fine! I got the picture," he said to the wind.

Ben brushed himself off as best he could and plodded back up the hill to Jason's place while he contemplated how to move forward with his life. He didn't know what his future might hold. He was as lost as a ship that broke anchor in the night, rolling with the waves, without direction or footing, being cast about without a destination or mooring.

Ben had a hard time seeing himself back in Hawaii, especially after his head injury. Besides, he thought, he wasn't able to fly any more than he could dive right now, and he certainly couldn't do his job, even if he could return. That reality struck him to the core. Diving was his whole life. He had absolutely no idea how to move beyond it.

Stepping Stones, he thought, was now his only option, but with Becky's vanishing act, it seemed highly unlikely that she wanted him to be any part of it. He shrugged off that thought with a shiver.

Ben thought about all the ideas he'd had for their venture together, and he found it maddening that, of all the people in all the world, he had to work with Becky Mills, the sad little girl from his past, who'd grown into a stubborn, infuriating, remarkable woman.

"Mrs. G., you have a devious mind," he said as he shook his head.

He took in another deep breath, then continued toward Jason's place. By now, more time had gone by, and he could just imagine what Jason might think to see his car there and not him, so he picked up his pace.

He was freezing and ravenous by the time he'd reached the house, but Jason still wasn't home. Ben tugged off his wet clothes and hopped in the shower to wash off the remnants of the salt water and the chill of the night. Before long, he rummaged through the fridge, but saw nothing appealing. He wished Foster's Clambake was open for the season because he was craving one of their lobster rolls and clam chowders. As his stomach continued to growl, he decided to head on over to the Ship's Cellar Pub for a bite, but thought he'd give Jason a heads up. He scooted out the door and tapped Jason's number, but it went straight to voicemail.

"Hey, Jason. Wasn't sure if you were heading back yet, but if you were, thought you might join me for a bite at the Cellar Pub. I'm heading there now. If not, see you back at your place."

He disconnected and drove to the Inn. The one thing he missed about not staying at the Inn was just walking next door from his unit, but he was grateful to have Jason's place nonetheless.

The inn and its pub were a welcoming sight. The windows glowed and white twinkling lights adorned the outside, giving it an enchanting appearance. Ben parked and entered through the inn's main entrance. He'd gone that way so he could warm himself by the fireplace before heading downstairs to eat. A wood-burning fire was something he sorely missed living on the island, and he didn't want to miss the opportunity while he had it.

Ben approached the large stone fireplace and rubbed his

hands together, taking in the warmth, then found one of the leather chairs empty and had a seat. He noticed Julie working behind the upstairs bar, and Julie didn't take long to notice him as well. She gave him a bright smile and a quick wave, then held up one finger, indicating for him to wait a minute.

By now, Ben's hunger gnawed at his stomach, and as much as he'd like to say hello, he thought it best to go downstairs and get a table. He stood and gathered his coat off the arm of the chair and slowly moved across the wooden floorboards to the top of the staircase.

"Hey, there," said the cheery voice behind him. Ben turned to once again see Julie's big smile and sparkling eyes before him.

"Hey," Ben said with a questioning grin. "I'm surprised to see you up here."

"Yeah, once in a while I help up here. I like it though."

A young couple was climbing the stairs and Ben moved out of the way to let them by. They nodded thanks to Ben and Julie and wished them a good night. Right about that time, a staff member brushed by and told Julie he'd see her tomorrow, then he whisked off, in a hurry, toward the dining room.

Ben shifted back to the stairs landing and hesitated. "I was just heading down to grab a bite. If you're done for the night, would you care to join me?"

Without blinking an eye, Julie said she'd be delighted to, but would need to grab a sweater out of her car first because she didn't think it was appropriate to wear work attire in front of patrons.

"I'll be right back. Oh, but go ahead and get us a table. Get one by the fireplace if you can. I think you'll like it there." She gave his hand a squeeze, then scampered off.

"Will do." His gaze followed her as she left, but all he thought was that he hoped he wasn't making a mistake. The last thing he needed was having Julie think he was interested. He had enough to deal with and didn't need to add another woman to the mix. At least he was safe in that he didn't have a room next door. And he wasn't cleared to drink alcohol, which was a saving grace.

He got a table near the fire and was perusing through the menu, which he realized was kind of ridiculous because he knew it by heart. He'd decided on a burger and a lobster corn chowder by the time Julie made her way toward him. She'd loosened her braid and her hair lay long and wavy over her shoulders. She pulled out her Windsor-backed chair and plopped down with a huff.

"Did you order drinks?" she asked.

"Nope, not yet. You may know my usual drink of choice, but I have absolutely no idea what you might like."

"I'll have anything you're having." She crossed her arms, placed them on the table, and leaned forward. "Surprise me."

Ben raised his eyebrows. "Okay, you asked for it. You will definitely be surprised."

The server approached, and Julie exchanged pleasantries with him before Ben ordered. "We'll have two ginger ales on the rocks, please."

Julie's confused expression was priceless. She couldn't tell if he was kidding or not, and so he added, "Julie, would you like a lime with yours?"

"Ah, sure—why not? A lime would be great." Julie squinted her eyes and cocked her head to the side as the server left. "Okay, I thought you were a whisky kind of guy."

"I'm a man of mystery," he teased.

"I guess you are at that." She opened her napkin and lay it on her lap, then tapped her temple. "So, what's with the big bruise and stitches?"

"I got into a fight with a desk and lost."

"Aah, I see. I've been known to get in a fight with the leg of my couch on occasion. We came to an understanding. I told it that if it happened again, it was outa there. I think it listened, but time will tell."

"Yes, the cantankerous old couch leg. They're a menace to society and should be outlawed."

Julie picked up her drink. "Here, here!"

Ben followed suit and clinked their glasses together. They ordered their meals and then passed some time making up stories about the other guests, guessing at what their conversations might be until their food arrived. He had to admit that he was enjoying himself, but deep down, he wished Becky sat before him, wearing her Cheshire-cat smile. Ben blew on his spoon of chowder, and Julie cut into her salad.

"You know what? In all the times I've served you, I've never asked what brings you here to York Harbor. Are you here for work?"

Ben pondered her question while he tore open a small bag of oyster crackers. "Kind of? Well, not originally for that reason. I was here to say goodbye to a friend. She was more of a grandmother figure, I guess." He dipped his spoon in the chowder and gave it a slow stir. "Now, though, I'm not so sure why I'm here."

"And the mysterious, desk-fighting man remains aloof." She popped a cherry tomato in her mouth. "Next you'll be telling me you're a—'consultant.'"

Ben chuckled. "I'm not trying to be cryptic. It's just

that I'm seriously not sure what I'm doing here." He went to explain what had happened with his head injury and the fact that he could no longer do his diving job.

"So, you're kinda stuck here."

"Maybe?" he said as the server placed their entrées in front of them.

"When I asked if you were here for work, you said, *kind of.* What does kind of mean if you're not able to dive?"

"Now there lies the million-dollar question. I thought I was going to start a business with a friend. But now, I'm not so sure how that's going to play out." He took a bite of his burger.

Julie cut up a piece of asparagus. "Okay, I'm intrigued."

Ben dabbed his mouth with his napkin and took a drink, then explained the business concept that he and Becky had laid out. Time ticked by and his burger grew cold as he became more animated and excited about the venture. He shared a couple of his job training ideas: the service industry, baking, fishing, and the trades. Then expounded on teaching basic living skills like budgeting, using coupons, cooking, and anything else that would help kids that might otherwise fall through the cracks. He couldn't remember the last time he'd been this excited about anything.

"Ben, you might not be able to dive the way you used to, but maybe you could at least teach some of the basics of it to some kids? That would be considered job training, right?"

"That's a great idea, but I can't dive now." *Or maybe ever.* "I know someone who can though. Diving really centered me when I was going through some pretty hard times. I mean, sure, I was in the military when I started, but that doesn't have to be the case now, does it? It could open doors they wouldn't have otherwise."

"So, what's stopping you, then?" Julie's enthusiasm stoked his.

Ben took a couple more bites of his cold burger. *What is stopping me?* He thought about Becky and the fact she wasn't speaking to him, and made the decision that their venture was bigger than the two of them. He would not sit it out or take no for an answer.

"You know what, Julie. I was stopping me, and I'm not going to let that happen."

"Good for you! I think that calls for strawberry cheesecake, don't you?"

"Absolutely."

"How about you make that three slices of strawberry cheesecake?" Ben looked up to see Jason standing at their table. "I thought you got lost on your way back to the house, Benni Boy, and thought I better check up on you."

Jason turned toward Julie and placed his hand on her shoulder. "Is he driving you crazy yet, Jules?" He slid a chair over. "I can take him off your hands if you need me to."

"I'm barely surviving, but I think I can make it through dessert. By then, I might have reached my limit, though."

They laughed at Ben's expense, and Jason flagged the server down.

Ben was at a loss for words as he took in their comradery. "So, I take it you know each other?"

"Nope. I just randomly seek out strange women and join them for dessert. It's kind of my thing," Jason said.

"Yeah, and I especially liked that he's psychic, since he knew my name." She stood up to face Jason. "Consider me dazzled and amazed." She bowed, fluttering her cloth napkin in Jason's direction.

"Oh sure, go ahead, make fun of the man with a brain injury. I see how it is," Ben said, as if deeply hurt, then cracked a smile. "Guess it's strawberry cheesecake for three then," he said to the server. "And please add a strong black coffee. I'm going to need it to keep up with these two."

"So, are you solving third-world problems?" Jason asked.

"Not quite, but I think Ben has a pretty good start for some kids in transition."

"Cool. You patched things up with Becky, then?"

Ben grimaced and shook his head. "Not yet."

Jason gave him a stern look. "You gotta make it happen, Bud."

"I know, but it's in her court now."

Julie swallowed the last bite of her cheesecake and put her fork down. "Wow, Ben, after what you just told me about your project being bigger than the two of you, you're going to sit back and see what she decides to do?"

"Julie's right, Ben. You don't have time to just sit back. You told me yourself that there's a clock ticking."

Ben looked at Julie, then Jason. They sat staring at him. *I've never shied away from what I wanted. So why am I allowing Becky's stubbornness, or whatever it is she's dealing with, dictate our future? We need to do this. Mrs. G. chose us to do this. We just need to move forward—together.*

Ben got up from the table and dropped his napkin on his plate. "You're right. You're absolutely right."

CHAPTER 28

Rebecca stood at her kitchen counter slathering butter over a warm slice of Emily's freshly baked bread, then scooped up a spoonful of leftover beef stew. She closed her eyes while she chewed, enjoying its flavor. Mrs. Getchel had taught her how to make the beef stew on a cold winter day, much like today.

She'd come home from school feeling rather down, per her usual self, and Mrs. Getchel was browning steak tips on the stove. Rebecca had always enjoyed seeing her wearing an apron and working in the kitchen. Mrs. Getchel was a stocky, large bosomed woman of average height. She had graying chin-length hair, and wore her wire-rimmed glasses on the tip of her upturned nose.

Rebecca recalled standing in front of the pot of browning beef as Mrs. Getchel wrapped her arm around her shoulder and pulled her in close, with an added squeeze for good measure. She'd talked her through the step-by-step instructions on how to make a great beef stew. Rebecca smiled at the realization that she could reproduce the great beef stew.

Mrs. Getchel had taught her much over the years, and Rebecca was grateful to have had her in her life. She placed her soup bowl in the dishwasher while she contemplated the next quilt she'd make. Rebecca was more caught up than she thought she would be with the quilts for her list of kids. She'd sent a few away for some long-arm stitchwork. The others she'd machine stitch or tie, but for now, she needed to do something for herself.

I'll make one for me and Mrs. Getchel.

Rebecca went to her closet full of fabric and picked colors that represented the home that had now become hers. The fabrics comprised a pale yellow for the house, white for the porch, green and floral for the gardens and trees. And if she was lucky, she'd use one of Mrs. Getchel's aprons for the edging. This tiny quilt would hang in the living room, next to the one she'd done of the home where she'd grown up.

Rebecca stood at her worktable and drew the designs on paper. She carefully measured each shape and placed the pieces together like a puzzle. Time had gotten away from her, and she could feel an ache in her lower back and hands.

Rebecca examined her overall layout and was pleased with its outcome. Before calling it a night, she removed each stencil paper and laid them on top of the fabric that they belonged to. Next, she set up her portable Janome sewing machine. It would be easier to use for such a small project. Then she called it a night.

Getting her mind off Benjamin and Stepping Stones for a while was good. Thinking of what they could have had together tended to derail her. She'd lived too much of her life wishing things could have been different.

She removed her clothes and before she threw on her nightshirt, her reflection in the mirror caught her attention. Rebecca stood stoically while she stared at her image, hating her vast patchwork of rippled skin. Not only was her scarred skin ugly, but it represented the worst of herself. It stood for her selfishness, stubbornness, and rebellious nature. Her body was a tapestry of anguish, regret, and unforgiveness. At times, she thought she shouldn't hide it, but show it to the world as a warning of who she was.

Yes, it was good that Ben was going back. He deserved better than what she offered. She deserved to remain alone.

Rebecca pulled her nightshirt over her head and welcomed sleep. In sleep, the world wasn't real. It couldn't torment her the way her waking moments taunted her throughout the day. She felt as if the day teased her into thinking that life could be different, but it ended with another bitter pill to swallow. She cursed herself for thinking that maybe her fate had changed, that Ben was her answer to a new hope—a new beginning. Now, she had absolutely no idea of what her future could hold.

She finally climbed into bed and pulled the blanket up under her chin, hoping sleep would come easily. Ben still circled around in her mind. She touched her lips, recalling his mouth upon hers, and wished she could still feel his warmth. Did he ever think of her? Was he sleeping and dreaming wonderful dreams of the sea and all it held in its depth, or was he, too, lying awake wondering what his future held?

Rebecca worried for him and prayed that he'd get to dive again someday. It brought him solace and joy. She couldn't help but think of Ben in Hawaii and imagined what his world was like there. Rebecca pictured him frolicking in the waves like they used to do when they were kids. Oh, how she longed to see him carefree again.

He'd been a lanky kid, but now, his shoulders were broad. He had muscular legs, and could pick her up and throw her over his shoulder as if she were a ragdoll. She smiled, thinking about his excitement. Had she only laughed instead of screamed, their lives would be on a totally different track— one with a future together.

Sleep didn't come. Soon the blanket felt heavy on her chest. She kicked it off with a fit, rolled over as if she were a child having a tantrum, and pounded her pillow. Rebecca didn't want to admit it, but she wasn't ready to let go of Benjamin Daly. He'd come back into her life for a reason, but for what? Perhaps he was only there as a catalyst for her new venture, and she was meant to pursue it on her own.

She certainly couldn't consider him a romantic interest because he hadn't given her any sign that he was attracted to her, with the exception of that spontaneous kiss, and she was sure he'd quickly regretted that kiss. Rebecca thought again about his warm, soft lips and the feel of his strong arms around her. She shook her head, rejecting the impossible.

No, she thought, *he's leaving*.

An aching of sorrow and disappointment found its way in to her heart. The same ache that came after every loss in her life. Before long, her sorrow turned into acceptance. She'd lived without him before, and she could live without him again.

Rebecca fell into a restless sleep and woke with a jolt. She remembered something the lawyer had said, scrambled through the papers scattered on her desk. Hands shaking, she reread the part about the trust's conditions. *Develop and operate equally and jointly.* There was no work around. They *must* do this together, all of it, or they'll disappoint Mrs. Getchel by failing to fulfill her wishes. And she'd lose her home.

CHAPTER 29

Daylight was breaking as Ben lay in bed or as near as you could call a bed. His back and shoulder hurt from the mattress. His feet hung over the end in the too-small a bed. He was grateful to have a place to stay, but it would not do for much longer. He sat up and rubbed his hand. It had fallen asleep, and he couldn't feel his pinky finger. As soon as the tingling of his hand awakened, he stirred from the bed.

Clyde, Jason's cat, leaped onto the bed and meowed so intensely that he sounded as if he were half starving, but Clyde's looks suggested otherwise. He rubbed the cat's head before placing it back on the floor, then pulled on a pair of jeans. "Let's get you something to eat, fatso."

Ben's bare feet were cold against the tile floor. He scooped out Clyde's food. Clyde's black-and-gray fur weaved around Ben's ankles in anticipation of his breakfast.

"My turn now," he said as he gave the cat another rub on the head.

He opened the fridge and took out a container of almond milk, then rummaged through the cupboard for some cereal. He grabbed the Wheaties and poured them in to a bowl, then peeled a banana. As he sliced the banana, he noticed Jason's car wasn't in the driveway. He tried to remember if he'd heard him come home in the night, but nothing came to mind, and Ben figured Jason had left for work early.

Once again, the cat graced Ben with his presence. This time Clyde had leaped onto the table and poked his nose toward Ben's bowl. "Oh, no you don't," he said. "This is all mine."

As Clyde pushed his nose toward Ben's, Ben reciprocated. Clyde's yellow eyes peered into his as if searching for his deepest thoughts. "You don't want to hear about it, you fur ball."

The cat meowed as if he disagreed.

"Okay, you asked for it," Ben said in a soothing tone.

Clyde slid his body down, sprawling across the table.

"Didn't Jason teach you it's not polite for you to lie on the table?" Ben waited for Clyde to respond. "No? Well, who am I to tell you otherwise, then?"

Ben scooped up the last slice of banana with his spoon while he considered what his deepest thoughts actually were. "Well, Clyde, I gotta tell ya. I'm confused, and I don't take that lightly. I'm usually pretty decisive." Ben stared at the cat's mesmerizing eyes. "But you don't know Becky Mills. She'd got me befuddled and, I dare say, her eyes are darn near as beautiful as yours."

"So, you're hitting on cats now?" Jason said as he sluggishly made himself a coffee.

"Good Lord, Jason, you about scared the crap out of me. You just getting home?"

"Nah, well, kind of. Stayed out until the wee hours. Sure as heck feels like an all-nighter, though."

"Where's your car?" Ben once again looked out the window. Jason's spot in the driveway was empty.

"Left it at the Inn," Jason said dryly.

"Oh?" Ben leaned back in his chair and shifted in his seat to see Jason more directly, "Do tell."

Jason removed his coffee cup from the Keurig and pulled out a chair. "Julie and I stayed in the common room most of the night talking."

"Talking," Ben said with a snicker.

"Yes, talking."

Ben considered Jason's story, and he could see how that might be possible. She was a pretty great conversationalist, and Jason was too.

"So, what's with the car, then?"

Jason took a drink from his mug. "Well, between the drinks, the warm fire, and exhaustion, let's just say I wasn't in the best driving shape."

"She had to drive you home?" Ben laughed and slapped his hand on the table.

"For the love of all things holy." Jason cradled his head in his hands. "Please, take it down a notch, will ya?"

"Oh, I'm sorry," Ben said in a near holler. "I didn't mean to give you a headache, because believe you me, I know what a headache feels like."

"You're an ass," Jason said in a whisper.

"Maybe you should go take a nappy and sleep it off."

"I can't. Got a meeting at work."

"Alrighty then." Ben stood to grab a coffee for himself. "Need a lift to your car, or is Julie picking you up?"

"She was my second choice." Jason held his mug to his chin, breathing in the heat.

"I'm flattered." Ben gave him a devilish grin and sat down.

"Oh, get over yourself. I figured you'd be up with nothing better to do, and that way, Julie could get some sleep."

"Well, don't you have me all figured out. That's me—the guy with nothing better to do." Ben leaned back in the chair and rubbed his finger on the rim of his coffee cup. "How long do you think I should give her to call me before I try to reach out again?"

"Rebecca?"

"Yes, Becky." Ben threw his hands up. "Who else do you think I could be talking about?"

"Well, you were taking a pretty good liking to Clyde."

Ben swatted Jason on the back of the head. "Now look who's the ass."

"What the heck!" Jason moaned as he rubbed his temples. "Seriously. I need to be at work by 9:00. Are you good with that?"

"You bet." Ben downed the rest of his coffee.

"Thanks—and about Rebecca. Don't tell me you didn't go see her last night and deal with it?"

"No, I thought maybe it was best if—"

"Ben, buddy, you know you can't wait for her to call you. You know her well enough to know that she's stubborn and always has been. I'd suggest you make another move before too much distance grows between you again."

Ben let that percolate for a moment, then nodded. "I'm

going to hop in the shower, and I'd suggest you grab yourself another cup of coffee." Ben set his mug in the sink and headed toward the door. "And Jason . . . thanks."

Jason waved him off. "Don't mention it."

Clyde scurried to catch up to Ben. He skidded around the corner and up the stairs, nearly tripping Ben as he climbed the treads. "You are an ornery little guy, aren't you?"

Clyde's tail pointed straight up as he pranced the rest of the way up the steps.

Once again, Ben's thoughts drifted to Becky. Her reaction to cats surprised him. He took her as someone who might enjoy them for company. He found it odd that she'd included a cat in her quilted picture that hung in her living room.

Ben splashed warm water on his face and lathered up, recalling Becky's bathroom debacle of broken glass, cut fingers, and busted toe. But it was her scarred skin that caused him to wonder, *What happened to you, Becky?* His heart broke for her. He couldn't imagine the pain she must have endured. A shiver went up his spine before he took the last upward swipe of his razor.

The steaming shower felt good on his cold feet. He made a mental note to purchase some slippers along with a list of other items he'd need because he planned to stay in York Harbor for the rest of the winter. He hurried along so Jason wouldn't be too rushed, especially because he was running at an exceptionally slow pace. Ben laughed silently, picturing how the rest of Jason's day would go.

***

Ben pulled into the parking lot at the main gate of the base. Jason unbuckled, climbed out of the passenger's seat.

"Go see her. Now," Jason said, then shut the door behind him. Just about the time Jason made it to the front of the vehicle, Ben laid on the horn, nearly knocking Jason off his feet. Ben gave him a big smile and a wave goodbye, and Jason gave Ben the finger.

The sun was shining, and the water sparkled in the light. He pulled his shades off the visor and set them on his nose while he drove away. Ben assumed Becky would be at work by now. He'd check if her car was in the drive at Proposals and see if she could get away for a few minutes. If she wasn't there, he'd head to her apartment.

A gust of wind brought on an unexpected snow squall that lessened visibility, but he found it mesmerizing and beautiful as he took the corners. Oh, how he'd missed New England. The snow tempted him to roll down his windows to take in the coastal air, but he didn't want to fill his backseat with the fluffy stuff, so thought better of it.

Ben arrived at Becky's apartment. His chest quickened when he saw her car was in the driveway and questioned whether he should intrude. Maybe she was getting ready for work. Then he realized that if she was working her morning shift, she would have left by now.

He made a U-turn and parked in front of her place, pulled his sunglasses off and rested them on the dash, then stepped out of the car and straightened his jacket. The snow squall had turned into a more consistent steam, so he turned up his collar to the wind and hurried to her front door's landing. He didn't know what to expect. He just hoped she wouldn't slam the door in his face.

A quilted wreath wrapped with fabric patterns of holly berries, red and green plaid stripes decorated her door. A crumpled bow stared back at him. He grabbed hold of the bow and tugged on the loops to straighten the wire.

There, that's better. His nerves vanished, and he knocked on the door.

CHAPTER 30

Rebecca had seen Ben's car pull up. She couldn't believe her eyes as she spied through the window curtain. *What is he doing?* It appeared he was sticking a note on her door or something, then he knocked, which made her jump out of her skin. She momentarily considered pretending she wasn't there, but she knew he had to know she was.

Her heart raced at the thought of him seeing her in her not-expecting-company appearance, and spying no less. She hadn't showered, and still wore her nightshirt and robe. She couldn't remember if she'd brushed her teeth. She certainly hadn't run a comb through her hair.

He knocked again. *Dang it.*

"I'll be right there!" she said, as she ran to the bathroom. *He's just going to have to wait.*

She grabbed a pair of jeans out of the dryer and put them on, pulled a sweatshirt over her head, swished her mouth with some mouthwash, and ran her hands through her hair. By the time she'd reached the door, her hands were shaking, and her adrenaline was in overdrive. *I'm not ready for this.* He'd said she was supposed to reach out to him when and if she was ready to see him. And ready she was not.

Rebecca could see him through the sidelights of the door. *You're always so put together,* she thought, *and dang it if you aren't gorgeous.*

She didn't know what to expect. She hadn't seen him since his surgery. She had butterflies in her stomach and, yet, she was still hurt he planned to leave.

Rebecca had intended to reach out to him today and tell him that he couldn't just fly away, that they needed to make their venture work, *together.* Now here he stood on her doorstep, and she was thrown for a loop. *Stepping Stones needs us. The kids need us.*

She put on her cool, unphased face as best she could, and calmly opened the door. "Hi, Benjamin."

His big brown eyes penetrated through to her heated core. She couldn't quite tell if he was angry or happy to be standing face to face with her again.

He stood just outside the door with his hands in his pockets, shifting back and forth from leg to leg. His nose and tips of his ears were bright red. It was freezing out there, but she was hesitant to let him in as if everything was okay.

"Hey Becky," he said as he continued to dance back and forth. "Could I come in, please?"

Rebecca searched his face for some indication as to why he was there. His eyes pleaded with hers as he shivered.

"Yeah, sure, come on in." She opened the door wide and stepped aside, giving him room to enter. By now, she too was shivering from the cold. "It's—ah—good to see you."

"It's good to see you too, Beck." He rubbed his hands together to warm them up. "Wow, it really got cold out there. Did you see the snow?"

"No, I'm afraid I missed it. I was in the back room, focused on work." Rebecca gestured toward the hallway. A look of confusion crossed Ben's face. "My quilting room's back there."

"Oh, that's cool. It must keep you pretty busy—back there," he said as he, too, gestured down the hall. "You working on another kid's quilt?"

"No, not right now. I'm doing another wall one for myself." She pointed toward the ones that hung on her wall.

An awkward discomfort filled the room, and neither one of them knew quite how to act.

Ben blew warmth into his hands as he walked toward the small framed patchwork wall quilts, then reached out and straightened one frame that had previously caught his attention. "I'd like to see how you make these. I always thought there were patterns or something and never realized that you can just make them up."

By now, the small talk agitated Rebecca, and she wanted to know what his game was.

"What are you doing here, Ben? I'm pretty sure you didn't come to learn about my quilting." She crossed her arms, shifting her weight to one side, awaiting his response.

Ben cleared his throat. "Did you happen to go to the house recently?"

"Yes, I did. I saw the note you left for me. Thanks for not just leaving without a goodbye this time."

Ben cocked his head to the side with a squint. "I'm not following."

"You'd said you'd be leaving as soon as you can fly." She broke eye contact and played with her rings. "Which is fine. I mean you don't really owe me anything."

"I know I don't owe you anything, Becky. And honestly, I don't think you owe me anything either. But what I don't understand is why you didn't visit me at the hospital or even check to see if, I don't know, if I was dead or alive?" Ben's jaw drew tight and he seemed to have a hard time figuring out what to do with his hands. "I know you care about me, but you have to know that was kinda harsh, don't you?"

"Kind of harsh?" Rebecca could feel her face flush. She hated it when that happened because it often led to anger, and anger made her cry. She wasn't about to let Benjamin Daly see her cry—again. "You know what, Ben? If you must know, I saw you in the hospital. A lot. In the beginning anyway. What I think is harsh is you just walking away. What's harsh is having you back out on your commitment. What's harsh is you taking the easy way out again!"

By now, Ben's nostrils were flaring as he paced back and forth. "And how was I supposed to know that, Beck?"

He has a point.

Ben threw his hands in the air. "I never saw you and it's a little hard to keep a commitment when the person you're supposed to keep the commitment with doesn't talk to you and falls off the face of the planet. Wouldn't you agree?"

"Well, I learned from the best, didn't I?" Becky gritted her teeth and stared him down.

"When will you let it go, Becky? I was a kid for crying out loud. A kid that needed to make his own way in the world. The military was my best way out."

"Yep. There it is. You said it. You needed to make your

own way. Well, what about me? You said you'd always be there for me. And you weren't."

Ben sat down on the arm of the couch and clasped his hands on his lap. "Becky, what did you expect me to do if I'd stayed?"

Rebecca knew she was caught. She didn't have a clue of what he could have done for her, but the fact remained: he left her without the courtesy of keeping in touch. "I don't know for sure, but you didn't even write me. You're the one that dropped off the planet. Not me."

"So, this whole not-seeing-me-in-the-hospital thing was nothing but revenge?" Ben's face dropped. He stood up and shoved his hands in his pockets, shaking his head in disbelief.

"No! It had nothing to do with revenge," her voice softened at the realization that she was as much to blame as he was. "Not even a little bit."

Rebecca crept toward him, reached out, and rested her hand on his forearm. She slid it ever so gently down to his wrist and took hold of his hand. She didn't want to admit it, especially to him, but she wanted to say that her staying away was because she loved him and didn't want to see him get hurt because everyone she loved left her. But she couldn't say it. She wouldn't. So she skirted the truth. "I did it because I care too much for you."

Ben nodded, then pulled his hand away from hers. "You sure have a funny way of showing it." He walked toward the door. "I'm just gonna go." He turned toward her and half-cocked his mouth with a sigh. "Because I care for you too much."

With that, he stepped out and shut the door behind him.

Rebecca swung open the door as he trundled down the

stairs. She wanted desperately to ask him to stay, to say why she'd done what she'd done, and to tell him she needed him— that she'd always loved him. But the sight of his back walking away choked back her will to speak.

Rebecca shut the door and pressed her back on it. She slid down until she sat on the floor as silent tears dripped down her cheeks, soaking her sweatshirt's neckline.

Rebecca wiped her cheeks with her hands and pulled up to a stand. She peered out the window. His car was gone. Then she sluffed off toward the kitchen to make a cup of tea and grab a bite to eat, even though she wasn't hungry. Just the act of eating would give her some comfort.

Rebecca replayed what they'd said. *I cared too much. He cared too much. He left me. I wanted revenge.* The words ran through her mind like a broken record. *I said he took the easy way out, but I'm the one that's taking the easy way out.*

Rebecca slathered some honey on her English muffin, and watched as it soaked into the crannies, then took a bite. She just wished that the sweetness of the honey would make everything right, but she needed to make things right. Rebecca didn't want to beg him to stay where he wouldn't be happy because that would mean that she was the selfish one.

He was right. He had been a kid when he'd chosen to leave her to join the military. It was the best possible thing that he could have done, under the circumstances. Instead of being proud of him, she'd pouted like the child that she was. He needed to live his life, and now she needed to live hers, with or without him.

Rebecca stuffed the last of the muffin in her mouth and licked the sweet honey off her fingers, downed the rest of her tea, and strode off to get ready for work. She figured if she was ready, she could work on her quilt, right until she had to leave. At least, she thought, Proposals would calm her heart.

Today was a day of designing, drawing, and selecting. Rebecca enjoyed the research aspect of her job. She would take the bride's wish list of colors, and overall shape of the bouquets, then run with it. Yes, this work was just what the doctor ordered, a relaxing office day while Sophie pieced together arrangements, and Emily baked.

By the time Rebecca got out of the shower, she had a whole new outlook on her day. Ben still weighed on her mind, but Proposals and her patchwork quilts were what brought her joy. Joy over anguish would win the day.

CHAPTER 31

Ben felt as though he had whiplash. As he walked away from Becky's, he could sense that she was watching him, but he wasn't about to turn back. He figured he'd met his quota of rejection, and the last thing he wanted was to have her shut the door in his face.

Ben had gone there with such hope, thinking that they could at least talk about their relationship or at least about Stepping Stones, and maybe come to some kind of understanding. Some of what he'd said stung, but he was justified. It had been harsh of her to not give him a second thought when he'd needed her. After all, he'd been seriously injured at her work place. He couldn't help but think that a complete stranger would have acted in a kinder way.

Maybe he didn't know her at all. Maybe nostalgia had blinded him, but he realized she hadn't actually changed that much. She'd been withdrawn and shut him out even then. And yet, he was drawn to her like a seagull was to a french fry.

Ben was just about to turn into Jason's road but thought better of it. He'd just end up staring at the walls. He was going stir crazy and needed to be around people.

Grounds Coffee Shop seemed the place to go, he thought as he pulled up to the curb. Even with the drop in temperature, diehard customers still showed up. He stuffed his hands in his pockets while he waited for his turn to enter. Steam covered the windows, and he watched in amusement at a kid doodling on the glass. Much to his surprise, the doodles of sea life were skillfully done. The kid, who Ben thought to be around fifteen or sixteen, no sooner drew one thing before erasing it with his sleeve and breathed on the glass to form a new palette to draw another.

The aroma of freshly ground coffee beans helped to ease Ben's simmering anger. He grabbed a table for two, which happened to be next to the artistic prodigy. Ben's back was to the mother and child, and he couldn't help but overhear their conversation.

"I'm sorry, Nathan, but we can't afford it," his mom said in a hushed voice. A few seconds ticked on before she quelled the silence. "Enough with the eye rolling. That's rude."

The squeaking of the glass, indicating that the kid was once again drawing a new creation and choosing to ignore his mother. Ben had to smile. He'd been much like this kid when he was that age.

"We took you in because we wanted to help you succeed, but we never intended to—"

"I get it! You can't afford it." His voice was snarky, and Ben could only imagine how that had landed.

"Honestly, Nathan. It's as if you think we have done nothing for you at all." Her rise in pitch made her exasperation clear.

Ben took a sip of his coffee, then set it back down on the table. He rubbed his finger around the cup's brim, thinking about the woman's words to the kid: "We took you in because we wanted to help you succeed."

Ben recalled those same words spoken to him. Mrs. G. had been kneading bread. Her large hands, covered in flour, pushed the dough, then rolled it over, repeating the process. Her sturdy hands working in the dough had mesmerized him. He'd let her down that day, but for the life of him, he couldn't remember what specifically he'd done. She was the first person in his life that he didn't want to let down. Ben wondered about this Nathan kid.

"Surely there has got to be a more affordable camera for you to capture sea creatures, of all things."

"Not that can reach the depths that I need! It's not like I can swim down there myself."

"You are very talented. I'll give you that, but money doesn't grow on trees. So, if you want it bad enough, then I suggest you get a job."

"How am I supposed to do that, Mrs. Connor? I don't have any job experience, and even if I did, who'd want to hire me?"

"Nathan," she said with a softened tone, "you sell yourself too short."

"No, I don't. I know I can do whatever they ask me to do, but no one will give me a chance. It's so stupid. They want experience, but how the heck am I supposed to get experience if no one will hire me?"

Ben felt for the kid. He'd been there himself at that age. He wished he could help. He laughed silently, thinking that his funds would run out before too long, and he'd need to find employment as well. That was, unless he and Becky could get Stepping Stones up and running. At least that way, he'd have access to his portion of Mrs. G's estate.

"Can I get you a refill, Ben?"

Ben snapped out of his daydreaming at the sight of the familiar, smiling face staring down at him.

"Refill?" Jillian asked again, holding the pot at the ready.

He was grateful that her name was embroidered on her shirt, because he couldn't recall it to save his life.

"Sure, Jillian, thank you." He slid his mug closer to her, and she poured. "Seems you've got an artist on your hands." Ben tipped his head in the kid's direction.

"Seems I do. He's been improving since he first started coming here. At least it's harmless enough. One never knows what can happen with idle hands."

"Might I suggest a winter scene? I bet he'd do a great job for you." Ben didn't think it was possible, but her smile became even broader, and her eyes lit up.

"That's a great idea! Poor kid lost both his parents over the past year. His dad used to bring him here. He was such a great guy." Her gaze drifted toward Nathan and a sadness washed over her.

"Well, thanks again for the refill," Ben said, trying to bring her back to the here and now.

"Absolutely." Her bright smile once again shined, and she shot him a wink. "Now if you'll excuse me, I need to hire an artist. I might even get a busboy out of it too."

Ben sat back, taking in the conversation. Nathan jumped up and nearly toppled Jillian over, coffee and all, after Mrs. Connor had agreed to allow him to work. He'd hugged them both, and Jillian's joyous laughter filled the room.

Nathan's enthusiasm renewed Ben's own intent to move forward with Stepping Stones, whether Becky liked it or not. Nathan wasn't alone in his quest for purpose and the wish to succeed. All those kids needed was a little help, and he and Becky were the ones to do it.

He gulped down the rest of his coffee, threw on his coat, then stepped up to the counter to order a ham-and-cheese bagel sandwich to go. By now, Jillian was behind the counter, digging around for an application. He placed his order, and Jillian told the cashier that it was on the house.

"That's not necessary."

"I insist." Jillian ripped an application form off the tablet, then flung her arm in the air with triumph. "I just got a bus-boy, and I'll have the nicest looking windows in the village. I'd say the bagel sandwich is well worth it."

"Well, it looks like we have three wins, then. Thank you, Jillian."

"The thanks are all mine. It was really a good thing that you did there, you know. It isn't often that people go out of their way like that to help."

"I've been on the other side of it myself, and if it wasn't for a great lady that taught me a good deal about helping kids out, I don't know how my life would have worked out. I only hope to fill her gap."

"That sure sounds like our lovely friend, Mrs. Getchel. God rest her soul."

"The one and the same."

"She was such a kind lady. I miss seeing her popping in."

"I bet you do," Ben said, realizing that he, too, missed seeing her. Being away for so long, he hadn't given her much thought, but since he'd returned, he'd regretted that he hadn't made more of an effort. She was pivotal in his life, and she'd deserved more than a letter now and again.

Jillian was now around the counter facing him. Her jovial manner had dissipated. He didn't need or want her sympathy, and he could tell she was biting at the bit to continue the conversation. He was grateful when the girl handed him the brown paper bag that contained his sandwich.

"Jillian, thanks again for this," he said as he waved the bag in his hand. "But I have to get going, and I think Nathan is waiting for that." he nodded toward the paper she held in her grasp.

Jillian glanced down at the paper in hand as if it were a foreign object she had no idea how it got there. Her momentary memory lapse vanished. "Seems you are correct. It was nice to see you here at Grounds again, Ben."

"It was good to be seen."

With that, Ben scooted out the door to his car. His next stop would be Mrs. G's. He really didn't know what he would do when he got there, but he was sure it was where he needed to be.

CHAPTER 32

The goings in and out, meetings with clients, and an impromptu tour of the venue made the day go by quickly. Rebecca was relieved that she could focus on the work and not wallow on her altercation with Ben. She flipped over the Closed sign and lazily trod through the parking lot to her car.

A whisper of laughter spilled through the night air. Sophie and Brady were in their kitchen. Sophie was stirring something in a large pot on the stove, while Brady entertained Samantha. Little Sam sat on the island's countertop. Her bunny slippers dangled over the edge.

Rebecca's mind raced back to the times that she, too, had sat on the counter of her childhood home. Her father had made rabbit ears with his fingers while his deep voice sang out the tune of *Little Bunny Foo Foo*. He'd been such a wonderful dad. If she'd only realized then that she'd have such a short time with him, she would have made every moment count.

Now, she stood there in the world, as though she were

looking at life in a snow globe from the outside. Life was happening all around her, but she wasn't a part of it. She was simply an observer, a non-participant in this thing called life.

Ben creeped back into her life, and she was, unwilling to embrace the little time that she had with him. *I haven't learned.*

She was just about to climb into her car when Sophie flicked on the porch light and opened the door. Daisy came pouncing out, then stopped abruptly as if she'd hit an invisible wall. The cat stared at her, then cautiously approached. Rebecca's pulse quickened as Daisy sat at her feet, peering up as if to say, "I'm here for you."

Rebecca didn't expect her sudden burst of emotions. Her cheeks were cold as a brisk wind blew across the tears that ran down her cheeks. She wiped the tears away while Daisy continued to look at her. All she could think about was her own beautiful cat from her childhood. The one that changed her life forever. Rebecca brought her hand to her chest and thumped her chest a few times. That simple act made Daisy spring into her arms, just as her cat Greta had always done.

"Well, what do you know, Daisy May? You know that trick, too."

Rebecca caressed Daisy, and the cat responded with a purr and nuzzle under Rebecca's chin. The softness of her fur warmed the chill running through her. She hadn't held a cat like this since that fateful night, and she missed it. The comfort of holding Daisy as she peered into her eyes, led her to believe that the cat understood the pain that she'd gone through, the tremendous loss, the uncontrollable waves of guilt, the hatred that she had for herself, and the fear of abandonment.

Rebecca had kept those feelings bottled up inside, a kind

of self-inflicted punishment for what she'd done. Yet, the cat she held seemed to ease the cork ever so slightly. Surprisingly, Rebecca was reluctant to put the cat down, but it was getting late and she wanted to stop by the house to search for one of Mrs. Getchel's aprons. She gave Daisy a kiss on the top of her head and set her on the ground. Daisy strutted off with her tail raised high, as if she knew she'd accomplished something significant.

Life is too short. If I can hold a cat without the world caving in, then maybe I can let Ben in, too.

She'd known the expression, better to have loved and lost, than never to have loved at all. She'd heard that adage more times than she could count, but that expression came from people that had never had the kind of loss she'd borne. They meant well; she knew that. But the sentiment had been lost on her, until this moment. *Life is too short.*

Rebecca made sure she could see Daisy, put the car in reverse, and navigated to Mrs. Getchel's.

The moon was full and cast shadows, but she no longer feared the shadows. They were almost comforting. It was as if they were saying, "It's okay to not fully expose everything. It's okay to hide your pain—your scars—to stay in the safety of hiding because when the light comes, the shadows will be gone." For now, the shadows would remain and that gave her peace, knowing that she could step into the light when she was ready. Daisy had given her every reason to believe that, one day, she'd stand firmly in the light, exposing all of who she was and what she'd done.

As she approached the house, she noticed that the lights were on. *I didn't leave the lights on, did I?*

She hadn't noticed Ben's car until she was pulling into the

driveway. An instantaneous jolt of adrenaline shot through her body. Rebecca sighed, closed her eyes, and slouched into the seat, trying to calm her emotions. What would she say to him? The longer she sat there, the more anxious she got, so she took a deep breath, let it out, and opened the car door. *Life is too short.* She proceeded to the side entry with her heart pounding, hoping that their time together wouldn't end in another confrontation.

"Bohemian Rhapsody" blared and Ben sang along, using a massive wrench as his microphone. She stood back and leaned against the door. *Well, what do you know? He can hit the high notes.* He was in his own little world. Once again, she envisioned the snow globe syndrome, and no longer wanted to be on the outside, looking in.

She wanted to be a part of the fun. It was as if she were standing on the edge of a diving board afraid to jump, but she took the step anyway. So, when the lyrics, "Let him go," began, she sang out as loudly as she could. Ben didn't miss a step. He twirled around and continued to play the part of Freddie Mercury, much to her delight. Their duet ended in laughter.

"What are you doing here, besides the obvious on-stage performance, of course?" she asked.

"I was bored and figured there would be stuff to do around here to keep me busy," he said as he held the mock microphone in his grasp.

Rebecca now noticed the cabinet doors under the sink were open. A corroded pipe fitting lay on the floor. He'd replaced the old sink fixture.

"Alrighty then. You've been busy, but it was just a drippy faucet. You really didn't need to—"

"It drove me crazy—the dripping. Figured I'd just replace

the whole thing. It wasn't good for large pots anyway, and I use a lot of large pots when I cook."

He cooks? She could envision him with no shirt, and an apron wrapped around his hips, soup spoon in hand. A warmth ran through her body. "And what is it you plan on cooking?"

"Anything we want."

The word *we* didn't slip by her unnoticed. Butterflies fluttered at the idea of *we. Perhaps we've turned a corner.* She smiled at the concept before putting him to the test. "Anything you say?"

"Anything," he said with a smug confidence.

"Okay then. It's too late tonight, but tomorrow, I think I'd like to have chicken and dumplings. From scratch."

"Of course, from scratch. There's no other way. Unless you don't want good chicken and dumplings."

"Oh, I don't want good chicken and dumplings; I want superb chicken and dumplings," she said with a flick of her fingers to her lips.

"Is there anything else you'd wish, mademoiselle?"

Indeed, there is. She tried to shake the image of his ripped abs and low-lying apron from her mind as best she could. "Nope, that should do it." Her cheeks warmed as she stepped toward the new faucet and turned it on. "Well, I sure hope your cooking is better than your plumbing."

Ben squatted and reached into the cabinet and turned a valve. Water poured out with no leaks. He brushed his hands together, with obvious enthusiasm at his success.

"I made a rough list of repairs that need to be done around here. That way, I can work on it while you're at Proposals." He added the monkey wrench to the makeshift toolbox and set it on the counter.

"Are you sure we should do that? We don't even know if the town will approve Stepping Stones, and if they don't, you'll have done all the work for nothing?"

"Hogwash. We'll get the approval."

Rebecca couldn't help but wonder what had changed since their last heated discussion, but she didn't want to bring it up and ruin the good time they were having together now. "Seems to me you need an actual tool box before you work on anything else." She pointed to the old wooden box. "Where did you get that?"

"It was in the garage, way in the back. I'll scrounge around some more, as well as in the basement, to see what else she might have lying around, tool wise. I'll run to the hardware store for whatever else I might need."

"We need to get crackin' on a budget, too." The light-heartedness of the earlier moment drifted out of the room like a fog rolling over the water. "If we're really going to do this thing, we need to do it right."

"Agreed, so let's do this thing," Ben said as he reached out for a handshake, and she reciprocated. "Okay then, if you could name one room in the house that makes a house a home, what would it be?"

"The kitchen, without question. Everyone bonds over food, don't you think?" Rebecca replied.

"Absolutely. I think it's where I've had my most meaningful conversations. I can't tell you how many talks Mrs. G. and I had in front of this sink and at that table." He sighed and a slight grin washed over his face. "Many times, you were the topic of that conversation."

"I was not!" A wave of contradictory thoughts rolled through her mind. *He did like me. Or, maybe, they were talking about how pathetic I was. But he was smiling when he just said that.*

"Indeed you were." A wider grin appeared.

"Well, you can't just lay that on me and expect me to brush it under the rug." She stepped away from Ben, who leaned against the counter, and sat down at the table. He now wore a full-on smile as he walked toward her and pulled out a chair of his own.

"Spill it, Benjamin."

"She worried about you, you know."

Her heart sank. *So, it was about me being a pathetic kid.* "She worried about all of us, including you." Rebecca leaned forward, and traced the pattern of the tablecloth with her finger.

"I imagine so, but she seemed to take a personal interest in you. I think she saw something in you she didn't want you to lose."

She saw something in me? "I don't know about that. As you know, I'm a pretty closed book. Even you've told me as much."

"Truer words have never been spoken, but nothing says that book needed to be opened for others to see your essence. Maybe you'd been writing a new one all along. A book that started with a word, paragraph, page, and before you knew it, you'd written new chapters. With each word, you exposed more of yourself than you may have realized. But your story is far from over, Becky. In fact, I believe you're in the middle of writing a series, the series of Becky Mills—after the pain."

Rebecca's throat tightened at his words. Words she'd never imagine coming from Ben. She dropped her head and closed her eyes. *I'm still in pain. I'm always in pain.*

She pulled her hand away at the unexpected touch of Ben's against hers. "Sorry, I…"

"It's okay. I just wasn't expecting that." She shook her head to snap herself out of her downward spiral. "Surely you and Mrs. Getchel must have had more interesting conversations," she said as she leaned back in the chair.

"Yep. For one, she'd noticed that I'd taken a liking to you, and she had, on many occasions, strongly suggested that such a relationship wouldn't be wise because you were too young."

"You didn't!" Becky could feel the heat rise to her cheeks. "We were just friends." The lightheartedness found its way into her heart once again. Elbows on the table, she leaned closer to him. She chewed on her thumbnail while she tried to read his expression.

"Yeah, only because she warned me enough times. You didn't see all the times she'd swat me with a hand towel, or give me 'the look.'"

"Trust me, you weren't alone in that regard, but I learned to be quicker than the towel. Then she'd point her finger at me, along with 'the look.'"

"Ah, you got the double I'm-watching-you treatment," Ben said with a smirk.

"Yep. I think between us, we were a handful because we'd had some similar conversations while snapping green beans and peeling potatoes."

Ben and Rebecca spent the next couple of hours eating takeout, meatball subs and chips from the pizza place up the road, and writing a wish list of what needed to be done to the house. They'd considered opening the kitchen up into the living area, but after much consideration, they agreed to keep it set apart from the rest of the house. Too many moments of growth had happened in the confines of the intimate kitchen.

However, Ben wanted to at least update the cabinetry and fixtures. Rebecca pictured herself standing in front of the sink, washing potatoes, or sitting at the table, snapping beans just as Mrs. Getchel had done and imagined the faces and lives of those who'd sit across from her would be. The realization of what she and Ben were about to undertake was, by any stretch of the imagination, the biggest thing she'd ever do in her life.

"I miss her, Ben."

"So do I, honey, so do I."

CHAPTER 33

Rebecca sat hunched over her quilting table and hand stitched the last letter onto the quilt for a young man who'd recently been placed in the system. Rebecca learned he was a local teen that enjoyed drawing and that his specialty was sea life. As she ran her fingers across the silken threads, hoping that she'd chosen the right words.

I,

Nathan Monroe,

am talented and will shine

The patchwork revealed ocean waves in hues of blue, green, gray, and white. A border of anchors and sea creatures encased a background of navy. The center of the quilt featured a ray of light beaming out, as if the water had burst open to allow the sun to shine.

Her hope was that each sentiment she stitched would instill in each child the will to live up to the message. Even though God hadn't answered her prayers in the past, she closed her eyes and prayed that Nathan would have a great life ahead of him, and that he'd be brave while he struggled to find his footing.

She wrapped the quilt in tissue paper and set it in a box. Rebecca made it a point to wrap each gift and not simply place it in a gift bag. Wrapped boxes, in her opinion, showed special care and purpose. To her, they showed love. She tied the navy package with natural raffia ribbon and attached a card with a sand dollar design that read, "*Made especially for Nathan Monroe.*"

Rebecca placed the gift next to the door so she wouldn't forget it when she headed out. She filled another thermos of coffee and looked over the tasks they'd completed for Stepping Stones, and the ones still left to do. Rebecca was ecstatic with the progress she and Ben had made with Stepping Stones over the past few weeks, and she was grateful that she was able to edit the planning and zoning forms to better match their vision. The town meeting was set for next week. She and Ben had decided to have Stepping Stones be an in-transition place for kids who'd aged out. It would provide counsel, skills, and job training, as well as an after-school and summer learning center for teens still in the system.

Next on her list was to pound out the details with Sophie and Emily about the gala that she and Ben would hold at Proposals. Sophie and Emily had thrilled her when they'd approached her a few weeks prior, asking how they could help, knowing that getting Stepping Stones ready would pull her away from Proposals. She'd never considered having a gala, and their expertise at throwing events was just what she and Ben needed.

The gala's goal would be to bring potential mentors for the trades, arts, and professional apprenticeships to the kids at Stepping Stones, as well as fundraising. She was beyond pleased when Sophie had offered to mentor time-management and event-planning skills. Emily offered a baking class, and Brady was excited to bring on an apprentice for both construction and photography. Even Proposals' sweet elderly neighbors, and constant patrons, Mr. and Mrs. Templeton offered to teach kids about gardening and transplanting.

Ben, on the other hand, was pleased to offer a water safety course and an introduction to scuba fundamentals, but Ben reluctantly had to hand off the diving aspect to Jason.

Even Jillian wanted in on the excitement and offered to mentor restaurant management skills, while Duncan would teach music or accounting.

Rebecca was at a crossroads. She needed to spend much of her time running the day-to-day tasks at Stepping Stones, but she hoped she could find time to offer some sewing classes, and perhaps a little floral arranging.

Rebecca reviewed the invitation to the gala and prepared the press release for the event. She was hoping beyond all hope that it would prove a smashing success. She still had her doubts and worries about the town's final approval. Rebecca didn't enjoy setting her hopes too high; she'd been let down too many times before. She took in a deep breath and envisioned success before letting out a slow exhale.

Well, Rebecca Mills, you are at the point of no return now. So, suck it up, and do what needs to be done.

She smiled at the memory of Mrs. Getchel saying that to

her for the first time. Rebecca had laughed when Mrs. Getchel had said, "Suck it up." It was as close to using a swear word as she'd ever gotten, but it had, in fact, caused Rebecca to suck it up.

Rebecca pulled her hat over her ears, threw on her coat, grabbed the gift quilt, and headed out the door. When she reached for her thermos of coffee part way to work, she found an empty spot. She'd left it on the counter. *To Grounds I go.*

She hadn't gone to Grounds in a while. She'd give a quick hello to Jillian and grab a couple of chais for Sophie and Emily. They were addicted to them, and Rebecca figured it would be a nice addition to their meeting.

Rebecca opened the door and a blast of warmth welcomed her. The aroma of coffee beans wafting in the air gave her a lift. Grounds was full, per usual, and the chatter and clinking spoons gave comfort to her soul.

She stood in line and noticed a new kid busing. He was a fair-skinned young man with untamed blond hair. The kid tilted his head to keep his bangs from getting into his eyes and kept his gaze on the task at hand, avoiding onlookers. His spindly arms lifted the tray of mugs and plates with relative ease as he wandered through the seats on his way to the kitchen. Jillian approached her with her bright smile.

"Hey, Rebecca. I hope things go well for your big meeting next Thursday. Oh, and Duncan told me about the gala you're planning; it sounds wonderful!"

"Thanks," Rebecca said as Jillian scurried past her.

"I'll be expecting an invitation!" She passed Margo Bennington and her group of adoring ladies that everyone secretly referred to as cackling hens.

Mrs. Bennington stiffened her back and her eyes lit up. "Invite? Do tell."

Oh great, just what I needed. Rebecca forced a smile. "Hello, Mrs. Bennington."

"What might you be planning? A soirée?"

Rebecca wanted to blurt out that it was none of her busybody's business, but she succumbed to the demands of polite society. "I'm planning a gala for Stepping Stones."

"So that's what you're naming your 'project'—Stepping Stones?"

"Yes, me and my business partner are opening a learning center for kids in the foster—"

"Yes," Mrs. Bennington snapped. "I'm quite aware of what you're attempting to do. Mark my words, the historical society will have a great deal to say about changing an historical home into an unseemly place of business."

Rebecca wasn't about to let her get under her skin. "Actually, it's called Stepping Stones: A Bridge to Success. I'm confident that we've done everything that we can to please the historical society."

"Oh, have you now? We'll see about that." She dabbed the corners of her mouth and glared at Rebecca. "Seems to me that those kids would be better served elsewhere than in the community of York Harbor."

"Oh, and why is that, Margo?" Rebecca was walking on thin ice, but she wasn't about to let Mrs. Bennington degrade Stepping Stones or her future kids.

She cleared her throat. "Norma Getchel did the best she could for those kinds of kids, but that time has passed and it's time to move on. Our community has done its good deed as far as we are concerned."

By now the buzz at Grounds had come to a halt and all patrons gazed at Rebecca, awaiting her response.

"Those 'kinds of kids' as you call them are also a part of this community, and have graciously contributed to it. Perhaps, Margo, if you are so concerned, you might wish to contribute your time to better their lives instead of dismissing them."

"My time is better served with people that can impact the community in a positive way, not on a bunch of delinquents that won't amount to anything. Surely you can understand—"

The crash of a tray behind her brought Mrs. Bennington out of her seat. Indignation spewed out of her in sputters at the coffee, tea, and cocoa that now dripped from her clothes and hair.

She turned her attention toward the busboy. He froze. "You did that on purpose, didn't you?"

"No! I—"

"And this is exactly what I was referring to. This is an example of one of your delinquents right here."

"That's enough Mrs. Bennington," Jillian snapped. "I think it's best you leave and get yourself cleaned up."

Jillian stood stoically, and Rebecca could almost feel the air in the room disappear with the inward gasps of those around her.

Margo Bennington's eyes glared and she pushed out her chest like the hen that she was and stared Jillian down.

"Now, Mrs. Bennington!" Jillian said, matching Mrs. Bennington's glare.

Mrs. Bennington gathered her belongings, and she and her fellow hens stormed toward the door with a huff. Mrs. Bennington stopped short, causing her hens to bump into each other. "You can be sure I will do everything in my power to stop this atrocity from continuing. York Harbor is no place for the likes of you." She pointed in the kid's direction. "Norma Getchel is gone. As sure as I stand here today, you can count on this project, this *disgrace* to our community will never open."

Margo stuffed her thick arms into the sleeves of her coat and clutched her handbag. Her eyes now bored into Rebecca's. "You, my dear, have crossed the wrong woman."

With that, she stormed out with her pointy nose high in the air, along with the hens, waddling behind.

A few people stood and cleaned up the broken dishes off the floor. Another customer wrapped her arm around the stunned boy and swept his hair out of his eyes. Jillian brushed her hands over her apron and swallowed hard.

"I'm so sorry for the interruption of your morning. I'd be happy to offer you a cup on the house for your troubles," Jillian said as she forced a smile.

"I don't need a free coffee," said one man. "But you can give that young man the cost of one as a tip."

"Here, here," shouted the patrons in unison.

Jillian's smile was now genuine. "I will be happy to do just that."

"Here's to Jillian!" a lady from the back of the room raised her mug.

By now, clapping and cheers filled the coffee shop.

"It's about time someone put that pompous windbag in her place!"

"I'll help with Stepping Stones, Rebecca," said a gentleman from the corner of the room.

"Me too," said a lady busy wiping the floor with napkins.

"Count me in too!" chimed others.

Rebecca stood with tears rolling down her face. Gratitude

was something she'd seldom experienced. She caught the eyes of the young busboy. A knowing glance of understanding passed between them. She nodded and gave him a grin as she wiped her tears. He smiled in return. This, she thought, is why she was going to do what she'd set out to do. She wanted to make an impact in a child's life. Kids like him—and like her.

"That was brave of you to stand up to Margo." Rebecca gave Jillian's hand a squeeze. "Thank you. I know with the likes of her that this has the potential of bad press for you and Grounds."

"Don't mention it. She's had it coming for a long time." Jillian patted the top of Rebecca's hand. "Besides, for all we know, it might have been good for business. She and her lady friends take up my tables for too much of the days, anyway. Now, if you'll excuse me, I need to make sure that young man is okay. Poor thing, with all his other troubles, it just breaks my heart."

"Of course." Rebecca's mind reeled in that moment. "Just a quick question for you, though. What's his name?"

"Oh, that's Nathan. He's such a sweet kid. Talented, too. I just hope for his sake he doesn't get too cynical and untrusting." She gave a pouty face, then shifted to a smile. "I must be off, but please know that I'm in your corner with the whole Margo thing and with Stepping Stones. But you already know that."

Jillian bounced off, her ponytail swaying behind her. Rebecca took in the scene of Jillian giving what she assumed to be pep talk to Nathan. *Nathan, hmm.* She thought about the quilt she'd just completed for a local teen named Nathan, then shook off the thought as ridiculous. Her mind quickly shifted as a few people approached her to learn more about

Stepping Stones and asked how they might help.

To her dismay, they had more questions than she knew how to answer. The only thing that she could come up with to tell them was the date and time of the planning meeting and that their support would mean a great deal.

By the time she left Grounds, her head was spinning. Mrs. Bennington's threat rocked her. She dreaded the thought of battling against Margo.

CHAPTER 34

Mrs. G's home was transforming right before his eyes. Ben stood back to see the living room as a whole with the old, yellowed-pineapple wallpaper removed. His hands were sticky with paste and strips of paper hung from his hair. Ben scooped up the piles of mucky paper from the floor and slopped them into the construction-size trash bag.

His head ached once again. His brain had, he hoped, enough time to heal by now, but pain still ebbed and flowed, causing him to get dizzy. He wobbled over to the overstuffed chair covered with a sheet.

The dreadful thought that he may never get to deep-dive again covered him like the sheet he sat on. It was almost as if he were homesick. A feeling of being somewhere that was supposed to be home, but wasn't. The gnawing feeling in the pit of his stomach he found unsettling.

Ben leaned over and took a swig of water from the gallon jug sitting on the floor by his feet. He wiped his upper lip with the back of his hand, then picked up his tools. He smiled as thoughts of Becky slipped into his mind once again. She'd given him the shiny red toolbox the day they'd finished their to-do list.

"Congratulations!" she'd said. "We've moved from planning to doing. So, you better get to it."

He'd told her that he was already doing it, and competently. His biggest concern with the work was that it might be in vain. He had a sinking feeling that Mrs. Bennington's attempt to stop Stepping Stones from proceeding would prove successful. She had an influence that stretched far and wide. They couldn't underestimate her.

Ben glanced down at his phone and realized that his alarm had never gone off. An instantaneous shot of adrenaline course through his body at the thought of being late for his and Rebecca's appointment with the attorney. Ben glanced around the room and huffed at the still-messy room. He'd hoped to have everything cleaned up before leaving, but at least, he'd finished the actual task of removing the wallpaper.

Ben took off toward the bathroom, grateful that he'd thought to bring a change of clothes. He'd showered there a few times before, allowing him the ability to jump right in the steaming water. The feel of the water rolling over him was refreshing, and for once, it didn't make his tender head injury sting. Within a minute, he was drying off and reaching for his clothes, which he now realized he'd left in a bag in the living room. *Damn it.*

Ben wrapped the thin terrycloth towel around his waist and swung the creaky bathroom door open. He slipped down the hardwood floor hallway, then skidded as he suddenly came face to face with Becky. She stared at him with a gaping mouth and wide-eyes. He couldn't stop and crashed into her, knocking them off balance. Becky gasped as they landed with a sprawl.

Ben scrambled to his feet, then realized that he'd managed to lose the towel he'd worn. He stood completely exposed. Becky's face reddened.

"Okay," he said breathlessly. "I say we're now even on the naked-bathroom thing."

"We are." Her smile grew wide and a giggle escaped her. Within moments, she was in full-fledged hysteria.

Ben wasn't sure whether to laugh or hide himself. He suddenly felt exposed in a way he'd never experienced before. Sure, he'd stood naked before women more times than he'd care to admit, but he'd never been laughed at.

Becky clutched at her stomach as her laughter rolled on. He retrieved the dampened towel Becky held up to him and wrapped it around his waist once again.

"We're gonna be late, you know," he said as he gazed down at her as she continued her laughing fit.

"I don't think. I've ever. Seen you so. Flustered," she said as she attempted to wipe the tears from her cheeks. "It's hysterical."

"Clearly," he said as the smile he could no longer contain fell across his face. "I'm just going to grab my bag." He pointed in the direction of the canvas bag on Mrs. G's chair. "Give me a minute?"

"Of course." Rebecca glanced at her watch. "But please hurry so we won't be late."

CHAPTER 35

Rebecca watched as Benjamin strutted along the hallway. The towel now draped dangerously low on his hips. She could make out the form of his tight bottom with each step he took. He was a handsome man, and she found it hard to look away.

She didn't mean to laugh when they'd collided, but the thought of being wrapped up with him as he lay naked over her had made her nervous. He was taking her laughter as amusement, and that was just fine with her. If he knew the true reason for her laughter, she would have died of embarrassment.

She could feel the ache between her legs intensify at the thought of being intimate with him. Rebecca wanted to experience what it would feel like to touch his warm, naked body entwined with hers. She wanted to bring his mouth to hers and take in his taste. She wanted so much, but her desires could never be fulfilled. They were business partners that once had childhood crushes, nothing more.

Rebecca ran her hand over the coarse plaster. The bare

walls were canvases of potential. She tried to envision what they would look like with the French-blue paint she'd picked. She wanted to provide the feeling of comfort and calm, something that would diffuse anxiety and stress. As much for her own wellbeing as those that would enter the doors of Stepping Stones.

Rebecca sensed him nearby, and turned. Ben's full figure stood with his arms crossed over his chest. It accentuated the muscles in his biceps, and she couldn't look away. He leaned carefree against the wall.

"Penny for your thoughts," Ben said it with a slightly cocked grin. "You happy?"

Again, she flushed, recalling her thoughts moments ago. "Yeah, I'm happy. You got a lot done today." She brushed her hands together to remove the damp remnants of plaster and paste sticking to her palms.

"It's progress." Ben sauntered toward Rebecca. The ever-present smirk deepened as he neared. "I'm pretty pleased with what I see, too."

Rebecca looked away from his gaze. "Yep, progress."

He reached his hand up and, ever so carefully, placed a loose strand of hair behind her ear. "We should get going."

Rebecca's breathing hitched, and she hoped he hadn't noticed. "Yeah . . .we should go. Don't want to be later than we already are."

Ben casually draped his arm over her shoulders. "Shall we?" He gestured toward the door. He grabbed his coat as they proceeded down the front porch stairs.

"I don't know why I'm so nervous," Rebecca said.

Ben stopped her before they reached the car. "We've done everything Mr. Howard has asked of us so far. We're just going to make sure our ducks are in a row for the planning meeting. I'm sure if there was a problem, he'd have let us know by now."

"You're probably right, but you don't know Mrs. Bennington the way I do. She's got a lot of power and connections. What if she knows something we don't?"

"Then we'll cross that bridge when we get to it." He gave her a peck on the forehead, then opened the car door for her.

Ben's confidence was reassuring, but still she couldn't ignore Margo Bennington's conniving ways. That woman was capable of just about anything.

Chapter 36

Ben and Rebecca took their seats in the unimposing attorney's office. They sipped their coffee as they awaited his arrival. Becky looked as though she were crawling out of her skin. She wouldn't stop fidgeting and her nervous energy was getting the best of him. Either that or the overly strong coffee. Ben rested his hand on her thigh to settle her nerves. She breathed a deep sigh and took another sip.

Ben set his mug down and rested his elbows on his knees, his thumb rubbed the inside of his opposing palm. He didn't want to admit it, but he was anxious, too. Mrs. Bennington's threats to stop Stepping Stones from moving forward put both of them in a precarious situation. He wasn't so much concerned about Rebecca's financial situation because she still had a career, but if this didn't work, he'd be without an income or the benefit of the inheritance. He was unsure of what he'd do at that point, and that realization didn't sit well with him.

Mr. Howard pushed open the doors with a stack of papers in hand. He wore a bright smile and walked on his toes as he approached.

"Ms. Mills." He nodded. Just as Rebecca and Ben started to stand, he added, "Mr. Daly. Please stay seated, be comfortable." The unkempt papers flopped in his grasp. "Thank you for coming in. Much appreciated."

"No problem," Rebecca said with a reassuring expression that Ben knew was forced. "Please call me Rebecca."

She prefers Rebecca over Becky... hmm.

"Great. Good. Well, let's look at what you've got for me, shall we?"

Ben pulled out a folder he'd stuffed between himself and the cushioned arm of the chair. He hoped they'd met all the requirements thus far.

Mr. Howard clicked his tongue and bobbed his head up and down as he scanned through the contents of Ben's folder. Ben sat stiffly until he realized Becky had rested her hand on his knee.

"You've been busy. Your receipts are in order. You're now registered with the state as a business and all that. Looks like you're well on your way to honoring Mrs. Getchel's wishes." He sat back, clasping his hands and rocking in his chair.

Ben leaned forward. "What about Mrs. Bennington?"

"You're a legal entity, and you're following the town's requirements to get your approvals. As far as I can see, unless she can prove that what you're doing is a danger to the community, unlawful, or breaches local ordinances, there's not much else she could do."

"That's a lot of unlesses, wouldn't you say?" Rebecca asked in a hushed tone. "She's quite capable of ruining everything."

"Not if I can help it." Mr. Howard sat up and riffled through his papers. "I'll need you to do some signing so I can disburse some funds to you, and some other documents, such as sub-contracting intent and contracts."

He flipped around the first document, set a pen next to it, and motioned for Rebecca to sign.

Ben picked up his pen, and his anxiety grew. The condition of receiving his portion of the inheritance and reimbursement for their out-of-pocket expenses wouldn't exist if this failed. His fears of being unemployed and his dwindling bank account weighed heavily on him. Ben's head pounded again. With every signature he applied to the papers, he grew increasingly uneasy.

"What happens if we commit to hiring help, signing on trades teachers and coaches, continue with the construction, and in the end, Margo Bennington wins?" he asked as he laid the pen on the desk.

"I understand your concern, Mr. Daly, and I'll do my best to make sure that doesn't happen. There are no guarantees when it comes to these things, but I'm hopeful."

Hopeful? That's the best he can come up with? As Ben's stress levels rose, he leaned back and took a closer look around the office. The paint was yellowed, reminding him of Mrs. G's dated living room walls. The drapes matched whatever decade the walls were last painted. The chair that Mr. Howard sat in was worn and dated. Even his suit was of poor quality. A lightbulb was out in the room's corner, and the plastic plant in the window wore a coat of dust. Mrs. Bennington could afford the most expensive attorneys in the state. He and Becky had to rely on Mrs. G's hometown boy. He ventured to guess Mr. Howard and Mrs. G. had been friends, and she'd wanted to throw him some support.

What have I gotten myself in to? He closed his eyes and rested his head in his hands. The pounding grew intense.

"Ben?" Becky said, but her words didn't register until she shook his shoulder. He picked his head up and Becky was leaning over him. Her eyes squinted with concern. "It's time to go."

They collected their belongings and headed outside into the sunny day. Much of the snow and ice that had accumulated was now disappearing. The air was more crisp than raw. He had every reason to be pleased. They were moving forward, and at a pretty good pace, but the feeling of dread washed over him like a storm cloud blotting out the sun.

"You're quiet," Rebecca said as she shut her car door.

"I'm good. Just a lot to take in, I guess." He didn't want to tell her of his doubts. He couldn't tell her he wanted more than anything to cut and run. Ben felt trapped in a sea of the unknown, but he didn't want to fail Mrs. G., and more importantly, he didn't want to fail Becky. Again.

Ben didn't mind taking risks when it was just him. Sure, his diving team depended on him, but technically they were all freelance, so they would do just fine without him. This was different; they weren't Becky. He vowed to himself that he wouldn't let her down again.

"Rebecca, mind if we make a quick stop?"

"That's fine. I'm free for the rest of the day." Rebecca leaned her head back in the seat and closed her eyes. "Do you really think we can pull this off, Benjamin?"

"Absolutely," he said without hesitation. *I'm going to hell.*

She turned to head to the side and looked out the window. "You know, it's not just Mrs. Bennington we have to get past? We still have to get approval to take in these kids with licensing and everything. What we're doing is pretty unconventional. What if—"

"We'll get the approval. We're not asking to take these kids in as foster parents. I mean, sure, we can be interims for emergencies, but what we're providing is resources to help them better transition into the real world. We've got this."

Rebecca was still looking out the side window. Her clasped hands rested on her lap. He wanted to reach out and assure her, hold her in his arms, and tell her everything would be okay, but he had to convince himself first.

Ben pulled into Ground's parking lot and was pleased to see the winter landscaped murals that now graced the windows. He hoped Nathan might be working and wanted to congratulate him on a job well done.

Rebecca swung her head around, staring him down. "You're not serious? You know who might be here, right?"

"We can't avoid Mrs. Bennington forever, Rebecca."

"Yes, yes, we can." Rebecca's brows raised. Mrs. G. had used the same expression on him more times than he cared to remember. Coming from Becky, he found it adorable.

"I understand you want to avoid that nasty woman, but we should still support Jillian's business. She stuck her neck out for us. Besides, after Mrs. Bennington's last eventful exit, I doubt she'd show her face anytime soon."

"I wouldn't count on that. Mrs. Bennington thinks she's above the rules." Rebecca sighed and shook her head. "Fine. You're right. But if she says one word—"

"She won't, if she knows what's good for her." He turned off the car. "You comin'?"

"Yes," she said with a roll of her eyes, then opened the door. Ben followed suit.

"Do you know what she drives?" he asked as they traipsed around to the front of Grounds. Ben eyed the white Lexus that crept toward them.

"Not sure I do."

No sooner had she responded, than his question was answered. Margo Bennington sat in her car, staring them down. Each time they made a step, she moved closer.

"Really? What is wrong with her?" Ben asked.

"I'm sure she's furious with me. I embarrassed her in front of everyone, but this is ridiculous."

Ben's blood pressure rose with each act of aggression. He stopped and stared back. Rebecca picked up her pace, leaving him behind. She stomped directly toward her adversary.

"Seriously? This is how it's going to be, Mrs. Bennington?"

Margo didn't say a word in response. She just sat with her lips pursed as if she were about to spit. She clutched the wheel hard, and revved the engine.

Rebecca swiveled to face Ben as he strode up beside her. "Is she kidding me right now?"

He took her by the arm. "Rebecca, let it go." He tugged toward the entrance. "She's not worth it."

Rebecca swung the front door open. "That woman is despicable."

Ben stopped her in her tracks. "Look at me."

Rebecca shut the door and stared at him. She was breathing heavily and her jaw was tight. The eyes that stared back at him were full of rage.

He rested his hands on her shoulders and gave them a

squeeze. "We have to play it cool and not let her know she's getting under our skin. It's what she wants." He could feel her tense body relax a bit. "Now, give me a smile." Ben gave her a goofy grin, and she obliged before sticking her tongue out. "There you go." He laughed. "That's the Rebecca I know and love."

Ben opened the door and scanned the room. He was relieved to see the reason for his visit busing a table. Ben caught Nathan's eye and gave him a wave. Nathan gave a shy wave in response. "Come with me, Rebecca. I want you to meet someone."

Rebecca cocked her head inquisitively. "Okay."

She followed behind as Ben maneuvered around the tables and chairs.

"Hey, Nathan. How's the job going?" Ben didn't bother to extend a hand as Nathan's was occupied with a tray of coffee mugs and small plates.

"It's going okay." Nathan gave them a sideways smile. "Do I know you?"

"Not really," Ben said. "I was here the day Jillian hired you."

"You're the guy that got me the job!" His eyes lit up, and he set the tray down on the table. Nathan reached his hand out and Ben reciprocated with a shake. "Thanks for what you did for me."

"No problem. All I did was give the introduction. You're the one that secured the job."

By now, Nathan was grinning ear to ear.

"Nathan, I'd like you to meet a friend of mine." He gestured toward Rebecca. "Nathan, this is Rebecca Mills. She's also my business partner."

"Hi. I remember you." Nathan's neck and cheeks turned pink. He lowered his head as if he wanted to crawl into a hole.

"I remember you too," Rebecca said. "I want you to know that I think you handled yourself really well that day. You need to understand that what that lady said was untrue. I hope you know that."

Ben took in the conversation between the two of them. Her tenderness toward Nathan was endearing, and her compassion when she spoke to him was palpable. That was when he knew they had to make this business work. The kids needed her, and he suspected she needed them, too.

Ben cleared his throat. "Well, we should probably let you get back to it." He tapped the top of the table with his knuckles a couple of times. "Just wanted to tell you that you did a super job with the windows. Keep up the good work."

"Thanks." Red cheeks bloomed across Nathan's face as he picked up the tray. He nodded goodbye and turned away with a bounce to his step.

"He seems like a great kid, Benjamin."

"Yep, and I'll be damned if we allow that woman to let kids like him fall through the cracks."

CHAPTER 37

Rebecca hummed the tune "Pure Imagination" that played in the shop as she tucked pink tea roses, fuchsia China roses, and pale pink Peruvian lilies into a petite, porcelain tea pot, imprinted with the same type of flowers. She turned the arrangement around several times, making sure that it looked equally beautiful from every angle. After she was satisfied, she was sure the recipient would be as delighted as she was.

Rebecca had felt unusually cheerful throughout the day, which wasn't hard to do with all the happy customers, popping in and out of Proposals. It was a new year, with new hope, and the spirit of generosity continued.

A touch of giddiness welled up inside. Her footing with Ben was feeling steadier, and they were well on their way into making Stepping Stones a reality. But she still couldn't shake Mrs. Bennington's vow to stop the project. Today, Rebecca tried her best to push aside the threat and keep moving forward. After all, she had Ben's support. They were in this together, and that realization hit her like a shaken up can of soda that was ready to explode.

Rebecca set the teapot arrangement in the refrigerator, then grabbed her laptop. Her next tasks were to do inventory and place orders for the Valentines' Day that was now less than three weeks away. Soon the shop would again be filled with red roses and candles, just as it had for the Christmas holiday.

For the first time, Rebecca was actually looking forward to Valentine's Day. Ben wasn't a love interest, but he was her friend, a male friend, and she secretly hoped that they'd spend the day together, even if it wasn't an official Valentine's thing. She just didn't want to spend it alone, again.

Rebecca blindly scrolled through the order screen on her laptop. *Maybe I'll offer to make us dinner.* No, he should make her the chicken and dumplings he'd promised her. After all, he didn't have anyone else besides her and Jason to hang out with. They could simply keep each other company. She smiled at the possibilities.

Time clicked by quickly and soon the door chimes of Proposals rang in the distance. Sophie was saying goodbye to a lingering customer. Emily clomped into the room.

"Hey, there. Almost done?" Emily asked as she leaned against the doorjamb.

"Almost." Rebecca closed the laptop and set it on the desk.

"Great! I was hoping you'd say that." Emily pulled her hair tie and gave her hand a quick run through her hair. "I'm alone tonight. Jack and the boys are doing guy stuff, and I don't feel like eating alone. Want to grab a bite?"

Rebecca's mind reeled. She and Emily rarely ever spent time with each other outside of work. It was usually a twosome of Emily and Sophie, not that she ever minded. She'd always been a loner. She'd intended to work on her quilting, but the invitation was a welcomed surprise.

"Sure! Where do you have in mind?"

Emily sat on the corner of the desk. "Let's go to the Inn. I'm craving a big juicy burger."

"Sounds good." Rebecca picked up a stack of receipts. "Just give me a minute."

"See you out front." Emily spun on her heels and headed down the hall. "I'll drive."

Within a few minutes, Rebecca slid into the passenger's seat of Emily's car. It surprised her to see the scattered candy wrappers and coffee cups strewn about. Rebecca had always taken Emily as a neat freak, and this, she thought, was refreshing. "Thanks for the invite. This is nice."

"Sure thing. We basically work on opposite sides of the shop, and I feel like we haven't connected in a while." Emily looked both ways at the end of the driveway before pulling out onto Route 1.

The Inn was only a stone's throw away, but Rebecca was grateful they weren't walking; she wasn't dressed for it. Rebecca was already feeling the awkwardness of not knowing what to say. At work, they'd talk about work or the guests. Not since their private talk about Mrs. Getchel, where she'd nearly had a breakdown and cried like a baby, and in the fiasco with Ben, had they discussed anything on a personal level. For the life of her, she was at a loss for words.

"Dang, it's cold." Emily adjusted the heat vents and turned up the temp, but it was still blowing cold air.

"I'll say." Rebecca crossed her arms, hugging herself. "I think it's as frigid as Mrs. Bennington's cold heart."

"That's pretty dang cold." Emily laughed as she pulled into the parking lot.

They scurried into the main entrance of the York Harbor Inn. Rebecca could feel her face blush as she recalled the last time she'd been there. The memory of plopping her breast in Ben's eggs Benedict was a memory she hoped she could some day laugh at.

The Inn was cozy, and the fire roared in the main room. The smell of wood smoke wafted in the air, subtle, but it still made her spine prickle. Anxiety fluttered in her stomach.

Emily stood looking up at her from the bottom of the staircase. "You coming?"

"Yes, sorry." Rebecca grabbed the smooth wooden hand-rail, steadying herself as she descended the stairs to join Emily.

She was still shivering, even her nose was cold, which made it beet red. She cupped her hands and breathed into them to warm up. Rebecca was pleased that they hadn't gotten a table near the windows so there wouldn't be any drafts.

"Is that curmudgeon of a woman still giving you trouble?" Emily asked as they looked over the menu, which was a mindless task, as they both knew they'd order burgers.

"Yep. She sure is."

"I say we have a hot toddy and make a toast to putting the great Margo Bennington in her place. Knocking her snobbery down a peg or two would do her some good."

"I think she needs more like twenty pegs," Rebecca said with a sigh.

"You do realize where you work, right?" Emily's eyebrows rose as she leaned toward her. Rebecca could tell Emily had something up her sleeve, but she couldn't fathom what Proposals had to do with anything.

"Well, of course I do, but—"

"Then you know we throw the best events in the area," Emily said.

Rebecca's mind raced as she recalled the numerous, extravagant affairs they'd hosted at Proposals, her favorite being Sophie and Brady's wedding. Proposals events were always the talk of the town and, often, their newsworthy events spread far and wide. "Yes, we do host some pretty amazing events, but I'm still not following you."

"Think about it. Can you just imagine having the who's who of Maine and New Hampshire at the gala, and not having Margo on the guest list?"

"I hear you, but I don't think she'd want to come. She doesn't want Stepping Stones to happen."

They handed the menus to the server and placed their order. Emily sat back in her chair with a mischievous grin on her face.

"What?" Rebecca asked, still not grasping Emily's thought process.

"What you don't understand about Margo is what her standing in the community means to her. Trust me on this one. She sees herself as the queen bee, and she would be humiliated if she couldn't attend, regardless of how much she detests what the event stands for."

Their hot toddies arrived and Rebecca took in the aroma of cloves, honey, lemon, and bourbon. The tall glass mug warmed her hands, and that warmth gave her a sense of hope.

"I see what you're getting at, but that would entail the guest list being, as you say, the who's who. I don't know the who's who." She took a tentative sip of the hot liquid and allowed the cup to linger at her lips.

"But Sophie and I do." Emily mirrored Rebecca with her toddy. An air of satisfaction drew up her mouth, and her eyes sparkled with glee. "Sophie's nearly done with the invitation list, and word has it, according to those that she's already spoken to, they're all in."

"Except for Margo Bennington, and her gaggle of adoring hens."

"Oh, no. Her hens will definitely get an invitation," Emily said with a smirk that became a laugh she couldn't contain.

"You're a devious woman, Emily Vassure."

"Indeed. Anything for a worthy cause."

Their burgers arrived, and Rebecca sank her teeth into hers with glee. The charbroiled juices dripped down her fingers, but she didn't care. Emily, on the other hand, dipped crispy salted fries in ketchup.

"It's good to see you happy for a change, Rebecca."

Rebecca swallowed and grabbed a fry. "Yeah, I am."

"Do tell."

"There's nothing to tell, really." She popped a hand-cut fry into her mouth.

"Aah, but your blushing face tells me a different story."

Her cheeks pinked every time she thought of Benjamin, and for the first time in a long time, she felt contentment. She and Ben had turned a corner. After all the years that had passed between them, she could finally open up to a future with him. Even though it was purely for business's sake, she ached for more. Perhaps because she'd been thinking of Valentine's Day all day. Deep down she knew she'd always loved the man, and she wouldn't shut that door if it opened to her.

Emily sat back, awaiting a response.

"It's nothing—really."

Emily's stare and smirk led Rebecca to believe she wasn't pulling the wool over her eyes.

"Benjamin and I kind of patched things up is all, and things are going pretty well—for the business."

"I see," Emily said and took a bite of her burger.

The last thing she wanted to divulge was how she felt about Benjamin Daly. She sipped her tea and the first thing that popped into her mind was to turn the tide. "You and Jack seem to be doing pretty well together. Have you made any special plans for Valentine's Day?"

Emily finished chewing and wiped her mouth and hands with no sign of discomfort at the change in focus. "We thought of going out, but honestly, I'd rather just stay home. He's gonna cook me one of his famous dishes, some Indian thing he learned during his travels. The boys plan to spend the night at their grandmother's. Should be an enjoyable night. You?"

Rebecca could see Emily's sparkling tease. "Nothing planned. I'll probably end up doing some work at the house. I want to start painting the upstairs rooms."

Emily rolled her eyes. "How romantic. You need a date."

Rebecca couldn't remember the last time she'd gone on a date. In fact, she couldn't recall ever going out for Valentine's Day. Again, her mind drifted to Ben. Just then his laugh rumbled from the stairs.

It couldn't be, could it? Rebecca's heart fluttered at the prospect of seeing Ben. She craned her neck to see if her ears were playing a trick on her. They weren't. Ben had his hand resting on the shoulder of a slender, dark-haired woman and leading her to one of the tables. She too was laughing as she took her seat. *Who is she?*

Rebecca could feel the blood drain from her face to her toes. Her naïve hopes of a Valentine's dinner with Ben swiftly melted away. She should have known better than to think he wouldn't date other women. She had no hold on him, but it was obvious that this woman wasn't new to him.

Rebecca couldn't take her eyes off of them. The woman squeezed his hand. He smiled in return. Rebecca overheard him say that she wouldn't have to drive him home, to which the unknown woman swatted him teasingly with her napkin, then responded, "I better not have to."

"Earth to Rebecca."

Rebecca's attention turned once again back to Emily.

"I lost you there," Emily said. "Everything okay?"

"Oh—yeah—everything is fine. I'm good. I just remembered that I had something I needed to do tonight. Would you mind if we head out now?" Rebecca hoped her request was convincing as it was all she could do not to run toward the side exit.

"Sure thing. I'm done anyway." Emily placed her napkin on her plate and spun her head around to look for the server.

"Perfect timing," Rebecca said as the server placed the check on their table. She slid a twenty and a ten in the check's jacket and nearly dropped her wallet on the floor as she frantically tried to return it to her handbag. Laughter from Ben and the mysterious woman flowed to her ears again, and she needed to escape. "I'll meet you outside. Okay?"

When Rebecca stood to leave, Emily's dazed and confused expression vanished. "Isn't that—"

"Yep. Doesn't matter." Rebecca flung her coat off the back of the chair, then dashed out the side door with a lump in her throat.

Rebecca didn't make the car ride back to Proposals easy on Emily. She was in no mood to talk about Ben, or anything else, for that matter. She simply stewed in her own self-pity.

At least she didn't resort to crying like a lunatic in front of Emily again. She'd done enough crying to last a lifetime, and yet, tears now bubbled up inside of her. She was angry that she'd let hope of a relationship with Ben enter her dreams.

CHAPTER 38

Rebecca climbed the few stairs to her apartment and opened the door. A rush of garlic, onions, and pot roast she'd thrown in her crockpot that morning filled her senses. In her haste to join Emily for dinner, she'd completely forgotten about preparing it that morning. Had it crossed her mind earlier, she would have invited Emily to her place instead. And avoided shattering her illusions about her future with Ben.

She removed her coat and her shoes and glumly headed to the kitchen. She opened the pot's lid and steam fanned her face. The roast drippings, potatoes, and carrots were tender as she stabbed them with a fork. She was relieved to see she hadn't overcooked it. At least, she hadn't had to eat alone again tonight. Had she not met Emily for dinner, she'd never have known about Ben's mystery date.

After transferring the pot roast and fixings to the fridge, Rebecca changed into a pair of fleece comfy pants and a matching teal sweatshirt. She stuffed her feet into her slippers and headed to her quilting room to finish the embroidery on the latest patchwork quilt for a young teen named Stella, which Rebecca had discovered meant star. The message would read:

I,

Stella Robinson

will shine bright in the face of darkness.

Rebecca stitched each burgundy letter with precision as her mind considered the life of Miss Stella Robinson. She hoped they placed her in a safe and loving home, a home that was nurturing, patient, kind, and forgiving like Mrs. Getchel's. She thought about what this quilt might mean to Stella and prayed it would bring her comfort in times of uncertainty and fear.

Rebecca was lost in her wandering thoughts when a heavy knock pounded on her front door. She set the quilt, needle, and threads down on her worktable and scurried to the living room to peek at who waited for her on the other side of the door.

Ben stood with his back to the door, rocking back and forth with a hand in his pocket, carrying a plastic bag in the other. He was looking toward the heavens, without a care in the world. She, on the other-hand, felt her armpits sweating, which infuriated her. She took a deep breath, convincing herself that she was in control and that his visit was no big deal whatsoever, then opened the door.

His broad smile and shining eyes stared back at her, and she swallowed hard.

"Hey, what's up?" Even she surprised herself at how calmly she'd asked the question.

"I come bearing gifts," he said with a jovial flash of the bag.

She couldn't imagine why he'd bring her a gift, especially because he'd just been with someone else.

"Okay. I'm intrigued," she said as he stood there with an unfettered assurance that all was right with the world. "Come in."

"It so happens that I just had dinner, and when the server told me that tonight's special was chocolate cream pie, I thought of you." Ben handed over the plastic bag as if it were the most normal thing in the world to do after having been on a date with another woman. "It's your favorite, right?"

Rebecca stood dumfounded. "Yes—right. My favorite."

"I made sure they didn't put whipped cream on yours."

She couldn't believe that he'd remember such a mundane thing as her not liking whipped cream, or that she loved chocolate cream pie. Mostly, however, she couldn't believe he was standing in her living room as if he hadn't just had dinner with another woman. His intoxicating scent of masculinity only added to her confusion. She could pick out notes of spice, a hint of wood smoke, and leather from his gloves. That, along with the chocolate, made her feel unsure, and she didn't know what to make of her contradictory feelings.

"How thoughtful of you, Benjamin."

All the disappointment she'd experienced just a short time ago at the Inn drifted away like seaweed among the waves. *Maybe I'd gotten it wrong?*

Ben followed her into the kitchen, and she felt self-conscious. Perhaps it was because if she were following him, she'd be looking at his strut and the shape of his body, and assumed he might be doing the same. For a moment, she almost forgot how to walk normally.

She set the bag on the table and pulled out the containers, then carefully opened them. "Where did you get these?" she asked, knowing precisely where they'd come from.

"The Cellar Pub," he replied nonchalantly. He pulled out a chair and reached for his portion of pie. "Looks pretty good."

Rebecca grabbed a couple of forks from the drawer. How far should she go with her questions? "Coffee?"

He glanced down at his watch. "Sure, why not?"

She plopped a K-cup in the machine and watched as the rich, brown liquid filled his mug. "Cream and sugar?"

"Nah, black's good."

Rebecca nodded, realizing that she knew exactly how he liked his coffee. Their morning at the Inn had seared it in her mind.

She could sense his gaze on her as she then placed her mug on the machine's tray to await its reward. Rebecca stood quietly as the steam rose. She hadn't heard Ben approach until his warm hand touched her shoulder.

"Is everything okay?"

"Yeah—sure." She bit her lower lip. "Why wouldn't it be?"

She didn't sound convincing, but she wasn't ready to say more. She didn't want to act like a jealous woman, or humiliate herself.

Ben turned her toward him. His eyes were tender and his manner relaxed. "Talk to me, Rebecca."

Rebecca pulled away and retrieved the now full mugs. "Don't want the coffee to get cold," she said, as carefree as she could muster.

He rubbed his hand across his mouth and sighed, then sat back down at the table.

"Have you done any more of your quilts?" He scooped up a fork full of decadent chocolate.

"Yes. Actually, I just finished one before you came in. It's for a girl named Stella. Did you know Stella means star in Latin?"

"Never thought about it." He shrugged. "That's cool. Makes sense."

Rebecca welcomed the diversion to her more sordid thoughts. She was happy to move on for the night, but resigned herself to clear the air when the sting wasn't so new.

"I think she'll like it. It has a kind of Van Gogh-Stary Night kind of look."

"Clever. I bet she'll love it." Ben shoved the last bite in his mouth and leaned back contented. "Can I see it?"

Before she knew it, she was opening the door to her workroom. Ben stepped inside with eyes wide. He wandered around, taking in the room. She had one of her larger planning patterns hanging on Mrs. Getchel's tablecloth's backing against the right-hand wall.

After Ben slowly walked along the wall of windows, he came to the ribbed stitching of a folded work that was ready for delivery. He gently ran his fingers along the ribbing before continuing to view the large space. There was a small piece in the center of the room near her sewing machine. The tiny quilt of Mrs. Getchel's home, or at least the version of the house as she now saw it.

Ben held the small square in his grasp, sat on one of her stools, and examined it closely. "This is amazing," he said. "I can't believe all the details. You even have her porch swing."

"I tried to get as much as I could. It's a little hard with the pieces being so small."

"It's remarkable, Rebecca." He flipped it over and paused. Her heart pounded with his praise. She loved what she did, and it felt good to see that he, too, appreciated her passion.

"I used one of her aprons for the border and backing. Not that anyone will see the back, since it's gonna be in a frame, but I'll know it's there."

Rebecca approached Ben as he continued to look at the piece. She leaned in, resting her hand on his back, and ran her finger across a worn section of the apron, trying her best to swallow the lump forming in her throat. "I miss her, Ben. I miss her so much."

"She'd be so proud of you, Rebecca." He pulled her to him and sat her on his knee. "We're going to do good by her. You just wait and see."

The feel of his arm around her was comforting. She laid her head on his shoulder, and he draped her knees over his lap. Her heart's steady rhythm matched his, and she felt safety being held in his care. A silent tear trickled down her cheek, dampening his shirt.

Ben's hand brushed the hair from her eyes and tucked it behind her ear. "What is it, Hon? Please talk to me."

She closed her eyes, and couldn't untangle her memories: the feeling of her dad's arms around her, her mom's tender touch on her cheek, Mrs. Getchel's heartbeat, a nurse's soothing shushes, a firefighter's strength. A whirlwind of sadness, emptiness, self-pity, and guilt tore at her. All these feelings needed to escape and make themselves known. Oh, how she needed him to know, to understand what she had done to those that she'd loved.

She wept until no more tears would fall, and he rocked her back and forth as if she were precious to him. When her stiff body fell into his, he lifted her up and carried her to her bed, removed her slippers, and tucked her under the blanket. Ben leaned in and placed his warm lips on her forehead and tenderly kissed her.

"Please don't go," she whispered, as she tried to recall the last time anyone had tucked her in. Another tear dripped from the corner of her eye and fell on the pillow.

"I'll stay as long as you wish," he whispered, then stepped to the other side of the bed. He removed his shoes and nuzzled up next to her. "I'm not going anywhere, Rebecca."

"Ben?"

"Yes."

"I like it when you call me Becky," she murmured.

Ben brushed her hair with his fingers. "Okay, Hon. Becky it'll be. Now, try to get some rest." The warmth of his words and his breath on her neck lulled her to sleep.

CHAPTER 39

Ben lay beside her, watching her. The hazy glow of the moon shone across her face. He took in her petite features. She had a button nose and high cheekbones. Her lips were rounded and full with a slight downward turn, as if she were dreaming of something not agreeable. She twitched, and he could see her eyes move from side to side. He considered waking her, but pulled her closer, hoping she'd continue to sleep and help vanquish her bad dreams.

Ben lay awake for hours. He wanted to sleep, but all he could think about was needing to get closure in Hawaii, figure out where he'd live long term, and see if Becky would mind him, temporarily using Mrs. G's car, so he could get rid of the rental. And getting Stepping Stones off the ground without Mrs. Bennington's interference.

Ben thought of Nathan and the other kids that lay awake in the night, wondering where their life would lead. Mostly he thought of the incredibly strong woman lying next to him.

She'd endured a heavy trauma in her past, and he wished that she'd trust him and finally open up to him so that she could fully heal the wounds of her past. But he didn't want to push. No, he mustn't press her. If he did, she'd withdraw more. She'd talk when she was ready, and he'd be there when that time comes.

He breathed in the sweet scent of her lavender shampoo and drifted off to sleep.

***

Ben woke to the familiar aroma of freshly baked cinnamon and raisins. *Mmm, muffins?* He rolled over and stretched. He ran his tongue across his teeth, wishing beyond anything else for a toothbrush. He yawned and sat up, resting his feet on the floor, allowing him time to fully awaken. By now, the faint sizzle of sausage or bacon frying in a pan reached him. He slid on his loafers and headed toward the welcoming aroma.

"Good morning!" Rebecca said with a big smile as she popped a blueberry into her mouth. She wore a pale pink bathrobe that tied around her small waistline and her ratty slippers. Her hair was tied up, creating a sloppy bun. He found the whole look refreshing.

"Good morning. It smells amazing in here." Ben approached the counter and breathed in the warm muffins. "I love cinnamon-raisin muffins."

"I remember. It's Mrs. Getchel's recipe. I found her stash of family secret recipes."

"I knew it! This is awesome." He reached in and plucked the top muffin and stuffed it in his mouth.

"Benjamin Daly!" She swatted a hand-towel across his chest. Ben wasn't going to let the flick of a towel deter him.

"It's so good," he mumbled while he snatched another chunk of the scrumptious cinnamon-raisin muffin top, then half-heartedly ran out of the range of her towel with a laugh.

It pleased him that Becky had turned a corner from the previous evening's emotional state.

"Anything I can do to help?"

"Nope," she said with a wide sweep of her arms. "I got everything under control."

Before long, they were digging in. Rebecca relayed her and Emily's earlier conversation regarding Mrs. Bennington's lack of invitation to the gala.

Rebecca ran the last bite of toast across her plate, moping the remnants of egg yolk. "Now, my question to you is: do we go ahead, as Emily suggested, and invite Mrs. Bennington's gossiping hens, or do we leave them out as well?"

Ben watched as she opened wide and stuck the crusty edge of the toast in her mouth. He never wanted to take his gaze off her. *You have no idea how damned adorable you are.*

She reached for an orange in the fruit bowl and peeled it open.

"Well?" She tore off a section of the orange. "Do we invite them or not?"

"I say we invite them." Orange spray permeated the air, and he could no longer resist. He grabbed one and tore it open, releasing more of the sweet scent.

Rebecca shrugged, then stood to remove their plates.

"No ma'am. I've got this." Ben plopped the rest of the orange into his mouth, rejoicing that it left him with a better taste than morning breath. He slid his chair back and picked up the plates.

"You really don't have to. I've already taken up a ton of

your time. And you were nice enough to stay last night."

"It's no trouble." Ben opened the dishwasher, scraped off the plate, and placed them inside.

Rebecca joined him. "The least I can do is help. It feels funny just sitting there in my own kitchen."

She drained the bacon grease from the heavy cast-iron skillet into an aluminum can, then proceeded to place the rest of the cinnamon muffins into two separate containers.

Ben suspected he'd be cleared to fly any day now, and he needed to get back to Hawaii so he could collect his things. He thought about having Holokai or Smithers ship his stuff, but he was afraid they wouldn't be thorough. Besides, he still needed to take care of his lease, and figure out how to get his motorcycle and car back on the mainland or, at least, sell them. He figured there was no time like the present to broach the subject.

"Becky?"

"Yep," she said as he maneuvered around her as if they were in a choreographed dance.

"So, I was thinking . . . if all goes well with getting the town's approval, and since Sophie and Emily have been helping so much with the gala plans, we could maybe squeeze in some downtime for a little while, right?"

Ben placed the last of the dishes in the dishwasher and rinsed out the sink as Rebecca wiped down the table.

"Yeah, won't that be nice? All we need is the town's final stamp of approval, but the attorney thinks it should go smoothly enough. Unless, of course, Mrs. Bennington raises enough fuss." Rebecca pulled out a chair. "But I think we're ready to meet any questions or concerns that they might have, don't you?"

"Absolutely." He straddled a chair, relieved. The timing could work out. It would be tight, but he thought the sooner his side of things were done, the sooner he could move on to giving Stepping Stones his full attention.

Ben fidgeted with a loose thread on her shirtsleeve. "I figured after the town meeting, it would be best if I got back to Kauai. Will you be okay with that?"

Ben could see Rebecca's body stiffen. She sprang up from the table and pulled a glass from the cupboard. "If that's what you need to do, then I think you should do it." She turned on the faucet and filled her glass, then gulped it down without looking in his direction. "So, your doctor's cleared you to fly, then?"

"He will, I'm sure of it. I won't be diving anytime soon, or likely ever for that matter. But I'll be able to fly because the cabin pressure is regulated. So, there's that."

"I see. Well, that's good." Rebecca still had her back to him. He got up from the chair and approached her, but she moved out of reach. "I guess the sooner you get going, the better. Don't you think?"

"Sure, but—"

"You know what? I should really get ready for work." Rebecca whipped around him and headed toward the hallway before turning to address him again. "Thanks again for last night. I hope I wasn't too much of a burden."

"Becky, you weren't—"

She slammed the bedroom door.

Ben stood staring down the now empty hallway. *You are infuriating, Becky Mills.* Once again, he wondered what had just taken place and threw his hands up in the air in defeat. *I don't get it!*

CHAPTER 40

Rebecca stood in her bedroom and paced the floor, wringing her hands until the front door closed. "Seriously!" She fumed. "He's running off! Again!"

She yanked off her sweatshirt and threw it on the bed. "You're the world's biggest loser, Ben!" She struggled with the knot at the waistband of her fleece pants. "And I'm such a sucker!" In her frustration, she ripped them off and kicked them across the room.

"You know what, Ben? You can date any beautiful woman you choose! She shouted into her closet. "You probably have women from island to island and seacoast to seacoast! Woopie, I'm Mr. Good Looking. Look at me with my huge pecs, massive thighs, and tight butt. All I have to do is smile my pearly whites, and they'll jump into my arms."

She shoved the hangers from side to side. "So, what if he's got some gorgeous woman at the inn for romantic dinners." She made her choice of what to wear. "For all I care, he can have Miss Hawaii herself standing at the airport, holding a big friggin' welcome home sign."

She pulled on her robe and cinched the belt. "Well, Benjamin Daly, they can have you because I certainly don't need you! I never have, and never will." She spewed the words. "I'm quite capable of making the gala and Stepping Stones a success without your sorry ass getting in my way!"

Rebecca gathered her clothes in her arms and flung her bedroom door open. "Do you hear me, Benjamin Daly?" She opened the bathroom door, and caught a glimpse of Ben scurrying across the end of the hall's entrance.

She froze.

No. He's not! He couldn't be.

Rebecca slid into the bathroom, then peered down the hall, hoping she'd imagined him. She debated if she should call out. No, he was there, and worse, he'd heard her gush of anger. She could pretend that she hadn't said anything at all, or she could step out and give him a piece of her mind for having the audacity to eavesdrop.

Rebecca stepped out to face the humiliation of her outburst. As she tightened her robe, the thought of him listening to her pushed the embarrassment aside and renewed her anger. She stomped down the hallway to see him leaning against the kitchen's archway.

"Busted," he said, giving her a sheepish grin before turning it into a smirk.

"You can wipe that stupid grin off your face right now, Benjamin," she said with a clenched jaw. "What makes you think you have the right to stand out here and invade my privacy?" She clenched her fists at her side and wanted nothing more than to punch him in the Adam's apple.

He took a step toward her and his smirk turned into a seductive grin.

"Oh, no, you don't," she said as the pounding of her heart grew stronger. She felt fully exposed. No bathrobe could hide her feelings toward him, and she wished she could fully hide within it and disappear.

"So, you like my tight butt, do ya?" He took a step closer.

"No, I don't. I—I was just being dramatic. It meant nothing."

She stood her ground, determined to not let him see her vulnerability. She would not allow him to put her guard down.

He bit his smirking lip, then flashed her a smile.

She stared up at him, refusing to give into his charms. "Why are you here, anyway? I heard you leave."

"Forgot my muffins. Good thing I did or I wouldn't have known you think I'm good looking."

By now, he was within a few inches of her and caressing her arm with his fingers. He didn't shudder at the feel of her scarred flesh through her thin robe. He'd seen her scars, but that acceptance had been out of pity. Rebecca's knees grew weak and her resolve faltered, so she took a step back to escape his irresistible pull.

"I will not be one of your flings, you know. So don't think you can waltz in here, uninvited, mind you; eavesdrop, then try to seduce me. I know you too well, Benjamin." Her spine straightened and her pulse quickened.

Ben took a step back. "So that's it. You have your mind made up about me. I'm, what did you say? Let me think. Yes, I remember now. I'm a loser."

"You're not a loser. Haven't you ever heard of being hyperbolic?"

"What do I have to do to make you understand that I'm not going anywhere, Beck?" His eyes softened, and he leaned in to her.

Rebecca fidgeted with the neckline of her robe and pulled her hair back to gain her composure. "You just told me you wanted to go back to Hawaii! So, tell me how that's supposed to convince me otherwise?"

"Yes, I said that, but it's only so I can pack up my stuff and tie up loose ends."

"Oh." She gulped. "So, you're not—"

"I'm staying here." He reached his hand up to her chin, lifting it up. "This is where I want to be. Right here, with you."

"Okay then. Good—that's good." She shifted, not sure where to look and what to do next. *He's staying.* "I should ah . . . get showered. I'll just, ah." She pointed toward the bathroom. "Get ready for—"

"For work. Yeah, of course." He nodded and took a step back. "I'll just head out then."

"Cool, okay." She tried to sidestep him, and his body rubbed against hers. He lingered, and she could feel the heat of him. A warmth tumbled through her, causing her breath to catch. "Don't . . . forget your muffins."

Ben shot her a mischievous glance. "I'm thinking maybe I should."

CHAPTER 41

Ben left the doctor's office with a renewed energy. He got his approval to fly, and he was on cloud nine, save for the fact that he'd leave Rebecca behind to deal with the mounting list of to-dos for the gala. But he thought leaving would only get more difficult later, once Stepping Stones were open for business.

He mused at the thought that Rebecca liked him in the romantic sense. Seeing her standing before him that morning, after overhearing her confessions, took all his willpower to not pull her into him and taste her succulent lips. He was growing to adore this woman, with all her charms and stubbornness. He never expected to get attached to a woman or anyone, for that matter. He liked it better when he was unattached. Having a serious relationship was as unknown to him as being raised by a mom and dad who loved him.

By the time he reached Jason's place, he decided he really knew nothing about love, or what it meant to love someone.

Have I ever been loved? Maybe, he thought. But if anyone had felt that way toward him, he hadn't reciprocated.

He considered Mrs. G. *Had she really loved me?* He shoved off the notion, as simply the act of caring. *Yes*, he thought, *she cared for me.*

Ben greeted Clyde at the door. His purring filled the room. "You don't love me either, do you Clyde?" He swiped his hand across the cat's back. "Nope, you just want your breakfast. That's all I am to you, nothing more than the hand that feeds you."

He threw his coat on the back of the kitchen chair and set Rebecca's muffins on the kitchen table. He smiled and shook his head at his good fortune. "She likes me, Clyde, and the best part is, I like her back." Clyde meowed incessantly. "I know. Isn't it great?"

Ben grabbed the can of cat food out of the fridge and popped off the plastic cover. Clyde leapt onto the counter and nudged his arm impatiently with his nose. "It's coming already. Jeez."

He set the dish on the floor and gave a brisk rub on Clyde's head, then sat down to watch him eat.

He'd never considered having a cat, or any pet for that matter. Growing up, it had been out of the question. Once, he recalled, one of the foster homes had a dog, but it was an outside dog. Thinking back, he was terrified of it. It had an enormous head with a big jaw, and he thought it would eat him alive if it got too close. The dog would growl and bare its teeth at anyone that passed its way. It had a thick, heavy chain that it dragged around over the dirt. He didn't remember anyone playing with it, or even so much as petting it. The fosters would throw him a bone once in a while, but that was about the only comfort he vaguely recalled. *Maybe that's why it was so mean*, he thought.

The memory of the chained dog brought him to a place that he'd buried away long ago. He closed his eyes, remembering being locked in his room at that same house. He must have been around eight or nine years-old. Yes, he'd been in third or fourth grade at the time. It was the year that his teacher, Miss Trigs, had brought him into see the school nurse and some other guy that asked him a lot of questions.

Ben sighed as the memories came pouring back. With his eyes still closed, he rested his head on his hands and leaned his elbows on his knees. Ben remembered being really hungry; he was always hungry. He, too, was treated like the dog and had gotten a figurative bone tossed to him occasionally. Bile rose to his throat at the memory. They had tethered him to his bed by a thick rope, a bed without sheets or a blanket.

Ben mindlessly rubbed his ankle where the rope had chaffed. In his mind's eye, he could almost hear the dog growling and howling outside the filthy upstairs window of that cramped room. Ben recalled hearing an empty dog dish, and heavy chain clanging together over and over as the dog paced back and forth. He too had had just enough room to pace in the small room that smelled of urine.

Clyde's chubby body rubbed against Ben's leg. He reached to pick the cat up and set him on his lap. He hadn't realized that his face was damp with tears until Clyde licked his chin. Ben swallowed hard. *Thank you, Miss Trigs. You saved me.*

Ben took a deep breath and released the memory into the never again space that he'd created long ago; his special place where fear, pain, hunger, and anguish lived. He gave Clyde a snuggle and set him on the floor just as Jason burst inside, juggling an armful of grocery bags.

"Hey, how'd it go with the doc? You cleared?"

"Yeah, I'm good to go," Ben said, while he swiped his face dry.

"Cool. Did ya tell Rebecca yet?" he asked as he unloaded groceries.

"She knows I'll be heading out, but doesn't know I'm cleared."

Ben helped Jason with the unpacking. "You got some pretty good, lookin' steaks here," he said as he pulled the package out of the bag. "And a bottle of merlot." Ben slapped Jason on the back. "Someone's got a date."

"As it happens, I do." Jason flashed a grin and pulled a bouquet out of one of the grocery bags.

"Dude! You didn't get them from Proposals?"

"Crap, I never gave that a thought. Next time."

"Sure, if there's a next time. Without me there as your wingman, I seriously question your ability to have another."

"Shut up," Jason said, giving Ben a shove. "It's not my fault that you couldn't come up with a date."

"I didn't know I was supposed to. You never once said you were having dinner with Julie last night." Ben tore open a bag of Lays potato chips. "I felt like a complete idiot when she said she was meeting you there, but that you were running late."

"Yeah, sorry about that. I thought I texted you."

"Well, you didn't." He popped a chip into his mouth. "Do you know how much I detest being a third wheel?"

"It was last minute. What can I say? She called, and I invited her to join us. Get over it."

"Suppose you'll want me outta here." Ben rolled up the

chip bag and shoved it in the cupboard. "I'll grab some stuff and head to the house. There's a few projects I'd like to finish up, anyway, so I'll hang there for the night."

"Are you sure you don't want to stick around? I can put out another plate for you, being that you're now our designated third wheel and all."

Jason's deadpan expression stared back at him.

"You're an ass."

"So, I've been told," Jason said, then twisted the top off a bottle of water.

CHAPTER 42

Rebecca strode over the cobblestones leading to Proposals' barn behind the shop and main house. She smiled as she reflected on the morning she and Ben just had. She paused for a moment to take in the sun's warmth on her back and lifted her gaze skyward.

The large stained-glassed, intertwined wedding bands above the massive double doors of their event center sparkled, offering a sense of hope and happiness to anyone who entered its doors. She was beyond grateful that Stepping Stones' gala would take place there, as the wedding bands, weren't just a symbol representing weddings, they were also the coming together as a community, sharing a common purpose, supporting one another, and committing to a goal. Yes, there wasn't a better place to host the event.

Rebecca opened the barn doors and wasn't surprised to see that the room, once again, took her breath away. She marveled at the sun's reflection through the stained-glass window, across the exposed-beamed rafters, and wooden floors that sparkled and shimmered along with the three grand chandeliers that hung above. Rebecca pictured the room full of donors and worthy entrepreneurs, willing to open their hearts—and wallets—to teach, lead, and inspire the kids in the foster community. She only wished her parents and Mrs. Getchel could be here to share the moment.

"It will be perfect, Rebecca."

Rebecca turned. Sophie's silhouette stood in the doorway. "I hope so."

"I know so." Sophie came to Rebecca's side. She, too, took in the rays of light pouring through the barn.

"You don't think Mrs. Bennington will ruin it, do you?"

"Not if I can help it. Between you and Ben, me and Brady, Emily and Jack, and Duncan and Jillian, not to mention all of your guests, I don't think she'd stand a chance."

"I guess you're right." Rebecca shrugged as if shaking off the negativity. "I just need to stop worrying about it."

"It's going to be great. You just wait and see." Sophie's bright smile was reassuring as she gave Rebecca's hands a squeeze. "Now, let's go over the plan again. Of course, it could change, depending on how many tables we need, but I'm suspecting we'll be at capacity."

Rebecca chatted away with instructions and Sophie tapped notes into her tablet.

"Have you thought about incorporating a silent auction?" Sophie asked.

Rebecca paused, considering the idea. "That's brilliant! Of course, I'd have to get donated items, which will make a lot more work, but I think it's doable. Don't you think?"

"Absolutely. I can think of some items even as we speak.

I'd bet Brady would donate a print, or even a portrait sitting. I'm pretty sure Emily would donate one of her mom's paintings. Oh, and you could make one of your quilts. For that matter, you probably already have one made." Sophie got more animated as her enthusiasm grew. "I'd be willing to give a subscription plan for bouquets. Rebecca, don't you see? The possibilities are endless!"

Sophie's effervescence was contagious, and the worry that Rebecca had carried was lifting. "It's really a great idea, Sophie. Thank you."

"My pleasure." Sophie flipped the leather top of the tablet closed and held it to her chest. "I think we're all set for now. Really, not much has changed since we last talked. So easy peasy. I'll be sure to have an area set up for the silent auction." Sophie pointed to the left of the fieldstone fireplace that showcased the back wall. "Okay then, I best get back in there. The Kingsburys will be here in a bit to go over their wedding party's bouquets."

Sophie headed back to the shop with Daisy, who'd joined her, prancing along without a care in the world.

Rebecca slid the large barn doors together and took in the crisp sea air. The sun was on its descent and the sky was turning shades of orange, pink, and yellow, which left her feeling happy. Her mind shifted once again to Ben.

She'd been moved when he'd said he belonged right here with her. Yet the word *belong* hit her more than anything else. Ben now knew where he belonged. Now she, too, embraced the feeling of belonging. Between everyone at Proposals, and Ben, the feeling of homesickness was lessening. It had taken her a long time before she could describe her emptiness—the homesickness. Sure, she'd lost her physical home as a kid, but the emptiness was more than that—much more.

A home wasn't about a place; it was about the people in that place.

Since her parents' death, no matter where she'd gone, she's always carried a deep sadness, a longing for home that never ceased. Until now. She feared that this sense of home would once again disappear. Her contentment was now slipping away, the same way the sun was. She questioned if Ben would want to return to Maine once he'd gone back to paradise. *I can't believe he's leaving before the gala.* She shook her head in disbelief. *That's it. It's impossible for me to say no to that man.* She grinned. *No, Rebecca Mills, he told you, this is where he wants to be.*

A gust of wind and the drop in temperature left Rebecca shivering, but also exhilarated and refreshed. She took in a deep breath, inhaling the winds of change, and with it, hope for her future. A future with Ben.

Rebecca pulled her phone out of her jacket pocket and pressed Ben's phone number. As it rang, she felt like a teenager. She'd called him a million times since he'd arrived in town, but it was always business related. This time, she was asking for a date. She was just about to give up when he picked up.

"Hey, there. I was just thinking about you."

Just hearing his voice calmed her trepidation. "You were? Good thoughts, I hope."

"Always. What's up?"

"I was wondering if you'd want to join me for dinner?" Rebecca held her breath as she waited for his response.

"I already fed you, and you're tipping the scale as it is."

Rebecca was speechless. She wagered he'd been drinking because there was no other explanation. *He couldn't be that cruel.* If he meant it to be funny, he had a gross sense of humor. "Excuse me?"

"Oh, no, not you! I'm sorry. I was talking to Clyde."

Rebecca ran a list of common acquaintances and the name Clyde didn't ring a bell. "Who's Clyde?"

"Jason's cat. Sorry, you were saying?"

"I was asking you over for dinner." Rebecca once again awaited his response when finally, he laughed—an uncontrollable laugh.

"You—you thought I—I was talking about you? You were inviting—me to dinner—and…" His laughter made his breath catch and squeal.

"Are you quite done, Benjamin?" she asked.

"That sounds great," he said with a snicker. "How soon can I be there?"

Rebecca bit her lower lip in relief. "Give me an hour."

She hung up and slid her phone back into her pocket. "Benjamin Daly, I hope you're ready for an unforgettable night."

CHAPTER 43

Ben freshened up with a clean shave and, after several attempts, chose a buttoned-up, navy-blue shirt he hoped Becky would like. *Why am I nervous?* He tucked his shirt into his jeans. *It's just dinner.* He shook his head and buckled his belt, then slid into his loafers. He nodded with approval at his reflection. As excited as he was about being cleared to fly, his need to tell her was waning. He wanted the night to be perfect: no upsets, no arguments, no drama. He wanted, as Becky put it, unforgettable. He grinned at the thought.

Ben glanced at his watch. He had time to kill before he headed to Rebecca's. Instead of pacing the floor at Jason's, especially because Jason was busy preparing for his date, he decided to make a run for a bottle of wine for Becky.

Ben drove down Congress Street, in Portsmouth, per Jason's suggestion, in search of LaBelle Winery. To his delight, he found a parking space across from its entrance and snagged it.

Portsmouth had transformed since he'd last spent time

there. The historic seaport had grown, and the bustling vibe was palpable. He crossed the street toward the large green archway in the heart of Market Square and stepped inside LaBelle Winery, taking in its welcoming atmosphere. A young lady greeted him with a pleasant smile, and was kind enough to direct him to one of their wine experts to assist him with his purchase. He then dashed off to Rebecca's, knowing he'd be cutting it close. He was grateful the traffic was manageable.

Ben pulled into the parking spot but hesitated to get out of the car. *Don't screw it up.* He gave the steering wheel a confident squeeze, grabbed the wine he'd selected from LaBelle Winery, and strode toward the steps that lead to Rebecca's door. To his delight, she opened the door for him.

"Hello, Benjamin," she said with a glint in her eyes and a wide smile.

He sure liked the carefree Becky standing before him. Her hair was loosely gathered atop her head. A few wisps escaped, leaving her adorably sexy.

He stepped in, and to his surprise, she gave him a warm peck on the cheek.

"It smells amazing in here. What are we having?"

"It's my homemade marinara simmering. We're having chicken parmesan. You like chicken parmesan, right?" she asked as he handed her the paper bag with the wine. "More gifts?"

"Just a little something to go with dinner." He removed his coat and draped it over the arm of the living room chair as she peeked in the bag. "I wasn't sure what we were having, so I got both a red and white alchemy."

"Perfect! One for dinner and one for dessert." She marched toward the kitchen, and he followed.

Perfect indeed.

She opened the fridge and placed the bottle of white alchemy in the door, and set the red on the table. He was about to sit when she spun around and grabbed him by the hand. "I want to show you something."

They headed toward her quilting room. Her happy-go-lucky demeanor transfixed him, and he couldn't imagine what she'd want him to see.

"Sophie gave me an idea today. She suggested that we have a silent auction at the gala, and I want you to help me select one of my quilts to sell. I need to start marketing the items as soon as I can and figured I'd start the ball rolling with my own contribution. What do you think?"

Before he could get a word in, she continued, "Good idea, right?"

They stepped inside the room. "They're over here."

She dragged him to the big, wooden worktable, where she'd had three different quilts laid out. "Well?" she asked, staring up at him. "What do you think?"

She was happy. Her green eyes were full of fire, and her cheeks were flush, giving her a glow that was appealing. *How can I ever leave now?*

He reluctantly pulled his gaze away from her and examined the quilts. One was a series of stars, and each star was a combination of pale pink, mint, in both solid colors and floral prints. Another appeared to resemble how he'd built log cabins when he was a kid with varying lengths of rectangles placed in square patterns. The last one used numerous triangles that formed diamonds. Ben liked the last one the best. Its colors were bright and reminded him of the colors of the ocean, with its blues, teals, and greens.

He picked up the quilt, intending to open it up. "Do you mind?"

"Of course." She leaned back against the worktable and rested her palms on its edge.

"Wow, it's big. It must have taken you forever."

"Nah, it's a pretty basic pattern, really. After you do enough of them, it comes together pretty quickly." Rebecca stepped closer. "I also sketched out another idea that I could make instead. It's the Nubble Lighthouse—come see."

Ben refolded the quilt and laid it back on the table, then stepped to another table just below the bank of windows. She sifted through papers strewn about the tabletop to find the one she wanted.

"This is something I've been wanting to do forever. As you can see," she pointed out, "it's Nubble—obviously. But I want it to look like a sunrise behind the lighthouse with calm waters."

Ben considered her vision. "I'd be like depicting hope or something. A new day, peace…"

"Yes—exactly," she said before her once cheerful disposition transformed before his eyes.

"What is it, Becky?"

"With everything else I have to do, I'm not sure I can pull this one off, but it makes the most sense, right?"

"It's a landmark and it could get more bids for Stepping Stones." He thought about the huge task of adding the auction to the gala's agenda, and the workload in his absence would fall on her. "What if I could take collecting the auction items off your plate? Would that help you find the time to make your quilt?"

"That would be great, but as soon as the doctor clears

you to go, you'll be leaving." She cast her eyes to the floor and crossed her arms.

He placed his hands on her cheeks and lifted her face toward him. Her sadness tugged at his heart. She'd been through too much disappointment. He couldn't, he wouldn't cause it again. "I already saw the doctor. He said it's going to be a while before I'm cleared to fly again." He hadn't wanted to lie, but he didn't want her to think he was only staying out of guilt.

Rebecca's lips quivered.

"I thought you'd be happy," he said, trying to understand.

"I—I am. I'm sorry you can't go back, but honestly, it feels like a weight has lifted."

A tear trickled down her cheek, and he gently wiped it away with his thumb. Her supple lips forced a meek grin, and he leaned in and kissed her. Her taste was salty as he drew her to him. She didn't pull away; she embraced his advances. Ben lifted her and set her on the edge of the table as their mouths explored each other's. Becky's warm hands held his cheeks, and she pressed closer. Ben took in the sweet scent of her and her tender touch. He ran his hands down the length of her sleeved arms, savoring her—caressing her, but she tensed and pulled away, once again a look of sadness filled her eyes.

"We should stop." Rebecca put her hand on his chest, pushing him away, and slid herself off the table. "I'm going to work on our dinner."

She walked away, leaving him baffled and feeling utterly confused.

He turned to sit on the edge of the table. He replayed the event in his mind and couldn't make sense of it. He thought he'd read her well, that she was open and ready for a more intimate relationship. *What happened?*

CHAPTER 44

Rebecca stood in the kitchen, having left Ben in her wake.
What's wrong with me?

She'd gotten an answer to her prayer. He was staying. He was committing. And he'd wantonly kissed her.

She rubbed her hand down her arm the same as he'd just done, and could feel her rippled skin beneath her shirt sleeve. *He touched me.* He'd already seen her scars, and they didn't seem to bother him, but they bothered her. Rebecca didn't feel pretty or sexy. She felt ugly, and that ugliness was a constant reminder of her selfishness.

Rebecca was wrong to wish he'd stay in York Harbor. He was only staying because he had no other choice. He didn't want to or wasn't choosing her. Self-pity bore down on her like an anvil. He pitied her too. She just knew it.

Ben treaded softly as he approached while she spread marinara sauce over the chicken breasts. She could feel herself tense up again and forced herself to relax.

"Would you mind opening the wine for me?" she asked, thinking keeping him busy might help.

"Sure. Which one?"

"Let's start with the red alchemy, but we'll have to save enough of it for our dinner. We can let the white continue chilling while the chicken bakes."

She dug through the drawer in search of a corkscrew and handed it to Ben. He opened the bottle in silence as she placed two glasses in front of him. Still, he was quiet. She could hear the glug of wine filling each glass. As he handed the goblet to her, she drew in the sweet scent of the grapes.

They stared at each other, daring one another to take the first sip. He seemed detached as he peered over the rim. He was seeing right through her; Ben was there, but not really. He was simply going through the motions.

"I'm sorry, Ben."

"You have nothing to be sorry for. I misread. I shouldn't have pushed."

Rebecca gulped down a big swig of the red alchemy. The rich blend of fruit, spice, and woodland notes warmed her throat and eased her angst. "It's not you. Really."

She could only imagine what he might be thinking. *It's not you, it's me.* The cliché wasn't lost on her, but it was a true statement. She didn't want to push him away. On the contrary, she never wanted him to leave, but her insecurities took over. If he shied away from her body, there was no going back from that. She would be crushed and demoralized. The tension between them would put the project at risk, and she couldn't allow that to happen. Stepping Stones was more important than her need to be loved.

Ben took a drink. "I can't figure you out. I'm sorry, as much as I try, I'll be damned if I can."

"You're not alone." Rebecca took another swig. "I'm not trying to be aloof—truly, I'm not."

Rebecca sprinkled parmesan cheese over the sauce and placed the chicken dish in the oven. Ben had pulled out a chair and had a seat. His silence, she noted, wasn't that of a pouting man. No, it was patient and concerned.

She took another long drink of the wine before turning to face him. "I'm afraid, Benjamin."

He squinted his eyes and cocked his head. "You're afraid of me?"

"Goodness, no." She knelt in front of him and rested her hand on his knee. "I'd never be afraid of you. You've never given me a reason to." She bit her lip, then bit the bullet. "I'm afraid that if you see me for who I really am, you'll wish you hadn't, and that would mess up everything."

"Because you still don't trust me, Becky."

"No. It's not that. It's not that at all."

"Then what is it? What could possibly be so bad that you're afraid I'd walk away?"

Rebecca took his hand in hers and came to a stand. "I'd like to show you something."

She was dizzy as she stood and wondered if the wine was hitting her hard or if it was the sheer nervousness of what she was about to expose that caused her to waver.

Ben followed her down the hallway to her bedroom.

"You can sit there." She pointed to a chair in the corner of her room.

She swallowed hard and proceeded to her closet. She got on her hands and knees and moved a few pairs of shoes to the side. She lifted the hem of one of her longer skirts and retrieved a box. Her hands shook as she held the box to her chest. She paused to gain her composure and carried it to where Ben sat.

"I'd like to tell you a story, a story that I've never told anyone." She paused with a sigh. "I'm telling you this because you deserve to know the truth about me. Then, whatever decision you choose to make about us, I'll accept. I promise." Rebecca bit her lower lip and willed her heart rate to slow. She handed him the box.

Ben took the white box. It covered his lap, and he looked at it as if he wasn't sure he should open it. "You don't have to do this."

Ben removed the box from his lap and set it on the floor. He stood and stroked the loose tendril of hair behind her ear, then ran his finger across her quivering lips. "You don't owe me anything. It's me that owes you."

"I need to Benjamin. It's something I think I really need to do."

"Then let's do it together." He picked up the box and took her by the hand, leading her to the edge of the bed. "Sit." He patted the bed. She obediently sat, and the weight of him sat down next to her. He placed the box over both their laps. "I'll lift the lid with you." He kissed her temple. "When you're ready, go ahead, and I'll follow."

Rebecca leaned into his shoulder, grateful for his kindness, then sat up and slid the cover off the box up. To him, the content wouldn't mean much, but to her, it meant everything.

The lifted cover exposed a folded quilt. Rebecca removed the quilt from the confines of the box and set the box aside, then handed the quilt to Ben. "Go ahead, open it up."

Ben's puzzled look didn't surprise her. He unfurled the quilt and memories washed over her. The patchwork design had a multitude of fabrics: some were floral, some checked, others solid, and others had images of childish creatures, such as bunnies, chicks, butterflies, and kittens. The quilt was tattered with an unraveled edge, but it was large enough to cover a twin bed. A singed swath caught Ben's attention.

"I don't understand."

"My mom made this quilt for me for my tenth birthday. All the patchwork is from various clothes that I'd worn as a child. She told me she only used her favorite ones, the ones that meant something special to her." Rebecca pointed out a few of the squares. "This one was from the first dress I wore when I was born. This one is from my first birthday."

Ben touched the section and glided his finger over the pattern of ribbons.

"And there's one from my first day of school, and that one is from my favorite blanky." Rebecca could feel her throat tighten. She swallowed the lump down, forcing herself to continue. "I kept this quilt at the foot of my bed, slept with it, and carried it with me when I watched tv, and spent the night with friends."

She flipped the quilt over to reveal the back side. It was worn with thinning threads, loose knots, and stitches. In the lower right-hand corner was some embroidery that was barely legible because of the singeing. "This says, '*Rebecca, my darling daughter, and love of my life, may you always be wrapped in love, Mom.*'"

Rebecca could no longer stop her tears from falling. She closed her eyes and leaned into Ben. After a few moments, she pulled herself together and wiped her tears.

Ben wrapped his arm around her, holding her closely.

Rebecca reached for the quilt and Ben loosened his grip on her as well as the quilt. She straightened up and continued. "You must be wondering what any of this has to do with anything."

"A little." He turned to face her. "I know this is hard for you, but I'm listening."

Rebecca took in a deep breath and exhaled, willing herself to continue. She ran her trembling fingers along the singed edge of the quilt. "This is here because I was selfish, and my selfish actions caused those that I loved to die. That changed the trajectory of my life forever." Her lip quivered, and she sniffed back her tears. "It was the worse day of my life. And it was all my fault."

Ben gathered hold of her trembling hands and held them tight as he pulled them to his lips. He kissed them tenderly and between each kiss he whispered, "Let it go, it's time to let all of it go."

Rebecca closed her eyes and continued. "It was the evening of Thanksgiving. I was fourteen years-old. We'd had such a great day with friends over. We'd watched football, played cards, and I had my fill of all of the pumpkin pie I could eat." She fiddled with the edge of the quilt. "After everyone had left, I helped to clean up. It was getting pretty late at that point, and my mom started to blow out the candles. I wasn't tired and was going to stay up, so I asked if she could leave the one in the living room lit. It smelled like sugar cookies, and I liked the glow and the way it flickered."

Rebecca paused to collect her thoughts. Ben patiently waited for her to continue. "Mom insisted that she'd blow it out, but I promised I wouldn't forget."

"But you forgot," Ben said.

"Yes, but what made it worse is that I brought the candle

up to my room first. That's when I fell asleep. My cat must have knocked it over, because the next thing I knew, smoke alarms were going off, and my parents were pulling me out of my bed. My mom grabbed this quilt off my bed and wrapped it tightly around me to keep my hair from catching fire as we fled the house."

"I don't understand. You all made it out?"

"Yes, we did." Rebecca couldn't hold in her anguish any longer. A flood of tears spilled out. Her nose ran. She could barely catch her breath.

Ben grabbed hold of her, the quilt sandwiched between them, and cradled her to his chest. He didn't utter a word; he just rocked her in his arms.

Several minutes ticked away before she felt able to continue telling her nightmare. "When we were safely outside, awaiting the firetrucks, I realized that Greta—my cat—was still inside. Without thinking, I took off running toward the house. I can clearly remember hearing my parents shouting my name, but all I could think about was getting my cat out of the house. I still had this quilt around me. I thought I'd be safe. I was fourteen." She shook her head at her foolishness.

"Anyway, I hadn't realized it, but my parents had come after me. I'd heard Greta meowing through our smoke-filled living room. I grabbed her in my arms. As I headed toward the front door, the staircase collapsed. Part of it hit me and knocked me down. My quilt had slipped off one side, and Greta jumped out of my arms and bolted. That's the last I saw of her."

Ben caressed her shoulder as she collected her will to continue.

"The next thing I knew, a firefighter was throwing me over his shoulder and carrying me out of the house, then I passed out. I didn't come to right away, but when I did, I had an oxygen mask on my face, and I was calling for my mom and dad."

"They never made it out alive."

"Their bodies were found upstairs in my room."

"I'm so sorry, Honey. I'm so very sorry."

"It was all my fault. I killed my parents because I wanted a stupid candle lit, and I wanted my cat."

"You were a kid…"

"I know, but there's still no way of changing the fact that it was all my fault. All I have left of my past life, is this quilt, and—"

Rebecca removed the quilt from her lap and placed the fullness of it on his. She stood up and pulled her light-weight sweater over her head, revealing her scared body. "And this."

Rebecca stood shaking as she exposed her rawest self to him. He'd seen her before, but now he saw the full extent of the damage. "This is what I deserved." She ran her hand over her shoulder, arm, and torso. "And I need you to see me for who I am. I'm the selfish one, Ben, not you. I'm the one that hurts those around me. You deserve better than me."

By now, she wasn't feeling self-pity, but confidence. She knew her truth. And now so did Ben.

"Did you think I'd judge you?" Ben asked. "Because, I'd never judge you. In fact, you amaze me. You are a strong woman, Becky. Hell, I served in the military, and you've dealt with more pain than I ever have."

"I'm no hero, Ben," she said, just as the smoke alarm screeched from the kitchen.

CHAPTER 45

Terror shot through Rebecca's eyes and she froze. She trembled and all he could think to do was cover her up. He grabbed the quilt and wrapped it around her.

"It's just the chicken in the oven, Honey. It's okay. We're okay." But she wasn't okay. Rebecca was growing paler by the second and then she collapsed on the floor.

Ben was torn. He made a split-second decision to leave her alone and run to the kitchen. Smoke billowed out of the oven. The piercing sound of the alarm hurt his ears. He searched for pot holders, but gave up. He plucked a damp dish towel off the counter and dropped the oven door down. Ben grabbed the pan of charred chicken, rushed it out the door, and set it in the snow. The glass baking dish burst and shards of glass flew.

"Damn it!" With the door still wide open, the smoky air poured outside, but the alarm still shrieked. Towel still in his hands, he ran back in and waved it madly under the smoke alarm.

"Stop. For bloody hell, stop!" He wanted to hurry and get to Becky. She was in shock and he was furious that he wasn't with her instead of waving at a blasted alarm. It finally stopped.

He ran down the hall and took the corner to her room. She sat on the floor, wrapped in her quilt, staring blankly at the floor.

"Becky. It's me, Ben. There's no fire. No fire. It was just smoke from the chicken, Hon. We're okay. Everything is okay."

Rebecca slowly turned her head toward him. "I want to go home."

"Aah, Sweetheart, you are home. I'm right here with you." His heart ached for her. He wanted to take her pain away and hold her until she felt safe.

"I want to go home," she repeated.

Rebecca carefully came to her feet and removed the quilt from her shoulders. She moved past him. She retrieved her sweater off the chair and pulled it over her head, drawing it down ever so gently to cover her scars. She continued to move in slow motion toward him, and he reached for her.

Rebecca no longer shivered, but her paleness remained. He pulled her to him and held her as close as he could.

"Please take me home," she whispered.

Ben couldn't hold his emotions back any more. The dam broke, and tears rolled down and dampened Rebecca's silky hair. "I want to, but I don't know where home is."

"Our home, Ben. Take me to our home."

It clicked. *Mrs. G's.* Alright. I'll take you home, but we should get you some things to take with us."

"Okay," she said in a childlike voice.

Ben had seen a small suitcase in her closet when Rebecca

had retrieved her quilt. He rummaged through a few drawers and gathered some of her necessities, then pulled a pair of slacks and blouse off their hangers, and grabbed a green sweater he'd seen her wear before. He threw them in the suitcase, then headed to the bathroom and collected her toothbrush and other personal items. Lastly, he grabbed her robe and slippers. He walked her to the living room and set her and her bag on the couch.

"I'll be right back." He scooted out to the car and started it up. Within a moment, he ran back inside. He checked to make sure he'd turned off the stove and the lights.

"Are you ready to go?" he asked.

"I think so."

He took her hand, helped her off the couch and walked her to the warm car, then buckled her in.

"I'm just going to get your bag."

He stepped inside the living room and did a double checked before he remembered the quilt. He gathered her pillow and the quilt, then slid them into the back seat. Before long, they were on their way to Mrs. G's.

As Rebecca sat silently beside him it occurred to him she'd said, their home; not her home. *Their* home.

"Sweetheart, I need to make a couple of stops, if that's okay."

She nodded, and he veered off Route 1. He headed toward Jason's to collect some of his own belongings. He wanted to be near Rebecca and get out of Jason's way, so it was the best solution. In addition, he wouldn't have to drive back and forth while he fixed up Mrs. G's place. Next, he'd have to ditch his rental car, which he should have done weeks ago. Keeping it was costing him a fortune, and he no longer had money to waste.

Everything he now had was subject to the adherence to Mrs. G's wishes. They needed to get Stepping Stones up and running as soon as possible.

He couldn't believe he'd even considered leaving so soon. *I'm an idiot.* He decided he'd have Smithers sell his car and ask Holokai to put together his personal belonging and his dive gear, and ship it to Maine. His apartment was rented and furnished when he moved in, so at least he didn't have to burden anyone with that. The proceeds of his car would pay for shipping his stuff to the mainland. He'd have enough left over for a good-sized down payment on a car here. Feeling relieved at having a plan, he bolted into Jason's, grabbed his things, and scribbled a note explaining where he'd be.

When he hopped back in the car, she was leaning her head against the side window, which he thought had to feel cold, but she didn't seem bothered. He jacked up the heat anyway and decided to forego the second stop until after he'd settled her in at the house.

He'd looked forward to an evening without drama, and to his utter dismay, it had turned into a disaster. If the alarm hadn't gone off, she would have been well on her way to healing the torment she'd carried with her all these years. It pissed him off that she'd had a setback.

He thought of her excitement about her quilt for the fundraiser. Then it hit him. All of her quilting equipment and supplies were at a place she no longer wanted to call home. Quilting was her lifeline, and he needed to do something so that she could continue her work.

He remembered hearing that Brady, Sophie's husband, was a photographer, but also a general contractor.

Ben's wheels turned in his head as they approached the

house. He put his thoughts on hold and helped Rebecca out of the car. She seemed frail in his arms as they made their way inside.

He thought about what they had available in the house. *Tea. We have some tea.* He'd seen it in one of the cupboards, outside of that, there wasn't much else to eat, and his stomach was growling.

"I'm going to get you some tea, and then run to the store to grab us something to eat. Would you like to stay down here and watch tv, or would you rather go lay down upstairs?"

"I'd like to lie down upstairs."

"Okay, you got it."

As they stood at the top of the stairs, he was perplexed as to where to bring her. It didn't seem right to take her to her childhood bedroom, but he also wasn't sure if she'd be comfortable in Mrs. G's room. To his relief, she led the way to Mrs. G's room. She curled up under the covers, and he tucked her in.

"I'll be back up with a cup of tea." He left a kiss on her cheek and caressed her hair back to expose the depth of her deep green eyes, eyes he couldn't live without.

CHAPTER 46

Rebecca awoke and looked around the room. *Where am I?*

She stretched and sat up against the headboard. A full cup of tea waited on her nightstand. She dipped the tip of her finger in the liquid to see if it was hot or cold; it was stone cold. She turned to face the window. Still nighttime. She glanced at her watch, surprised to see that it was eight-fifteen. Her mind reeled as memories of the evening flashed by. She remembered telling Ben about her quilts and the auction, but the rest was fuzzy until she saw her quilt folded up at the end of the bed. *I told him.*

Clarity soon came, and she put the pieces of the night's events together. *I told him everything.* She tossed the blankets aside and moved to the edge of the bed. Her tattered slippers sat on the floor at her feet. She smiled. Ben had been so sweet to bring them. *Where is he?*

Rebecca slid on her slippers and smoothed the crease of her childhood quilt. The quilt had been a turning point in her life back then, and now, it was a turning point again. She stepped into the hallway and crept downstairs. It smelled heavenly as she turned the corner, toward the kitchen.

Ben was lifting a lid off a large pot and savoring the aroma of the steam.

He hadn't noticed her, so she watched him as he hummed to a tune. She smiled, remembering him singing at the top of his lungs in that same spot. He seemed at home, and that warmed her heart.

"Hi," she whispered as she approached.

He turned and beamed her a broad smile. "Hi, I was just about to wake you up."

"Whatcha making?"

"The best chicken and dumplings that you've ever had in your whole entire life."

Rebecca leaned in as he brought a wooden spoon filled with broth to her lips. She'd never tasted anything so divine. She savored the richness of thyme, sage, and a hint of cloves. The texture was silky to her tongue, and it warmed her to her soul. "When can we eat?"

"Whenever you put your sweet little butt in the chair, which I hope is right now, because I don't know about you, but I'm famished."

She took a seat at the metal-legged table and didn't miss the fact that he'd cleared off his tools and placed one of Mrs. G's plastic tablecloths over it. He set two shallow, wide-rimmed bowls down and ladled the steaming chicken and dumplings.

"I can't believe you did this."

"I promised you chicken and dumplings, and I figured what could be better to make you than a little comfort food? You needed it." He took a seat and cut open one of the dumplings. "I hope it helps you feel a little better. You had me worried."

"Sorry—I…"

"Becky, would you please stop apologizing? It was timing, is all. I'm sure you would have responded differently if you hadn't just been telling me about what happened in your past. I completely understand." He reached out and held her hand. "Okay?"

"It's just that I feel so foolish. I must be the most high maintenance person you know."

"Not even close. I wish you knew my friend Holokai. Now that's someone that's high maintenance." The corners of his eyes wrinkled as his smile grew. "And don't even get me started on Jason."

"He can't be that bad. As far as I see it, he's been taking care of you." Rebecca flashed a teasing grin.

"Oh, you do, do you?"

"Yes, I do."

"Well, let's see now. I bet you never had to make me date-sit for you." He took another spoon full and raised his eyebrows at her over the spoon's handle.

"No, I can't say as I'd ever had to do that." Rebecca rolled that thought around in her mind as she too took a spoonful.

"But at least we got some chocolate cream pie out of the deal. So I guess, all things considered, it wasn't so bad."

She smiled in recognition. "His high maintenance was our gain."

It tickled her to realize that the women she'd seen him with wasn't a romantic interest, and it certainly made her feel better about him coming to see her afterwards. *He's a pretty good guy.*

"Benjamin, I truly appreciate everything that you've done for me. You've been with me when I was most vulnerable. Too many times, I might add. I need you to know how regretful I am to have left you alone while you were recovering. It—"

Ben set his spoon down. "It's water under the proverbial bridge."

"No, it's not. I need you to understand why."

"Really, it's—"

"Please. Let me continue."

His face softened and his shoulders relaxed. "I'm listening."

Rebecca drank a bit of her water and dabbed her mouth as she considered how she'd like to say what she needed to say. After a moment's hesitation, she realized that she'd already laid her dirty laundry at his feet. Adding a bit more wouldn't make a difference.

"Remember when I said that I cared too much, and then we had a big fight afterward?"

Ben nodded.

"Well, I want you to know that I meant it. What I mean by that is that everyone I care for ends up leaving me. I couldn't bear it if something happened to you because of something I'd caused."

She mindlessly played with the food on her plate. "You see, it scares me because it just seems like bad things happen to those I—love."

She didn't dare to lift her eyes to his. How he'd take her confession would be written all over his face, and as much as she wouldn't blame him, his rejection would be unbearable. "Safe to say, Benjamin, I was afraid for you and for me. I thought it best if I just stayed out of your life."

He was considering all that she'd just said, but his silence ate at her insides. Her heart shattered into pieces, pieces she never could mend. She'd been broken for most of her life, and it seemed nothing could heal her wounds.

CHAPTER 47

Ben didn't know how to respond. He understood the words she'd just spoken, but he couldn't quite comprehend them. *She was so afraid I'd leave her, so instead, she left me.*

He clasped his hands under his chin as he tried to make sense of it. He wasn't sure if he felt sad for her because of all that she'd been through to cause her to think that way, disappointed that he wasn't worthy of her, or hurt that she trusted so little. But knowing that she loved him wasn't lost on him either. He just questioned if she even knew what love was. He sure as hell didn't.

Ben stood up, picked up his bowl and spoon, and carried them to the sink. She'd opened up to him and bared her soul, which he recognized was brave. She'd trusted him with her story. Her trauma afterwards, well, that was regretful. She was still in pain as she sat looking like a worn-out ragdoll. He owed her some kind of response, but the words wouldn't come.

He wasn't used to caring so deeply for anyone. If it had

been someone else, he'd never have allowed the relationship to get to this point. His relationships were shallow, which he hated to admit, but it was true. He walked away after the first sign of drama. He'd had enough drama in his own life, and he'd never intended to add more. But the truth was, he cared too much for Rebecca, and he had no idea what to do with his feelings.

He'd always compartmentalized his life. There was work. Those losses of life or the saving of them weren't about him; they were other people's problems. His social life was as he wanted it—strictly social and superficial. Family was non-existent, so there was no issue there. Romantic relationships were to satisfy his needs and nothing more. This, however, threw him for a loop. He had absolutely no idea what to make of it.

He sauntered back to the table and sat down. She'd barely eaten a thing, and she was, once again, pale. Ben wanted nothing more than to talk this out, but she was clearly fading again, and he was worried about her.

"I want you to know that I've heard what you've said—all of it—and I know it was a really hard thing to share with me, especially after our history together. So, thank you for trusting me with it."

He got up from his seat and stepped closer to her. He kneeled at her side, wrapped his arm around her waist, and grasped her clenched hands on her lap.

"I think. . ." He hesitated. "I think it might be best if we talk more about this once you've had some more rest."

Her head jerked to face him, and her eyes were wide. As he spoke, he touched his fingers to her lips.

"Honey, please. Once we've both had a full night's sleep,

we can talk more, but for now, I really think maybe we should call it a night."

"Fine. Sure. Tomorrow then."

Rebecca removed his hands and slid her chair back, nearly knocking Ben off balance. She picked up her bowl. She pulled open the drawer that held the trash and spooned her remaining chicken and dumplings in the bag, then pushed the drawer closed with her foot. She placed the bowl in the sink and walked out of the room while he stood there, dumbfounded.

"What did I say?"

As Rebecca clomped up the stairs, she stopped. "It's what you didn't say, Benjamin."

He could hear her race up the rest of the stairs, then slammed the door to Mrs. G's room shut.

Ben sighed. *Well, that could have gone better.*

CHAPTER 48

Rebecca was floored at his non response. *Wait until tomorrow! I just poured my heart out and confessed how I feel about him, and that's what I get?* She was mortified. Sure, he'd listened to her, and he didn't seem to judge her, but this rejection was too much. It infuriated her that he wasn't man enough to admit that he wasn't interested in her. Pity, she confirmed, was the worst feeling ever.

"Honey this and Honey that," he'd said, but his Honey was sour. He was appeasing her and nothing more. She was sure of it.

She pounded her pillow, then flipped onto her back, staring at the ceiling. *What am I doing here, anyway?* she thought, then remembered it was precisely where she'd asked him to take her.

She'd never stayed in Mrs. Getchel's room before, save for the time she'd had a nightmare. She'd crawled into her bed like a child. Mrs. Getchel had simply pulled her into her breast and caressed her hair, asking her to tell her all about it, but her dreams were too close to reality, and she hadn't wanted to open up that can of worms.

She lay there, once again, wishing that she could tell Mrs. Getchel everything that was swirling around in her mind. Rebecca missed her friend nearly as much as she missed her own parents, but she found herself getting angrier by the minute, and the urge to throw something was building.

Mrs. Getchel had manipulated her and Ben and, because of her meddling, Benjamin Daly had weaseled his way into her heart once again, only to leave her empty in the end.

What were you thinking by bringing us together and forcing us to do your bidding? Rebecca thumped her fists on the bed in frustration. Just knowing Ben was downstairs, probably going about his business as if nothing important had just taken place. She screamed into her pillow, then threw it across the room, which knocked down a framed collage to the floor.

Rebecca sat up and her attention went to her carefully folded quilt at the foot of the bed. She reached for it and brought it to her chin. The words of her mother fell open in her lap. *May you always be wrapped in love.* Her words felt like a proverbial slap in the face. The inescapable feeling of loss crept over, hovering like a storm cloud ready to burst wide open at any moment.

Rebecca thought about the quilts she'd made over the years. Each message she'd embroidered was meant to bring hope to their recipients. Now, she realized, they might have only brought on disappointment. Even the joy of creating her quilts seemed futile.

A knock on the bedroom door snapped her out of her

downward-spiraling thoughts and soon another, but louder, rapping came.

"What do you want, Ben?"

"Can I please come in?" His voice seemed strained and unsure.

She considered her reply.

"Please, Becky."

She rolled her eyes and stepped out of the bed, then released the latch that held the door locked. Rebecca sighed, then opened the door. Ben's distress was apparent as he stood, acting as if he was unsure of what to do with his hands.

"You may as well come in." Seriously, she thought, how could this night possibly get any worse?

Ben entered the room. His eyes caught sight of the wall hanging lying on the floor, then he turned toward her. "May I sit?"

"Sure." She made a flippant motion to the spot next to her on the bed.

He sat down and shifted to face her. His tongue found the inside of his cheek and his gaze roamed the room as if he were searching for words.

"I'm sorry. I realize I didn't handle what you shared with me appropriately. Or even how I'd intended." His gaze fell on her as he straightened his back. "This is all new to me, and I confess, I'm not sure what to do with it." He hesitated and looked at the ceiling. "I've had no one in my life that I really cared about, in this way. I have to admit that it scares me a little."

Rebecca was stunned. His confession was the last thing that she'd expected from him. At each turn, he ended up surprising her. She sat silently, realizing that her silence did not differ from how he'd responded to her after she'd poured her heart out. She now understood how he'd been feeling. She regretted her hasty and juvenile retreat, but she still couldn't bring herself to reply with any sort of coherent response.

"I don't know how to do this, Becky. I keep trying to show you how I feel about you. Doing stuff is all I know how to do. Words, well, words about how I feel, as you now know, don't come easy. But know this; I do care for you, deeply. Maybe that's what love feels like." Ben cleared his throat and looked in her direction. "I honestly don't know, but I'm willing to figure it out if you are."

Rebecca could no longer hold back her overwhelming relief. He loved her and that consuming thought came out as tears. But for the first time she could remember, they were happy tears.

His exasperated expression was short lived. She threw her arm around him. His embrace matched hers with a need that devoured them both. His embrace was more comforting than her beloved quilt. Her mouth found his with a hunger and desire she'd never known.

***

Rebecca sipped her coffee, welcoming the new day both literally and metaphorically as she peered out the window of Mrs. Getchel's kitchen. The morning sky burst with crimson and orange, which led Rebecca to dare to believe that brighter days were ahead.

Ben came up from behind her. His arms found her waist, and she leaned against him. A sense of safety enveloped her and gave her a long kiss on the top of her head. She took in the scent of his shaving cream and his warmth, wishing the moment would never end.

"Sleep well?" He swayed them back and forth as if they were dancing to a song that only he could hear.

"Mmm," she murmured. "I sure did, and you?"

"Like a baby." He turned her toward him.

Rebecca set her coffee down on the counter. She wrapped her arms around his neck and they continued the dance. "I'm guessing this is what love is supposed to feel like?"

"I'd like to think so."

She pressed her cheek on his chest and listened to his beating heart. They swayed in time to its rhythm. Thump, thump. Thump, thump. Thump, thump played the music of their souls, a dance of unity of mind and spirit.

Ben pulled away and kissed the tip of her nose. His warm hands lingered on her cheeks with a tenderness that melted away any worry for her day. "It's nice to see you smiling again."

She flashed him a grin from ear to ear. "It feels good to smile again."

"Good." Ben kissed her on her forehead and took note of her coffee. "Any of that left?"

"Yep. We got lucky. There was a container of coffee in the cabinet. Enough for a small pot."

Ben pulled a mug from the cupboard and poured a cup and topped hers off with the remaining coffee. "Are you still planning to go to work today?"

"Yes. I've got a bride coming in for a consult." She enjoyed the time she spent with brides-to-be. Seeing them walk in unsure and then leave confident in their choices was satisfying. It was the part of her job that made it all worthwhile.

That and the actual wedding day when everything was perfect. Today, she'd much rather just spend the day with Benjamin.

"Okay, then. I'm taking this with me." He lifted his coffee. "While you're getting ready, I thought I'd take care of the broken glass at your apartment, check on things for you, and pick up some breakfast sandwiches. I put your handbag with your phone on the entry table last night. Hopefully it's charged. I didn't think to grab the charger." He pursed his lips. "Anyway, call me when you're ready, and I'll come back and pick you up."

Rebecca couldn't recall what he was talking about. *My baking dish.* A shiver crept up her spine at the memory of thinking her apartment was all ablaze. "Thank you, but—"

Ben touched his finger to her lips. "I've got this."

"No. What I mean is, I have nothing to wear, and I don't even have a toothbrush." She cringed as that reality sank in and prayed she didn't have horrid morning breath.

"Everything you should need for the day is upstairs. If I forgot anything, then we'll swing by your place on the way to Proposals."

"You packed a bag for me?"

"Of course."

Of course, he did. What could I have been thinking? She shook her head. "Okay, then."

"Great. The sooner I get going, the quicker I can get back."

He was right. She needed to get ready and wanted to leave some extra time to swing into the attorney's office. He had a packet of info that they'd need for the town meeting that was now only two days away. She wanted to look at everything in advance in hopes of giving her a little peace of mind and settle her angst.

"Thanks for taking care of everything, Benjamin."

He gave her a peck on the cheek, and headed out the door.

Rebecca gulped the rest of her coffee and headed up stairs to the bedroom. The fallen collage of her temper tantrum caught her attention. She retrieved it from the floor and examined the frame. Outside of the cracked glass, she was relieved to see the frame had no sign of damage. Glass was replaceable.

She carried the frame to the bureau, carefully removed the backing, and withdrew the 8x10 collage and the two glass pieces. The backing of the patchwork of photos had a handwritten note. She assumed it was in Mrs. Getchel's hand until she read the name. It read, "*Mrs. Getchel, Thank you for giving me a family. Happy Birthday, Ben.*"

She flipped the paper over and examined the images more closely. The photos were photocopies of the originals. Each picture was cut to bring out the faces and shape of the kids. Mrs. Getchel's image took the center spot. Rebecca had seen the photo before in one of the albums downstairs.

Mrs. Getchel had taken special care to make scrapbooks of her foster kids and recorded their accomplishments. This photo of her was one taken in the backyard when Rebecca had lived there. She remembered the day as clear as a bell—the fourth of July, and they were having a barbecue. Mrs. Getchel had arranged to have a badminton set in the yard, along with a variety of other games, and a water sprinkler.

Rebecca remembered the laughter and the antics of the other kids. When evening came, and Mrs. Getchel lit the fire in the pit, Rebecca had withdrawn from the others.

Ben and Jason had roasted marshmallows and made s'mores while the younger kids lit up sparklers and danced around the yard, making swirling motions with their arms. The fire and the sparklers had caused her to tremble. Fire, in any form, was still a cause for PTSD to take over, but Mrs. Getchel had taken notice. She took her by the hand and walked her toward the side yard.

A large apple tree and flowering shrubs appeared as silhouettes in the moonlight. Rebecca could still see the shimmering sparklers dancing in the distance as Mrs. Getchel pointed out lightning bugs floating through the air all around them. They twinkled their lights, as if welcoming her to share in their fun. Rebecca caught a handful and watched them blink on her fingers. She marveled at the little flying creatures.

Ben had joined them, carrying a s'more in each hand. He'd handed her one. She could see in her mind's eye his beaming smile before he took a bite of the melting chocolate. They hadn't known the magnitude of what those two gracious acts of kindness meant to her, but she'd never forget.

Rebecca read the inscription again. "Thank you for giving me a family."

She flipped to the photo side again and examined the other photos. They were all there: she and her fellow fosters: Benjamin, Jason, Frida, and Amy—her new family. She wondered if Ben had foreseen their future. Had he envisioned them as they now are, or had it been Mrs. Getchel, all along, that had seen their future? Rebecca's questions continued as she set the collage on the bureau and collected her belongings to go take a shower.

She was dressed by the time Ben opened the front door, announcing he was back. Her heart skipped a beat just knowing he'd returned. She couldn't get the smile off her face when she heard him whistling. *He's home.*

Rebecca joined him in the kitchen as he pulled ham-egg-and-cheese sandwiches out of bags from Grounds Coffee Shop. She hadn't realized how hungry she was until he'd opened the wrapped sandwich and handed her one.

"Thank you. This is perfect." She took a big bite and egg yolk oozed down her chin.

"Good." He used his thumb to wipe away the drip from her chin. "I thought about us eating them on the way to Proposals, but honestly, I couldn't wait another minute. It was all I could do to not devour mine in the car."

At that moment, she saw Ben in a whole new light. He had shown her all along that he wasn't selfish. It wasn't just the sandwich that pulled at her heartstrings, it was all his acts of kindness over the years. Sure, he'd left all those years ago, but in doing so, they'd grown into the people that they were today. Had that not happened, they wouldn't be where they were right now: two people that were bonded and meant to be together. They were ready and able to fulfill Mrs. Getchel's final wish.

They finished up their sandwiches, grabbed their coats, and headed toward the door.

Ben stopped dead in his tracks. He pointed to the tattered slippers on her feet. "Where are your shoes?"

She peered down at her slippered feet, forgetting that she'd had them on. "I'm—I have absolutely no idea."

CHAPTER 49

Rebecca was relieved when her consultation with the bride-to-be ended, and she was able to say her goodbyes. She was anxious to go over the documentation regarding Stepping Stones' upcoming town meeting. Everything was on the line, and they couldn't afford to have any hiccups. When Mr. Howard told them he'd received a certified letter from Mrs. Bennington the previous day, about some issues regarding the historical significance of the house, it had thrown them for a loop. Seemed Mrs. Bennington's letter stressed that they were in violation of a town ordinance. If that was the case, it would stop the project in its tracks, with less than two days before the meeting, no less.

Rebecca could still see Mr. Howard's trepidation when Ben had been irate at hearing this and demanded that Mr. Howard take care of it immediately. She wasn't reassured when Mr. Howard stuttered and stammered his response, that he'd do just that.

Rebecca sat at her desk and pored through the documents, and reviewed the overall plans, hoping that they'd dotted all the I's and crossed all the T's. All she could think about was the ramification should Mrs. Bennington be right.

Rebecca had already pictured her and Ben welcoming kids in and helping them to recognize their full potential. The thought of anything jeopardizing that was more than she could bear.

They had some renovations that needed to get done before they could open, but she was relieved that those structural and cosmetic plans were ready to go. Once they got the town approval, the work could begin, so long as they raised enough money. Beyond what Mrs. Getchel's trust account held, the gala was just the thing to make that happen.

She looked over the invitation list that Sophie and Emily had helped put together and hoped, once they were sent out, the replies would be a resounding yes. She and Ben needed every volunteer they could get and hoped the attendees would have deep pockets. Otherwise, Stepping Stones would be in jeopardy, and she'd lose the house. Her *home*.

Rebecca sat in her office, thinking of Ben. They'd come so far since she'd seen him at Mrs. Getchel's funeral. She never dreamed that her life would have changed so drastically in such a short amount of time. She couldn't help but think that Mrs. Getchel had known all along what would happen. She smiled and had to believe that Mrs. Getchel was watching over them and cheering them on.

A knock at the door drew her away from her daydreams.

"Come on in," Rebecca said, expecting Sophie so she could debrief her regarding the appointment she'd completed, but to her surprise, Ben entered.

"Hey, beautiful," he said with a broad smile as he stepped into the room. All she could think was about the last time he'd come there. She could still picture him lying on the floor unconscious.

"Hey, you." Rebecca stood to meet him. "What are you doing here?"

"I know, it's early." He took her into his arms. "But I was nearby and couldn't resist coming to see you."

"I'm glad you did."

Rebecca took in his masculine scent, and strong embrace, as if she were savoring it for a lifetime.

"I'm sorry about losing my temper with the attorney this morning." Ben kissed the crown of her head. "I hope I didn't upset you."

"No, you didn't; Mrs. Bennington did."

Ben released her, and Rebecca motioned for him to have a seat opposite the desk. He ran his hand along its edge. "I'm guessing this is where I hit my head?"

"Yes," she said as sorrow poured through her. "I'm so sorry for how I—"

"Please don't apologize. I should have listened to you. I was wrong. And now, after hearing what you went through, I never would have—"

"I know. It's okay." Rebecca could see the despair in his eyes. "We're okay."

He gave her hand a squeeze just as Sophie opened the door.

"Oh, hi, Ben. I didn't realize you were here. I can come back."

"No, no, no. You two have work to do. I'll step out." Ben stood to go and gave Rebecca a wink. "See you in a bit."

"You better."

Rebecca took in his broad shoulders and swagger as he made his way out the door. She was grateful to have him in her life once again. *Thank you, Mrs. Getchel.*

***

Ben and Rebecca pulled into the parking lot of the York Library for their long-awaited town meeting.

"Is this really happening?" Rebecca asked as they stared at the front doors.

"It's really happening." Ben gave her a reassuring nod. "We've got this."

Ben's words were said with certainty, but Rebecca wasn't so sure. Her stomach was flip- flopping. She just wanted the whole ordeal over with.

As they walked through the lot, Rebecca shifted her head from side to side in search of Mrs. Bennington's car, but didn't see the white Lexus. They took the stairs to the lower-level, hand in hand, and Ben gave it an extra reassuring squeeze when they entered the room.

The meeting hall had filled up quickly. Ben and Rebecca took their seats at a folding table toward the front of the room, facing a sprawling, curved desk. The dais with six chairs and six microphones looked intimidating. The Town of York's round emblem adorned the dais' front. Rebecca was trying her best to keep her anxiety at bay. Ben briefly rested his hand on her knee to steady it, and she breathed in deeply.

She glanced behind her toward the entrance, anticipating their attorney's arrival. Friends and co-workers, and neighbors spilled in to support the project. Sophie gave her a thumbs up. Some patrons from Grounds Coffee Shop, as well as Jason, were also present. It warmed her heart to see so many people there, showing their support of Stepping Stones.

To her relief, their attorney stepped in, along with, who she assumed was a member from the Historic District Commission. Mr. Howard had called earlier in the day and mentioned someone from the commission might be joining him. Mr. Howard and a stranger advanced to another folding table next to hers and Ben's. He unpacked documents and maps, then he took his seat just as the six planning board members filed in.

Ben nudged her with his elbow and shot her a look. He tossed his head toward the entry door. Mrs. Margo Bennington bulldozed through the crowd. Murmurs filled the room. Rebecca's heart nearly beat out of her chest. She lifted a silent prayer, *Please help us*. Rebecca took a deep breath and slowly exhaled, urging her heart to steady. *We can do this. Be strong, Rebecca.*

Mrs. Bennington plopped in a chair directly behind Rebecca and Ben's table, and Rebecca couldn't resist making eye contact and saying hello.

Mrs. Bennington pursed her lips tight and squeezed the handbag on her lap without saying a word. Rebecca giggled nervously at the woman's silence, knowing full well that her booming voice would soon make a spectacle of the proceedings.

The six-member board took their seats, and the meeting began. As the proceedings continued, Rebecca was relieved at their attorney's competence. She wiped away her earlier opinion of him, and fully understood why Mrs. Getchel had him on retainer. He stood with microphone in hand and explained, in great detail, how Stepping Stones would fit into the community and adhere to the town ordinances and regulations. He addressed parking, esthetics in keeping of the house's historic features, and a multitude of other aspects that both the planning board and historical commission required.

Now, the time she and Ben dreaded had come. The community had an opportunity to take to the lector and argue against the project or show their support.

Mrs. Bennington hoisted herself from her chair and plodded across the carpeted floor to the podium. As she introduced herself, the mic squealed with piercing feedback. The crowd winced. Rebecca and Ben, pleased with Mrs. Bennington's botched introduction, eyed each other with a look of delight. Mrs. Bennington proceeded, her accusatory tone and finger pointing only added to their amusement. Her tirade of judgement included the words delinquents, lacking character, uneducated, troublemakers. The negativity eroded Rebecca's confidence.

Mrs. Bennington spewed about what a nuisance to the community having cars going in and out, bogging down the village center would be. How the grand home would turn into nothing more than a commercial enterprise.

With each accusation, Rebecca watched the nodding heads and tight brow lines of the planning board members. She squeezed Ben's hand, hoping that they could persuade them to vote in their favor.

Mrs. Bennington's tirade went beyond the five-minute timeframe allotted, and the board interrupted her. Rebecca wished the board had a giant hook they could use to pull her away from the microphone. She was making a spectacle of herself. Her face grew redder by the moment as she spit and sputtered her objections. One of her hens approached and finally got Margo to take her seat.

The next twenty minutes nearly brought Rebecca to her knees.

As others from the audience took to the mic and introduced themselves, she learned that many of them were past foster kids Mrs. Getchel had helped. To her delight, several teens spoke of their support and how much Stepping Stones was needed for their future and the benefit of teens in transition.

Nathan stood up and shared the story about how Ben had helped him get a job, and how Rebecca had supported him when Mrs. Bennington had ridiculed in public. Rebecca could no longer control her emotions. She was smiling as tears of joy fell down her cheeks. She couldn't believe that Nathan would stand up and share his story about being in the system. He told of his need and desire to succeed in life, and from what he'd heard at the meeting, Stepping Stones: A Bridge to Success was just what he and others like him needed. His heartfelt words moved the audience and the board. As Nathan stepped away from the podium, the crowd clapped in appreciation.

Rebecca's hands shook as she held her pre-written notes and approached the podium. She swallowed hard as she saw the onlookers staring back. She cleared her throat and stepped closer to the microphone.

"Can you all hear me, okay?" she asked as she raised her eyes. She was greeted with encouraging smiles and nods, but she put her focus on Ben. He blew her a kiss and mouthed, "You got this."

Rebecca glanced at her notes and the words blurred on

the paper. She closed her eyes. *Just speak from the heart.*

"For those of you who don't know me, my name is Rebecca Mills. I lived in a loving home, filled with encouragement, laughter, as well as tears. I was blessed to have been taught that success was defined by doing something that you are passionate about, and living a life that fuels those passions."

Rebecca paused and locked eyes with several people in the crowd.

"Many of you are living proof of living a life of success. You may own a business that provides decadent sweets so others can celebrate milestones. Or make flower arrangements that delight. You may be a builder that sees a vision and makes that vision into something tangible for others. You could even serve coffee with that special ingredient called love. Some of you might serve in the military, for which I am so grateful. Others snap photos to capture loved ones so those images can last for generations. And, there are those who are teachers and mothers, who nurture, guide, listen, encourage, cry with, cheer for, believe in, and dream much bigger dreams than we could have ever imagined for ourselves."

Rebecca paused and cast her eyes down. She placed her hand on her heart and readied herself to continue.

"I was lucky enough to have lived in a family that offered me a chance to succeed, but that was taken away from me, as it was for so many others. You see, I was one of Mrs. Norma Getchel's kids.

"Mrs. Getchel, who lived in this community for her entire life, opened her home to foster kids just like me. And contrary to some of what we heard here tonight, I can assure you, these kids, through no fault of their own, are simply those who no longer have parents that can care for them. They are good kids that just need a break and mentors who can help them through their circumstances."

"As I look around, I recognize many among us, that were also blessed to have spent time in Mrs. Getchel's loving care."

"Mrs. Getchel wasn't just a foster care worker. She was our teacher, our mother, our grandmother, our friend. She entrusted two of her 'kids' to carry on her legacy. She chose that man, right there." She pointed to Ben. "Benjamin Daly and myself."

Rebecca gave Ben a nod. "But, as Mrs. Getchel would often say, we should always leave things better than how we found them."

"She chose us because we have a passion for helping kids bridge the gap from dependance to independence, so that they, too, can pursue their own passions, and live a successful life. And so, I ask you, grant us the ability to serve this wonderful community, and the children who need us, by bringing Stepping Stones to life. Thank you."

Rebecca glanced over at the board members as she took her seat. Ben gave her a peck on her cheek. The members wheeled their chairs toward each other. The chairperson covered his microphone, and they whispered among themselves.

Rebecca leaned toward Ben's ear. "Do you think we did enough?"

"I think so, but Mr. Howard told me that the board has to follow the town's zoning, planning ordnances, and historical commission guidelines. The emotional level probably won't come in to play."

"I know," Rebecca said with a sigh.

"Becky, you have to know that regardless of the outcome, I am so proud of you."

"Thanks." She grinned. *I'm proud of me too.*

The board members swiveled back to their original places.

"They all look so serious," she whispered. Ben nodded.

The chairperson thanked the community for their input. Rebecca noticed Mrs. Bennington stick out her chin and glance around, grinning at everyone as if the chairman had spoken only to her. Mrs. Bennington stopped short when she got to Rebecca and snickered.

"We, the board," the chairperson said. Rebecca held her breath. "Approve the plan for Stepping Stones. May it live up to its name, providing a bridge to success for generations to come."

With that, the chairman banged the gavel. Mrs. Margo Bennington stormed out of the room in a huff.

CHAPTER 50

Ben gave Rebecca an embrace and shook Mr. Howard's hand, still high from the town's approval of their project.

The audience was dispersing, and Ben wanted to find Nathan before he left. Sophie, Brady, and Emily approached, and Ben indicated he'd be right back. He spotted Nathan from the corner of his eye. He was with Jillian and the guy Rebecca had introduced as her accountant, Duncan. They were headed in Ben's direction.

"Thank you, Nathan." Ben gave him a squeeze on his shoulder and shook his hand. "That was pretty brave of you to stand up there. It means a lot to me."

"Thanks," Nathan said proudly.

By now, everyone from Proposals came over to join them.

"Well, you did a fine job." Ben introduced him to the others. "Brady, you're going to love this kid. Nathan here shares your love of photography. He's quite the artist."

"Sure is," Jillian added.

Nathan and Brady kibitzed about different cameras for underwater use. Rebecca had tugged on Ben's elbow, pulling him aside.

"Benjamin, when I'd met Nathan at Grounds, I knew I recognized the name, but I wasn't sure until tonight that he was *the* Nathan Monroe."

Ben didn't have a clue what she was talking about, but her expectant eyes led him to believe that he was supposed to know. "I'm not following."

"I made one of my quilts for a Nathan Monroe," she whispered. "He got one of my quilts."

"Oh. That's pretty awesome. You should tell him."

"Are you kidding me? That would be so awkward. For both of us."

Ben shook his head, not understanding her reasoning. He didn't dare question why it would be awkward, and so he didn't ask.

"I've never actually met any of the kids I make them for, and now I have a face to go with the quilt."

"I see." He still wasn't quite following, but just seeing her excited was reason enough.

"I don't make them for recognition, Benjamin. Just knowing he has one makes me happy, is all."

He found her delight and giddiness adorable, and he wanted to plant a big kiss on her chatterbox mouth, but he resisted. "I'm glad you're happy. I'm sure Nathan is pretty happy to have it."

Rebecca joined the rest of the group as introductions and congratulations continued. Ben stood back and took in the sight before him. Those people had knit their way into his world, and that was an unexpected addition he'd never dreamed of.

Rebecca was beaming, and her excitement was contagious. She and Sophie discussed the invitations to the gala that was now only three weeks away. Emily was sharing about some of the desserts Jillian planned to serve as Duncan and Nathan were gathering their things to leave. Ben wanted to get Brady's attention before he left and discuss the idea rolling around his head since the wee hours of the morning.

Ben caught Brady's eye, and walked to the edge of the room, avoiding the people stacking chairs.

"What's up?" Brady asked, joining him.

"I'm hoping you can help me out with a project. A secret project."

"Do tell," Brady said.

"I'd like to take you up on your offer to help with some remodeling and construction at Stepping Stones." Ben leaned his shoulder against the wall, and Brady listened. "Rebecca wants to move into the house, but the problem is, her quilting studio is at her apartment. Obviously, she can't keep paying rent just so she can work."

"Obviously."

"Yeah, so, I was thinking, if you're willing, would you be able to duplicate her studio in the area above the garage at the house."

"How big are we talking?"

Ben pulled out his phone from his pocket. "I was at the studio this morning, and I took some photos of the space. Most of it is her equipment, work table, and shelving."

Brady leaned in as Ben swiped through the images. "As you can see, it's mostly wide open except for the walk-in closet. It's where she keeps all her fabric, so I don't think it would be too difficult. We'd just need to add a bank of windows for light. Since Stepping Stones will be teaching skills, I thought it would be good to add some extra work tables. You know, so Becky can teach quilting. Kind of multipurpose classroom."

Ben relinquished his phone to Brady, who zoomed in on some shots. "This looks pretty doable. We'd just need to get a building permit. That won't be an issue if we're just adding windows to the back. Everything else is interior." He nodded as he handed the phone back over.

"So, you'll do it then?"

Brady stepped back and took a broad stance, then crossed his arms. "Sure. I'll do it. I like surprises, and as it happens, I'm in a lull with projects."

"Oh, man, thanks." Ben shifted and slid his phone back into his coat pocket. "I think she'll be thrilled."

"I think so, too, but how do you suppose we can pull this off without her knowing?"

Ben thought for a moment, and then his eyes lit up. "I have an idea, but it's going to take some strategizing."

***

Ben crept out of bed. His wandering mind had kept him awake most of the night. With his hope of falling asleep waning, he gave up before the sun came up. He dressed in a pair of jeans, a hooded sweatshirt, and threw on some sneakers. Then shoved his arms in his coat and headed out the door.

The call to the water brought him to York Harbor Beach just as the skyline awakened. He pulled his hood up and stuffed his hands in his pockets. A light, icy wind hit him on the back as he navigated the stones at his feet and headed toward the entrance of York's Cliff Walk.

He entered the narrow path and weaved through the

sleeping shrubbery. His gait was lazy. Ben took the crisp sea air into his lungs as if it were his last breath. He sighed as the weight of his new reality sunk in. The waves sloshed against the cliffs, beckoning him, nudging him to once again dive and become one with the water. It was not meant to be.

Ben ascended the cliff's path and tried to focus on all that was going well: he and Becky were hitting it off, Stepping Stones got its approval, the gala planning was well underway, and his surprise plan for Becky's quilting room was on schedule. These things, he thought, should make him happy, and they did. Somehow, it just wasn't enough. Ben was an adventurer, and he missed the excitement of diving. He'd never seen himself as someone who settled down, but he had to admit it had its advantages. He could no longer see his life without Becky in it.

Ben stopped and picked up a smooth stone and rolled it around in his fingers, then tossed it. The rock's splash got lost in the crashing waves below. He broke off a thorny twig and plucked the thorns off as he continued his mile-long walk. His mind shifted to Margo Bennington's embarrassing spectacle the night before. He chuckled at the sight of her face when she realized she'd been defeated. Yes, he and Becky made quite a team. He thought of Nathan and his bravery at speaking out for what he knew was right, and of Rebecca's heart felt words that made even him want to live up to.

Ben turned the clock back to when he was around Nathan's age; a time just before Rebecca arrived at Mrs. G's home, his home. He'd been a lost soul, and he felt then just as he was feeling now: lost. A sense he wasn't whole.

He made a turn in the path and caught sight of Millbury Lane, the end of the road. He dropped the twig at his feet and took the small stone stairs to the rocky coastline. He noticed the tips of black fins peeking in and out of the water's surface. Ben sat on the last step and watched the diver move through the water. He wasn't far, nor was he in deep waters, but he seemed content, lingering as if something caught his interest.

Ben's hands grew stiff and the rocky steps on which he sat sent a chill to his bones. He stood to get his blood circulating again just as the diver stood in the water. He navigated the fins over the smooth stones and headed in Ben's direction.

"Find anything interesting out there?" Ben asked.

"Enough." The diver pulled his mask off and peeled his neoprene suit off the top of his head. The stranger made it to dry rocks and sat down. He removed his fins, then sauntered toward Ben. He appeared in his late sixties or early seventies with a full head of gray hair, and a robust physique. Ben guessed former military from his swagger.

"You got some great looking equipment there. Did you serve?" Ben asked.

"Yep." He ran his hand through his hair and gave it a shake, sprinkling salt water through the air.

Ben considered his age and took a guess. "Nam?"

The man cocked his head. "Indeed. You?"

"Navy—USS Carl Vinson. Name's Ben." Ben reached his hand out.

"Roger," he said with a sturdy shake.

"Is that a Zeagle Ranger you're wearing?"

Roger glanced down at his BCD vest. "Yep."

"Cool. I haven't seen one up close."

"You a diver?" Roger asked.

"Was—until recently. I was doing salvage dives, but I can't do it anymore."

"Oh?" Roger leaned his hip against a post near the base of the steps and crossed his arms. "What's stopping you?"

Ben tapped his finger near his temple. "Head injury."

"You and me both. Took some shrapnel during combat."

"How is it you're able to dive?"

Roger shrugged. "Time. It was a good while before I could get back in there." He gestured toward the water. "Can't do the deep stuff anymore, but I can still play."

Roger bent over and retrieved his fins.

He could still dive? "Question for you. Do you know if it's possible to teach diving with our limitations?"

"Don't see why not." He shrugged. "Five feet, fifteen or fifty. It's all the same." Roger gave a shiver and reached his hand out to Ben. "Nice meeting you, son."

"Pleasure was all mine." Ben took Roger's gloved hand with both of his and squeezed. "You have no idea what you've done for me today."

With that, Roger gave him a nod, headed up Millbury Lane and vanished.

Ben wanted to jump up and down like a kid who'd just won the Little League world series. He whooped and hollered into the morning sky as he double timed it back up the path. Ben didn't need to do deep dives to find pleasure. He could be perfectly content with less. He was excited about the prospect of teaching the skill. Healing would take time. Roger's injuries might not be the same as his, but just knowing the possibility existed gave him hope. His previous feelings of loss dissipated as quickly as the morning mist upon the water.

***

Before heading back to the house, Ben decided to pull into Grounds Coffee Shop. Nathan might be working on a Saturday morning. Ben's assumption was correct. Nathan was bussing a table and shot Ben a smile the second he entered the room. Jillian was speeding around tables with her coffee pot. He gave Nathan a wave and then stepped to the counter to place an order of breakfast sandwiches. Claire, the girl behind the counter, knew what he'd order before he could get the words out of his mouth. "I come here that much, do I?"

"Any friend of Jillian's is a friend of all of us. Remembering her special friends' orders comes with the job description." She gave him a grin as she punched his order into the system.

"Now you're just stroking my ego." Ben reached for his wallet. "You know my order, and now I'm a friend." *You can't beat that.* He gave a lighthearted laugh and paid.

Ben maneuvered around the tables until he reached Nathan. "So, Nathan. I heard you talking to Brady Owens about the pics you like taking underwater. Right?"

"Yeah, I like drawing sea urchins, natural underwater formations, things like that." Nathan tossed his head to the side to get his hair out of his eyes and placed plates and cups in his bus tub. "Oh, thanks for introducing me to him, by the way." He rested the tub on the table. "He's a pretty cool guy."

"You're welcome."

Ben heard his name getting called, announcing that his breakfast sandwiches were ready for pickup, but lingered for a minute while Nathan finished cleaning up the table.

"Have you ever considered learning to scuba dive? You'd get some really great shots that way."

"Who hasn't?"

"What if I were to teach you?"

Nathan's mouth just about dropped to his chest. "Are you kidding me right now?" But his excitement abated just as quickly as it had arrived. "It's gotta be *way* out of my price range, though, and I'm saving for a camera."

"Tell you what. You keep up the good work here and keep your grades up, and I'll see what we can do. Deal?"

Nathan's eyes grew wide. "I will. Promise, I will."

"Good." Ben gave Nathan a slap on the back, grabbed his sandwiches, then strutted out the door with a smile on his face as big as the ocean.

CHAPTER 51

Rebecca lazily opened her eyes and was surprised to see that the sun was already up. She was excited to start her day at Proposals. Now that Stepping Stones' approval was done, she could focus on the gala. She and Sophie were going to make some final revisions to the gala's guest list and finally get the invitations in the mail. Rebecca gave a little squeal, knowing that Stepping Stones was really going to happen. The outpouring of support the night before encouraged her. She was confident that they'd raise the revenue for scholarships, necessities, as well as have ample volunteers to teach the kids, not only life skills, but skills that would open their eyes to creativity and gifts that they could use throughout life.

Rebecca's thoughts went to Nathan. A flood of gratitude poured through her. She was thankful to know he had one of her quilts. She recalled the message she'd stitched: *I; Nathan Monroe, am talented and will shine.*

Shine he did, she thought, and it solidified her need to continue. The messages that she stitched into the quilts and the care that she took in creating each one wasn't just a name on paper; they were kids that needed some comfort, needed to know that someone cared for them and believed in their potential.

Rebecca stepped into the bathroom to get showered and dressed. She was surprised to see Ben had scrolled a note on the mirror. It read, "Good morning, beautiful. Coffee's made. Grabbing us breakfast." He'd used one of Mrs. Getchel's lipsticks; one Rebecca had seen her wear almost daily. Between the message and seeing the petal pink lipstick, Rebecca, for the first time she could remember, she was happy looking into a mirror.

Before long, she traipsed down the stairs, ready for the day. Ben was talking in the kitchen. As she got closer, she realized he was on his phone. She didn't want to interrupt him, so she held back. His tone was soft, as if he was purposely trying to speak quietly. Perhaps he was afraid he'd wake her. Surely, he'd heard her in the shower. So why the secrecy? She stepped a little closer and stood behind the wall between the kitchen and the living room.

Her pulse quickened. She didn't want to eavesdrop, but was compelled to do so. She wanted to trust him. He'd certainly proved himself trustworthy lately. Even so, she couldn't help herself.

He was looking out the back door window, with his back to her. "I told you last week that they cleared me to fly."

He hesitated, and she could hear him pace. "Would you listen to me, Holokai? If you'd shut up for a second, I'll tell you." His pacing stopped. "Yes," he said in frustration, "that's what I've been saying. As soon as the gala's over, I'll be seeing your ugly mug." Ben laughed. "I hear you."

He walked toward the living room, and Rebecca held her breath, hoping he wouldn't catch her listening in. "On the upside," he continued, "at least I'll be leaving this friggin' weather. Hey, I gotta go. Rebecca's going to come down here any minute. Yeah, I'll keep you posted. We'll talk soon."

He hung up and cleared his throat, then hollered toward the ceiling. "Hey, Beck! Sandwiches are getting cold!"

Rebecca couldn't move, not because she didn't want him to see her, but because she was stunned. *He lied to me?*

Confusion and disappointment spilled over her like a glass of cold water. She could feel fury rise in her. *He's been cleared to fly?* She fumed. *After he promised to stay, he has the audacity to leave?* Blinking back tears, she cursed herself for falling for him once again. *I thought he loved me.*

She continued to hide. *Was he planning to leave me all along? Was he just using me to get his inheritance?* She bit back her desire to lash out and expose the secret he was trying to keep, but she wanted to see how far he'd keep up the charade.

Rebecca got her breathing under control and tried her best to relax before she was comfortable enough to safely step into the archway.

"Hey, thanks for getting sandwiches again, but I'm not hungry." She rubbed her stomach, showing her discomfort at the idea of eating. "There's just too much to do for the gala."

"Beck, you should try to eat a little something. Just a bite. It might make you feel better."

"Yeah, I know. I'll grab something at Proposals. Emily's always got stuff in the fridge."

Ben gave her a puzzled look. "Oh, okay." His dejected

expression almost appeared disappointed. He picked up the sandwich. "You could take it with you."

"No thanks." She waved it off. It felt like a bribe. "Just doesn't sound appealing."

Rebecca looked at the time, realizing that she'd be too early for her meeting with Sophie, but she wanted to get out of there. "Wow, time got away from me. I—ah—need to go. I don't want Sophie waiting for me." She did a two-step and spun to leave. "Not sure how long I'll be today. I—I've got a ton to do."

"Anything I can help with besides collecting the auction items?"

Rebecca faced him again, trying her best to keep her cool. "No, we've got it under control."

Her need to leave was building to the point she wanted to run. The fact that he was being so kind, knowing that he was making plans to leave her, caused her stomach to turn sour.

Ben set the sandwich back down and made a step in her direction. "See you at dinner, then?"

"It's probably best if we're on our own tonight. Like I said, I'll be working late." She pushed up her sleeve and glanced at the time. "I've—um—I gotta run."

With that, she ran toward the door, grabbing her coat and handbag along the way.

She got to her car and felt sucker punched. All her excitement from the night before, this morning, and for her future, had vanished. *He's been lying to me this whole time.*

***

Proposals was quiet, except for the hum of a mixer coming from Emily's kitchen. She could smell freshly made bread and the heavenly scent of baked cinnamon. Her stomach growled, and she needed a strong, hot coffee. She kicked herself for not thinking to swing into Grounds on the way. It would have eaten up some time she had to kill.

The humming stopped, and Emily opened the oven door. The rush of baked cinnamon, pastry and cardamom nearly took her breath away. She couldn't resist any longer and slipped behind the counter toward the kitchen. Emily was sliding the cinnamon twists off the baking sheet and placing them on a cooling rack.

"There's nothing like the glorious aroma of your cinnamon twists, Em."

Emily nearly jumped out of her skin and flung a cinnamon twist into the air. It whirled to the ceiling and landed on the floor, leaving flaky pastry scattered on the tile.

"Good grief, Rebecca. You scared the hell out of me."

Rebecca fought back a grin. "Sorry about that."

Emily reached down and picked pieces of pastry off the floor. "What are you doing here so early?"

"Have you ever caught someone in a lie, and it was all you could do to not to punch 'em in the face?"

Emily removed the large bowl from the standing mixer and poured its content into the awaiting muffin tins. "Yes. All the time, but I've also come to realize that I tend to jump to conclusions and overreact. Even Sophie's been known to jump to conclusions from time to time."

Rebecca leaned against the counter, snagged a cinnamon twist off the warming rack and broke off a piece. "I don't think I'm jumping to conclusions." She popped the bite-size piece into her mouth.

"Hey! That's two, I'm down now."

With a full mouth, Rebecca mumbled, "Sorry." She made herself a cup of coffee. "Honestly, I'm not even sure I can be in the same room with him right now."

"Who?"

"Ben."

"I see." Emily placed the muffin tins in the oven and wiped her hands on her apron. She poured herself a cup of coffee, and joined Rebecca at the counter. "It's none of my business, but is there a chance that it might be a misunderstanding?"

"No. I heard him clearly say that his doctor had cleared him to fly when he told me he wasn't. Then I heard him say he was going back to Hawaii as soon as the gala's over." Rebecca could feel her blood pressure rise again. Her head throbbed. Her sweet treat no longer appealed to her. She set the twist down and stared at her coffee as if she were reading tea leaves. "I mean, can you believe that?"

"I do find that hard to believe, but maybe there's more to the story than meets the eye. He's got to go back at some point to deal with his life back in Hawaii, right?"

"Yep. Hawaii." She played with a small flake of pastry. "I suppose, but something isn't adding up."

"Trust me, you don't want to take advice from me about times that things don't feel right. My record is impressive on that account. Just ask Sophie and Brady."

"You sell yourself short, Em."

"I beg to differ with you on that one." Emily gave her a nod, then shuffled to the refrigerator. "You said you overheard him, correct?"

"Yes. He was on the phone. He didn't know I was in the next room."

"I see." She nodded. "You know what? If I were you, I'd consider how he's cared for you. I mean, you'd have to be blind to not realize how much he's head over heels for you. And look at everything he's done for Stepping Stones. That must count for something, don't you think?"

"Sure, but…"

"There you are," Sophie said as she stepped into the kitchen. "I thought I heard you in here."

Rebecca took a quick sip of her coffee and placed the mug in the sink. "Yeah, I got here a little early, and I've been indulging myself with one of Emily's cinnamon twists. You ready?"

Rebecca mouthed, "Thank you" to Emily, then headed out of the kitchen, ready to set Ben's big secret aside and focus on the more pressing issue of the gala. She was determined to not let the likes of Benjamin Daly derail her plans of making the gala a smashing success. She'd act as if she'd never heard his lie. At least until the gala was over.

Chapter 52

The past few weeks flew by as Rebecca focused on preparing for the gala, and Ben concentrated on all the work at Stepping Stones. Now, the night of the gala was here, and Rebecca had to face the reality that Ben would be leaving. She'd hoped Ben would have brought it up over the past few weeks. A simple, "Hey, by the way, I'm heading to Hawaii after the gala," would have kept her from feeling like a fool. She couldn't for the life of her understand why he hadn't trusted her enough to tell her the truth, unless he never intended to come back. That thought was enough to rip her heart out.

Rebecca walked up the incline to the barn. Proposals bustled with activity. Black table linens covered the many round tables throughout the barn. Gold chargers with black napkins, in the shape of bow ties with gold crystalized napkin rings at their centers circled the table tops, along with gold-rimmed champagne flutes. Each table's centerpiece had varying heights of clear cylinder vases. Each vase contained weighted floating orbs of gold, along with white roses, and gold painted willow branches. Gold candle sticks with black candles completed the dramatic look for an awe-inspiring formal gala.

The tables along the wall for the auction items were covered in shimmering gold sequin, and boasted large, clear balloons filled with gold confetti. Rebecca had displayed her quilt of the Nubble Lighthouse, as well as the multitude of other offerings Ben had collected.

Duncan and his brother's band were setting up. Their contribution was to play cocktail music while everyone was eating dinner. The massive stone fireplace provided the backdrop for the food display.

Ben was setting out the chairs, and Rebecca took in his rhythm as he flipped each chair off the cart and set it into place, being careful to place each one just so. She'd have thought he wouldn't have cared so much, knowing he'd be leaving as soon as it was over.

She'd envisioned this evening differently when they were a team, a couple. Rebecca had pictured them working side by side, flirting and teasing. She pulled her gaze away.

When everyone was done with their tasks, Rebecca stood at the entrance and took in the shimmering spectacle. She didn't even mind that Ben had joined her. She was happy with the results she, and her friends, had achieved. Nothing, not even Ben's presence, would hamper the incredible feeling of joy that filled her to overflowing.

Ben joined her in her admiration of the scene before them. "It's absolutely stunning, Becky. You've done an amazing job planning this."

"With a lot of help." She couldn't wipe her broad smile off her face. "It is pretty amazing."

Ben took Becky in his arms. "This is going to be a smashing success. I can just feel it. Can't you?"

"Well, we have the who's who coming. I just hope they donate both talent and funding. The last thing I want is to have them use this event to schmooze."

"Me, too, Hon. Me, too."

Rebecca's back prickled when he called her Hon, but she pushed it aside. "Well," she said as she pulled away from his embrace. "We need to get ready. I brought my stuff here. Meet you back in an hour?"

Ben had a momentary blank expression. "Sounds good." He hesitated for a moment, then reached to slip a piece of her hair behind her ear. "Becky, is everything okay?"

"Of course. I don't know how you can ask that. Just look at this place."

"No, I mean between us? You've been so distant lately. Have I done something wrong?"

"There's a lot riding on this gala. I just want everything to go well." She headed out the exit toward the main house of Proposals to get ready, stuffing down her feeling at Ben's betrayal.

***

Rebecca stood at the full-length mirror examining herself. She'd decided tonight was the night where she'd be bold because Mrs. Getchel deserved nothing less from her. Rebecca stepped into her sleeveless violet-colored gown and pulled the narrow straps onto her shoulders. The scoop-neckline plunged just enough to bring out the one and only piece of jewelry Mrs. Getchel had owned: a string of pearls. Rebecca had found it in the top drawer of Mrs. Getchel's dresser in a little wooden box.

Rebecca slipped on her taupe leather high heels, touched up her makeup and hair, which she wore in a swirling updo. That style was also a first for her. She stepped up to the mirror again and breathed in. *I can do this. I can be brave.*

The fact that Ben saw her the second she entered the barn pleased Rebecca. He braced himself with the back of a chair, and his smile lit up the room. She couldn't help but notice that he was gorgeous in his black tuxedo.

"Oh, Becky, Honey, you look stunning." He took her by the shoulders and kissed her cheek with tender lips, then pulled away slightly to take another look. "Just stunning."

"Thank you. You look pretty terrific yourself." She gave his hand a squeeze. "Shall we do this thing?"

"You bet."

Guests in their formal best filed in, and the bubbly energy was palpable. Champagne flutes clinked. The auction table was ticking upward with generous bids. Music filled the room. The candles flickered, and the fire burned, providing a warm glow that shimmered and reflected off the crystal chandeliers and stemware.

Everything was going along beautifully until Rebecca saw Mrs. Bennington making an entrance. Margo was all smiles and opened her arms to greet several of the guests. She gave pecks on their cheeks, then removed her fur coat and handed it to an attendant, as if she'd been cordially invited.

Oh, no you don't! You are not going to ruin this evening for me.

Rebecca scurried over toward Emily and Sophie, who stood near the microphone and podium at the far corner of the barn. Her heart was racing, and her blood drained to her feet, making her feel as though she was about to faint. Ben came up behind her and grabbed her before she stumbled to the floor.

"What is *she* doing here?" Ben asked. His teeth clenched with anger. "I thought she wasn't invited?"

"She's not. I can't let her ruin everything."

By now, Sophie and Emily had joined them.

"Should we get rid of her?" Emily asked with alarm in her eyes.

"I can have Brady escort her out right now," Sophie added.

Rebecca paused and squared her shoulders. She could tell Ben was ready to drag the woman out on his own.

"Ben, can you trust me?" she asked.

"I—yes—but—"

Rebecca whispered in Ben's ear. "I'm going to make her pay." Then Rebecca gave him a wink and turned toward Sophie and Emily. "Don't worry about her. I've got this."

Rebecca stepped up to the microphone and got Duncan's attention so he could check the sound. She tapped on the microphone, giving it a thump, and Duncan gave her a thumbs up.

"Ladies and Gentlemen, it is our privilege to welcome each one of you to the gala," Rebecca said, making sure to look at Mrs. Bennington. "It is our sincere hope that you will put Stepping Stones: A Bridge to Success on its path to success. Benjamin and I are thrilled that you have joined us. We ask that you enjoy the food, entertainment, and the company of those around you, but more importantly, we ask for your generosity."

She lifted a hand toward Margo Bennington. "Without further ado, I'd like to invite our esteemed guest of honor to come up and say a few words. She has been a pillar in the community. You will soon learn she is not only generous with her time, but also financially. Her substantial contribution to Stepping Stones is so much appreciated. We hope that her donation will inspire you to match or exceed her generosity for this noble endeavor. Will you all join me in welcoming Mrs. Margo Bennington up to say a few words?"

Rebecca held the microphone in the air and gave a wide smile at Mrs. Bennington. The old bat's jaw dropped, then she quickly recovered as the attendees all turned to face her, giving her a resounding applause. Her face flushed, and she fanned her chest as she strutted across the room to join Rebecca.

Rebecca smiled, shook Mrs. Bennington's hand and moved her closer to the microphone. She whispered in her ear, "How kind of you to come, Mrs. Bennington."

***

Rebecca plopped on one of the chairs that sat askew. She removed her shoes and massaged her foot. The last goodbye was in the books. The gala was a smashing success and would be the talk of the town for years to come.

Ben pulled a chair up and across from her. "Let me do that," he said, and took her foot and massaged it. "I have to tell you, Becky. What you did with Mrs. Bennington was brilliant. Absolutely brilliant."

"She deserved to be put in her place," she said.

"You appealed to her ego. I bet she was dying inside when she thought you'd been talking about someone else." Ben released a laugh that filled the room. "Brilliant, just brilliant.

And it cost her a bloody fortune."

Ben leaned in to give her a kiss, and she pulled away. "So, now that the gala is over with, I guess you can be on your way."

Ben grimaced at her remark. "What are you talking about?"

"I heard you, Ben. The talk you had with your friend Holki something or other."

"Holokai?"

"Yeah, him."

"What did you hear me say?"

"I heard you say that as soon as the gala was over, you'd see his ugly mug." She could finally tell him that she knew his secret. She no longer needed to pretend that everything was okay. An overwhelming sense of loss was causing her heart to break. "So, ya better get going."

"Becky." His eyes were soft and a slight grin formed. "Yes, I did say that, but—"

"But what? You've been lying to me, Ben. There is no but." Tears blurred her vision and the words choked in her throat.

"But, Honey, you're coming with me."

"I'm what? I don't understand."

Ben nodded with a smile.

"Hey, Rebecca," Sophie said. Emily stood at her side. "We've got it from here."

"I don't understand." She was trying her best to make sense of what was happening. Sophie and Emily stared down at her with the same Cheshire cat smiles.

Emily rested her hand on her shoulder. "Ben is taking you away for a belated Valentine's week. He seems to think you need a vacation away from us."

"I can't imagine why?" Sophie chimed in, followed by a grin.

Rebecca stood in utter awe. "But we have so much to do to get Stepping Stones up and running."

"It can wait," Ben said as he took her by the hand. "Sophie and Emily will make sure all the funds are deposited and check in on your apartment. Brady can handle the renovations on the house by himself. Everything else can wait until we get back."

She turned to Ben. "We're really going to Hawaii?"

"Yep, we're really going to Hawaii. Right now."

"No, wait, what? Right now?" she asked in utter shock.

Emily slid a suitcase at her feet.

"But how?"

"No more questions," Sophie said. "Brady's waiting right over there." She pointed outside. "He's taking you two to the airport."

Before Rebecca could say another word, Ben whisked her out the door.

Epilogue

When they'd arrived back at the house, Rebecca had a sun-kissed glow. Even though the flight back was long, it filled her with energy. She took notice of the newly painted walls in the living and stairwell. She was pleased to see the note Sophie had left taped on the railing. She'd been kind enough to stock the refrigerator and turned the heat up as the change in climate was making the already cold temperature seem even colder. She gave a shiver, and Ben took her into his arms.

"Honey, why don't you go change into your comfies. By the time you come back down, I'll have a hot chocolate waiting for you."

"That would be great. Thank you." Her mind instantly went back to the time he'd brought her the s'more. *He's a good man.* She'd already apologized a million times about doubting him and his integrity, but she still didn't think she could ever forgive herself for having jumped to conclusions.

She stepped into the bedroom and pulled a pair of sweat-pants and a sweatshirt from a shelf in the closet. The warmth of the fleeced lining felt soft on her still sunburned shoulders. She reached for her slippers, and to her surprise, a new pair sat where her old pair had been. *He got me new slippers?* She slid the slippers on. They fit perfectly. The alpaca lining felt luxurious and cozy. A perfect fit.

"Do you like them?" Ben asked as he held the two mugs of hot chocolate in his hands.

"I love them." She wiggled her toes and stared down at them.

Ben handed over her mug. "Come with me for a minute. I want to show you something."

Rebecca didn't dare ask, because he once again wore a grin that said he was up to something. She didn't think her heart could take any more.

They walked toward the back end of the house where the old service staircase in the kitchen was located. He took her by the hand, careful not to spill his hot chocolate. They proceeded up the stairs and down a small hallway that led to the top of the expansive garage. Her pulse was racing at what felt like a billion beats per minute. *What is he up to?*

He opened the door at the end of the hall and switched on a light. The room lit up. She gasped. Everything was there: her worktable, her sewing table, all her fabrics, Mrs. Getchel's tablecloth backing even hung on the wall, just as it had in her apartment. There were more work stations and duplicate tools of the trade lying on each workspace. Rebecca burst into tears. She handed her hot chocolate to Ben and walked along the wall of materials, and ran her fingers over the fabric. Tears kept flowing.

Ben stepped away, set the mugs down and pulled her into his embrace. "Do you like it?"

"Oh, Benjamin. I love it—every part of it. How did you make this happen? How was this possible?"

"I had a little help from our friends," he said with so much love in his eyes that she wished she could climb into them and never leave.

She wiped her tears. "This is why you took me to Hawaii, isn't it?"

"It was one reason, but the biggest reason is because I love you. With all my heart and soul. I love you, Becky Mills, and I never want to spend a day without you."

Rebecca wrapped her arms around his neck and looked into his deep brown eyes that stared back at hers. "I love you too, Benjamin Daly." She kissed him with every ounce of passion she possessed.

They were finally home.

The End

THANK YOU FOR READING
PATCHWORK TO HEALING.

To learn more about Karen's books, insights, upcoming events, blog, and more:

www.KarenCoultersAuthor.com

Join her Newsletter @

https://karencoultersauthor.com/newsletter/

Follow her @

www.facebook.com/Karencoultersauthor

www.instagram.com/Kcoulters

Email her @

KarenCoultersAuthor@gmail.com

Invite Karen to your Book Club @

https://karencoultersauthor.com/book-clubs/

Your review of *Patchwork to Healing* and her other works would be greatly appreciated, as they provide readers with valued information. Your review will also aid in Karen's novels reaching a greater audience. Reviews can be accepted anywhere books are sold, as well as social media.

Made in United States
North Haven, CT
04 June 2023

37350940R00228